THE CHOICE

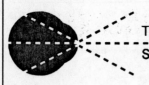

This Large Print Book carries the
Seal of Approval of N.A.V.H.

THE CHOICE

ROBERT WHITLOW

THORNDIKE PRESS
A part of Gale, Cengage Learning

GALE
CENGAGE Learning®

Detroit • New York • San Francisco • New Haven, Conn • Waterville, Maine • London

GALE
CENGAGE Learning®

LT
MYS
WHITLOW
ROBERT

3 1257 02404 5279

© 2012 by Robert Whitlow.
Scripture quotations are from King James Version of the Holy Bible; and THE HOLY BIBLE, NEW INTERNATIONAL VERSION® NIV®. Copyright © 1973, 1978, 1984, 2011 by Biblica, Inc.™ Used by permission. All rights reserved worldwide.
Thorndike Press, a part of Gale, Cengage Learning.

Thorndike Press® Large Print Christian Mystery.
The text of this Large Print edition is unabridged.
Other aspects of the book may vary from the original edition.
Set in 16 pt. Plantin.

LIBRARY OF CONGRESS CATALOGING-IN-PUBLICATION DATA

Whitlow, Robert, 1954–
    The choice / by Robert Whitlow.
        pages ; cm. — (Thorndike Press large print Christian mystery)
    ISBN-13: 978-1-4104-5332-7 (hardcover)
    ISBN-10: 1-4104-5332-4 (hardcover)
    1. Large type books. I. Title.
PS3573.H49837C48 2012b
813'.54—dc23   2012031046

Published in 2012 by arrangement with Thomas Nelson, Inc.

Printed in Mexico
1 2 3 4 5 6 7 16 15 14 13 12

To mothers. You give away part of your life each time you bring a baby into the world. May you be blessed for your selflessness.

Her children arise and call her blessed.

— Proverbs 31:28 NIV

PART ONE

ONE

Rutland, Georgia, 1974

Sandy Lincoln nervously twirled her long blond hair around her index finger. A magazine with a picture of Olivia Newton John on the cover and a feature article about Cher's recent breakup with Sonny lay unopened in her lap. Her mother stared unseeing across the waiting room.

"Why is it taking so long?" Sandy asked.

Her mother checked her watch.

"It's only been thirty minutes. Do you want to go home and let the doctor call?"

"No," Sandy replied immediately. "What if Daddy answers the phone?"

"You're right," her mother answered with a heavy sigh. "I don't know what I was thinking."

A dark-haired nurse in her thirties stuck her head in the room.

"Miss Lincoln, you may come back now."

As soon as the nurse spoke, Sandy instinctively grabbed her mother's hand for a second and then released it. The two women followed the nurse down a narrow hallway to an examination room.

"What did the test show?" Sandy asked anxiously.

"Dr. Braselton will be with you in a few minutes," the nurse said as she held the door open. "He'll discuss it with you then."

There was one chair in the room. Sandy hopped onto the examination table and let her feet dangle. The white paper that covered the table felt cool against the back of Sandy's bare legs. She repositioned her short skirt. The queasiness that had greeted Sandy each morning for the past two weeks returned. She put her hand to her mouth to stifle a burp.

"Stomach upset?" her mother asked.

"I'm scared," Sandy replied in a voice that sounded more like that of a seven-year-old girl than a seventeen-year-old young woman. "The test is positive, isn't it?"

Before her mother could answer, Dr. Braselton swept into the room. The white-haired doctor was older than Sandy's parents. His two children had already graduated from Rutland High, and one now attended medical school in Augusta. Sandy's mother started to get up from the chair.

"Keep your seat, Julie," the doctor said with a wave of his hand. "I just saw Bob at the Rotary lunch a couple of hours ago."

"Did you tell him we were —"

"No, no. I didn't know Sandy was coming in until I checked my schedule when I got back to the office."

The doctor turned to Sandy and opened a thick folder in his hand. Dr. Braselton had been treating Sandy since she was a baby. Her chart contained a record of everything from childhood vaccinations to follow-up care after an emergency appendectomy. He rubbed the side of his nose and looked at Sandy with a depth of kindness that made tears suddenly flow from her eyes. The doctor grabbed a couple of tissues from a box and pressed them in her hand.

"Sandy, you're pregnant," he said. "And based on the information you gave my nurse, you're about eight weeks along."

Sandy wiped her eyes with the tissues. Through blurred vision she could see her mother was also crying.

"I'm going to write a prescription for prenatal vitamins until you can see an ob-gyn," Dr. Braselton said, then turned to Sandy's mother. "You go to Bill Moore, don't you?"

Julie nodded.

"I can set up an appointment, or —"

"I'll do it," Julie said with a sniffle.

"Okay."

Dr. Braselton waited until Sandy's tears slowed to a trickle and her mother's natural stoicism reasserted itself.

"I'm here to help you in any way I can," he said. "Do you have any questions?"

Sandy looked at her mother, who shook her head. Dr. Braselton was a good man who'd served two terms on the city council and was the head of an important committee at the church. Sandy didn't want him to have a bad impression of her or her family.

"I know who the father is," she said, trying to keep her voice steady. "There's only one person it could be. I didn't want to do it, but things got out of hand, and I didn't think I would get pregnant. I mean, I know it can happen, but —" She stopped in midsentence.

"Does the boy know you're here?" the doctor asked.

"No." Sandy paused. "Not yet."

"You have a lot of important decisions to make," Dr. Braselton said, closing his folder. "If you want to talk to me about anything, call Patricia and tell her you want an appointment."

Tears stung Sandy's eyes again. The doctor patted her on the shoulder. Sandy saw him glance at her mother.

"Julie, that goes for you and Bob too."

"Thanks," her mother mumbled.

Outside the office, Sandy opened the passenger-side door of the car and shifted her cheerleading outfit to the backseat. Embroidered on the uniform front were four stars, signifying the number of years she'd been on the varsity squad.

"You won't be needing that," her mother said as she started the engine.

"But Friday night is the Caldwell County game," Sandy protested. "As long as I don't do any stunts, there's no reason why I can't cheer. And Brad and I are going out with a group for pizza after the game. I told him before I left school today that we need to hang out with other people instead of always being off by ourselves."

"You should have thought about that eight weeks ago."

Sandy didn't answer. She was guilty and without any excuse.

"Do you remember the talk we had about premarital sex?" her mother asked as she backed out of the parking space.

"Yeah, when I was fourteen."

"When did you decide to forget about it?"

15

Sandy stared out the window and didn't answer. They turned onto Campbell Street and passed her father's insurance agency. A sign in front of the one-story, red brick building read Lincoln Insurance Services.

"Are you really going to make me quit cheerleading?" Sandy asked in a subdued voice.

"Did you hear what Dr. Braselton said about big decisions?"

"Yes, ma'am."

"That's not one of them."

Not sure what her mother meant, Sandy kept her mouth shut during the remainder of the short drive home. Her mother pulled into a garage that a previous owner had added to the 1940s colonial two-story, wood-frame house. Sandy's car, a bright-yellow VW Beetle with flower decals on the fenders, was parked at the curb. Carefully maintained bushes in rows across the front of the house reflected the orderliness inside.

Sandy went upstairs to her room. From her window, she could see the symmetrical maple tree that she and Jessica Bowers had loved to climb when they were little. Beneath the tree was a gabled Victorian-style playhouse built by Sandy's father. The playhouse was still in good shape. Sandy kept it free of cobwebs, and every few years she and her father applied a fresh coat of pink paint. Her mother told her friends the playhouse was waiting for grandchildren. Sandy regretted that her mother's wish was about to come true much sooner than she'd expected.

Sandy slipped on her favorite pair of jeans and sucked in her stomach to button them. The jeans had been snug the previous week. Now they were downright uncomfortable. Sandy took off the jeans and put on a pair of baggy gray sweatpants with Rutland High School printed in large red letters down the sides of the legs.

She heard the front door slam as her little brothers, Jack and Ben, came bounding into the house. The boys, ages ten and thirteen, shared a large, airy bedroom across the hall from Sandy's room. She stepped into the hallway as they raced up the wooden stairs. Ben slowed down and crouched low as he approached her.

"Hey, let me show you the move I learned in wrestling today. I flipped Andy onto his back like a turtle."

"Not now." Sandy held up her hands. "I'm not feeling well."

Ben stood up. With his brown hair, dark eyes, and broad shoulders, everyone said he looked like his father. Jack was still a skinny towhead. Sandy could hear Jack banging around in the boys' bedroom.

"Is that why you went to the doctor?" Ben asked.

"Uh, yeah."

"Did he give you any medicine?"

"Vitamins."

"You already take vitamins."

"But you don't," Sandy replied.

Ben flexed his right bicep, which seemed to have doubled in size the past year.

"Can you imagine how huge my muscles would be if I did?"

"Yeah, but who beat you in arm wrestling last week?"

"As soon as you feel better, I want a do-over."

Sandy left Ben and walked downstairs to the kitchen. Her mother was on the phone. She looked up as Sandy entered.

"I'll call you back later," she said, returning the receiver to its cradle.

"Who was that?" Sandy asked.

"Linda."

Julie Lincoln's older sister, Linda, lived in Atlanta. Sandy glanced over her shoulder. Her brothers weren't in sight.

"Were you telling her about, you know —"

"Yes."

"Why?"

18

Sandy's mother sat down at the rectangular table where the family ate their meals. Behind the table was a bank of windows. Sandy could see the maple tree, the playhouse, more flower beds, and the expanse of green grass carefully maintained by her father.

"Because I'm confused and need her advice."

Sandy wasn't used to her mother admitting weakness.

"I don't know how to talk to your father about what you should do with the baby, what we're going to say to Brad's family, your schooling. You're thinking about cheerleading. I'm worried about the rest of your life."

Sandy plopped down and rested her head in her hands.

"I'm worried about talking to Daddy the most and Brad and his family second," she said. "Mrs. Donnelly is a nice lady. I think she'll understand when —"

"You have no idea how Kim Donnelly is going to react," her mother said, cutting her off. "They moved here less than a year ago. Who knows what the Donnellys believe? Someone at the beauty shop told me they've both been divorced."

"That was a long time ago," Sandy said,

avoiding eye contact with her mother.

She'd not disclosed to her parents the background information revealed so casually by Brad. Divorce in small Georgia towns in 1974 still carried a significant social stigma.

"It happened before Brad and his brother were born," she said.

"Were they married when Kim conceived Brad?"

"Sure," Sandy replied, then realized she didn't actually know the answer. "I mean, they were adults."

"Do you think that makes a difference?"

"No, ma'am," Sandy admitted. "I don't feel grown up."

"Because you aren't, except in the way that got you into this mess."

Tears stung Sandy's eyes again. She'd never been so emotionally fragile.

"That sounds harsh, but it's true," her mother continued. "You're not ready for life on your own, much less the responsibility of a child."

"I know." Sandy sniffled. "But it helps that Brad loves me. He told me so at the dance after the first home football game. Together, we can work things out."

Her mother covered her face with her hands for a moment, then looked up.

"Sandy, please don't say things like that. A high school romance isn't something you can build a future on."

Sandy didn't have the strength to argue. Shame had sapped her normal spunkiness.

"I'm going outside," she said.

"Go ahead," her mother replied. "It's not a good time for us to talk. I'm as upset as you are and need some time to think before your father comes home. I'm disappointed in you, but I don't want you to take the brunt of his reaction."

Sandy went into the backyard. Most of the leaves had fallen from the trees. Her brothers had raked them into the compost pile at the rear of their property. The grass was a rich green following the fall dose of fertilizer.

Sandy opened the tiny door to the playhouse and crawled inside. She leaned against the bare counter that had served as a make-believe stove, sink, and changing table. A young girl's imagination can be as strong as her childhood reality. Sandy pulled her knees up to her chin and closed her eyes. When she opened them, nothing had changed. She felt trapped. Imagination had lost its magic. Her present reality left no room for pretending.

She was still pregnant.

Two

"Coach Cochran came by the office today to increase his life insurance policy," Bob Lincoln said as they sat around the supper table. "Did you know his wife is pregnant again?"

"No," Julie replied.

Sandy kept her eyes focused on the lasagna on her plate. She'd nibbled around the edges but wasn't hungry. Her mother often prepared meals from scratch, but this supper had gone directly from the freezer into the oven and then to the table.

"He's not going to give up till he gets a boy," her father said. "One more girl and he'll have enough for a basketball team. I'm going to talk to some guys in the booster club and see if we can't scare up some extra cash for him by the end of the season. It'd be a shame to lose him to a big-city school over a few bucks. He's doing a great job."

"The players like him," Sandy offered in a

soft voice.

"And they play their hearts out for him," her father replied. He took a quick sip of sweet tea and leaned forward. "Do you know what else Coach Cochran told me?"

Not waiting for anyone to guess, her father clapped his hands together.

"He believes Brad Donnelly is a bona fide Division I prospect at wide receiver! Cochran has been getting calls from coaches at a few SEC schools." Sandy's father raised his hands as if signaling a touchdown. "Including Auburn. War Eagle! Sandy, if Brad gets a scholarship offer, you could go to Auburn and try out for the cheerleading squad. I'm not trying to pressure you, but wouldn't it be a blast if Brad made the team and you were on the sidelines? Cheerleading in college is a huge commitment, and your studies would have to come first, but being part of that would be something you'd be proud of for the rest of your life."

"Would we get to go to the home games?" Ben asked.

"Every single one of them," his father answered. "And we might go to a few away games too. The whole thing got me as excited as a kid."

"Your lasagna is getting cold," Julie said.

Sandy's father looked down as if suddenly

discovering there was food on his plate. He took a big bite.

"This is great, honey," he said, his mouth partially full. "Better than what they serve at Mama Rosario's."

After supper, Sandy helped her mother put the dishes in the dishwasher. The two women worked in silence. The males in the family went into the den to watch TV for a few minutes before the boys did their homework.

"When are we going to tell him?" Sandy whispered as she rinsed Jack's plate. "I sure didn't think about college all afternoon."

"I did," her mother replied. "But not, of course, like your daddy. It's a forty-minute drive to the community college in Carteret. You could probably schedule classes two days a week or go at night after the baby is asleep."

Her mother's words made Sandy's head spin. She suddenly pictured herself in her bedroom with a crying infant in what had once been her grandmother's yellow wicker bassinet. Sandy and her brothers had each spent the first few months of their lives in that bassinet.

"I would stay here after the baby is born?"

Her mother pressed her lips together tightly for a moment.

"Sandy, this is a bad situation, but we're not going to put you out on the street."

A moment later, Bob Lincoln walked into the kitchen and placed his hand on Sandy's forehead.

"Feels fine to me," he said. "Ben told me you went to the doctor today, then mentioned something about getting a prescription for vitamins."

Sandy backed away from her father until the kitchen counter stopped her.

"Yes, sir," she said.

Her mother looked toward the den.

"Where are the boys?"

"There wasn't anything decent on TV, so I sent them upstairs to do their homework. What's going on?"

Julie dried her hands on a dish towel. Sandy held her breath. The queasiness she'd felt in the doctor's office returned, only worse. Her mother wrung the towel tightly in her hands for a moment before laying it on the edge of the sink.

"Sandy's pregnant," she said.

No preamble. No buildup. No effort at damage control before dropping the bombshell. Sandy had watched her mother handle her father for years. Sometimes she could change his mind and make him think it was his own idea. This was a radically different approach. It was her daddy's turn to step back. Sandy and her father faced each other across the kitchen with her mother standing in the middle.

"How?" he managed after a few seconds passed.

"I think you know the answer to that," Julie replied matter-of-factly. "She's about eight weeks along. It explains why she hasn't been feeling well when she first gets up in the morning."

"You've had morning sickness?" Sandy's father asked with a bewildered look on his face.

"I threw up today, but you'd already left for the office."

Her father's face suddenly turned red. His mood could shift in seconds. Sandy braced herself.

"Who did this to you?" he sputtered.

"Brad Donnelly," Sandy replied. "It happened toward the end of summer. Do you remember when we went to the lake —"

Sandy's father swore and slammed his fist against the countertop.

"I'll get him kicked off the team and expelled from school! He rides in here from Houston and takes advantage of you." Sandy's father looked wild-eyed at her mother. "Do the Donnellys know about this?"

"No," Sandy responded. "I didn't want to tell Brad until I saw the doctor and talked with you."

Sandy's father checked his watch. "Let's go over there right now."

"Mr. Connelly is out of town on a business trip," Sandy said. "I asked Brad about it this morning without telling him why I wanted to know."

"Carl Donnelly is a salesman," Julie added. "Most weeks he leaves on Monday and doesn't come back till Friday. Sometimes he comes to the games with a suit on."

"He should have spent more time at home telling his son how to treat innocent young girls!"

Even though her father was wrong about both her innocence and age, Sandy wasn't about to disagree with him. She was relieved that, so far, his anger had been focused outward. There would be time later to rehabilitate his attitude toward Brad. She relaxed a little bit. Then her father's gaze turned to her. Sandy felt her face flush. Her heart started pounding.

"I'm sorry, Daddy," she began, fighting back tears. "I never wanted to do anything to embarrass you and Mama. I wish —"

Before Sandy could continue, her father opened wide his arms.

"Come here, sweetie," he said.

Sandy flew across the kitchen and into his embrace. Her father held her close as tears soaked his shirt. When they separated, Sandy felt both drained and strengthened.

"We'll talk tomorrow," her mother said. "There are some things your father and I have to discuss first."

Sandy nodded. She'd received what she needed — assurance that she would have the support of her family as she faced the future.

The following morning Sandy spent fifteen minutes in the bathroom unsuccessfully battling nausea. Her face remained pale when she checked herself in the mirror. Her father was waiting for her in the foyer when she came downstairs. The house was quiet. In the light of a new day he looked serious, not angry. Sandy checked her watch. If she didn't leave soon, she'd be tardy for homeroom.

"Where are Mama and the boys?" she asked.

"She took them to school this morning so you and I could be alone. Are you going to talk to Brad today?"

"Yes, sir. I thought I'd wait until sixth-period study hall. That way he won't have to think about it all day during classes."

"But he won't go straight home after school. He'll have football practice."

"I know."

The grandfather clock in the foyer chimed the quarter hour.

"Your mama and I stayed up late talking last night. We believe we should meet with the Donnellys as soon as possible, even if Carl is out of town. That means Brad needs to talk to his mother as soon as he gets home. We'd like to do it tonight."

The thought of a larger group that included Brad, his mother, and both her parents didn't help Sandy's nausea. The meeting was inevitable, but that didn't make it easier. Bracing herself, she asked the question that had been uppermost in her mind as she lay in bed the previous night unable to fall asleep: "What are you going to say to Brad?"

"That he has to take responsibility for his actions. What that means at this point is one of the things we'll discuss."

"Like Brad and me getting married?"

"Sandy," her father said in a tone that instantly put an end to any debate. "If you want our help, you're going to have to let us

29

guide you through this."

"Yes, sir."

"Get going," he said, opening the front door for her. "I'll be home early from work."

It was one of the longest days of Sandy's school career. The first time she saw Brad, the lanky young man with reddish-brown hair and green eyes was standing in front of his locker. He had on the same shirt and pants he'd worn the night the baby was conceived. Sandy shuddered and ducked into the girls' bathroom so she could avoid him. She tried to act normally at lunch. Brad pressed his leg against hers beneath the table while he joked with his buddies. Sandy wanted to pull away but forced herself to remain still.

During fifth-period chemistry, Jessica tapped Sandy on the shoulder when Mr. Cook stepped out of the room for a minute.

"What's wrong?" the tall, dark-haired girl whispered. "You don't look so well. Do you think you're coming down with something?"

Sandy touched her right cheek. She'd applied the usual amount of makeup before leaving the house.

"No."

"And you didn't say a word at lunch. Did you and Brad have a fight?"

Sandy and Jessica had known each other so long that they were as sensitive to each other's feelings as natural sisters. Unwelcome tears suddenly came to Sandy's eyes. She looked straight ahead so Jessica wouldn't see and shook her head.

Mr. Cook returned to the room, and Sandy tried to focus on the day's lecture about complex carbon compounds. But all she could think about was what lay ahead in sixth-period study hall. She wanted to come across to Brad as mature, not whiny, but doubted she'd have much control at all.

"Let's hang out in study hall," Jessica said as they gathered up their books. "I'll cheer you up."

"No, I need to talk to Brad."

"What's going on?" Jessica demanded.

Sandy knew the truth would devastate her friend. She started toward the door with Jessica right beside her.

"You're going to tell me eventually," Jessica said. "Open up and get it over with."

They jostled their way down the crowded hallway.

"Not until after study hall," Sandy said. "I'll give you a ride home. Then we'll talk."

"Are you forgetting that you have cheerleading practice, and I have to work on my solo routine?"

Jessica, with her long, graceful arms, was head majorette and could juggle three flaming batons at once.

"I'm skipping practice," Sandy said. "I'm not sick, just tired."

Jessica grabbed Sandy and spun her around. Several people bumped into them. Sandy tried to pull away, but Jessica forced her into a gap between two banks of lockers.

"You look sick and feel tired, and it's Brad's fault?"

Sandy blinked her eyes and didn't answer. Suddenly, the blood rushed from Jessica's face.

"You're not — ?" Jessica stopped.

"Please," Sandy pleaded. "I need to get to study hall and make sure I can get alone with Brad."

Sandy left Jessica and reentered the sea of high school humanity flowing down the hallway. Sixth period was in the library. Flushed after her encounter with Jessica, Sandy walked rapidly. Brad, his back to the door, was seated at a table in the rear of the room with three other members of the football team. Sandy marched up to them. One of the other boys, a hulking offensive lineman named Larry Babineaux, saw her coming.

"Look out, Donnelly," he said. "You're in big trouble."

Brad glanced over his shoulder, saw Sandy, and smiled. Brad's smile exuded unlimited charm. Normally, when he directed it toward Sandy, it made her feel like the sun had burst from behind the clouds. Today it had lost its power.

"No, I'm not," Brad said, pulling back a chair so Sandy could sit down. "We're talking football, but Sandy knows more about how to run an offense than you do."

"Brad, I need to talk to you," Sandy said. "Alone."

"See," Babineaux replied in triumph. "I can read a girl's body language better than you can."

"If that's true, why don't you have a girlfriend?" one of the other boys asked.

"Can it wait a few minutes?" Brad asked Sandy. "We're in the middle of something."

"No."

Brad hesitated for a moment, then shrugged his shoulders and got up from his seat.

"See that?" Babineaux observed in a voice loud enough for everyone within earshot to hear. "Sandy is small but tough. Notice what happened, guys. She took down Donnelly harder than the cornerback from

Barnwell on that busted play across the middle last week."

Sandy walked away from the table. She took a couple of steps and glanced back to see if Brad was following. He made a parting comment that made the other boys laugh, then joined her.

"Don't do that to me, baby," he said in a low voice. "It was embarrassing."

Sandy didn't respond. There was a small, unoccupied table near the biography section. She led the way and sat down. Brad, a puzzled expression on his face, sat across from her and leaned forward.

"What's going on?" he asked.

Looking into Brad's eyes, Sandy's carefully researched speech flew out of her head. Tears stung her eyes. She took a deep breath and tried to steady herself. Her life was about to change forever.

"I went to the doctor yesterday. I'm pregnant."

Brad sat up straight in his chair with a shocked expression on his face. Then, almost immediately, a smile creased his lips.

"That's a rough way to get back at me for joking around with you in front of the guys."

"It's not a joke. Dr. Braselton gave me a pregnancy test, and it came back positive."

Brad stared at Sandy. She watched as reality hit him. He gripped the edge of the table with his large hands.

"That's impossible. Take another test."

"I can do that, but there's no doubt in my mind. Everything about my body says I'm pregnant. I've been throwing up most mornings for the past two weeks."

"And you're sure I'm the father?"

Before she knew what she was doing, Sandy reached out and slapped Brad across the face. He stared at her in stunned shock.

"What? Why?"

"How dare you ask me that?" she whispered intensely.

One of the study-hall proctors, a student teacher named Mr. Phillips, came up to the table.

"What's going on over here?" he asked.

"Nothing," Brad answered. "We're talking."

"I thought I saw her hit you."

"No, she just patted me on the cheek."

"Keep it under control, or I'm going to have to separate you. No physical contact is allowed in here."

"No problem," Brad answered.

Phillips gave them a skeptical look and turned away. Brad's cheek was turning red where Sandy had hit him. She tried to feel sorry for striking out but didn't. Her eyes blazed.

"Who else do you think might be the father?" she asked.

"No one. You caught me off guard with this, and I didn't have time to think." Brad looked past Sandy for a few moments. "How unlucky can we be? One time, and you're pregnant."

"The first and only time," Sandy reminded him.

"Yeah, the girls in Houston knew how to avoid stuff like this."

Sandy had suspected Brad was more experienced than she, but he'd never blatantly admitted it.

"Oh, you're blaming me?"

"No, no. It's on both of us. But you're the one who's going to have the rougher time. I hate that."

At the hint of sympathy, Sandy relaxed slightly.

"I talked with my parents, and they want to get together with you and your mom tonight. I know your dad is out of town."

"No way." Brad shook his head. "Your father isn't going to come over to my house and chew me out in front of my mom. She's going to have a nervous breakdown when she finds out anyway, and it will take a week and two-fifths of vodka to calm her down."

Brad had used vodka stolen from the family liquor cabinet to concoct a fruity drink that lowered Sandy's inhibitions the night she conceived.

"Whether you want to get together or not, she's going to find out today," Sandy replied. "My parents are going to call her this afternoon. She can hear the news from you after football practice or from them on the phone. And I can't control what my father is going to do. Last night he was super mad, but he seemed calmer about it this morning."

"Man, I can't believe this happened."

"Do you still love me?" Sandy asked in a subdued voice.

"Yeah, but it doesn't help that you hit me."

Sandy didn't want to apologize but forced the words from her lips.

"I'm sorry."

"Just don't ever do that again. I'd never hit you, no matter how mad I got."

"I know."

Brad tapped his finger on the history book in front of him.

"Will they make you drop out of school?" he asked.

"Probably. When Sally Holmes got pregnant last year, she was expelled and didn't get to walk at graduation."

Brad said a swearword. "It wasn't like that in Texas. Girls could go to class right up to the time they went into the hospital."

"And her boyfriend was kicked off the football team," Sandy continued. "They ended up getting married. I think they're living in the basement of her parents' house. I don't know if she had a little boy or a girl."

"No way." Brad bowed his head.

Sandy wasn't sure if he was reacting to the possibility that he might not get to play football or the prospect of marrying her and living with her family.

"We don't have a basement," she said.

Brad raised his head and looked at Sandy as if she were crazy.

"I've been to your house. I know that."

"I was just —" Sandy stopped. "So, are you going to tell your mom when you get home?"

"Yeah, but she's not going to want your parents coming around. Your mother has looked down on her since we started dating, and your father is a nut."

Sandy wanted to defend her folks, but there was a grain of truth in Brad's words. She felt a tap on her shoulder. It was Jessica.

"Hey, Brad," Jessica said with a fake smile

plastered on her face. "Is it okay if I steal Sandy away for a few minutes?"

"Sure," Brad replied. "We're done."

THREE

Jessica took Sandy by the arm and guided her around the corner so they were standing between two long rows of bookshelves. She peeked through the shelves toward the table where Sandy had been sitting with Brad.

"He's going back to the table where the other football players are sitting," Jessica said. "I saw you slap him."

Sandy winced. "It happened so fast I didn't know what I was doing. Where were you?"

"Right here." Jessica pointed down at her feet. "I could see Brad's face but not yours. I thought you heard me gasp when you hit him. Then Mr. Phillips came over to the table, and I got scared, but Phillips is pretty dense. What did Brad tell him?"

"That I patted his cheek."

"How lame. Why did you hit him?"

"Because of what he said. And please,

don't ask me to repeat it."

"Then tell me what's going on. Are you pregnant?"

Sandy looked at her friend and nodded. Tears once again stung her eyes. Jessica leaned over and wrapped her arms around her. The two girls held each other.

"I knew it," Jessica said when they parted. She took a tissue from her purse and handed it to Sandy. "And not just since chemistry class. You've been feeling lousy for weeks and walking around like you had something on your mind. Then when you left school yesterday to go to the doctor with your mother, I couldn't get the idea out of my head that you were getting a pregnancy test. I mean, I didn't want to believe something bad about you, not that it's horrible to have a baby, but in a way it's a huge disaster."

"Yeah, I've felt all those things."

"Did Brad know something was going on?"

"He had no idea, and my daddy said I had to tell him today."

"How far along are you?"

"Eight weeks."

"Eight weeks! How did you keep your mouth shut?"

"I was scared."

"What did your parents say?"

41

Sandy summarized the events of the past twenty-four hours. "I was going to tell you next, but I owed it to Brad to let him know."

"Then he acts like a total jerk." Jessica's eyes flashed. "This is ninety-nine percent his fault. You wouldn't have done this if he hadn't put tons of pressure on you. He's used to having his way with girls at a big-city school. You're not like that. I've been worried about you ever since you started going steady with him. I've prayed about it every night before going to bed."

"Girls," a male voice interrupted them. "This is a study hall, not a social hour."

It was Mr. Phillips. He raised a long index finger to his lips.

"Yes, sir," Jessica replied sweetly.

Sandy and Jessica moved to a table on the opposite side of the library from Brad and the football players. They passed notes back and forth. When the bell rang ending the school day, Sandy hung back until she was sure Brad was gone.

"Please don't let anyone see those notes," Sandy said to Jessica.

"I'll tie them up in a plastic bag and put it in the trash can. Call me later and let me know how things go."

"Are you going to say anything to your mom?"

"Not if you don't want me to. I mean, eventually she'll find out."

"I know." Sandy sighed. "But I can't stand the thought of her being disappointed in me."

"She'll freak out, but I won't breathe a word until you say so." Jessica ran her fingers across her lips. "These are sealed."

On her way out of the building, Sandy stopped by Mrs. Winters's classroom. The brown-haired math teacher in her midthirties was Sandy's favorite instructor and coach of the cheerleading squad. Sandy stood in the door of the classroom until the teacher looked up.

"I won't be at practice again today," Sandy said. "I'm still feeling sick."

"What did the doctor say?"

Sandy edged away. "I'm sure I'll be fine by Friday night, but don't practice any stunts that include me getting tossed in the air."

As she fled down the hall, Sandy thought she heard Mrs. Winters calling after her. She didn't slow down.

Sandy's mother left a note on the refrigerator that she was taking the boys to the barbershop. Emotionally and physically exhausted, Sandy dragged herself upstairs and fell into bed. She'd not taken a nap since fourth grade. She closed her eyes and didn't wake up until she heard a knock on her door. It was her father.

"Hey, Daddy," she said, blinking her eyes. "I was tired so I decided to lie down for a few minutes."

She glanced at the clock on her nightstand and realized she'd been asleep for more than an hour.

"Are Mama and the boys here?"

"Not yet. They were going to stop by the grocery store after finishing at the barbershop. Did you talk to Brad?"

"Yes."

"Is he going to tell his parents?"

"I think so."

"You're not sure?"

Sandy sat up and swung her legs over the edge of the bed.

"I told him during study hall this afternoon. He doesn't think we should get together tonight to talk."

"He's worried about what I'm going to say to him?"

"Yeah."

"He should be."

"Daddy, please don't make things harder than they already are," Sandy pleaded.

"I'm going to say what needs to be said.

What's happened to you affects all of us."

"Can we practice-talk? You know, like in a play at school."

Her father gave her a puzzled look. The front door opened as Sandy's mother and brothers returned.

"We can't talk about that now," her father said.

Sandy went into the bathroom, brushed her tousled hair, and went downstairs. Her mother was unloading the grocery bags in the kitchen.

"How was school?"

It was a reflex question her mother had asked thousands of times since Sandy had gone to Miss Mary Lou's kindergarten with her hair in pigtails.

"I guess that's not what I need to ask you today, is it?" her mother said before Sandy could respond. "Help me put away the groceries."

Ben and Jack appeared at the kitchen door demanding a drink and a snack.

"We'll have supper in an hour and a half," Sandy's mother responded. "You can have a glass of juice but no snacks. Go outside and burn off some energy. You acted like hoodlums at the grocery store."

The boys each gulped down a large glass of apple juice and ran out to the backyard to throw a Frisbee. Sandy's father came into the kitchen.

"Tell your mother about your conversation with Brad," he said.

Sandy knew her mother would want details. She provided a toned-down version that left out everything immediately before and after the slap.

"That's it?" her mother asked.

"Most of it."

Her mother put a fresh roll of paper towels on the holder above the sink.

"Of all days, I saw Kim Donnelly at the grocery store," she said.

"Did you talk to her?"

"About the price of bananas and the ski trip she and Carl are planning to Colorado during the holidays. Nothing about you and Brad."

"He's getting home from football practice about now," Sandy said.

Her parents exchanged a long look.

"If we don't hear from Kim Donnelly in an hour, I'm going to make the call," her father said.

Sandy's mother nodded. After her father left the kitchen, Sandy stayed to help prepare supper. It was something she rarely did because of cheerleading practice. She chopped onions for a meat loaf and cut several pieces of day-old bread into tiny squares. Her mother spooned the mixed ingredients into a loaf pan and put it in the oven. When she closed the oven door, the phone rang. Sandy jumped. Her mother picked up the receiver. Sandy held her breath and waited.

"Hello, Kim," her mother said, raising her eyebrows at Sandy.

Sandy wanted to slide into a hole in the ground and never come out. Her mother listened for a moment.

"It was a shock to us too."

Kim Donnelly continued to talk. Sandy's mother glanced at the floor, then the kitchen clock.

"If Carl will be home by eight o'clock, what time would you want us to come over?"

After a brief response, her mother nodded her head.

"All right, we'll see you at nine-thirty at our house. The boys will be in bed by then."

She hung up the phone.

"Kim called Brad's father with the news, and he's driving in from Savannah. She agrees we should get together as soon as possible, and we're going to do it here. You'll need to straighten up the living room after supper."

"Okay. I'm glad we're not going to the Donnellys' house."

The living room at the Lincoln home was immaculate, but Sandy didn't argue. Her mother never had to worry about unexpected guests finding the house a mess. While the meat loaf was cooking, Sandy went upstairs to her bedroom. On her thirteenth birthday, her parents installed a telephone extension in her room, and Sandy picked out a pink princess phone that was now a joke rather than a prized possession. She called Jessica.

"It's better that they're coming over here," Sandy said to her friend. "Brad's house is kind of creepy."

"It's because of all the drinking that goes on over there. And who knows how his parents treat each other when no one is around."

Jessica's parents didn't allow alcohol of any kind in the house. Sandy's father would drink a cold beer while watching a football game on Saturday or after cutting the grass on a hot day. Brad never told Sandy if his folks argued a lot, but his father regularly yelled at the referees during football games.

"What are you going to say?" Jessica asked.

"I'm not sure."

"Keep your mouth shut. Let your daddy take up for you."

"What if he starts in on Brad? It could ruin everything."

"Maybe it will make him realize what he's done to you."

"And then dump me?"

"Sandy, I'm just telling you how I feel. We've been best friends since we were three years old. I'm worried to death about you. I couldn't concentrate during majorette practice and dropped the baton more than I have since ninth grade. When I got home I went straight to my room and haven't come out, because I know my mom will figure out that I'm upset and start grilling me."

"Do you want to tell her?"

"Yes, but not so she'll know the latest gossip before anyone else. If I ask them, my folks will pray during your meeting with the Donnellys."

Sandy knew she needed all the help she could get, especially if her daddy and Brad's father got heated up.

"Okay, I guess you can tell her." Sandy paused. "I feel like dirt on the bottom of a shoe."

"That's not what I think."

"I know, and thanks for not judging me."

"And I'll take up for you at school. All the

girls who've been jealous of how cute and popular you are will be totally catty about it, but I promise to do what I can to protect you."

"Love ya," Sandy replied gratefully. "If I make it through tonight, I'll see you tomorrow."

Sandy was surprisingly hungry and went back for a second helping of meat loaf and green beans. After the meal, she dutifully vacuumed the spotless living room, dusted the dust-free furniture, and pretended to straighten the pictures and knickknacks that were already in perfect position. On one wall of the living room were large portrait pictures of Sandy and her brothers, taken three years earlier and retouched by an artist to make them look like real paintings. She paused to look in the eyes of the fourteen-year-old girl who stared back without any hint of how radically her life would change in such a short time.

Ben and Jack sailed through the evening, oblivious to the dark cloud that hung over the family. Sandy could hear them working on a model ship while they were supposed to be doing their homework. Normally, she would have stepped in to straighten them out, but tonight she didn't feel like correcting anybody's wrongs. She tried to study for a chemistry quiz, but the letters and symbols on the page ran together. She watched the clock; time dragged by. Closing her chemistry book, she laid out several outfits on her bed before selecting a modest skirt and a yellow sweater. Stepping into the hall, she met Jack returning from the bathroom where he'd brushed his teeth.

"Are you getting dressed up so you can sneak out later and meet up with Brad?" he asked.

"No."

"What's going on?"

Sandy tried to come up with a quick answer that wasn't a total lie.

"Can't I play dress-up if I want to?"

"Yeah, but it's kind of weird."

Downstairs, Sandy found her mother in the kitchen brewing a pot of coffee. A plate of light hors d'oeuvres rested on the counter.

"You're serving snacks?" Sandy blurted out.

"I hope this is going to be a civilized meeting," her mother replied evenly. "Get your great-aunt's silver coffee service from the cupboard in the dining room and six cups with saucers of the fine china."

On her way to the dining room, Sandy realized her mother was right. It would be hard to start shouting while holding a delicate Wedgwood cup between two fingers. When she returned from the cupboard, her father was in the kitchen. He'd taken off his tie before supper but now had it freshly knotted around his neck.

"Satisfied?" he asked Sandy's mother.

"Yes."

By 9:25 p.m., everything was neatly laid out on the coffee table in the living room. Sandy occasionally drank coffee while trying to stay warm at cold football games. Tonight she might shiver, but it wouldn't be from the cold. The doorbell chimed.

"Stay here," her mother ordered. "Let your daddy answer the door."

Sandy's father opened the door. Any greetings he exchanged with the Donnelly family in the foyer were muffled. Sandy's heart started pounding. Brad and his parents came into the living room. Brad was wearing jeans and a T-shirt with the name of his old high school in Houston printed across the front. He gave her a grim look. Kim Donnelly, a tall woman with brownish-red hair, didn't look at her. Carl Donnelly, also wearing a tie, looked around the room as if making sure there wasn't someone hiding out of sight.

"Before we sit down," Sandy's mother said in a tense voice, "would anyone like a cup of coffee?"

Everyone except Brad and Sandy clustered around the coffee service. Sandy watched Brad, who seemed to be studying a piece of carpet. Sandy wanted to say something to him but didn't. After everyone's coffee cup was full, Sandy's mother directed them where to sit. Sandy and her parents sat on the sofa with Sandy in the middle. She put her hands beneath her legs. Brad's mother and father were close together on a love seat opposite the sofa, with Brad next to them in an upholstered chair. Sandy's father took a long sip of coffee and cleared his throat.

"Thanks for coming over on such short notice," he began. "Sandy went to Dr. Braselton yesterday, and he confirmed that she's pregnant. Brad, do you have any doubt that you're the father of the baby?"

Brad touched his cheek where Sandy had slapped him. She held her breath.

"Not if Sandy says so," he replied.

Everyone looked at Sandy, who blushed.

"Brad is the daddy," Sandy said in a soft voice. "We were only together one time."

She saw Brad grimace. Carl Donnelly rolled his eyes.

"She's eight weeks along," Sandy's father

53

said. "But a lot of decisions are going to have to be made, especially —"

"Eight weeks?" Brad's mother interrupted in her high-pitched voice. "Is that all? There's only one decision that needs to be made. Sandy should have an abortion. And the sooner the better!"

FOUR

Sandy had studied the recent U.S. Supreme Court decision in *Roe v. Wade* and memorized enough facts about the case to answer a question on a quiz before forgetting about it.

"There are several new women's health clinics in Atlanta that provide excellent care," Kim Donnelly continued. "I called two of them this afternoon. Sandy can get an appointment next week and get this taken care of quickly. That way our kids can put this behind them and get on with their lives."

"We'll pay for it," Carl added. "As Brad's parents, we don't want to dodge our responsibility. Sandy is a fine young woman, and no one will need to know what's happened. We want to protect her reputation."

Sandy was shocked. The possibility of terminating the pregnancy hadn't crossed her mind.

"That's something we haven't had a chance to discuss," her father said.

"And won't," her mother added emphatically.

"Hold on, Julie," her father said. "We've asked the Donnellys to come over here so we can discuss options. This is one of them."

"One option you can forget is forcing the children to get married," Kim said firmly. "They still may have shotgun weddings around here, but we're not going to let Brad ruin his life by getting married, dropping out of school, and living in a trailer park."

"I left my shotgun locked up in the garage," Sandy's father replied grimly. "And there's no need to start tossing around accusations. My wife is entitled to her opinion."

Sandy had always thought Brad's father was the dominant partner in the Donnelly marriage. Now she wasn't so sure. Kim Donnelly's face grew red, and her voice climbed even higher.

"We may be newcomers to Rutland, but when it comes to our son, we're not going to be bullied or dictated to by you or —"

Sandy felt the human volcano sitting beside her on the couch about to erupt. She tensed.

"You'd better shut your mouth if you want

to stay another minute in this house!" her father roared.

In a flash, Kim Donnelly was heading to the front door. Carl followed. Before he could take three steps, the front door slammed as his wife left the house. He spun around and pointed his finger at Sandy's father.

"Don't ever speak to my wife like that again," he said in a cold voice. "And keep your trampy daughter away from my son. Come on, Brad, let's get out of here."

Sandy and her mother both grabbed Sandy's father as he started to launch himself off the sofa. Brad hurried after his father without looking back at Sandy. The front door opened and closed again. Sandy's father jerked loose and bolted toward the foyer.

"When I get my hands on him —"

"Bob!" Sandy's mother cried out. "Let them go. They're in the car by now."

Sandy's father turned around. There was an expression of anguished rage on his face unlike anything Sandy had ever seen before. Panic rose up inside her as she realized her father might do something so violent that it would scar their family forever, perhaps even worse than the humiliation she was already bringing. He turned toward the door.

"Daddy, please! Stop!" Sandy cried out.

"Dad!" Ben called from the top of the stairs. "What's going on down there?"

Sandy's father paused and ran his right hand across the top of his head.

"Nothing!" he roared.

A few seconds later, Sandy's brother appeared in the doorway. He was wearing too-small pajamas that Sandy had given him the previous Christmas. He rubbed his eyes.

"I heard yelling, and the front door slammed. Are y'all having a fight?"

"No," Sandy's mother answered. "We'll talk about it later."

Ben stepped into the living room and saw the coffee table and plate of untouched hors d'oeuvres.

"Can I have a snack? I'm hungry."

Sandy braced for another explosion from her father. He stared incredulously at Ben for a second, then waved his hand toward the food.

"Go ahead. Eat all you want."

Sandy's father left the room and headed toward the master suite at the rear of the house. Ben began wolfing down the snacks. Sandy and her mother carried the coffee service, cups, and saucers into the kitchen.

"What now?" Sandy asked as she poured the steaming coffee down the drain.

"Another sleepless night," her mother answered.

"I'm sorry," Sandy said.

Sandy had already apologized, but there seemed to be no end to the opportunities to do so. As her mother bent to open the dishwasher, Sandy thought she saw lines on her face that hadn't been there before.

"This is one of those things a parent knows can happen but doesn't believe ever will," her mother said. "It's going to be one day at a time for all of us, and I don't have anything left for this one."

As she lay in bed that night, Sandy thought about her parents suffering in their bedroom. She knew the Donnelly house was also in an uproar. What Brad's parents said stung, but the coldness she felt from Brad hurt worse. She turned over and buried her face in her pillow.

The next day news of Sandy's pregnancy had become common knowledge at Rutland High by third period. Jessica swore she hadn't mentioned it to a soul, which meant Brad said something to one of his buddies, who then told a girl, any girl. That one spark of information triggered a firestorm of gossip that swept through the school faster than an atomic chain reaction. When Sandy walked down the hall toward her locker before fourth period, she felt every set of eyes she encountered staring at her. She stood in front of her locker for a few moments, then closed it without taking out her Spanish textbook. Instead, she walked directly to the school office. Mrs. Branson, the school secretary, saw her come in. She picked up the phone before Sandy spoke.

"Mr. Pickerel, Sandy Lincoln is here to see you."

Sandy stood with her hands folded in front of her. The door behind the secretary opened, and the bald-headed principal came out.

"Hello, Sandy," he said. "Come in."

Sandy sat down in a chair in front of the principal's desk.

"I guess you heard," she began. "I'm pregnant, and Brad Donnelly is the father."

"Yes."

Sandy looked down at the floor. "If it's okay, I'd like to go home."

The principal picked up a slip of paper and scribbled something on it.

"Here's an excuse to leave campus for the day. Sandy, you're an outstanding student and I want to help in any way I can, but my hands are going to be tied by your circumstances. Ask your mother or father to call me as soon as possible."

Sandy left the office, glad that the halls were now empty of students. She stopped by her locker to get some books and then walked toward the rear of the building. The parking lot for seniors was between the main classroom building and the football field. As she walked toward her car, a male figure emerged from the locker room beneath the home side of the football stadium and started walking toward her.

It was Brad.

Sandy stopped in her tracks. She didn't know whether to return to the classroom building or dash to her car and flee. Before she could make up her mind, Brad started jogging in her direction. There was no avenue of escape. He met her a few feet from her car.

"Hey," he said.

"Hi."

Brad took another step forward. Sandy flinched. Her arms were full of books, and she hoped he wasn't going to give her a hug.

"I'm sorry about last night," he said. "My mom acted like a jerk."

Sandy searched Brad's face. He seemed sincere.

"My daddy shouldn't have yelled at her," she said and sighed. "The whole idea of getting together with our parents to talk things over was a disaster."

"Yeah." Brad looked past Sandy toward the school building. "Where are you going?"

"Home. I can't take the way people are staring at me."

"Who? If anyone hassles you, I'll put a stop to it."

"How did the word get out?" Sandy asked. "Did you tell someone?"

"Only Coach Cochran. I met with him before school started."

"You didn't say anything to your friends?"

"No, but everyone knows."

"It would have happened eventually." Sandy shrugged. "What did Coach Cochran say?"

"The school board will have to decide if I get kicked off the team."

Sandy started to get upset that Brad's thoughts went to football, then realized that's how her mother must have felt about cheerleading. That conversation now seemed a long time ago, when life's trivial activities still seemed important.

"Let me take your books," Brad offered.

"No, I'm just going to my car."

Sandy started forward. Brad kept pace

with her.

"Why aren't you in English class?" he asked.

"How could I listen to old Mrs. Brooks talk about grammar and composition?"

They reached Sandy's car. She opened the passenger door and put her books in the front seat. Brad rested his left hand against the roof of the car.

"Did you get sick this morning?" he asked.

"Just a little queasy. If I drink a glass of milk, it seems to help. I guess my body needs vitamin D."

"Yeah."

Sandy waited. Brad looked into her eyes.

"Did you think any more about what my mother said about taking care of the pregnancy?"

"You mean getting an abortion?" Sandy bristled.

"Don't get mad. We're just talking."

"No, I didn't."

"We made a mistake," Brad said. "And I didn't handle the news very well. I need to apologize to you about that. Since then, I've had time to think things over. Really, it's all I've done since study hall." He looked at her earnestly. "Here's what I know. I care about you a lot and don't want you to suffer."

Sandy softened. Brad continued.

"And while our parents might not think so, I believe our relationship is something special that could lead to marriage. But the pressure of having a baby in high school doesn't make sense for either one of us. When it's the right time, I want to be a father. That should be something planned, not accidental."

"But an abortion?"

"Will let us go back to the beginning and do this thing the right way. If you want, I'll go to Atlanta with you."

Sandy wavered. Carl Donnelly paying for the procedure meant nothing to her. The offer of personal support from Brad was tempting.

"I'd have to talk to my parents. I know my mama won't like the idea."

"It's your choice. Nobody should make you do something you don't want to do. Not her, not anybody."

"Let me think about it."

Brad leaned over and, before Sandy could pull back, kissed her on the lips. She didn't resist, but when their lips parted she quickly glanced toward the school.

"If a teacher saw that we could —"

Brad laughed. "Get in trouble?"

■ ■ ■ ■

That evening Sandy and her parents told her brothers about the pregnancy. Ben's face turned red. Jack looked puzzled. Sandy could see the wheels of Ben's mind turn as he processed what had happened between his sister and Brad Donnelly. He sat with his arms across his chest and didn't say anything.

"Where is the baby going to sleep?" Jack asked.

"We've not decided that yet," Sandy's mother replied. "There are a lot of questions about the future that aren't going to be answered tonight, but we wanted you to hear the news from us. Now, both of you go upstairs and do your homework."

The seriousness of the moment prevented the boys from arguing. They dutifully trudged up the stairs.

"That went well," Sandy's father said when the boys were gone.

"I'm not so sure about Ben," Sandy answered.

"You're right," her mother agreed. "I'll talk to him one-on-one later."

"Your mother mentioned that you came home early from school," her father said.

"What happened?"

Sandy told how she felt in the hallways as news of her pregnancy spread. Her mother's eyes grew teary.

"So I went to the office and Mr. Pickerel gave me permission to come home. He wants one of you to call him."

"I'll do it," her mother said, wiping the corner of her right eye.

"And on my way out to the car, I ran into Brad in the parking lot," Sandy said.

"Did he say or do —" her father said, his voice getting louder.

"He apologized for how his parents acted last night," Sandy broke in, then paused. "And told me he'd go to Atlanta with me if I decide to have an abortion."

"Sandy —" her mother began.

"Please, Mama, let me finish."

Sandy repeated the rest of her conversation with Brad, except the part about marriage.

"That's Kim Donnelly talking," her mother said. "She prepped him. I can hear her voice secondhand."

"You should have seen his face. It didn't come across that way at all."

"An abortion is a disgraceful thing that used to be performed in back alleys in unsanitary conditions," her mother shot

66

back. "Your granny would turn over in her grave if she knew you were considering something like that."

Sandy had loved her maternal grandmother, a country woman with kind blue eyes and the recipe for the best sugar cookies on earth. Sandy's father put his hands on the table.

"I want to say something," he said. "And hear me out before either of you cut me off. Last night I got upset with Brad's mother, but today at the office I thought about what she said." He looked at Sandy's mother. "Regardless of the source, I don't want us to rule out any option without a good reason. I went by to see Reverend Frost and asked his opinion about abortion. He told me there are different beliefs about when a baby becomes a human being. A lot of people think it has to be able to survive outside the mother's body to be a person. Before that, it's a collection of cells that only has the potential to be a person. If that's true, the most important question for us to answer is what's best for Sandy. Ending the pregnancy would allow her to get back to normal: going to school, cheerleading, planning for college, and enjoying everything that her senior year in high school is supposed to be."

"Reverend Frost told you Sandy should have an abortion?" Sandy's mother asked.

"No. But he said it wasn't a clear-cut situation, and because it's so early in the pregnancy, we should consider Sandy's needs first."

Sandy wanted to think about herself too. Two days into knowing she was pregnant was enough time to convince her that it might be smart to end the problem before it got worse. A fresh start following a hard lesson learned sounded more and more like a good idea. And the minister's words to her father eased her conscience.

Brad's face swam into view. She cared about him a lot. Otherwise she wouldn't have done what she did with him. Daydreams about marriage to the handsome football player weren't new, but they'd been squelched during the past forty-eight hours. Away from their parents' interference, she just knew the two of them could work things out. Sandy was glad her mother couldn't read her mind.

"I had a conversation today too," her mother said. "With Linda. She thinks —"

"Why did you have to invite her to stick her nose in this?" Sandy's father interrupted with obvious exasperation. "I get tired of her always running her mouth and spouting her opinion as if it were written in red in the Bible."

"Linda has more sense than anyone else in this family, and we're so emotionally involved it's hard for us to think straight. I let you finish. Now it's my turn."

Sandy's father grunted. "I just don't like it when she pretends to be your mother."

"She took care of me when I was little, and now that my folks are gone, I'm glad I have someone like her in my life. You won't think she's just trying to be nosy when you hear what she's offered to do."

FIVE

Before her mother could continue, the phone on the kitchen wall rang. Sandy got up and answered it. It was a classmate from school.

"Becky, there's nothing else to tell," Sandy said. "Look, I've got to go. I'm talking to my parents." Sandy paused and listened for a moment. "No, that's not true, and if you're my friend you won't repeat it."

Sandy hung up.

"What did she say?" her mother asked.

"Nothing."

"You said something wasn't true. What was it?"

Sandy rolled her eyes. "Becky Allen heard that Brad and I were going to elope and get married in Las Vegas."

"Who started that rumor?" her mother asked.

"Lynn Jordan. I've tried to be nice to her, but she's hated me ever since I was elected to the sophomore homecoming court and she wasn't."

"There's going to be all kinds of crazy talk," Sandy's mother said, shaking her head. "Anyway, Linda has offered to let you live with her until the baby is born. She got in touch with a special school in Atlanta that will accept you so you can graduate on time. I can talk to Mr. Pickerel tomorrow, but we all know he's not going to let you stay in school while you're pregnant."

Sandy's mouth was dry. She'd always been intimidated by her spinster aunt. After earning a biochemistry degree from Vanderbilt, Linda had worked for years at the Centers for Disease Control in Atlanta. Sandy wasn't sure exactly what she did, but it had something to do with scary-sounding viruses and bacteria that, if released, could kill half of humanity. The thought of living in the same house with her aunt made her skin crawl.

"I don't think that's a good idea," Sandy said.

"Do you have a better one?" her mother asked.

"Live here. You told me yesterday you weren't going to kick me out onto the street."

"But it's going to be hard for you to be in

71

Rutland during the pregnancy. You didn't last a whole day at school, and it's only going to get worse."

"But if I stayed with Aunt Linda, where would I go after the baby was born?"

"Come back home until you leave for college in the fall. Linda and I agree the best thing to do is place the baby for adoption. There are plenty of couples who can't have children and desperately want one. While Kim Donnelly was calling abortion clinics, Linda contacted several adoption agencies in Atlanta. She's narrowed the list down to two that only work with middle- and upper-middle-class couples. Kim can say all she wants about getting rid of an accidental baby, but it's not the baby's fault that it's inside your womb, and in about seven months the 'it' is going to be a tiny boy or girl who deserves a chance at life, even if you're not in a position to raise it."

Her mother's words intensified the inner war in Sandy between teenage self-centeredness and budding maternal instinct. She placed her fingers lightly on her stomach. And felt something move. She sat up with a start.

"Is it too early to feel the baby move?" she asked.

"Yes," her mother said. "Quickening

doesn't happen until around four or five months."

"It's probably gas," her father added. "That happened a lot to your mother when she was pregnant with you and your brothers. She had terrible gas."

Sandy's mother cut her eyes at Sandy's father and then continued. "You'd meet with someone from the adoption agency who'd explain everything to you shortly after you move to Atlanta. The agency makes all the arrangements for prenatal care and notifies the hospital of your situation. Once the baby is born, you sign papers allowing it to be adopted."

Sandy's stomach was in knots.

"Would I see the baby?"

"I wondered about that," her mother said. "Linda didn't know. I think it would be hard to see the baby and then give it up."

"Me too," Sandy said slowly. "I'd hate to go through the hassle of the pregnancy for nothing."

"We don't have to make that decision tonight," her father said.

"He's right," her mother added. "I think it makes sense to place the baby for adoption so you can get on with your life, but I don't want you having regrets down the road when things are hard."

"It's already been hard," Sandy said. "And it's going to get worse."

"Let's all sleep on it and talk more tomorrow," her mother said.

Later that evening in her room, Sandy faced the question she hadn't brought up with her parents. How would Brad react to her decision? She picked up the pink phone in her bedroom and slowly dialed the Donnellys' number but hung up before the call connected. Five minutes later her phone rang. It was Brad.

"Can you talk?" he asked.

"Yeah, I'm in my room with the door closed. I started to call you but chickened out," Sandy said.

"You could have. My parents went out to dinner and left me home to watch Nate. It's their way of punishing me."

Brad's eight-year-old little brother was a brat.

"I hauled the TV from my parents' bedroom into his room, then locked him up with it turned to a scary movie."

"You didn't."

"No, he's watching a rerun of *Bonanza*." Brad paused. "I had to get off to myself because all I can think about is you."

Sandy sat on the bed and crossed her legs.

"What have been thinking?"

"How much I want to be with you."

"Really?"

"Yeah. If our parents weren't going nuts, I believe we could figure out what we should do."

"Cool. I was thinking the same thing."

Brad was silent for a moment.

"You know," he said, "I've never felt what I do for you with any other girl, and I meant every word I said to you at the lake and the dance."

Sandy melted.

"Me too," she said. "I went steady with Chris Stevens for over a year, but I've never really loved anyone before."

Brad was quiet for a moment.

"Hey, I have an idea. You'll think it's crazy, but at least listen."

"Okay."

"What if we took off on our own?"

Sandy's eyes opened wide. "You mean, like Las Vegas?"

"No, we can't drive all the way across the country. But Jack Harris told me that a seventeen-year-old girl who's pregnant doesn't have to get her parents' permission to get married."

"We'd elope?" Sandy's head was spinning.

"Why not? Once we were married, our

folks would have to deal with it and couldn't boss us around."

Sandy had always imagined herself walking down the aisle of the church holding on to her father's arm and wearing a flowing white gown.

"Would you still want me to end the pregnancy?" she asked, using the phrase she'd picked up from the conversation with her parents.

"Yeah, but that doesn't keep us from loving each other. And if we're married and don't have any money, you can get an abortion for free."

"For free?"

"Yeah. I found the notes my mom wrote down yesterday and called one of those clinics in Atlanta myself. I didn't give the woman who answered the phone my name, but I told her the whole story, and she said not to worry about the money. They just want to help girls like you who are in a jam."

"Where would we get married?" Sandy asked, hardly believing the words were coming out of her mouth.

"I thought we could drive over to Richfield and see a justice of the peace. They have a place across the street from the courthouse where you get the blood test."

The nearby town had a well-deserved

reputation as a marriage mill.

"When would we go?" Sandy found herself asking.

"I'd like to do it right now, but it'll have to be when the courthouse is open."

"You're sure you want to marry me?" Sandy needed to hear it again.

"Hey, this pregnancy thing hit me like a load of bricks, but I'm getting my feet under me now. I can't live without you."

"I feel the same way about you," Sandy said. "I love you."

"And I love you." Brad paused. "Hold on. Nate is pitching a fit. I've gotta go. We'll talk tomorrow."

Sandy slowly lowered the phone to its cradle. That night sleep was impossible. As she tossed and turned, Sandy's mind raced through so many possible scenarios for the future that she felt she was going crazy. At 3:00 a.m., she sat bolt upright in bed.

"Stop it!" she cried out.

She listened, afraid that she'd awakened one of her brothers, but the house remained silent. She tried to command her mind to calm down, but it wouldn't obey. She knew her mother kept an extra bottle of sleeping pills in a cupboard in the kitchen, and Sandy had to have something to knock her out. Going through four more hours of torment wasn't an option. She walked softly down the hallway to the top of the stairs, placed her hand on the railing, then stopped in her tracks. She was pregnant, and a sleeping pill might be dangerous to the baby's development.

Sandy slid to the floor with her feet curled beneath her. She leaned her shoulder against the top post of the stair railing and buried her face in her hands. How could she walk into a clinic and ask a doctor to end the pregnancy when she couldn't force herself to go downstairs to take a sleeping pill? She'd talked seriously with Brad about getting an abortion, but she actually had no idea how the procedure was performed. She lifted her head and pushed her tangled hair away from her face.

"I can't do that," she muttered.

She remained in a huddled mess at the top of the stairs and waited for a counterargument to surface. A couple of minutes passed. Nothing came. Pulling herself up, she shuffled back to her bedroom, where she collapsed into bed and fell into a fitful sleep.

The following morning Sandy was nauseated again and threw up in the bathroom. As she finished, there was a light knock on the door. Bleary-eyed, she opened it to find Ben, forlorn-looking and wearing his too-small pajamas.

"Are you throwing up because you're pregnant?" he asked.

"Yes."

"I'm sorry."

"I feel better now." Sandy forced herself to smile as she ruffled Ben's hair. "Get ready for school."

"I think Brad Donnelly is a creep. You deserve a boyfriend who is tons better than him."

"Don't say that about Brad."

"I can if I want to."

Ben pushed past her into the bathroom.

Sandy went to her room and didn't come out until she heard the boys leave the house. Then, still in her nightgown, she went downstairs. Her mother was sitting in the breakfast nook drinking coffee.

"Rough morning?" her mother asked.

"And night."

Sandy poured herself a glass of milk and put a piece of bread in the toaster.

"When are you going to call Mr. Pickerel?" she asked while she waited for the toast to pop up.

"This afternoon. Or I may go by the school in person."

"Why not call him?"

"I want to ask him to check out the school Linda found in Atlanta."

"Don't do that. Not yet. That's not what I want to do."

"Do you have another idea?"

"No, but I feel like you're rushing me."

"You'll feel more like talking later in the day," her mother said. "Mornings were always hard for me when I was pregnant with you and the boys."

"Don't talk about me that way!" Sandy raised her voice.

She spun away, knocking her glass of milk onto the floor, and ran out of the kitchen. Slamming her bedroom door, she lay facedown on the bed and put her pillow over her head. After a couple of minutes, there was a knock at the door. Sandy raised her head.

"Leave me alone! I'll clean up the mess!"

The door opened.

"You don't have to say anything, and I cleaned up the milk. Here's your toast. I put butter on it and poured a fresh glass of milk."

Her mother set the milk and toast on the nightstand.

"Thanks," Sandy muttered. "I'm sorry."

Her mother held up her hand. "We're not

going to talk now. Drink your milk and eat the toast. I have a dentist appointment in twenty minutes, then I'm going to the nursing home to see Mrs. Belhaven. It's been over a month since I stopped by for a visit."

Mrs. Belhaven was a former neighbor who'd sold her house and moved into a nursing home when her health declined. She'd taught Sandy how to bake peanut butter cookies. Sandy sat up.

"Please don't tell her about me."

"I won't. But even if I did, she wouldn't remember it by the time I reached the parking lot. She's going downhill fast."

"Then give her a hug from me."

"Okay. I'll be gone for several hours."

Sandy lay on her bed until she heard the front door close behind her mother, then got up and went downstairs to the laundry room. There was a load of the boys' dirty clothes waiting to be washed. She put the clothes in the washer and started the machine. She glanced at the clock in the kitchen. If she was at school, she'd be in her honors Spanish class.

Unlike most of her classmates who despised foreign language study, Sandy enjoyed both speaking and reading Spanish. She'd brought home her Spanish textbook and the original Spanish version of *Don Quixote.* Returning to her room, she read a few chapters in the classic novel. Cervantes's portrayal of Dulcinea, the peasant girl whom the delusional Don Quixote believed to be a noblewoman, touched her. Sandy had never experienced life as an outsider looked down upon and laughed at by others. Until now.

When she went back downstairs, the clothes were ready to be put in the dryer. After they were finished, she neatly folded them and carried them up to the boys' bedroom. She hoped doing the laundry would be acceptable penance for her blowup in the kitchen.

Her mother hadn't come home by noon, and Sandy fixed an elaborate sandwich containing two meats, three cheeses, a tomato slice, lettuce, pickles, mayonnaise, and spicy mustard, all between two thick slices of French bread. She was amazed how quickly she could transition from nausea to famished hunger. She ate every bite of the sandwich and washed it down with two large glasses of water.

After lunch, time dragged by. To go from the frenetic pace of a high school senior to complete inactivity was a severe jolt. Sandy tried to take a nap but couldn't. Lying on her bed, she imagined what Brad was doing at school. She knew exactly where he would be throughout the day. In her absence he would have to endure all the scornful stares and snide behind-the-back comments.

At around two-thirty her mother returned. Sandy went downstairs to the kitchen.

"Thanks for doing the boys' laundry," her mother said.

"You're welcome. It was boring around here. Did you talk to Mr. Pickerel?"

"Yes, and he went out of his way to be helpful. He made a couple of phone calls about the school in Atlanta while I waited in his office."

"What did he find out?"

Her mother took a small notepad from her purse and flipped it open.

"It's one of the few options you have. Pregnant girls go to Metro High, along with students who've been expelled from schools in the Atlanta system, and are sent there for one last chance. The school also accepts students who've come through the juvenile court system."

"That sounds horrible," Sandy replied, her eyes wide. "It's a school for juvenile delinquents."

"But Mr. Pickerel said the principal has a good reputation, and the overall graduation rate is fair. Remember, most of your credits for college will be from Rutland High. All you'll have to do is finish out the year in Atlanta."

"You want me to go to this place?" Sandy asked in shock.

"The Atlanta school is one option," her mother replied. "There are at least three others. You could leave school and be a dropout."

"I wouldn't do that."

"Good. Second, you could withdraw from Rutland and reenroll next year after the baby is born. Mr. Pickerel assured me they'd let you return. Finally, you could take the GED test. If you did that, you'd have a high school certificate, but it would be hard to get into a good college."

Sandy quickly realized that passing the GED test might be the best path to take, especially if she married Brad. As a young wife, she'd probably attend a community college that wouldn't be picky about admissions.

"I bet I could pass the GED test now," she said. "And I wouldn't have to leave home for seven months."

Sandy immediately felt a twinge of guilt for deceiving her mother. Marrying Brad would mean moving out and finding another place to live, even if it was somewhere in Rutland.

"I thought about that," her mother admitted. "But I really want you to consider going to Atlanta."

"Daddy doesn't want me to go."

"He's considering it. After I left the high school, I went by his office and talked to him for a long time."

Sandy knew that eventually her father wouldn't be able to resist her mother's will. "It's my life," she said, then braced herself for her mother's reaction.

"Yes, it is," her mother replied simply. "And you're going to have to live with whatever decision you make."

The unexpected shifting of responsibility to her shoulders caused Sandy to step back.

"You're not going to make me do something?" she asked in surprise.

"No," her mother replied. "I'm not."

Six

A couple of hours later, the front doorbell chimed. Football practice wasn't over yet, so Sandy knew it couldn't be Brad. She ran downstairs and peeked through the sidelight. It was Jessica. Sandy opened the door. Jessica came in and gave her a long hug.

"I missed you today," her friend said. "When are you coming back to school?"

"Let's go up to my room."

The two girls had spent countless hours in Sandy's bedroom talking, giggling, sharing secrets, and staying up late. They sat opposite each other on the floor. Sandy told Jessica she wasn't going back to Rutland High and went over her educational options.

"The place in Atlanta sounds scary," Jessica said.

"Yeah, I can't believe my mom is pushing it. My parents say they aren't kicking me out of the house, but that's what it feels like to me." Sandy took a deep breath before continuing. "I just want to work things out between me and Brad."

Jessica glanced down at the floor.

"What?" Sandy asked.

"I don't know," Jessica replied without looking up. "It may not be anything."

"What are you talking about?" Sandy asked in alarm. "Tell me."

Jessica sighed. "I saw Brad talking to Crystal Bradshaw at her locker after second period. I didn't think anything about it until sixth-period study hall. I had to get a book for that research paper I'm writing on Clara Barton for American history. When I went to the biography section against the back wall, Brad and Crystal were together again, talking and laughing. As soon as Brad saw me, he put his arm around Crystal's waist, and they moved away. Everybody knows Crystal is a terrible flirt, so it was probably all her fault. I mean, she calls guys on the phone to try to get them to ask her out. Nobody does that."

Sandy felt the color drain from her face.

"He put his arm around her waist?"

"Yeah."

"How did he look at her?"

"I don't know. He seemed uncomfortable."

"Was that before or after he saw you?"

"Uh, after, I guess." Jessica ran her fingers through her hair. "Hey, I shouldn't have said anything about it. You've got enough going on without me making it worse."

"No," Sandy said, trying to regain her composure. "I need to know what's going on so I can ask Brad about it. I'm not there at school to keep track of stuff myself. I'm sure he has a good reason for talking to Crystal. You know, I can't expect him to ignore everyone except me."

"Yeah, you like to joke around with Barry Maxwell."

"Barry and I have been friends since kindergarten. There's never been a bit of romance between us. He's not my type."

"And Crystal isn't Brad's type. I mean, why would he be interested in her if someone like you is willing to date him?"

"I guess so," Sandy said without much confidence in her voice.

Shortly before supper, Sandy's pink phone rang. It was Brad.

"Hey," he said. "I missed you today."

"I missed you too. It was super lonely here." Sandy paused. It didn't feel right to immediately bring up Crystal.

"I want to see you tonight," Brad said. "I've got a plan."

Sandy's heart skipped a beat.

"What kind of plan?"

"Tell your mom that you'll go to the grocery store to pick up something for her. Before you leave the house, call me and we'll meet up."

"Then what?"

"We'll drive to the overlook. It should be deserted on a weekday evening."

"I don't know . . ." Sandy hesitated.

"I have to see you. It's driving me nuts being apart."

"And then I'll come back home?"

Brad was silent for a moment, then laughed.

"What's funny?" Sandy asked.

"We're not running off to get married tonight, but we do need to work out the plan."

Sandy felt embarrassed.

"Okay, but I'll need to come up with more of a trip than to the grocery store. What are you going to tell your parents when you leave?"

"Nothing. They won't care. Call me and I'll meet you."

Sandy helped her mother set the table for supper.

"Where are the paper napkins?" Sandy

asked after checking the usual place.

"We must be out. Use the cloth ones, and I'll wash them later."

"Do you want me to go to the store after supper and pick some up?" Sandy asked, trying to sound nonchalant. "I've been cooped up in the house all day and need to get out."

"That's not necessary, but if you want to go out, you could take a peach pie I baked this afternoon to the nursing home where Mrs. Belhaven is staying. I told the administrator I wanted to donate a dessert as a prize for their bingo tournament later in the week. It would also be good if you could stick your head in for a minute and say hi to Mrs. Belhaven."

Sandy smiled. "Sure."

Each time during supper that Sandy thought about her rendezvous with Brad, her heart beat a little bit faster. Her brothers wolfed down their food in between monosyllabic responses to their mother's questions about school.

"When is Sandy going back to school?" Jack asked. "It's not fair that she gets to stay at home."

"We're not sure," Sandy's mother responded. "But while she was home, she washed and folded your dirty clothes."

"That's why I couldn't find my brown shorts," Ben said.

"They're in the third drawer of your dresser," Sandy replied.

"I'd moved them to the second drawer," Ben said. "The third drawer is where I keep stuff that I don't wear too much."

After supper, Sandy didn't stay in the kitchen to clean up. She went directly upstairs to her bedroom, closed the door, and called Brad.

"Perfect," he said when she told him about the nursing home. "Great idea. When are you leaving the house?"

"In about ten minutes."

"See you in the parking lot at the nursing home. I'll park on the opposite side of the building from the main entrance."

"But we won't have time to go to the overlook. The nursing home parking lot will be private enough."

"Not for what I have in mind."

"No," Sandy replied emphatically. "We need to talk, not —"

"Relax, baby," Brad interrupted. "See you there."

The peach pie was covered with clear plastic wrap. Sandy could see a few places where the juice had seeped through the top of the brown crust. Her mother had perfected the art of flaky crusts and knew exactly how much sugar to add to fresh peaches without ruining their slight tartness.

"I'm leaving with the pie!" she called down the hallway to her parents' room.

"Thanks. Don't go anywhere else!" her mother answered.

Sandy didn't reply. She carried the pie out of the house and carefully positioned it on the floorboard of the car.

The nursing home was about two miles away. The one-story building was constructed in the shape of a T. There was no sign of Brad's car when Sandy parked on the right-hand side of the building.

She delivered the pie to a woman on duty in the administrator's office, then went down the hallway to Mrs. Belhaven's room. The door was closed, and Sandy cracked it open. The elderly woman was asleep on her back with her mouth open. Sandy tiptoed into the room and wrote a short note on a pad to let her know that she'd stopped by.

When she left the building, Sandy saw Brad's car. He'd backed into a space beside her VW. Sandy looked both ways as she crossed the parking lot. No one was in sight. Brad was wearing a Rutland High baseball cap. He leaned over and unlocked the passenger door of his car as she approached.

As soon as she got in the car, Brad leaned over, put his hand behind her head, and gave her a kiss. Sandy responded for a moment, then pulled back.

"What's wrong?" Brad asked.

"It feels weird kissing in the parking lot of the nursing home."

"That's why we should go to the over-look."

Sandy shook her head. "Not tonight. I can't stay out long."

Brad shrugged. "Pretty soon we'll be kissing whenever and wherever we want." He took a sheet of paper from his pocket. "During study hall I wrote down some stuff we need to talk about."

"Was that before or after you hung out with Crystal Bradshaw?"

Brad's eyes narrowed. "I knew Jessica would tattle to you about that and turn it into a big deal. Look, Crystal is a cool girl, but there's nothing between us. She knows what we're going through and was decent enough to call me and tell me everything is going to be okay. That's way better than the people who are talking behind our backs and running us down."

"She called you at home?"

"Yeah."

"How many times?"

"Not that many. Come on, Sandy. I didn't want to get together with you to talk about Crystal."

"Okay," Sandy replied defensively. "But not being at school makes me worry about things —"

"That you shouldn't worry about." Brad glanced down at the sheet of paper. "I've written down the name, phone number, and address of the clinic in Atlanta. I talked to the lady again this afternoon, and she says there's no reason for you to wait until after we're married to have the abortion. That makes sense to me. Then we can get married, and have an awesome honeymoon. It would be weird being together and knowing you're pregnant. After we were married, I thought we could call our parents and tell them we're going to the mountains for a few days. They have these honeymoon cabins in Gatlinburg —"

"Please," Sandy interrupted. "You're going too fast."

"Hey, it's my job as the man to plan our future."

"But I haven't decided if I'm going to have an abortion."

Brad's mouth dropped open. "Why not?"

Sandy told him about the sleeping pill

incident.

"So?" Brad replied. "You were half asleep. That's not the best time to make a big decision."

Sandy placed her hand on her stomach.

"I just can't think about the baby as a glob of cells."

"But that's what it is. The woman at the clinic told me they use a vacuum cleaner sort of thing that sucks it out in a few seconds."

Sandy felt suddenly nauseated. She put her hand to her mouth.

Brad spoke slowly. "I told you in the school parking lot that I wasn't ready to be a father. Bringing a kid into our lives makes no sense." He pointed at Sandy's abdomen. "You're going to have to choose between me and it."

Sandy swallowed. She wanted to cave in but couldn't force the words out of her mouth.

"What if I let someone adopt the baby?" she asked hopefully. "My aunt in Atlanta has offered to let me stay with her until the baby is born and adopted out. Then we could get married."

"I'm not going to put my life on hold for nine months while you're in Atlanta."

"It's only seven months. I'm already eight

weeks along."

"It doesn't matter." Brad frowned. "Once you have a kid, you're used up."

Sandy stared at him in shock.

"Used up?" she asked.

Brad turned away. A horrible thought hit Sandy.

"Do you really want to marry me, or are you just trying to talk me into getting an abortion and then you'll dump me?"

Brad faced her.

"You're psycho," he spat. "Get out of the car."

"It was just a question." Sandy felt panic rising up in her throat.

"And I'm not going to answer it. I don't have to put up with your stupid jealousy about Crystal and craziness about a baby. This pregnancy thing has turned you into a different girl, and I don't like her. If you're not going to go along with my plan, we're finished."

Sandy didn't know what to say. Shaking, she put her hand on the door handle.

"If you change your mind, call me before you go to bed. If I don't hear from you, I'll rip up this sheet of paper, because it'll be over between us."

Sandy drove home through a haze of tears.

She dried her face with a tissue before she went inside the house, but when she glanced in the rearview mirror, she saw that her eyes were bloodshot. She quietly opened the front door and tiptoed toward the staircase.

"Sandy!" her mother's voice called out from the kitchen.

"I'm here!" Sandy said, her left foot on the first stair.

Her mother came into the foyer.

"How did it go at the nursing home?"

For a split second Sandy thought her mother knew about the meeting with Brad.

"Uh, I delivered the pie. Mrs. Belhaven was asleep, but I left her a note."

"Why were you gone so long?"

Sandy turned her head slightly.

"You've been crying," her mother said, concern coming into her voice. "What happened?"

Sandy plopped down on the second step of the stairs as fresh tears rolled down her cheeks.

"I saw Brad."

She buried her face in her hands. Her mother joined her and put her right arm around Sandy's shoulders. Her mother left for a moment and returned with several tissues that she pressed into Sandy's hand.

"He says we're finished unless I get an

abortion," Sandy said, her chest still heaving. "Did you know they use a thing like a vacuum cleaner to —"

Sandy couldn't say the words. Her mother began to gently massage her upper back.

"He says he wants to marry me," Sandy continued. "But he's not ready to be a father."

"Do you think he's ready to be a husband?" her mother asked softly.

Sandy thought back to the conversation in the car. She'd felt bullied and belittled.

"No, and I don't think I'm ready to be a wife and mother either."

She stared at the front door where Brad and his family had stormed out of the house.

"Brad said I was crazy. Maybe I am. But what he wanted us to do was crazy." She turned toward her mother. "I couldn't make myself go along with him. I love him, but I don't trust him."

"Then trust your heart."

"I don't know what it's saying."

"I think you do."

Sandy shook her head, then remembered what had happened the previous night at the top of the stairs. Brad's words rang hollow compared to what she'd felt in that moment about the baby she was carrying. Every cell in her body rebelled against the

98

idea of harming the life inside.

Her mother slipped from her seat on the stairs and knelt at Sandy's feet. She took Sandy's hands in hers. Tears pooled in her mother's eyes.

"Mama, don't," Sandy protested.

"Sandy, we love you. And I've —"

"I know, I know —" Sandy tried to stop her.

"Let me finish. I've treasured every moment of your life from the time I first saw you as a tiny infant in the hospital to watching you run onto the football field as head cheerleader two weeks ago. I don't want you to leave our home. I'll miss you terribly. But sometimes love doesn't get what it wants; it has to do what's best."

Her mother's words had a calming effect on Sandy.

"You really think I should stay with Linda and place the baby for adoption?" she asked.

Her mother put her fingers to Sandy's lips and shook her head.

"Don't say anything now. Wait until you're sure in your own heart."

Later in her bedroom, Sandy stared at her pink phone and tried to visualize herself picking up the receiver to call Brad. Each time she played out a possible conversation, it ended with an argument. Suddenly, the phone rang. Sandy jumped. It continued to ring as she debated whether to answer. Finally, deciding she'd regret not finding out what Brad had to say, she picked up the receiver.

"Hey."

"Sandy, it's Linda," her aunt said in her crisp voice. "I hope it's all right to call your personal number. I know you like to use the phone in your bedroom for conversations with your friends."

Sandy sat on the edge of the bed.

"No, it's fine. I've not been getting a lot of calls from my friends. I don't think they know what to say."

"I understand. Well, I'm not ready to stamp a scarlet letter on your forehead, and if you decide to accept my invitation to live with me, you're not going to get any lectures about the mistakes you've made. I assume you've figured that out on your own."

"Yes."

"Good. That doesn't mean I'll pamper you either. I intend to treat you like an adult."

"I don't feel like an adult."

"You aren't, but we're going to start pretending that you are. Your grandmother taught your mother and me that adversity is the crucible for character formation. That's what I want to see happen in your life over the next few months."

Sandy wasn't sure exactly what Linda meant. It sounded like a threat, but the words weren't spoken in a threatening way.

"Did Mama ask you to call me?"

"No, we haven't talked since yesterday morning."

Sandy paused for a moment.

"Thanks for inviting me to stay with you," she said. "It's very generous of you."

"It was one of those things that can't be logically explained. I immediately knew I had to extend the offer. It's up to you and your parents whether to accept."

"Mama is letting me decide."

"Good. I know that's hard for her to do. Whatever you choose, I'm going to support you."

When the phone call ended, Sandy slowly lowered the receiver into the cradle. Linda had always scared Sandy. Her father thought she was a busybody. But now, for the first time, Sandy saw how being around someone strong like her aunt might be good for her.

Sandy didn't call Brad. He didn't call her. Crawling into bed, she dreaded the return of the frantic anxiety that had harassed her the previous night. However, no night terrors assaulted her. She closed her eyes and woke up with the hazy rays of early morning light peeking through her window.

Within a few minutes, she was in the bathroom throwing up. When she finished, she went downstairs and told her mother and father that she wanted to go to Atlanta, the sooner the better.

"Are you sure?" her mother asked.

"Yes." Sandy touched her heart. "It's the only thing I can think about that feels right in here."

Her mother looked at her father and raised her eyebrows.

"Okay," he replied, throwing his hands up in the air. "If she can survive seven months with Linda, she'll be able to handle anything life throws at her down the road."

SEVEN

Ben wouldn't let Sandy carry the heavy suitcases downstairs from her bedroom. She watched as her brother wedged her third suitcase into the backseat of the car.

"Thanks, Ben," she said.

Ben looked at the ground and didn't respond. Sandy's father and Jack came out of the house.

"Where's Mama?" Sandy asked.

"She went upstairs to make sure you didn't forget anything," her father said.

"It's only a two-hour drive to Atlanta," Sandy said. "And I'm planning on coming home most weekends. I can get anything I need the next time I'm here."

Sandy's mother came out of the house carrying a blue dress Sandy had left in her closet on purpose. Sandy started to protest, but she kept quiet and let her mother lay the dress across the suitcases in the back-seat of the car.

"You look nice in this. Wear it if Linda takes you out to dinner. She doesn't cook every night, you know."

"Okay."

"Are you sure you know how to get to her house?" her father asked for the second time.

"The directions you gave me are on the passenger seat, and I'll remember the landmarks."

Her father checked his watch.

"You should get to Linda's house in about two and half hours. You're not going to stop along the way, are you?"

"No, except for gas and a bathroom break."

"Do it before you get to Atlanta."

No one spoke. They stood in a ragged circle in the driveway. A car passed on the street, and the driver honked the horn. It was Chip Cash, a boy who'd wanted to date Sandy about the time she'd fallen for Brad. If she'd gone out with Chip instead of Brad, maybe she wouldn't be getting in her car to leave for Atlanta.

She hadn't heard a word from Brad since the night in the nursing home parking lot. Jessica confirmed that Brad and Crystal were now an inseparable couple at school. The previous Saturday night they were seen snuggling in a booth at a local pizza restaurant. And Crystal proudly wore one of Brad's game-day jerseys to a big pep rally on Friday afternoon.

Sandy hugged Jack, who awkwardly pulled away after a couple of seconds. She turned to Ben, who wrapped his arms around her without reservation. She embraced her father, who patted her on the back. She then turned to her mother, who put her hands on either side of Sandy's face and looked into her eyes.

"You're going to get through this," her mother said. "And someday you're going to have a family of your own."

Sandy wanted to believe, but at that moment there wasn't room in her heart for a family other than the one standing in the driveway. Her mother kissed her on the forehead.

"Stay strong," she said. "Take everything one day at a time. And remember, I love you."

Sandy hugged her mother tightly, then planted a firm kiss on her left cheek.

"Thanks, Mama," she said. "I love you too."

Her mother wiped her eyes with the back of her right hand. Sandy got in the car, closed the door, and rolled down her window. As she backed down the driveway, the engine in the VW rattled like a giant sewing machine. Sandy waved one last time, then released the clutch and drove slowly away.

Every building and house Sandy passed was familiar to her. She knew many of the people who lived in the houses and a lot of the people who worked in the businesses. Her life was intimately intertwined with those in the nest where she'd been nurtured. Now she was departing on an unknown journey into a world of strangers with an uncertain end. She reached the city limits and pressed down on the gas pedal. The future rose to meet her.

The road from Rutland to Atlanta was two lanes wide. Near the halfway point was a locally owned convenience store/gas station. The store was familiar to Sandy because her father often stopped there to buy gas and snacks. She reached it and pulled off the highway. It was a sunny day. After filling up the gas tank, she went inside to pay and use the bathroom. A man she recognized from previous stops was at the cash register. Behind him a woman was stocking a shelf with cigarettes. Sandy paid for the gas with one of the crisp five-dollar bills her father had given her. After using the restroom, she paused in front of a drink cooler against the back wall of the store and tried to decide between apple and grape juice. Someone tapped her on the shoulder, and she turned around.

An old woman with a wrinkled face, bright-blue eyes, and white hair pulled tight in a bun stood behind her. The woman was wearing a blue-print dress similar to the ones Sandy's granny preferred.

"Excuse me," Sandy said, stepping aside. "I didn't know I was in your way."

The woman continued to eye Sandy without moving.

"Go ahead," Sandy said. "I'll wait."

The woman moved closer to Sandy and looked directly in her face.

"You're Rebekah," the woman said in a voice that cracked slightly.

"No. I'm Sandy Lincoln."

The old woman pointed at Sandy's abdomen.

"Like Rebekah, you have twin boys in there."

Sandy gasped and stepped back.

"How did you —"

"Are you going to raise them?" the old woman asked.

"Uh, I was thinking about adoption."

"Good, good." The old woman nodded

her head. "Just make sure that you separate them at birth."

"Why?"

The old woman leaned in closer. Sandy caught a whiff of a fragrance she couldn't identify.

"If they ever meet, one of them is going to die."

Sandy felt her skin grow cold.

"I don't understand."

The woman stared directly into Sandy's eyes with an intensity that made Sandy feel faint.

"Some choices bring life; others bring death. Choose well."

The old woman turned around, walked down the aisle, and left the store. Shaken, Sandy placed her hand against the cooler to steady herself. After a few moments and deep breaths, she grabbed a container of apple juice and took it to the cash register. There was no sign of the old woman in the parking lot. Sandy handed a dollar bill to the cashier, who rang up the sale and counted out the change in her hand.

"Do you know the older lady who just left the store?" she asked.

The man turned to the woman behind him.

"Sue Ellen, do you know who that was?

She came in but didn't buy anything."

"No," the woman replied. "But I saw her looking at cans of snuff."

"Did she bother you?" the man asked Sandy.

"Not exactly," Sandy said. "But she said something very strange."

"What was it?" the man asked.

Sandy shook her head. "Nothing."

Outside, Sandy glanced around apprehensively. Two cars were at the gas pumps with men standing beside them. There were passengers inside the cars, but Sandy didn't see anyone who looked like the old woman.

Sandy got in her car and drove slowly away from the station. At the edge of the highway she looked in both directions, not just to be safe, but to check for the old woman. As far as she could see, no one was walking along the shoulder of the road. Sandy pulled onto the highway and turned in the direction of Atlanta. She continued to search the roadside for a couple hundred yards but then gave up. The old woman couldn't have gone any farther than that on foot.

The odd encounter at the store cast a dark shadow over the rest of the trip. The fact that the old woman somehow sensed that

Sandy was pregnant was strange; the statement that Sandy was going to have twins was bizarre; and the dire prediction that if the boys ever met one of them would die was frightening. For Sandy, it was more uncertainty piled upon a mountain of existing ambiguity. And the haunting fragrance seemed to linger in the car. Only when she reached the outskirts of Atlanta with cars whizzing by on either side of the VW did her mind clear.

Linda lived in a small brick home a mile from Emory University, a liberal arts college for smart students who came from all over the country. With its cramped campus and the absence of a football team, Emory didn't seem like a real college to Sandy. Passing the main entrance to the school, Sandy turned left into a neighborhood developed in the 1950s. She passed quaint, modest houses built on heavily wooded lots.

Linda's house was at the end of a short cul-de-sac. There was a steep drop-off into a ravine at the rear of her property. A tiny stream flowed through the ravine, then disappeared into a large concrete pipe. Leaving her luggage in the car, Sandy walked to the front door. There wasn't a doorbell, so she clanged a brass knocker. A few seconds later, her aunt opened the door.

Linda, with her blue eyes and formerly blond hair, bore a physical resemblance to Sandy's mother, but the petite woman was more wiry than Julie Lincoln and filled with nervous energy.

"Come in," Linda said, giving Sandy a quick hug. "You're in the big city now where no one knows you're pregnant, and no one would care if they did. Where's your luggage?"

"In the car."

"It won't walk into the house by itself."

Linda's brusqueness was a dominant trait, and she showed little restraint in sharing her opinion about anything with anybody. She and Sandy carried the suitcases inside. Linda led the way through the small living room, past the kitchen, and down the hall to a guest room that contained a full-size bed, a wooden nightstand, a chest of drawers, and a closet concealed by sliding doors. A simple white bedspread covered the bed. It was a utilitarian room. Linda opened the closet door.

"I cleared out a space for your clothes," she said, "and the top two drawers of the chest are empty."

"Thanks."

Linda's two cats entered the room, meowing.

"Peaches and Lillo think this is their room, but I moved their litter box to the laundry room. If the door is closed and they start scratching, carry them there. They'll figure out the change in a few days."

"I wouldn't mind if they slept in here. Mama won't allow animals in the house."

"Well, there's no use having a pet if it's not part of the family, but I'd rather get them used to the laundry room."

Sandy didn't argue.

"I'll leave you alone to unpack."

Sandy took out her clothes and put as much as she could in the two drawers and in the closet. The things that wouldn't fit, she left in one of the suitcases. Although cozy, the house felt lonely, especially when compared to the hustle and bustle of her home in Rutland. The cats returned to the room and brushed up against Sandy's legs. She ran her hand down their silky backs.

"It's okay if they visit." Linda's voice startled Sandy. "It's only at night when you go to sleep that I want them in the laundry room. I should have made that clear."

"Okay."

"I'm going to put on some tea. Come into the kitchen when you're finished."

Sandy placed her prenatal vitamins on the nightstand. The pharmacist in Rutland had mistakenly put Julie Lincoln's name on the bottle, and when they picked up the prescription, the revelation that Sandy was pregnant was an embarrassing moment. The pharmacist's daughter, a member of the JV cheerleading squad, had looked up to Sandy like a queen on her throne. Now the queen's crown was shattered, the throne cracked.

Sandy entered the kitchen as the teapot started to whistle. From the breakfast nook windows she could see the wooded backyard. There was a row of birdfeeders on posts just outside the window. Several brightly colored birds were eating a snack.

"Do the cats go outside?" Sandy asked.

"No," Linda answered as she lifted the teapot from the stove. "Birds and cats can't coexist peacefully in the same backyard. Would you like some tea?"

"Yes, ma'am."

"None of that ma'am stuff around here," Linda replied. "It's Linda, plain and simple. You're not going to make me feel like your granny."

Linda poured the water over tea bags into mismatched cups. It was an act completely foreign to Julie Lincoln's universe.

"I assume you want sugar," Linda said.

"Yes, ma—" Sandy stopped.

"Good." Linda glanced up.

She sat at the table with Sandy, who dropped two cubes of sugar into her cup.

"Where do you get sugar cubes?" Sandy asked.

"The health food store," Linda replied briskly. "Now I'm ready for your questions."

Sandy picked up the steaming cup, but the tea was still too hot to drink.

"What questions?"

"Don't be silly. I'm sure you have loads of questions. Let's start with why I told your mother that you should place your baby for adoption. Thousands of women are streaming into the shiny new abortion clinics that have sprung up like mushrooms over the past year. Did you study the decision by the Supreme Court in *Roe v. Wade?*"

"We went over it in my honors history class."

"Did you read it?"

"No."

"Honors history? And you didn't read the decision?" Linda sniffed. "You should have. It shows how ignorant lawyers are when it comes to basic biology. How far along are you in your pregnancy?"

"About ten weeks."

"Did you know that by the end of week five your baby has a brain and a spinal cord? The heart starts beating and pumping blood

114

by the end of week six. And at seven weeks the baby may only be a quarter inch long, but she has nostrils on her face and arms with tiny paddles for hands."

Sandy thought about the conversation with the old woman at the gas store.

"Do you think I'm going to have a girl?"

"Who knows, but I think women deserve equal time in the language."

Sandy had heard her father accuse Linda of being a feminist, a first cousin to the communists. Sandy was more interested in boys and cheerleading than political and sociological labels. Linda took a sip of her tea.

"The Supreme Court ruled that an unborn baby has no protection during the first trimester of the pregnancy and doesn't become a person until she's old enough to survive outside the mother's body. That's illogical. If all the grocery stores in Atlanta closed, most of the people in the city would starve before they learned how to grow their own food. Does that mean we're not people because we're not as self-sufficient as my parents were on their farm in Dawson County?"

"Uh, no." Sandy sipped her tea. It had a sharp, bold flavor. "I just didn't feel comfortable with the idea of abortion."

"Your intuition was right, but you need to know there are good reasons for your feelings. You can't go through life making decisions without knowing the facts. The mush in your head needs to be taught to think in an analytical way."

As during their phone conversation, Linda's words sounded critical but didn't come across in a judgmental way.

"That isn't going to happen at the school you'll attend," Linda continued. "You'll probably make straight As without much effort, but it's going to be my job to teach you how to think."

"Will I be safe at the school?"

"You'll need to keep to yourself and avoid socializing off campus with other students. There are security guards on duty in the halls and cafeteria."

Even though she'd taken a sip of tea, Sandy's mouth went dry.

"Is it the only school in Atlanta that accepts pregnant girls?"

"Within a reasonable distance of the house. It's good that you can drive your car and avoid riding the bus. The adoption agency is on Roswell Road in Sandy Springs. The ob-gyn who treats many of the women placing their babies for adoption has an office in the same building."

"I thought you were checking out several agencies."

"And I settled on this one. I screened four caseworkers at two agencies and made arrangements for you to meet with the best one I talked to."

"Thanks for doing that."

Linda picked up a thick book that was on the corner of the table.

"Here's your first homework assignment. This is a text currently used in the human physiology classes at Emory. The first two chapters should bring you up-to-date on your pregnancy. Before you go to bed tonight, I want you to write a six-paragraph summary that includes a history of the study of fetal development through the latest research. There are amazing in utero pictures in the text. Do you know what in utero means?"

"No."

"You will by tonight. Do you know how to type?"

"Yes, I took typing in eighth grade."

"There's a typewriter you can use in the study across from the guest room. Double-space. I don't need the eye strain. No typos. Use correction tape if you make a mistake. I'll be checking your grammar too. You begin classes at the school on Tuesday."

Linda finished her tea and left the table. Sandy watched the carefree birds for a minute and then opened the textbook.

EIGHT

Sandy got out of her car and checked to make sure the doors were locked. She'd parked beside a vehicle that had a white door, a red hood, and splotches of rust everywhere else. On the other side of Sandy's car was a motorcycle with a skull-and-crossbones design on the gas tank. Walking to the school entrance, Sandy heard a boy whistle. She didn't turn around.

Built in the 1930s, the school building was a former junior high saved from destruction by the city's need to provide education for students who, for a variety of bad reasons, couldn't be placed in the regular school system. The tiles on the floor were discolored and cracked. The lights in the classrooms were archaic glass globes. The walls were painted hospital green. Many of the lockers in the hallways were missing latches. Sandy had learned the location of all her classes with the help of the guidance counselor who had set up her schedule the previous day.

She slipped into her homeroom class and sat in the front row. The teacher was a black man in his thirties. He was wearing a white shirt, black tie, and black pants. A group of boys were clustered against the back wall. Several of them looked old enough to be in their early twenties. About ten other students were scattered across the room.

"Hey, foxy lady!" a male voice called out.

Sandy kept her eyes forward.

"I'm not talking to you," the male voice continued. "You're no lady."

"And you're a punk," a female voice responded.

"Quiet," the teacher said, glancing at a clock on the side wall of the room.

The teacher called the roll. Before he reached Sandy's name, the door opened and a short Hispanic girl with long dark hair entered the room. She shyly approached the teacher and handed him a slip of paper.

"Take a seat," the teacher said.

The girl looked around. Her eyes met Sandy's, and she sat in the desk beside her.

A few names later, the teacher called, "Sandy Lincoln."

Sandy lifted her hand slightly.

"Here."

"Got it," a different male voice said.

The teacher ignored the boy and continued the roll call. When he finished he looked at the clock again and announced, "Eight minutes until you're dismissed to your first class. You may talk, but don't leave your seats."

Sandy rearranged the books on the desk so the chemistry text for her first-period class was on top. The dark-haired girl beside her didn't have any books. Sandy leaned over.

"Are you new to the school?" she asked.

The girl nodded but didn't speak. Sandy took a bold step and asked the question again in Spanish. The girl's eyes lit up, and she responded so rapidly that it took Sandy a second to understand her answer.

"What's your name?" Sandy asked.

"Angelica."

"Where are your textbooks?"

"I don't have any."

Sandy raised her hand.

"Nice fingernails," a male voice said.

The homeroom teacher looked at Sandy.

"What is it?"

"Angelica doesn't have any books or know her classes."

"Who did you talk to in the office?" the teacher asked the Hispanic student.

Angelica shrugged and looked at Sandy, who translated, then listened to her response.

"Señora Jansen," Sandy replied.

The teacher rolled his eyes.

"She doesn't speak Spanish. Take her back to the office and tell her to meet with Mrs. Matute."

Once they were in the hallway, Angelica started peppering Sandy with questions. Sandy had to ask her to slow down. They reached the office and found Mrs. Matute.

"How is she going to attend classes if she can't speak English?" Sandy asked the administrator.

"I speak English," Angelica said, to Sandy's surprise. "Talk slow."

"We have to give her a chance," Mrs. Matute said with a bored expression on her face. "Her transcript indicates she was in accelerated classes on the college prep track at a private school in Monterrey."

"Why is she here?" Sandy asked.

"Baby," Angelica answered, pointing to her stomach.

"Oh," Sandy said. "Me too."

Angelica's eyes lit up again, and she gave Sandy a hug.

"Here's your schedule," Mrs. Matute said to Angelica in Spanish. "Sandy, what courses are you taking?"

Sandy rattled off her classes. Mrs. Matute made a few pencil marks.

"Angelica is in four of your six classes, including chemistry, algebra II, civics, and" — Mrs. Matute looked up and gave a wry smile — "Spanish II."

Sandy and Angelica entered chemistry class together. The female teacher was already lecturing. She directed Sandy and Angelica to a table for two.

"We're on page ninety-six," the teacher said.

The teacher wrote a formula on the chalkboard.

"Can anybody complete the formula?"

Angelica looked at Sandy, who whispered the question. Angelica immediately raised her hand.

"Come to the board and finish it," the teacher said.

Sandy nudged Angelica, who walked to the front of the room. The teacher handed her a piece of chalk, and Angelica rapidly wrote the additional steps on the board.

"Correct," the teacher said and nodded approvingly. "Return to your seat."

Sandy spent the rest of the class taking notes and watching Angelica flip through the textbook until she reached the last fifty pages. When the bell rang, the teacher asked Sandy and Angelica to stay after class for a minute.

"I'm Mrs. Welshofer," the teacher said to the girls.

Sandy introduced herself and Angelica.

"Where did you go to school?" the teacher asked Angelica.

"Monterrey, Mexico."

"And you?" she asked Sandy.

"Rutland High."

Angelica spoke in a quick burst of Spanish.

"She says she likes chemistry," Sandy said. "It's her favorite subject."

"If her work today is any indication, she won't have a problem with this class," Mrs. Welshofer replied. "Sandy, can you translate quietly if she has a question?"

"Yes, ma'am."

"Then do so. I'll trust you to keep to the material."

The two girls were separated during the next period. Sandy went to a European history class that contained eight students. Two of the girls in the class were wearing wedding rings. When she reconnected with Angelica in algebra II, the Hispanic girl gave her another hug and an even bigger smile. Angelica's command of algebra paralleled her abilities in chemistry.

At lunchtime, Sandy and Angelica went to the cafeteria together. As they pushed their trays down the line, Sandy saw that Angelica was wearing multiple rings, but her ring finger was bare. As they carried their trays to a table for two against the wall, a large young man stepped in front of them.

"Hey, dolls," he said. "Some of my friends and I would like to get to know you."

He pointed at a long table where four boys and two girls were sitting. The girls arched their necks and eyed Sandy. The group didn't look rough, but Sandy wanted to be cautious.

"Not today," she replied. "I need to help Angelica with her English."

The boy, who had an unshaven face with thick black stubble, looked down at the Hispanic girl.

"Qué pasa?" he said to Angelica, who rattled off a response that drew a blank stare.

Sandy had to stifle a laugh. Angelica had told the boy that she wouldn't go out with a fat pig who had bristles on his face.

"Right, check you later," the boy said.

When they reached the table, Sandy asked Angelica what she would have done if the boy had understood Spanish. Angelica smiled and shrugged.

"His accent was terrible. And he didn't scare me."

The rest of the school day Sandy and Angelica stuck together. In civics class, Sandy spoke to the teacher, an older woman named Mrs. Borden, and received permission to help Angelica navigate the complexities of American government and culture. In Spanish II, the teacher, a young woman from South Carolina, called Angelica to the front of the small class to read a poem by a Spanish poet.

"I'm so glad Angelica has joined us," said the teacher when Angelica finished. "Her accent and pronunciation are so much better than mine. It's what you'd hear from a well-educated Spanish-speaking person."

After sixth period, Sandy asked Angelica if she could give her a ride home. The girl shook her head and pointed to her stomach.

"The father, he come for me."

They walked outside the building together. Parked next to the curb was a shiny blue Buick. A good-looking Hispanic man in his midtwenties and wearing a dark suit got out and called out sharply to Angelica. She gave Sandy a final hug and walked quickly over to the car. The man spoke in a harsh voice, but Sandy couldn't make out what he said. Angelica got in the car and left. Sandy had a sinking feeling that behind Angelica's infectious smile there might be a mountain of sorrow.

After supper, Sandy called home to report on her first day. Angelica's presence had totally changed her attitude toward the school.

"You almost sound excited," her mother said when Sandy paused.

"I know," Sandy replied. "It's like I've found something I'm supposed to do."

"You mean become a translator? I know you're good in Spanish, but I thought you wanted to study interior decorating."

"I'm not thinking that far ahead. I meant here at the school. I can help Angelica until her English improves. She's very smart."

Sandy's father was attending an executive board meeting for the Rotary Club and wasn't at home.

"Tell Daddy I kept to myself at school, except for Angelica, and nobody bothered me. It helped a bunch having someone to sit with in the cafeteria."

"How was the food today?"

"Yucky, but I'm eating healthy with Linda. She read a book about nutrition for expectant mothers and bought some extra groceries."

"Is she cooking?" her mother asked in surprise.

"We do it together. She says I need to learn how to live on my own."

"Okay, obey her without arguing," her mother said.

"Yes, ma'am."

After the phone call ended, Sandy went into the study. Linda handed Sandy a stack of papers.

"This is a copy of the Supreme Court's decision in *Roe v. Wade*. Read sections one through four. It's background stuff. Don't take notes. I'm going to ask you questions about it tomorrow afternoon when I get home from work."

"If you're going to ask questions, why can't I take notes?"

"Because I want you to remember what you read without a crutch."

"May I read it more than once?"

"Absolutely."

That night Sandy propped up in bed and read the first four sections of the case. Justice Blackmun went into great detail about whether a married woman who wasn't pregnant and a doctor who wanted to perform abortions should be parties to the lawsuit. While Sandy was hacking her way through the dense verbiage, Lillo came into the room meowing. Sandy put the cat in the bed and stroked her soft fur. The abortion case originated in Dallas. When she saw the word *Texas,* Sandy thought about Brad and wondered if the father of the pregnant woman in the lawsuit was the reason the plaintiff wanted the abortion. After the third reading, Sandy felt she was beginning to get a fairly good grasp of the material. It made her wonder if she had what it took to become a lawyer. She yawned and carried Lillo into the laundry room. Peaches was already curled up in the cat bed.

The following day Angelica didn't show up in homeroom. When the minute hand crept up to the time for first period, Sandy started getting worried. Although she'd only seen him for a few seconds, Angelica's boyfriend didn't look like a good guy. Sandy went to chemistry class but had trouble concentrating on Mrs. Welshofer's lecture. Halfway through the class, the door opened and Angelica, her head down, slipped into the room.

"Angelica, do you have a tardy note from the office?" Mrs. Welshofer asked.

Angelica looked at Sandy, who quickly translated the question. Angelica handed a piece of paper to the teacher, then joined Sandy at the table they shared.

"Why were you late?" Sandy asked in Spanish.

"I had a fight with Ricardo, the baby's father."

"Did he hurt you?"

"Girls, pay attention," Mrs. Welshofer said.

When class ended, Sandy herded Angelica into the restroom. Another girl was washing her hands. As soon as she left, Sandy put her hands on Angelica's shoulders and repeated her question. Tears came to Angelica's eyes. She started to cry and talk, which made it impossible for Sandy to understand what she was saying. The bell rang, and they had to separate. It wasn't until lunchtime that the two girls were able to talk. The same table where they'd sat the day before was empty, and Sandy headed directly toward it.

Angelica told Sandy her story. Angelica's father owned an import/export business that shipped expensive Mexican furnishings and artwork into the United States, and Ricardo worked for him as a salesman. Atlanta was the East Coast headquarters of the company and the location of a warehouse and sales office. Toward the end of the summer, Angelica came to Atlanta with her father for a visit and met Ricardo. A romantic attraction in a new place led to the pregnancy. Her father and mother decided it would be better for Angelica to remain in the United States until the baby was born rather than return to Mexico. No one in Monterrey except her immediate family knew she was pregnant. Her mother was telling her friends that Angelica was going to an exclusive school in the United States and wouldn't be back until late spring.

Angelica was sharing an apartment with a woman employee of her father's company. Ricardo had to drive her around and pay her expenses to keep from losing his job. If he got fired, Ricardo would be forced to leave the States. The previous evening he'd gotten mad at Angelica and hit her. Capitola, the woman she lived with, promised to keep the assault secret, but Angelica wasn't sure she would. Up close, Sandy could see a red splotch on Angelica's cheek.

"What are you going to do with your baby?" Sandy asked in Spanish.

"My mother wants me to leave it here with a family who wants a child."

"Adoption?" Sandy used the English word and explained its meaning in Spanish.

"Yes," Angelica said. "But Ricardo and I want to get married and keep the baby."

■ ■ ■ ■

When Sandy pulled into the driveway that afternoon, Linda came out the front door.

"Don't get out of the car," Linda said. "I called the adoption agency this morning and scheduled an appointment with your caseworker. We have to get going or we'll be late."

"I need to go to the bathroom."

"Make it quick."

Sandy returned and backed the car out of the driveway.

"Why am I driving?" she asked.

"Because I want you to know how to get there on your own. I won't be able to go every time."

Sandy tried to concentrate on the route; however, Linda began asking her questions about the *Roe v. Wade* decision.

"Not bad," Linda said. "Turn right at the next light."

They reached the adoption agency. It was in a modern business complex of ten or twelve identical three-story brick buildings, each surrounded by parking spaces.

"Park there," Linda said. "The doctor's office is on the first floor; the agency is on the third floor."

"Are they going to ask me to sign papers today?" Sandy said as they got out of the car. "I'd like Daddy to read anything before I sign it."

"Based on your insight into Justice Blackmun's reasoning, I think you already have a better legal mind than your father."

They went inside the building.

"Up the stairs," Linda said, steering Sandy away from the elevator. "You're young, and I need the exercise."

They climbed to the third floor. The entrance for the adoption agency was on the left. Sandy's heart began to beat faster. She followed Linda into a small, plainly decorated reception area. An obviously pregnant woman was sitting in a plastic chair reading a magazine. A middle-aged woman sat behind a glass opening. Linda introduced herself to the receptionist.

"We're here for an appointment with Mrs. Longwell."

"I'll let her know," the woman replied.

Sandy and Linda sat next to each other across from the pregnant woman, who ignored them. Sandy studied the woman and wondered about the path she'd taken to get there. Her clothes were plain, and she was wearing slightly dirty tennis shoes. She was chewing bubble gum. While Sandy watched, she blew an enormous bubble. Sandy's eyes widened as she waited for the bubble to explode across the woman's face. At the last instant, the woman sucked the gum back into her mouth. She looked up and caught Sandy staring at her.

"First time?" the woman said with an accent that revealed she wasn't from the South.

"Yes." Sandy nodded.

"Number three for me," the woman replied, rubbing her hand across her stomach. "My second baby at this agency. It's a lot better than the outfit I went to in New Jersey."

A door near the receptionist's window opened. A man stuck his head in the room.

"Tia, I'm ready for you."

The woman left. A few minutes later, the door opened again. This time a tall, middle-aged woman with brown hair came into the room. She shook Linda's hand and introduced herself to Sandy.

"I'm Stephanie Longwell. Let's go to my office and talk."

They went down a hallway lined with adoption-themed posters: "Babies Deserve a Loving Home" and "Every Child Is a Wanted Child." They entered a small office with three chairs in front of a wooden desk and sat down.

"Sandy, before we start, you need to know that I'm not going to ask you to commit to anything today. As I told your aunt, our goal is to treat you as gently as we would a newborn baby. I'm glad you're considering adoption, especially with the changes in the law over the past year, but no one at this agency is going to pressure you to do anything."

Mrs. Longwell had compassionate eyes and a calm voice that put Sandy at ease. She could understand why Linda had selected her. The caseworker asked Sandy a series of background questions. While Sandy spoke, Mrs. Longwell took notes.

"That's all the preliminary questions," Mrs. Longwell said. "Let me ask you an open-ended one. Why are you here?"

Sandy pointed at Linda. "She talked with my mother about adoption. At first, I wasn't sure, but now I think it's the best way to go."

"Can you tell me more about how you reached that conclusion?"

Sandy gave her a fairly lengthy version of the past few weeks' events. Of course, she left out the encounter with the old woman at the convenience store.

"Thanks for sharing," Mrs. Longwell said

when Sandy finished. "It helps me to hear from you. Now let me tell you what we can offer you and your baby."

The caseworker handed Sandy a brochure that explained the basics of adoption and went through the information with her. Sandy stopped her when she started talking about open and closed adoptions.

"Sometimes the adoptive parents stay in contact with the real mother after the adoption?" she asked.

"We prefer the term *birth mother.* When I first started working in this field, most adoptions were closed, with no contact or knowledge about the identities of the birth parents and the adoptive parents. The court would seal the records and rarely open them. That's been changing over the past few years, and various levels of contact between the parties are now more common."

Sandy turned to Linda. "I didn't talk about that with Mama or Daddy. What do you think?"

"I think it should be up to the child later in life to decide whether to initiate contact with the birth parents. It's my understanding you can leave your personal information with the agency in case the child is curious at a later time."

"That's one option," Mrs. Longwell said.

"We maintain a database that can be updated if you move or get married and have a new name. You can also decide to delete your information at any time if you want to."

"What if I wanted to find the child?" Sandy asked.

"That's okay if the adoptive parents agree."

There were a lot more decisions to be made than Sandy had imagined.

"I need to think about that."

Because Sandy was covered by her father's health insurance policy, her prenatal care and the hospital charges for delivery of the baby would not have to be paid by an adoptive couple.

"Which expands the pool of prospective parents for you to review," Mrs. Longwell said.

"You mean I'll have a say about who adopts the baby?" Sandy asked in surprise.

"Yes, except for their names and specific address, we'll give you a lot of information about the families."

Sandy's head was spinning.

"How can I know —"

"You'll do the best you can," Mrs. Longwell answered with a smile. "We administer a battery of tests to you and the prospective parents that will help us make recommendations. The tests aren't perfect, but they increase the odds of a good match. There are thousands and thousands of couples in this country who would love to adopt your baby. We have scores of them in our files. I'm sure there will be several excellent candidates in that group."

Another thought shot across Sandy's mind.

"What if I have twins?" she asked.

NINE

"Twins?" Linda blurted out.

"Is there a history of twins in your family?" Mrs. Longwell asked.

Sandy looked at Linda.

"Not that I'm aware of," Linda said. "Why in the world would you bring that up?"

"She told me I could ask any questions I wanted to."

"That's right," Mrs. Longwell replied soothingly. "There are no wrong questions in this office. What about the birth father's family? Any twins in his background?"

"I don't know."

Thirty minutes later Sandy left with a stack of information to read and questionnaires to fill out. They stopped by the office of the ob-gyn doctor on the first floor and scheduled an initial appointment.

"I liked Mrs. Longwell," Sandy said to Linda when they were in the car.

"I knew you would. And I thought it was

a good meeting, except when you threw in that off-the-wall question about twins. Where in the world did that come from?"

"Uh, I thought about it during the drive from Rutland." Sandy paused. "Is there someone famous named Rebekah who had twin boys?"

Linda thought for a moment. "There was a woman named Rebekah in the Bible. She was the mother of Jacob and Esau, who were fraternal twins. Why bring that up?"

"Just wondering."

They turned out of the parking lot onto Roswell Road.

"I'm more worried about Brad Donnelly refusing to consent to the adoption than finding a home for two babies," Linda said. "Contrary to what people claim, men can be much less logical than women."

Sandy thought about her last conversation with Brad and what he'd done since them.

"I think he'll do it."

"And you also thought you knew him pretty well before this happened, didn't you?"

"Yes," Sandy admitted. "And I was one hundred percent wrong."

Over the next two months, Sandy settled into her new life in Atlanta. Her morning sickness subsided, and she started cooking her own breakfast. The absence of extracurricular activities at school or a social life in the evenings opened up hours and hours of free time. Linda filled some of that space with reading material that she required Sandy to study and discuss. They covered such topics as Greek mythology, the Vietnam War, and the themes of sin and guilt in *The Scarlet Letter,* a book that Sandy now read more as fact than fiction. Because of their discussions, Sandy realized she'd spent most of her school career memorizing facts, not learning how to think.

She slipped into a routine at school. Sandy took the time to get to know her teachers, worked hard in her classes, and maintained a straight-A average. Her friendship with Angelica was the highlight of her school day. Once the predatory males realized Sandy wasn't going to respond to their lame come-ons, they left her alone. Her rapidly expanding abdomen also proved to be an effective deterrent.

Every other weekend Sandy returned to Rutland; however, she didn't go to high school football games and, except for Jessica, avoided contact with anyone outside her family. She didn't want to run into someone in the maternity section of a local store, so she shopped for clothes in Atlanta. And she didn't attend church. It was easier to withdraw from society than deal with the stares and silent judgments, a reaction Sandy shared with Hawthorne's Hester Prynne. She made no effort to get in touch with Brad. Jessica reported that he and Crystal went through a stormy and very public breakup after going steady for six weeks. Following that, no girls at Rutland High would go out with Brad, and he ended up dating a girl from a neighboring high school. Sandy didn't try to find out the details.

"You're different," Ben said one Sunday as Sandy packed her suitcase before leaving for Atlanta.

"Yeah, about fifteen pounds heavier," Sandy said and patted her midsection.

"No, you seem more grown up."

"Like Mama?"

"Nah, you're still you, only different."

"What do you mean?"

"It's like you know what to do without having to ask Mama or Daddy."

"I still listen to what they say, and so should you."

"Yeah, that makes you sound like a grown-up too."

Sandy laughed and gave her brother a hug.

On her trips to and from Atlanta, Sandy continued to stop at the gas store where she'd encountered the old woman who told her about the twins. Each time she entered the store, Sandy's heart beat a little faster. Part of her wanted to see the woman so she could ask her questions. Another part was scared that more knowledge would create more confusion. One day Sandy came out of the restroom and an old woman with white hair and wearing a print dress was standing in front of the drink cooler. Sandy cautiously crept closer and cleared her throat.

"Do you remember me?" she asked the woman.

The old woman turned and faced her. Instead of startling blue eyes, the woman's eyes were dark brown.

"No," she replied, revealing a mouth missing several teeth. "Do I know you?"

"Sorry," Sandy replied, stepping back. "I thought you were someone else."

The woman glanced down at Sandy's stomach.

"I have a granddaughter about your age who is about to have a baby. Her name is Lori Jefferson. Did you go to Caldwell County High?"

"No, ma'am. I'm from Rutland."

The Sunday that Ben told her she seemed more grown up, Sandy arrived in Atlanta to an empty house. Linda was in Chicago at a work-related seminar and wouldn't be home until Monday afternoon. Sandy's mother had been reluctant to let Sandy leave Rutland and spend the night alone, but her father stepped in and insisted she not miss school. Missing a day of classes wasn't a big deal, but Sandy was looking forward to seeing how it would feel to be on her own. Perhaps it was another sign of the adulthood Ben picked up on.

After taking care of the cats, Sandy curled up in a comfortable chair in the living room to read from a collection of short stories by Flannery O'Connor. She settled on "A Good Man Is Hard to Find" because the title seemed to be an accurate description of her life so far. But the story took a turn she didn't expect. When she reached the climax — the murder of the main character and her family on a deserted road — every creak and pop in the house was amplified. Sandy's left hand slipped from the arm of the chair, and Lillo brushed against it. Sandy jerked her arm away. Leaving the book in the chair, she doubled-checked all the exterior doors to make sure they were locked, then drank a glass of water in an attempt to calm her nerves.

The phone rang. Glad for the chance of a few seconds of human contact to help her escape from O'Connor's fictional world, Sandy answered it.

"Sandy?" a soft voice asked.

"Yes."

"It's Angelica."

"How are you?" Sandy switched to Spanish.

Angelica began to cry. In between sobs, Sandy was able to make out that her friend wanted her to come see her.

"Where are you?" Sandy asked.

"On the sidewalk."

"Sidewalk?"

"Yes, Ricardo left me here. I don't know if the buses run on Sunday night or which one would take me home."

"Do you have any money for a taxi?"

"I only have a few dollars, and I'm not sure how much it will cost."

"What about Capitola?"

"She's out of town."

Sandy twirled the phone cord between her fingers. Going out alone at night to try to find Angelina at an unknown location in

Atlanta was more maturity than Sandy was ready for.

"Are there any street signs near you?"

"I'm in a phone booth near a corner. Just a minute."

The phone was silent for a few seconds. Sandy heard a car horn in the background followed by male voices. Angelica returned and named two streets, neither familiar to Sandy. Sandy opened the kitchen drawer where Linda kept a map of the city.

"Tell me again," she said.

Running her finger down the list of streets, Sandy found one of the street names and turned over the map.

"Are you still on the phone?" Angelica asked.

"Yes, I'm trying to find you."

Sandy followed the street toward the downtown area until she spotted the connecting side street Angelica mentioned.

"Got it," Sandy said. "Why did you and Ricardo go there?"

Angelica started crying again.

"Will you please help me?" she begged.

Sandy set her jaw.

"I'm on my way," she said. "It'll take me a few minutes to figure out how to get to you from here. Stay close to the phone booth. Is there a streetlight nearby?"

"Yes."

"Don't wander off."

After she hung up the phone, Sandy wrote down directions to the intersection. Angelica was in a completely unfamiliar part of the city. It could be an avenue of mansions or a row of tenements. Taking a flashlight, the map, the directions, and her purse, Sandy carefully locked the outside door of the house and then got in her car. Before starting the engine, she stopped for a moment and prayed that she wouldn't encounter a "good man" who turned out to be a murderer. Then she locked the doors of the car.

There weren't many vehicles on the road. Every time she had to stop for a red light, Sandy avoided looking at the driver of the car that pulled up beside her. The image of the killer from O'Connor's story kept fighting its way to the surface of her mind. She gripped the steering wheel so tightly that her hands began to ache. The streets seemed to conspire against her as traffic light after traffic light turned yellow then red as she approached. She drove through a mixture of commercial and residential areas. She passed countless liquor stores, check-cashing outlets, and convenience stores. The houses got older and more run-down as she got closer to Angelica's location. Serious doubts that Angelica was safe rose up in Sandy's mind.

Then the neighborhoods began to transition. The homes were larger and included older houses that looked like they'd been restored. These were followed by several chic restaurants. She passed a major hospital, went down a hill, and noticed the connecting street as she passed by it, but she didn't see Angelica. She turned around. As she approached the intersection the second time, she saw Angelica standing next to a phone booth, hugging herself. Sandy pulled to the curb as a couple of young men approached. Sandy reached over and unlocked the passenger door.

"Get in," she said.

As Angelica stepped off the curb, one of the young men yelled something that Sandy couldn't make out. As soon as Angelica shut the door, Sandy stepped on the gas pedal so hard that the car lurched forward and died. In the rearview mirror she could see the young men laughing. Sandy started the engine and drove away more slowly. Angelica leaned her head against the back of the seat and closed her eyes.

"How do I get to your apartment from here?" Sandy asked in Spanish.

"I'm not sure," Angelica replied, opening

her eyes.

Sandy turned the steering wheel of the car sharply and entered the parking lot for the hospital. The lot was well lit by multiple lights on metal poles.

"I have a map —" Sandy began.

"No, not here," Angelica interrupted in a frantic voice. "This is where Ricardo took me when I started to bleed after —"

"After what?" Sandy asked in alarm.

Angelica looked at Sandy with dark eyes that were filled with sorrow. Before Angelica could answer, Sandy looked down at her friend's abdomen.

"You lost your baby?" she asked.

"No," Angelica answered as tears started to run down her face. "I let the doctor take it out."

Sandy's mouth dropped open in shock. Angelica had never mentioned any possibilities other than marrying Ricardo or adoption.

"Why?" Sandy asked numbly.

Angelica wiped the tears from her cheeks.

"Ricardo told me that he loved me and wanted to marry me, but he wasn't ready to raise a baby. He said once we were married we could have as many children as we wanted. He showed me the ring he'd bought me."

Sandy's face was grim. She'd heard that line before. She glanced at Angelica's finger. It was still bare.

"Yesterday he made me go to a place where the doctor took out my baby. The doctor had a machine that made a sucking sound and then it was over." Angelica paused and looked past Sandy as she seemed to relive the moment. The Hispanic girl shook her head. "I knew it was wrong and started to cry. Ricardo got mad and took me home, but he came back today and showed me the ring. We were sitting on the couch talking about the wedding when suddenly I started to bleed. I got scared, and he brought me here. I was here for hours and hours, but finally the doctor did something to make the bleeding stop. When Ricardo and I got in the car to leave, he said he'd had time to think about everything, and he didn't want to marry me. He was going to quit working for my father and move away where no one could find him. I begged him not to do it, but he got mad and made me get out of the car. That's when I called you on the telephone."

Sandy didn't know what to say. She wanted to hate Ricardo, but all she felt in her heart at that moment was compassion for her friend. She reached over and squeezed Angelica's hand.

"I'm sorry."

"What am I going to tell my papa and mama?" she wailed.

Sandy squeezed Angelica's hand again. Silent reassurance of her love was the best thing she could communicate to Angelica, who continued to cry.

"I want to go home," she said when she'd calmed down a little bit. "To Monterrey."

Sandy nodded. She understood.

"But first I have to get you to your apartment."

"Capitola isn't there," Angelica said. "She's visiting her sister in Birmingham, and I don't want to be alone."

"Then spend the night with me," Sandy offered immediately. "My aunt is out of town too."

Angelica sighed and seemed to relax.

"Yes. Thank you."

The return trip to Linda's house seemed much quicker. Angelica was quiet and spent most of the time staring out the window. When they arrived at the house, the cats greeted them. Angelica knelt down to stroke them. When she stood up, she winced.

"Do you want to change out of your clothes?" Sandy asked. "You can wear some of my pajamas."

"Could I take a shower?" Angelica asked. "I haven't felt clean since yesterday."

While Angelica showered, Sandy made up a bed on the couch in the living room and put on water for tea. Several minutes later, Angelica, her long, dark hair still damp, came out of the bathroom. Sandy's pajamas fit perfectly. Sandy had put on a blue nightgown. Angelica stared at Sandy's swollen abdomen for a moment. Sandy touched her stomach.

"I don't want to make it worse for you," Sandy said.

"Part of me feels pain," Angelica said, her face emotionless. "Part of me feels dead. Neither one is your fault."

The girls sat at the table and drank tea in silence.

"Are you hungry?" Sandy asked.

"A little bit."

"Would you like some popcorn?"

Angelica nodded her head.

"I love popcorn."

The popcorn made a happy sound as it tapped against the lid of a large pot on the stove. In a separate saucepan, Sandy melted butter. Angelica sat at the kitchen table and watched. When the popcorn was ready, Sandy divided it equally between two bowls and sprinkled it with butter and salt. Angelica took a bite and closed her eyes.

"This is good," she said.

Later, when Sandy lay in bed, she thought about Ricardo's betrayal. The same thing so easily could have happened to her. The baby inside her moved, and Sandy tried to shift into a more comfortable position.

As she lay on her side, Sandy prayed that someday Angelica would meet a good man who would treat her with the love and kindness she deserved — and that her sweet, dark-haired friend would have as many healthy, happy babies as she wanted.

TEN

The following morning Sandy took Angelica to her apartment before going to school.

"Are you sure you're okay?" Sandy asked.

"I need to rest. I was bleeding some last night, but it is better this morning."

Sandy reluctantly watched her friend climb the steps to the apartment and wave good-bye.

That afternoon when Linda came in from the airport, Sandy told her what had happened to Angelica.

"After I picked her up, I brought her here," Sandy said. "I hope it was okay that she spent the night."

"Certainly. Did the baby's father really leave town?"

"I'm going to phone Angelica later and find out. What he did was horrible."

"Men are the bane of women." Linda shook her head. "I'm happy I realized the truth."

"What truth?"

"That a woman can have a full and satisfying life without a husband in the picture. It was hard when I was younger and all my friends were getting married, but now I don't have any regrets. A lot of them are divorced and single with extra layers of pain to deal with." Linda paused. "Of course, singleness isn't for everyone. I tried to talk your mother out of marrying your father, but I'm glad she did. Otherwise, we wouldn't have you."

"You tried to talk her out of marrying my father?" Sandy asked in surprise.

"You've never heard that story?"

"No."

"When your mother asked me what I thought about your father, I had to give her an honest opinion, didn't I? Bob Lincoln's greatest ambition was to peddle life insurance policies to his buddies in Rutland and eat lunch at the country club. Your mother is one of the most gifted people I know. She could have landed a job with an interior design firm in Atlanta, Dallas, maybe even New York. Your granny had reservations about your father too, but she wouldn't say anything. That's not the way I'm wired. I have to be true to myself and those I care about. Anyway, once your mother went ahead with her plans, I determined to make the best of it. But your father never forgave me. Haven't you noticed how he feels about me?"

"Yes, but I didn't know why." Sandy remembered the book of photos from her parents' wedding. Linda, her blond hair cropped short and wearing dark-framed glasses, was her mother's maid of honor. "You were smiling in the wedding pictures."

"Because I'd said my piece. I've been willing to move on, but your father has been stuck in the same spot for twenty years."

Sandy sighed. "I liked it better when I was a little girl who didn't know what was going on."

"What's really sad is that age doesn't necessarily bring maturity."

Sandy kept trying to reach Angelica, but no one answered. Four phone calls, spaced about an hour apart, were fruitless. At 9:00 p.m., Sandy went to the study where Linda was working.

"No one is answering the phone at Angelica's apartment, and I'm getting worried. What if the bleeding came back worse than before?"

Linda pushed the chair away from the typewriter and took off her glasses.

"What do you want to do? Go over there?"

"I don't know. If someone was home, I'd think they would answer the phone. We could call the police, but what are we going to tell them? If Ricardo has done something else to her —" Sandy stopped, trying not to fear the worst.

"Put on your jacket," Linda said.

They took Sandy's car.

"It's a second-floor unit," Sandy said as she turned into the apartment complex.

Sandy didn't see Ricardo's blue car. She parked in front of the apartment building. No lights shone from the windows.

"Nobody's home," Sandy said.

"We've come this far," Linda replied. "I'm going to knock on the door."

Sandy wrapped her arms around herself against the chill as they walked up the single flight of steps to a metal door painted forest green. Sandy put her ear to the door for a second and heard nothing. Linda rapped the door sharply. They waited. She knocked again. Nothing. Sandy raised her hand and pounded the door with the side of her fist. There was no response.

"If someone is in there, they're not going to answer," Linda said. "First thing tomorrow, I'll call the manager of the complex and see if I can find out something. It may be a dead end."

Sandy didn't like the sound of Linda's last words.

Before eating breakfast the following morning, Sandy called the apartment again. The phone rang and rang. Just as she was about to hang up, a female voice with a Spanish accent answered.

"Capitola?" Sandy asked.

"Yes."

"It's Sandy Lincoln. Where is Angelica? I've been worried sick about her."

"On her way home to Monterrey. I took her to the airport last night and put her on a plane to Mexico City."

Sandy breathed a sigh of relief. Then the realization that Angelica was gone hit her.

"Is she coming back? I'd hate for her to drop out of school. We're near the end of the semester."

"No, her parents are going to send her to her old high school. After that she'll probably go to the Tec de Monterrey. It's one of the best universities in the country."

"She's good in science," Sandy said.

"Yes, and she told me what you did for her while I was gone. Thank you for your courage in picking her up when she'd been abandoned. Her father knows about your kindness."

Sandy had seen a photo of Angelica's father, an unsmiling man wearing a dark-blue business suit.

"Is Ricardo gone?" she asked.

"I haven't seen or heard from him. He didn't come to work and hasn't answered the phone at his apartment."

"I was worried he might have caused more trouble."

"He's a coward. Maybe someday Angelica can forget what happened here."

"Will you let her know I called and send me her address so I can write?"

"Yes, you were like a sister to her."

Sandy didn't trust herself to say anything else without crying. She hung up the phone as Linda came into the kitchen.

"That's a relief," Linda said when Sandy told her about the conversation. "But I know you'll miss her."

"Yeah, now I'm really going to have to learn how to be alone at school."

Several days later Sandy had an appointment with Dr. Berman, her ob-gyn. While sitting in the waiting room, she flipped through a magazine and found an article about a mother of twin boys. Sandy stared at the picture of the woman, a blonde like herself, who lived with her husband in Ohio. The boys were fraternal twins. As she read the story, Sandy rested her hand on her ever-growing abdomen. That morning at breakfast Linda had interrogated her about her food intake. Sandy defended herself.

"You know the meals in the cafeteria at school are terrible, and I'm not snacking in the afternoon" — Sandy paused — "except for the bag of chocolate-chip cookies I keep in the bottom drawer of my dresser. But that bag has lasted four days and the one before it even longer."

"No need to hide anything; however, ask Dr. Berman about your weight. And I think you should probably drink milk with your cookies. Vitamin D is important."

Taking the magazine with her when she was called for her appointment, Sandy stepped onto a scale in a centrally located hallway. The nurse pushed the weights to the right, readjusted the one on the bottom lever, and tapped the one on top a few more times until it balanced. Sandy didn't look at the result. After a nurse checked her vital signs, Sandy was left alone in an examination room. She continued to read the article about the twin boys who had distinct differences as well as close similarities. Dr. Berman entered the room.

The ob-gyn was a short Jewish woman with curly dark hair. She sat down, crossed her legs, and started talking while reviewing Sandy's chart.

"No more morning sickness?"

"Not for several weeks."

"Taking your vitamins?"

"Yes."

"All your vitals and blood work from your previous visit are good." The doctor flipped back a page, then returned to Sandy's current status. "Let's talk about your diet."

Sandy answered all the doctor's questions about her caloric intake.

"The baby's father is a football player," Sandy offered at one point. "He plays wide receiver."

"That might make your baby fast but not necessarily large." The doctor stood up. "Normally, I don't do a physical exam on this visit, but let's take a look."

Sandy watched the doctor's face as she measured and examined. Nothing about the physician's expression revealed any concern.

"You're a small-framed woman carrying a fast-developing baby," Dr. Berman said when she finished.

Sandy sat up on the edge of the examination table.

"I was reading an article about twins. Is there a chance I might be carrying two babies?"

"Any history of twins in your family?"

"No, but I'm not sure about the father's family."

"It would depend on your genetic disposition, not his."

"It was just a thought —"

"And a real possibility," the doctor interrupted, "based on your development. You're at twenty-one weeks but measure more like twenty-six."

"You're serious?" Sandy's mouth dropped open.

"The thought of multiples crossed my mind while examining you. If you're carrying twins or triplets, you'll likely deliver the babies around thirty-six or thirty-seven weeks."

"Triplets?"

"Are very, very rare. But twins are enough of a possibility that you might want to mention it to the adoption agency. Who's your caseworker?"

"Mrs. Longwell."

"She should know so they can have contingency plans."

"Is there any way you can check and make sure?"

"X-rays aren't recommended. There are experimental machines that rely on sound waves to create an image of what's in the uterus, but nothing that's been approved for use with patients. Would the presence of twins affect your decision to place the babies for adoption?"

Hearing the doctor say "babies" made it seem much more real than the words spoken by a strange old woman at a gas store.

"I don't think so. I'm less able to raise two babies than I am one."

Dr. Berman nodded. "We'll see how you've progressed at your next visit."

Leaving the doctor's office, Sandy took the elevator to the third floor.

"I don't have an appointment," she told the receptionist, "but if Mrs. Longwell has a few minutes, I'd like to see her."

While she waited, Sandy felt that her baby or babies were growing larger by the second. The skin across her stomach was tight. She couldn't imagine what she would look and feel like in seventeen more weeks. The door opened. It was Mrs. Longwell.

"Hello, Sandy," she said.

They went to the caseworker's office. Since her initial visit, Sandy had completed a battery of tests and filled out two long questionnaires. She'd learned that prospective parents had to complete even more paperwork.

"Thanks for seeing me," she said when they sat down. "I had an appointment with Dr. Berman, and she told me there's a chance I might be carrying twins."

"You mentioned that at our first meeting," Mrs. Longwell said, raising her eyebrows. "A woman's intuition about those types of things can be uncanny."

"It's nothing definite, of course, but the doctor said I should tell you."

"Right. Better to be prepared for the possibility than scrambling around trying to find a family willing to take twins at the last minute."

"Oh, I wouldn't want them to be placed with the same family," Sandy said.

"Why not? Our preference is to keep siblings together."

Sandy shifted in her chair. "But it's not a requirement?"

"No," the caseworker responded slowly. "But that doesn't answer my question."

Sandy started to tell Mrs. Longwell about meeting the old woman but couldn't bring herself to do it. It was a bizarre encounter, and to base a decision on it would make Sandy sound silly.

"I'd rather not say," she replied.

164

Mrs. Longwell studied her for a moment.

"If you insist on separate families, it's a huge decision that will affect the lives not only of your babies but of a lot of other people."

"I know. Could it be like the intuition thing you mentioned?" Sandy asked hopefully.

Mrs. Longwell tapped her pen against a pad on her desk.

"We have a psychologist who is available to meet with prospective mothers. Maybe you should see her. It doesn't mean there's something wrong with you; it's a way to gather information that will help you make the best decisions. Would you be willing to talk to Dr. Bondy? She's very insightful."

Sandy was feeling trapped and regretted bringing up the subject of twins with Mrs. Longwell.

"I don't know."

"Think about it," Mrs. Longwell said in her kind voice. "There's no need to cross that bridge today."

The caseworker swiveled in her chair and reached for a thick folder.

"I'm glad you stopped by. The results of your tests are in and have been collated with the answers on your questionnaires. I was going to discuss this with you when we met later this month, but it's not too early to begin thinking about placement options. You checked that you'd prefer a closed adoption without ongoing contact with the baby, right?"

"Yes."

"Why?"

"I talked to my parents, and we think it's the best way to go. That way, I can go on with my life, and the baby's family doesn't have to worry about me trying to meddle. Also, I went to high school in Rutland with twin girls who were adopted. They didn't know their birth mother and told me they didn't want to have any contact with her because it would make them feel confused, like they had to pick which mother to love. I don't want to cause that type of problem."

"Were these girls adopted by the same family?"

"Uh, yes." Sandy gave Mrs. Longwell a sheepish look. "But the Bergeson girls are identical twins."

"Is there something about their relationship that makes you want to avoid a single placement for twins?"

"No."

Mrs. Longwell waited, but Sandy wasn't going to explain.

"Okay," the caseworker said. "Deciding

whether to have an open or closed adoption is a decision that needs to be made early in the process. More adoptive couples prefer a closed adoption than an open one. If you go with a closed adoption, it gives you a broader selection of prospective parents to choose from."

"That's good, right?" Sandy asked.

"It can be."

"I want to do what's best."

Sandy left Mrs. Longwell's office with a timeline for future steps and an extensive questionnaire about the type of parents Sandy wanted for her baby, or babies. Getting pregnant had been so random. The adoption process was painstakingly intentional.

ELEVEN

Sandy finished the semester with all As and spent Christmas vacation in Rutland. When Ben saw her, his eyes got larger.

"Wow," he said. "You're really getting fat."

"It's not fat," Sandy's mother corrected him.

"It's okay." Sandy laughed. "I feel as fat as Santa. His fat jiggles; mine wiggles. Do you want to feel the baby move? He's gotten a lot more active the past few days. I think he's practicing some wrestling moves."

Ben backed away as if from a dog about to attack.

"No."

"Don't tease him," Sandy's mother said.

"How do you know it's a boy?" Ben asked.

"I have a fifty-fifty chance of being right," Sandy answered lightly.

Later that afternoon Sandy helped her mother fix supper in the kitchen. While they worked, Sandy filled her mother in on the book she and Linda had been discussing earlier in the week. While she talked, Sandy expertly diced onions with a sharp knife.

"You've learned a lot living with Linda, haven't you?" her mother asked.

"Yes," Sandy said, continuing to chop the onions. "And I think I did a lot better on the SAT than I did when I took it last spring. My body is making a baby, and my brain is getting smarter."

"That's unusual. Most women suffer 'pregnancy brain.' "

"What's that?"

"Getting really absentminded."

"That's not happened to me. At least not yet. I guess it helps that I don't have a bunch of extracurricular activities at school."

"Do you miss them?"

"Yes." Sandy put the onions in a small skillet. "But there's no use thinking about it."

"When you go to college, you can get back into circulation."

Sandy knew that was her mother's way of talking about dating. None of Sandy's current daydreams were about meeting the right boy.

"Linda told me about the advice she gave you before you married Daddy."

Her mother was rinsing carrots in the sink. Turning off the water, she turned around and handed the carrots to Sandy.

"She shouldn't have done that, but Linda never has had a proper filter on her mouth. Don't believe everything she tells you. Just because an opinion is strongly held doesn't make it true."

"I listen to her and don't argue."

"Which is what I've done since we were girls. Eventually, she moved past her opinion about your father, but he's never liked her."

"That's what she told me."

"Until now," her mother said. "When Linda offered to help you through this crisis by letting you live with her free of charge, your daddy was shocked. He'd always thought Linda was selfish and wouldn't believe me when I told him otherwise. One good thing that might come out of this is less tension between them. He even told me to invite her to spend Christmas Eve and morning with us."

Sandy rapidly removed the skin from the carrots, then began slicing off thin pieces to cook in brown sugar and butter.

"Do you have any regrets about giving up the possibility of a career and moving to Rutland?" Sandy asked.

Sandy's mother gave a rare laugh. Sandy

waited for a fuller explanation but none came. She put the carrots in a saucepan.

"I'm sure that I'm doing the right thing placing the baby for adoption," Sandy continued. "If I'm ever going to be a mother, this isn't the way it's supposed to be."

"I'm glad you feel that way. Even though you moved to Atlanta, I haven't been one hundred percent certain how your heart felt. I've had my struggles about adoption."

"How?"

Her mother kept her back to Sandy.

"I believe it's the best decision too, but the thought that my first grandchild will be raised by strangers is enough to break my heart."

It was Sandy's turn not to respond. Instead, she stirred the onions a bit more vigorously than necessary.

The only friend who came to see Sandy during the Christmas break was Jessica. They huddled up in Sandy's room, and Jessica bombarded her with an inexhaustible supply of questions about being pregnant.

"You'll find out someday when you're married to a wonderful husband and have thousands of dollars to decorate a gorgeous nursery," Sandy said at one point.

"You're the one who's going to marry a handsome guy and have a picture-perfect family. After all you've been through, I believe God has someone special waiting in the future."

Sandy thought about Brad's comment that she would be "used up." She rested her hand on her swollen abdomen.

"I'm not sure what sort of shape I'm going to have after this is over. Most men aren't attracted to girls who look like an overripe pear."

"Most of your weight is on the inside. You'll bounce back. But I didn't realize how fast the baby would grow. It makes me wonder if you might be having twins."

Jessica was inspecting her freshly painted fingernails while she talked. She looked up and saw Sandy staring at her.

"Did I say something wrong?" she asked.

"Uh, no."

It was Jessica's turn to stare at Sandy.

"Don't tell me. You think you might be having twins?"

Sandy nodded. Jessica screamed, then immediately clamped her hand over her mouth.

"Have you talked to your doctor about it? Isn't it too early to know that sort of thing? Can they take X-rays without risking damage to the baby, or babies, and find out?"

"Yes and yes and no," Sandy replied.

Jessica looked at Sandy's stomach with increased respect.

"How long have you known?"

Sandy studied Jessica for a moment.

"What is it?" Jessica asked. "Is something wrong?"

Sandy spoke slowly. "If I ask you to keep a secret, do you promise not to tell anyone?"

"Not even my mother?"

"My mother doesn't know about this."

"Wow." Jessica let out a sharp breath. "You and I have only had secrets about little stuff that didn't matter."

"It's something I haven't felt right talking about with anyone," Sandy replied. "But I believe I can trust you."

"I'll always be your best friend," Jessica said, crossing her heart with the fingers on her right hand. "And I promise to keep what you tell me secret from anyone. Forever."

Sandy told her about her encounter with the old woman at the gas station.

"I'm getting goose bumps," Jessica said, rubbing her arms. "Were you freaked out of your mind when the old woman was talking to you?"

"It happened so fast, but at the very end I thought I was about to faint. I wanted to ask her some more questions, but when I checked in the parking lot and along the road, there was no sign of her."

"Maybe it was an angel," Jessica said in a hushed voice. "I mean, she mentioned Rebekah in the Bible."

"I don't think so." Sandy shook her head. "She didn't have any wings, and she was looking at cans of snuff before I ran into her."

Sandy then told Jessica about her recent appointment with Dr. Berman.

"Will you know for sure about the twins before you go into labor?"

"We didn't get into that."

Jessica thought for a moment, then her eyes got big.

"If what the old woman said is true, your babies can't be adopted by the same family. They'll have to be separated at birth."

"Yeah."

"I just hope they're not identical like the Bergeson twins. That would make it tougher than if they're fraternal." Jessica paused. "How does that happen?"

"Linda has a book with pictures that explains how it happens. Two fertilized eggs produce fraternal twins. A single egg that splits causes identical twins. There are a lot more fraternal twins born than identical twins."

"Does Linda know you might have twins?"

"She heard me ask the caseworker at the adoption agency about it, but she didn't take me seriously."

After Jessica went home, Sandy hummed quietly while folding her clean clothes. All Jessica had done was listen, but it had felt good to unburden her heart. And if it turned out Sandy wasn't having twins, Jessica wouldn't make a big deal out of it. Their conversation would fit neatly inside the folder of fantasies the girls had shared since they were little.

Linda arrived in Rutland midafternoon on Christmas Eve. Sandy met her at the door and gave her a big hug.

"I see everything is in its place," Linda said, pointing to rows of perfectly wrapped gifts that lay in a semicircle beneath a tree decorated by scores of handmade ornaments.

"Yes. Always."

Sandy's mother came into the foyer from the kitchen and greeted her sister.

"Thanks for coming."

"Let's hope that's how you feel when it's time for me to leave," Linda replied.

"Where's Bob? I expected him to greet me at the door with a kiss on the cheek and a box of chocolates."

"He's scrambling around doing last-minute shopping and took Jack with him. Ben is over at a friend's house and won't be home until suppertime."

"The house looks nice," Linda said, glancing around. "I love the candles on the mantel."

"We're going to the candlelight service at the church later this evening. I hope you'll join us."

"Can I stay home?" Sandy asked.

The two women looked at her. Sandy put her hands over her stomach.

"You can't hide it with your hands," Linda said.

"Let's see what your daddy has to say about church," her mother suggested.

"I won't enjoy it," Sandy said, her lips pouty. "All I'll be able to think about will be the people staring at me and judging me."

"Shame on them," Linda said. "But I'm not surprised. The church your mother and I went to as girls was so full of hypocrites it should have been written on the sign out front. Most people's sins are hidden. Your problem just happens to be on display."

Sandy led Linda to the guest room on the main floor of the house.

"How are you doing?" Linda asked with tenderness in her voice as soon as they were alone.

"Except for getting fatter and fatter, I'm okay."

"I've missed you. And the cats haven't stopped roaming around the house meowing and looking for you since you left."

Linda put her suitcase on the rack at the foot of the high poster bed. Sandy started to leave the room but stopped at the door.

"Please be sweet to Daddy," Sandy said. "He's the one who asked Mama to invite you for the holidays."

"I'm not naive. I know this wouldn't have happened if His Highness hadn't extended his scepter in my direction. I'll be on my best behavior."

Sandy had doubts that Linda would make good on her promise.

Christmas Eve supper at the Lincoln house was a light but elaborate meal. The big holiday feast was reserved for a late lunch on Christmas Day. Sandy liked the variety of heavy hors d'oeuvres offered at the evening meal more than the massive ham that always occupied the center of the dining room table the following day. Ben and Jack were picky eaters who focused their attention on boiled shrimp with red cocktail sauce. As they gorged on shrimp, Sandy thought about all the time she'd spent peeling and deveining each one. She glanced over at Linda, who was nibbling a pastry filled with avocado and shredded chicken seasoned with Mexican spices. So far, her aunt had limited her conversation to the delicious food.

"Julie, this is divine," she said, holding up a tiny piece of the pastry before popping the final bite into her mouth. "Where did you get the idea for it?"

"I started looking up Mexican dishes after Sandy told me about her friend at school."

"Have you heard from Angelica recently?" Linda asked Sandy.

"Not since the letter that came while I was staying with you. But she sounded happy to be home. She's trying to put what happened in Atlanta behind her."

"What happened in Atlanta?" Ben asked as he inspected another shrimp.

"Her boyfriend dumped her," Sandy said, quickly glancing at her mother and Linda.

"When you get interested in girls," Linda said to Ben, "you'd better get your hands on a good book that will tell you how you should act. If your mother doesn't have one, I'll research it and find one for you."

"He talked to Mary Beth Wilkins on the phone the other night for thirty minutes," Jack cut in. "He sneaked into Sandy's room and used her pink phone."

Ben turned and punched Jack so hard in the arm that his little brother cried out in pain.

"Boys!" Sandy's father called out. "None of that at the table. And if either of you needs to know how you should treat a girl, you don't need a book to teach you. Ask me."

Sandy lowered her head and braced herself for a salvo from Linda that would sting twice as hard as the blow Ben landed on Jack's arm. Her father's reaction would then cause the plates in the china cabinet to rattle. Sandy glanced at her mother, who pretended to be preoccupied with a lettuce wrap.

"Your father is the first and best place to get information about girls," Linda said casually. "But you might want to talk to your mother too. Believe it or not, she used to be a girl and can give you good advice. A book would be your third option."

The rest of supper passed without a close call. Toward the end of the meal, Sandy's attendance at the candlelight church service came up. She begged to be excused and gave her father her most plaintive, pitiful, pleading look. She could tell he was wavering. Then, to everyone's surprise, Jack spoke up.

"I want you to come," he said. "We've always gone as a family. I don't care what other people think."

"And I've told my friends at school that you're doing the right thing letting your baby be adopted," Ben added. "The other day Jimmy Caldwell smarted off, and I —"

"What?" Sandy's mother asked sharply.

"Got him to stop," Ben finished.

Sandy looked at her brothers. She'd not thought much about what they'd faced because of the pregnancy. She felt ashamed at her self-centeredness.

"If you two want me to go, I will," she said.

Both boys nodded their heads.

It was a cold evening, and Sandy put on one of her mother's heavy winter coats. It wouldn't completely button in the front, but it helped mask Sandy's bulging abdomen.

"Can we sit in the back and leave as soon as the service is over?" she asked her father as they pulled into the church parking lot. "I don't want to go to the fellowship hall for hot chocolate and cookies."

"I'll fix a snack and make hot chocolate at home that will be better than anything the church has to offer," her mother said before the boys could protest.

Linda had driven her car and parked beside them. She came over to Sandy and linked arms with her.

"We're going to walk into that church together. Pretend that I'm old and weak and need a strong young woman to lean on."

The pressure from Linda's arm helped hold Sandy up, not the other way around. A cold wind was blowing, and people were hurrying into the sanctuary. Sandy saw several women look in their direction and whisper to their husbands. Her mother walked in front of the family with her head held high. Sandy knew she had endured a steady stream of gossip as the perfectionistic mother of the picture-perfect daughter who had turned up pregnant without being married.

Inside the church the two back rows were already filled, but there was room in the third row to squeeze in the family. Linda sat next to the aisle like a guard on duty. She helped Sandy slip out of her coat. Sandy didn't recognize the other people on the pew.

"Who's that?" she asked her mother, motioning to their left.

"The Morrows. They moved here a couple of months ago from Nebraska."

Sandy tried to get comfortable. The pew was padded, but it wasn't designed to support the unique weight distribution needed by a pregnant woman. The Christmas Eve candlelight celebration was one of the best-attended services of the year. Many familiar faces passed by on their way toward the front of the church. Fortunately, few glanced in their direction. The church filled to capacity.

The choir, cloaked in gold and red robes, entered from the back of the church singing "O Come, All Ye Faithful." They walked slowly down the aisle and into the choir loft behind the pulpit. The pageantry was both comforting and majestic. Sandy loved the combination of green wreaths, red bows, and gold and silver decorations. Her mother always helped prepare the church for the holiday season. Surrounded by family and warm feelings, Sandy began to relax. A small white candle that would be lit at the end of the service lay in her lap.

The service followed the usual format.

Congregational singing of Christmas carols alternated with special music from the choir, including a powerful version of "O Holy Night" sung by Mr. Sanderson, the choral director at the high school. When he reached the song's triumphant declaration, Sandy felt her own heart soar.

Reverend Frost, wearing a white robe with gold trim, took his place behind the pulpit. The minister was in his early thirties and a rising star in the denomination. Sandy's father didn't think he'd stay very long in Rutland before moving on to a bigger church. The minister opened the Bible and announced his text. Instead of the familiar Christmas story from the Gospel of Luke, he began in Matthew chapter 1:

Now the birth of Jesus Christ was on this wise: When as his mother Mary was espoused to Joseph, before they came together, she was found with child of the Holy Ghost. Then Joseph her husband, being a just man, and not willing to make her a public example, was minded to put her away privily. But while he thought on these things, behold, the angel of the Lord appeared unto him in a dream, saying, Joseph, thou son of David, fear not to take unto thee Mary thy wife: for that which is conceived in her is of the Holy Ghost. And she shall bring forth a son, and thou shalt call his name JESUS: for he shall save his people from their sins.

While the minister read, Sandy's imagination went on a two-thousand-year journey back in time to the events recorded in the ancient book. She saw Mary, pregnant and subject to ridicule. Mary's conception was without sin. Sandy's wasn't. But they shared a common bond of community shame. Sandy could guess the reaction of Mary's parents, her friends, the neighbors who'd known her since she was a baby, and the leaders of the synagogue. Electricity, automobiles, and running water didn't change what people thought and said. Mary would have suffered as much or more as a pregnant, unmarried woman in a small Jewish town than Sandy had in Rutland. Sandy's shame was justified. The reproach that fell on Mary was not. But their mutual humiliation touched Sandy in a deep, personal way. Her heart ached for Mary; it broke for herself. Never before had something in the Bible seemed so intensely personal. Sandy wiped a tear from the corner of her right eye.

Reverend Frost finished reading the scripture and began his sermon. Sandy stayed with Mary. She slipped a Bible from the rack on the back of the pew in front of her and turned to Matthew. As she read the passage again, she realized something she'd never noticed. Mary *voluntarily* accepted the humiliation of being an unmarried pregnant woman because of the importance of the baby she would carry. Her public reproach had a higher purpose, one that would affect all humanity.

Sandy had known that Jesus was the Savior of the world ever since she'd attended Mrs. Hartman's kindergarten class as a five-year-old. But in that moment, on Christmas Eve, in the beautifully decorated church, it became more than a well-known religious truth — it became relevant to her.

"Oh my," she whispered. "It's real."

Her mother glanced sideways, but Sandy ignored her. Jesus was not just the Savior of the world; he was *her* Savior. She'd done wrong, in many more ways than a one-night stand with Brad Donnelly. But Jesus made forgiveness possible. For that sin. For every sin. Something deep inside Sandy reached up to grasp the opportunity of forgiveness. And when she did, a huge weight rolled off her heart. She looked around the church and realized she wouldn't care if everyone in the sanctuary turned around at that moment and stared at her. Her shame was gone; she was forgiven by God. And that was all that really mattered.

A different kind of tears trickled from Sandy's eyes and rolled down her cheeks. These tears were tokens of the guilt being washed from her heart. She wiped them away with the back of her hand.

"Are you all right?" her mother asked.

Sandy nodded and kept looking straight ahead. She returned her attention to the sermon as Reverend Frost said, "In a few moments, we will light our candles, because the light of Christ has driven the darkness from our lives. Never forget — the blackest darkness must retreat before the light of the smallest candle. Go forth from this place and let your light shine before men, not just within the walls of the church, but wherever you are. Amen."

Ushers came down the aisles and lit the candle of the person sitting at the end of each pew. Linda passed her light to Sandy, who shared her light with her mother. After the last candle was lit, the electric lights in the sanctuary were turned off. The congregation stood and sang "Silent Night." For Sandy, the familiar phrases were filled with fresh meaning. *Holy infant . . . Jesus, Lord, at thy birth . . . dawn of redeeming grace.* Sandy's lower lip trembled as she sang. She had a nice singing voice, but tonight she had to sing softly. When the hymn was over, the congregation blew out their candles, leaving a single candle, the Christ candle, burning in the center of the Advent wreath at the front of the sanctuary. Sandy stared at the candle with deep gratitude. Reverend Frost pronounced the benediction.

The sanctuary lights were turned on, and the hubbub of conversation immediately broke out across the room as people talked and moved toward the aisles.

"That was a beautiful service," Sandy's mother said to her. "I'm glad you came."

"Me too," Sandy said, her eyes glistening. "This is the best Christmas Eve of my life."

TWELVE

In late January Sandy sat at the table in Linda's kitchen after supper with papers spread out in front of her. She'd read so many summaries of prospective couples who wanted to adopt a baby that the stories were running together. Reviewing the information impacted Sandy in one unexpected way — she was overwhelmed by the intense longing the anonymous people had for a baby. The way women, in particular, expressed their desire for a child deeply touched Sandy's heart. It made her wish there were enough babies for everyone who wanted one. Linda came into the kitchen.

"Here's one," Sandy said, picking up a piece of paper. "This couple lives in Virginia. The woman has had four miscarriages. After the last one, her doctor told her it would be dangerous for her to conceive another child. She's a third-grade teacher but wants to stay home and raise a child. Her husband is a salesman with a big corporation."

"Does he travel a lot?"

"Uh, he's over national accounts, whatever that means."

"He'd be gone a lot. An absent father is a missing influence."

Sandy thought about Brad's father and reluctantly slipped the packet into the reject pile. She felt bad doing so but couldn't take a chance. This would be her only opportunity to influence her baby's life for good.

"I wish I could see pictures," she said. "I can tell more by a person's face than I can by what they've written on a piece of paper."

"You have to trust the screening process at the agency. It's the most scientific way to go about it. Did Mrs. Longwell have any recommendations?"

Sandy reached for two folders, each with a note paper-clipped to the cover.

"Yes. One of them is on the East Coast and one on the West Coast."

"Still daydreaming about twins?"

Sandy rested her hand on her swollen abdomen.

"Dr. Berman doesn't say it's a daydream. Every measurement she's taken indicates I'm way ahead of schedule for a single birth."

"There's no doubt your body is working hard."

Sandy opened another folder.

"This couple lives in California. The woman is a speech therapist, and the husband does something with computers."

"We have a new computer at work," Linda said. "They installed it in a special climate-controlled room on my floor. My boss says computers are changing so fast it will be obsolete in a couple of years."

"Would the man in California have to travel a lot in that kind of work?"

"Not necessarily. It depends on whether he's an engineer who designs the machines or a salesman trying to market them. All I know is that it's a good field to get into. You might want to think about it when you go to college."

"Don't you have to be good in math? Math is my least favorite subject."

"Or good with languages. The computer has its own language."

"What? It talks?"

"Not now," Linda said. "You and I should learn about computers together."

Sandy shrugged. She wasn't interested in obscure scientific information that would never be relevant to day-to-day life.

"So you think I should consider the

California couple?" she asked.

"Yes. I've been to California several times for seminars. It's a big state, but every place I've been is beautiful in its own way. The weather is wonderful; the schools are excellent. I think it's a great place to raise a family."

"Okay," Sandy said, "but only if I actually have twins. I feel in my heart there's another couple that has to be the number one family. The family in the other flagged folder lives in Georgia. They've already adopted one baby, and I think a childless couple should get a chance before someone else receives a second child. Also, I don't like the idea of the baby being so close to me. If that happened, I'd be staring into every stroller I saw on the sidewalk and wondering if the baby inside was mine."

"You'll do that anyway. There'll always be that question in your mind."

Sandy knew Linda was right. It was an unsettling thought.

Several days later she was sitting in Mrs. Longwell's office.

"I've talked it over with Linda and called my parents," Sandy said. "The couple in California you suggested is my number two choice."

"Number two?"

"In case I have twins."

"Who's number one?"

"I haven't decided."

The phone on Mrs. Longwell's desk buzzed, and she picked up the receiver. She listened for a few moments.

"I'm on my way," she said, then hung up the phone.

Sandy stood up to leave.

"I have to go to our conference room for a few minutes. A question has come up that I need to answer in person. I'll be right back."

Sandy sat back down in her chair across from Mrs. Longwell's desk. She'd been in the office many times and everything was familiar to her. She looked again at the picture of Agnes, the caseworker's pet schnauzer. Agnes was lying on a reddish rug with a green chew toy in her mouth. Sandy leaned forward and picked up the photo. She could see the glitter of the rhinestone collar around the dog's neck. When Sandy returned the picture to its place, she saw another photo peeking out the edge of a folder. Glancing over her shoulder, she slipped it out with her index finger.

It was a woman.

The woman had short blond hair and

looked to be about thirty years old. She was standing in front of a two-story brick house beside a large palmetto tree. She had a happy smile on her face and eyes that seemed to look beyond the camera. Sandy devoured every detail of the picture. The woman was tanned and wearing a yellow blouse and light green skirt. A cream-colored Chevrolet convertible with a South Carolina license plate was parked in the driveway in front of a large two-car garage. Everything about the exterior of the house, yard, and car seemed perfect. Sandy turned the photo over. It was dated the day Sandy went to see Dr. Braselton and found out she was pregnant. There wasn't a name on the picture. After taking one last look at the woman, Sandy slid the photo back into the folder. A few seconds later, Mrs. Longwell returned to the room.

"Sorry for the interruption," the caseworker said. "Where were we?"

"Talking about my number one choice."

"Right."

Mrs. Longwell picked up a stack of four or five folders from the credenza behind her desk.

"Here are some other couples for you to review."

Sandy took the information. She wanted

to ask about the file containing the woman's picture but knew if she mentioned it, Mrs. Longwell would know she'd snooped.

"Thanks," she said.

The caseworker glanced down at her desk.

"Oh, and here's one more I meant to give you."

She picked up the folder and removed the photo before handing the information to Sandy.

"Let me know what you think. We need to identify your number one choice soon. Once that's done, I'll notify the couple and provide your background information to them. Then it will be up to the prospective parents to agree to the placement."

Sandy had seen the material given to prospective parents. It felt strange reading about herself as a "seventeen-year-old, blond-haired, blue-eyed, Caucasian female in excellent health with an above-average IQ, stable home environment, no history of illegal drug use, and regular prenatal care since eight weeks after gestation commenced."

"But that won't be a problem," Mrs. Longwell assured her. "You're the ideal birth mother."

The caseworker's choice of words made Sandy feel like a baby-making machine, but she knew Mrs. Longwell didn't mean the phrase in that way.

"And you're going to have two families ready in case I have twins?"

"Yes." Mrs. Longwell nodded. "I checked out what you told me with Dr. Berman, and she confirmed it. If it's a multiple birth, you may deliver earlier than expected."

Sandy had tried to avoid thinking about the actual birth process. She knew the combination of physical pain and emotional upheaval would be difficult. But she suspected the inner torment at hearing the baby's first cry and then having to face the hard reality that it would be the only sound she ever heard her child make would be worse than anything else. Birthing a second baby would multiply the pain on every level.

"I know." Sandy sighed.

"Are you okay?" Mrs. Longwell asked.

Sandy shrugged. "A lot goes through my head when I'm lying in bed at night trying to get comfortable."

"Is your commitment to the adoption holding up?"

"You've asked me that before."

"And I will continue to do so. Remember, my job isn't to force you to agree to an adoption. You can't legally surrender your parental rights until after the baby, or babies, is born; however, the decision of whether or not to place a baby with another family needs to be settled before you go into the hospital and pour so much of yourself into bringing a child into the world. Weigh all the factors —"

"I've done that," Sandy said. "Adoption is best for everyone."

"All right." Mrs. Longwell stood up. "Call me soon."

In the parking lot, Sandy slid behind the wheel of her car. Instead of starting the VW's engine, she picked up the folder that had contained the photo of the woman in the yellow blouse and opened it. The woman had been married for eight years. She was unable to have children following an unidentified surgery. She lived in South Carolina with her husband, who was an airline pilot. Sandy's heart sank. Pilots would be away from home more than salesmen. But Sandy kept reading anyway. The woman had a part-time job at a flower shop. As part of a brief personal statement each prospective parent was allowed to include in the packet, the woman wrote, "I believe Jesus will send us the child he wants us to love as he loves us."

Sandy looked out the windshield. The pilot father was a negative, but Sandy couldn't dismiss the woman's words. At lot of prospective parents mentioned praying for a baby. The woman's bold statement was different. It wasn't the way Sandy talked, but she liked the confidence it expressed. She thought again about the photograph. A shiver ran down Sandy's spine. She placed the folder on the passenger seat of the car and started the engine.

The following week Sandy phoned Mrs. Longwell and told her the South Carolina couple was her first choice.

"What happens next?" Sandy asked.

"I'll notify both couples that a baby may be available for them around the end of March or first of April."

"But you'll not mention the possibility of twins."

"I don't think keeping that a secret is wise," the caseworker said slowly. "What if several years down the road one of the children has a medical need, which can only be met by a sibling? It would be especially critical if the babies are identical twins, but it could still be potentially lifesaving information even if they aren't."

Sandy wanted to say she was saving the babies by keeping them apart but knew that explanation wasn't an option. She tried a different approach.

"Mrs. Longwell, have I been difficult to work with?"

"Uh, no. You're smart and mature for your age."

"Then please, let me do what I think is best. I've trusted you and the agency to find wonderful parents where my baby or babies will be loved and taken care of whether they know about a sibling or not. Don't fight me on this."

Sandy heard the caseworker chuckle.

"Sandy, I want you to call me in twenty years and let me know what you're doing with your life. You're a remarkable young woman and very persuasive in a disarming sort of way. Have you ever thought about becoming a lawyer?"

"A little."

"You should consider it. And even though I don't agree with you about separating twins, your request doesn't violate our guidelines. The records here will contain the information about siblings, and you can release your restriction on communication to appropriate parties in the future if you change your mind."

As the pregnancy progressed, Sandy started slowing down physically. She was fit, but the increasing baby load began affecting everything from her balance to her ability to breathe. There were other pregnant girls at the school at various stages of gestation, but by early March, Sandy was the most pregnant of the pregnant females. Her swollen abdomen attracted astonished stares. In her suffering she ignored them. She had to buy new shoes to accommodate her swollen feet and purchased a few maternity dresses that had as much style as the tents her father and brothers used when camping. Driving home for the weekends to Rutland was no longer possible, so her mother started coming to see her at Linda's house. One Friday in mid-March her mother drove to Atlanta so she could go with Sandy to her doctor's appointment. They sat together in the waiting area.

"It's nice having you with me," Sandy said, her legs stretched out in front of her. "Usually I'm all by myself. Some women come in alone, but others have their moms or husbands with them."

Sandy's mother managed a tight-lipped smile.

A few moments later, a nurse called Sandy's name and told her to stand on a scale. The nurse shook her head as she wrote down the number. Another nurse led Sandy and her mother to an examination room. After a short wait, Dr. Berman came into the room.

"This is my mother, Julie Lincoln," Sandy said.

"I can see the family resemblance," Dr. Berman said. "Your daughter has done an excellent job with this pregnancy. You should be proud of her."

The doctor helped Sandy onto the examining table.

"Are you having any contractions?" the doctor asked.

"Should I be?" Sandy asked in surprise. "It's almost a month to my due date."

"Even though it's your first pregnancy, I doubt you're going to make it that far. In fact, you could go into labor any day." Dr. Berman turned to Sandy's mother. "It's looking more and more like this might be a multiple birth."

Her mother's mouth dropped open.

"You mean twins?" she managed.

"Possibly. Or triplets. I've suspected the possibility of multiples for several weeks."

"Sandy, why didn't you tell us?"

"I guess I should have," Sandy said sheepishly.

"It wouldn't have changed anything," Dr. Berman said with a wave of her hand. "The main impact is on the due date. Twins usually arrive early; around thirty-seven or thirty-eight weeks is perfect. Sandy is almost ready for delivery now. Her blood pressure is stable, and my hope is that everything kicks in at the right time so we don't have to induce labor or deliver by caesarean section."

"I don't want an operation and scar," Sandy said quickly.

"And I'm not a doctor who does a caesarean at the drop of a hat. We'll keep close tabs on you to protect your health and the health of your baby or babies. I'll see you next week, if not sooner."

As soon as they were out of the doctor's office, Sandy's mother started firing questions at her.

"Yes," Sandy said. "Mrs. Longwell at the adoption agency is aware of the possibility of a multiple birth. I've selected two families in case I have twins."

"What about triplets?" her mother asked shrilly.

"There are plenty of wonderful people who want to adopt babies."

They got in the car. Sandy could tell her mother's mind was churning. Sandy shifted uncomfortably back and forth in the passenger seat and pulled the seat belt out to its farthest point and around her.

"Aren't there families that would take

both babies so they could be raised to-gether?"

"Probably," Sandy replied testily. "But that's not what I've decided to do."

"Twins," her mother repeated. "As far as I know, there's no history of twins in my family. Isn't it influenced by the maternal blood-line?"

Relieved that her mother had moved on in her thinking, Sandy nodded. "Yes, that's one part of the pregnancy Brad didn't have anything to do with."

Going to school became an increasing chal-lenge. It took all of Sandy's energy to drag herself from class to class. Unable to use a normal desk, she sat in a regular chair near the door and rested her textbooks on her stomach. Several days after her appointment with Dr. Berman, she received a note dur-ing homeroom to report to the principal's office. Sandy racked her brain to remember what she might have done wrong. Several times she'd had to leave class to go to the bathroom, but she couldn't think of any-thing else.

The head of the school was Dr. Walter Nichols, a former college basketball player. He came into the waiting area of the office as soon as the receptionist let him know that

Sandy was there.

"Come into my office," the administrator said.

Dr. Nichols was a tall, muscular black man who commanded the respect of the boys at the school. He had a no-nonsense approach to education and made it clear the school was the last chance of public education for the students who attended. Sandy sat down with a sigh. Dr. Nichols left the door of the office open.

"I'm not going to ask how you're feeling," the principal said. "That wouldn't be a fair question."

Sandy put her hands on the side of the chair to brace herself.

"I'm doing the best I can."

"Which is obvious to all of your teachers and the staff. Watching the way you've handled yourself has been an inspiration. So many of our students don't want to be here that to see someone who takes her schoolwork seriously encourages all of us to keep doing what we do."

"Thank you," Sandy said softly.

"But we're concerned about your health. How close are you to your due date?"

"A few weeks, but I may not make it that far. There's a chance I'm carrying twins."

Dr. Nichols raised his eyebrows. "What

does your doctor recommend about continuing with school?"

"She told me to do what I could."

"And we want you to do that without risking your health." The principal rested his hands on his desk. "I have a proposal for you if you'd like to hear it."

"Yes, sir."

"Your teachers are willing to prepare assignments so you can study at home and still receive credit for your classes. Mrs. Borden has offered to take the assignments to your house. Are you still living with your aunt near Emory?"

"Yes."

"Mrs. Borden's house is in the same area."

"That's nice of her," Sandy said. "But I'm not sure I can keep up —"

Dr. Nichols leaned forward. "Sandy, based on your academic performance, I would let you graduate right now if I could, but we need a way to satisfy the bureaucratic requirements for school attendance. A home-study program is one way to do that. Do the work you can, when you can. That will be more than enough."

Sandy had several years of perfect attendance in elementary school, and going to class was ingrained in her character. However, the chance to stay in her pajamas and read while sitting in the comfortable chair in Linda's living room sounded like a much-needed break.

"That would be great," she said.

"Good." Dr. Nichols sat up straighter. "Everyone here wants you to excel. You're a bright young woman with a great future ahead of you. If we handed out awards to outstanding students at the end of the year, you'd get the top one."

Sandy's eyes suddenly filled with tears. She'd been unaware that people at the school were watching her.

"Should I go to class today?" she asked, rubbing her eyes.

"If you feel like it. Mention to your teachers that we talked."

It was an emotional day. Sandy was overwhelmed by the response from her teachers. Mr. Vance, the algebra instructor, earnestly thanked her for her hard work. All of the women cried and hugged her. Mrs. Milton, the Spanish teacher from South Carolina, soaked through two tissues. Mrs. Welshofer, the chemistry teacher, held Sandy's hand and talked about the first day Angelica came to class and how Sandy agreed to help the Hispanic girl. Mrs. Borden retrieved a paper Sandy had written about the role of women in colonial society.

Placing it on her desk, she told Sandy it was one of the best pieces of student work she'd ever read.

When the final bell rang, Sandy was emotionally and physically spent. She sat in her little yellow car for a few moments and looked at the school. The overflow of love and encouragement from the faculty and the personal affirmation from Dr. Nichols touched her deeply. Ever since she'd fled in disgrace from Rutland High, she'd felt like a failure.

But Sandy wasn't a failure. She was an overcomer.

She'd done the best she could in a tough situation. And in God's mercy, she'd been surrounded by people who didn't judge her for her mistakes but encouraged her for the way she'd responded to them. She closed her eyes and let the words she'd heard during the day wash over her again and again. Over the past months, Linda, Dr. Berman, and the people in the run-down school building had lifted her out of the pit of self-condemnation. They'd helped save her life.

In the past, Sandy had dreamed of studying interior design like her mother. Since coming to Atlanta and meeting Angelica, she'd considered majoring in Spanish. Then Mrs. Longwell suggested she would be a good lawyer. Now Sandy wondered if teaching might be the best path for her.

Whatever she ultimately did in life, it would be profoundly influenced by what she'd learned at a school of last resort named Metro High in Atlanta, Georgia.

THIRTEEN

Linda drove Sandy to her next appointment with Dr. Berman.

"No change," the doctor announced after the examination.

"Should I be worried?" Sandy groaned. "I feel like I'm about to divide like an amoeba."

"I've never heard anybody put it that way." Dr. Berman smiled. "But every woman who has a child gives a part of herself to the baby. Trust your body and try not to worry. Anxiety has no positive side effects."

"Are you on call this week?"

Sandy knew Dr. Berman shared delivery duty with another ob-gyn physician, Dr. Castle. Sandy had seen Dr. Castle, a middle-aged man, a couple of times during her pregnancy, but she hoped Dr. Berman would be the one with her in the delivery room.

"Yes, then I'm off a week and on for two weeks."

"Those are good odds."

"Dr. Castle delivered both my boys," Dr. Berman reassured her. "He's a real pro. There aren't any bad odds in your future."

While Linda drove home, Sandy shifted uncomfortably in the passenger seat.

"I have an idea for a new invention," Sandy said while they waited for a stoplight to turn green.

"What's that?"

"A padded belt that will fit underneath a pregnant woman's abdomen and help support her baby. The ends of the belt could be attached to a brace that distributes the weight across the upper back and shoulders."

Linda chuckled.

"I can diagram it on a sheet of paper when we get home," Sandy continued. "It might not be the next Hula-hoop, but I would buy one."

"And you could offer them in different colors depending on the woman's outfit. That way each woman would want more than one."

"Yeah," Sandy grunted. "Like purses and shoes."

Sandy called her mother and told her

about the doctor's appointment.

"My suitcase is packed," her mother said. "If I didn't have to take care of Ben and Jack, I'd be there now. Anything I can do from here?"

"Uh, please call Jessica. I know she's thinking about me a lot."

"All right."

Sandy hesitated. There was one bit of news her mother didn't know.

"I talked to Mrs. Longwell yesterday. The lawyer for the adoption agency tried to get in touch with Brad about signing the surrender papers. Mrs. Donnelly told her to call Mr. Dexter."

Harold Dexter was a lawyer in Rutland. Sandy knew her father didn't like him but wasn't sure why.

"Is there a chance Brad won't sign the papers?" her mother asked sharply.

"Mrs. Longwell says that's always a possibility. Because Brad and I aren't married, Mr. Dexter would have to file some kind of legal papers if Brad wants to fight the adoption. Then it would go in front of a judge."

"Brad doesn't care about raising a baby."

"It's not him Mrs. Longwell is worried about. She said the paternal grandmother sometimes steps in and tries to get custody of a baby even though the birth father doesn't care."

"Kim Donnelly doesn't want to raise a baby either."

"I hope you're right." Sandy took a deep breath before dropping a bombshell. "But before I'd let that happen, I wouldn't surrender my parental rights to anybody."

"Let's not talk about that," her mother said with obvious tension in her voice. "We've made too many careful plans for everything to fall apart. I'd rather keep the baby than let Kim Donnelly get her hands on it, but I can't let myself think about that. And it's not healthy for you to either."

Sandy was so physically miserable that the possibility of legal problems with Brad and his parents, while catastrophic, couldn't make her feel much worse.

"I told Mrs. Longwell that I want Brad to sign first so the ten-day period he has to change his mind runs out before mine does. She thinks that's a good —"

"Stop it!" her mother said in a loud voice.

Startled, Sandy held the receiver away from her ear for a few seconds.

"I thought you wanted to know —"

"I'm about to have a nervous breakdown! I can't handle worrying about more things that could go wrong."

"I'm sorry," Sandy said.

"You've apologized enough, but that doesn't make it any easier. Tell Linda to call me as soon as it's time for me to come."

Sandy hung up the phone. When she turned around, Linda was standing in the kitchen doorway.

"Mama says she's about to have a nervous breakdown."

"Put yourself in her position."

"I try to, but it's hard to think about anyone but myself." Sandy paused. "Do you think I'm selfish?"

"Is that what your mother said?"

"Not exactly."

"And you want my opinion after living with you for six months?"

"Yes."

"Of course you're selfish. And your pregnancy isn't an excuse."

Sandy hung her head.

"The problem is that every person walking on two legs on the planet is selfish," Linda continued. "The bigger issue is, what unselfish choices are you making each day? You do a pretty good job with that, especially considering how lousy you must feel."

Linda's compliments, even when they came with reservations, lifted Sandy up.

"Inviting me to live with you was an unselfish choice," Sandy said.

"Before I called your mother, I was used to living here alone, doing what I wanted to do when I wanted to do it, not having to think about another person. As long as I kept the birdfeeders full and made sure the cats had food, water, and fresh litter, I didn't have to worry about anyone else. Yes, inviting you to come to Atlanta was an unselfish act. Sometimes such choices lead to difficult circumstances that cause regrets. But not with you. You're my niece, not my daughter, but the time we've had together is something I will treasure the rest of my life."

"Uh-oh," Sandy said.

"What is it?" Linda asked in concern.

Sandy put her hand on her back. "While you were talking, my insides tightened up and I felt a lot of pressure in my back."

"A contraction?"

"Maybe. It felt different from the Braxton-Hicks contractions I had the other day. Those were more across the front. I need to go to the bathroom."

When Sandy came out of the bathroom, she made it only to the kitchen door before the tightening sensation returned. She leaned against the doorframe. Her back ached.

"I left my watch upstairs on my dresser," Linda said. "I'll get it."

"I'm not going anywhere."

Sandy started walking up and down the hall. Dr. Berman had told her that walking sometimes made prelabor pains subside. Linda returned with the watch.

"Should I call your mother?" she asked.

"Not yet. Let's see what happens."

"Are you sure?"

"Yes," Sandy said. "I don't want her to come for nothing. Once she's in the car she'll be out of touch."

The pain returned and lasted forty-five seconds before subsiding. Sandy continued to walk through the downstairs area of the house. Linda, watch in hand, sat in the living room.

"It's starting now!" Sandy called out from the doorway to her room. She leaned against the wall until the pain subsided. "It's over!"

"Lasted forty-five seconds and twelve minutes apart!" Linda said.

Sandy went into the living room and sat down, but she couldn't stay in the chair.

"I've got too much energy to sit," she said, forcing herself up. "I'd rather be walking."

Back and forth she went through the house. Linda stayed in the living room, trying to read a book and recording the timing of Sandy's contractions on a piece of paper. After two hours, the contractions were coming in regular intervals ten minutes apart and lasting almost a minute.

"Call Mama," Sandy said when Linda showed her the sheet.

"Should I tell her to come here or go to the hospital?"

Sandy touched her stomach. "Ask the baby. I have no idea."

In a little over two hours there was a knock on the door. Sandy opened it. Her mother was standing on the step with her suitcase in her hand.

"The baby has dropped," her mother said, eyeing Sandy's abdomen.

"I know," Sandy replied. "If it drops much more, it's going to come out onto the floor."

Linda came into the kitchen from the living room.

"I think it's time to go to the hospital," Sandy said. "The contractions are coming six minutes apart."

"Do you want me to come?" Linda asked.

"Yes," Sandy responded instantly. "I'm going to need all the help I can get."

"I'm not sure what I can do. I've never had a baby. Your mother is experienced."

"You can let me know when I'm acting selfish," Sandy replied.

"What?" her mother asked.

"Linda will explain it to you. I'm going to

get my suitcase from the bedroom. Everything is packed."

Sandy rolled her suitcase into the kitchen. Linda drove. Sandy sat in the backseat with her legs stretched out across the seat. The contractions were getting more and more intense. She hadn't attended the prebirth classes sponsored by Dr. Berman's office when she found out husbands usually came. As a substitute, Dr. Berman gave her a pamphlet that Sandy had memorized. She tried to do the breathing exercises she'd practiced, but it was a lot more difficult when the pain was real. Linda stopped at a red light.

"Don't you think you could have gotten through that one?" Sandy asked.

"I didn't want to drive too fast."

"If you ever had a good reason to drive fast, this is it."

The rest of the trip, Sandy listened to Linda and her mother arguing about which lane to get in. Finally, Linda turned into the hospital parking lot and found a spot near the emergency room entrance.

"Did you call Dr. Berman's answering service before you left the house?" Sandy asked as they got out of the car.

Linda stopped in her tracks.

"It slipped my mind when your mother

arrived."

"The hospital can get in touch with her," Sandy said with a wave of her hand.

Thirty minutes later Sandy was in a labor room hooked up to monitors with her mother at her side. Linda opted to stay in the waiting room. A labor and delivery nurse informed Sandy that she was five centimeters dilated.

"You're going to have a baby tonight," she announced cheerfully. "I'll call Dr. Berman and let her know how you're progressing."

As soon as the nurse left the room, Sandy's water broke.

"The exam may have triggered it," her mother said. "I'll get the nurse and then check on Linda while they take care of you."

Now that the labor process was definitely under way, Sandy felt a sense of finality, like a runner who sees the finish line of a long race. Everything in her life since she'd found out she was pregnant had pointed to this event and this moment. For months she'd taken care of the baby in her womb and now wanted to usher him, her, or both of them into the world as healthy as possible.

The nurse returned with an assistant, who cleaned Sandy up and then changed the sheets on the bed. The nurse watched Sandy walk slowly around the room.

"I read your chart," the nurse said. "You're doing great."

"Thanks."

The nurse helped Sandy back into bed and reattached the monitors.

"I was adopted as an infant," the nurse said as she adjusted the knobs on the machine that measured the strength and frequency of the contractions. "I've never met my birth mother, but when I work with patients like you, I pretend I'm helping her."

Sandy peered up at the nurse.

"Do you ever feel mad at her for giving you up?"

The nurse stopped what she was doing and gave Sandy a look that reminded her of Linda.

"Every adopted child has questions. Some struggle with issues of abandonment and self-image. Others don't look in life's rear-view mirror at all. I'm kind of in the middle. I'm sure my birth mother had good reasons for doing what she did, but I don't know what those reasons were. Several years ago I contacted the agency that placed me, not to try to locate my birth mother, but to learn a little bit more about the circumstances of my adoption. I found out my mother had a say in where I ended up. That made me feel special, because I know she cared."

"I care," Sandy said softly.

"I know you do. I can see it in your eyes."

Sandy's mother returned, and Sandy told her about her conversation with the nurse. All talk ceased as Sandy dealt with a strong contraction.

"Linda called Mrs. Longwell," her mother said after the needle on the chart descended from the mountain. "She's going to get in touch with both sets of prospective parents."

"But not tell them about the possibility of twins."

"If that's what you told her. I still think it's a strange way to do this."

Sandy suddenly cried out. "Mama! Something's wrong!"

The needle on the graph shot up rapidly and kept climbing.

"What's happening?" Sandy asked, gritting her teeth.

"You're having a contraction."

"No, it's something else. Get the nurse."

Her mother hurriedly left the room. Sandy tried to control her breathing, but panic set in. The labor and delivery nurse rushed into the room and checked the chart.

"That's a strong one," she said. "It's at the peak and plateauing at a high level. You're making a lot of progress."

"Am I okay?" Sandy panted.

"Yes." The nurse watched the needle. "There, it's starting to go down."

The pressure eased slightly, but it was still excruciating.

"This is tougher than I thought," Sandy said, her cheeks hot.

The nurse patted her hand.

"That's why women, not men, have babies. I called Dr. Berman. She's on her way."

FOURTEEN

Sandy reached the limit of the pain she could endure, then found there was another level beyond it. Dr. Berman arrived and offered her an epidural pain block. Sandy's mother wiped some perspiration from Sandy's forehead.

"How close am I to delivery?" Sandy asked.

"Close," the doctor said.

"Will the epidural take effect before it's time to deliver?"

"Probably, but not by much."

Another contraction came, and Sandy had the strong urge to push.

"I want to push."

"Let's skip the epidural and get you to the delivery room."

Sandy's mother came with her. Sandy glanced up at the clock in the hallway as she passed by on a gurney. It was 1:30 a.m. She suddenly thought about Brad Donnelly.

He was lying in bed, sleeping peacefully through the night. Instead of getting mad, the ironic difference in their situations made her laugh.

"What is it?" her mother asked.

"Nothing, just a random thought."

Once they were set up in the delivery room, Sandy felt a strange sense of calm.

"I'm not scared," she said to no one in particular.

"That's good," said the labor and delivery nurse who'd accompanied her. "Your body knows what to do. Trust it."

A contraction came and Sandy pushed.

"Good," Dr. Berman said.

Several more strong contractions followed.

"That's it," Dr. Berman said. "Keep it up."

Sandy pushed.

"There's the head," Dr. Berman said. "A little bit more."

The next thing Sandy knew, Dr. Berman was holding up a reddish-blue baby. Hands quickly came in and started doing things that Sandy couldn't see.

"It's a boy," the doctor said.

"Is there another one?" Sandy asked.

Dr. Berman leaned to the side. Her lower face was covered by a blue mask, but her eyes were laughing.

"Yes."

"What do I do now?"

"You're doing it."

Sandy felt another contraction begin. She waited for the right moment, then pushed.

"What's happening?" she asked after the contraction subsided.

"Everything looks fine. The second baby is moving into position."

"How many are there?"

"There can't be more than two," Dr. Berman said. "The first baby weighed five pounds, two ounces."

Sandy glanced up at her mother, who was staring intently across the room.

"Is he okay?" Sandy asked.

"Yes," the delivery nurse said, popping into view. "His Apgar is six."

"Why isn't it higher?" Sandy asked.

"He's a little guy," the nurse said. "That's a great number for a baby this small."

For months Sandy had been determined to not try to see the baby or babies after they were born. But now, at the moment of birth, the maternal urge to have contact with her baby was overwhelming. Another contraction came, and she pushed. When the contraction subsided, Sandy glanced up at her mother, who was looking down at her.

"Should I see him?" Sandy asked.

223

"He's gone to the nursery."

"Did you see him?"

Her mother nodded without taking her eyes off Sandy's face. There was a deep sadness in her mother's expression.

"What's wrong?" Sandy asked.

Her mother simply shook her head. Another contraction came, and Sandy pushed. Several more followed. About fifteen minutes after the birth of the first baby, Sandy had an especially strong contraction and pushed.

"The head is crowning," Dr. Berman said. "Now, just like you did before."

A few seconds later, another reddish-blue bundle of humanity swept past Sandy's view. In a few seconds, Dr. Berman turned her attention to Sandy.

"Another boy," the doctor announced.

Sandy looked up at her mother, who was again focused on the area of the room where they'd taken the baby.

Sandy heard someone call out, "Apgar of five."

The delivery nurse appeared at Sandy's head.

"He's a little bit smaller than his brother. Four pounds, ten ounces, but he's a wiggly one. Don't worry. They're both fine."

"Are they identical?" Sandy asked.

"No."

Sandy could tell the nurse was about to provide additional information but stopped. Sandy watched her mother, who was absorbing every detail of what was being done to the second baby. When she looked down at Sandy again, her mother's eyes were red.

"They're both beautiful," her mother said softly. "And you did great. I hope the families that raise them do as good a job raising them as you have done bringing them into the world."

A pair of tears rolled down Sandy's cheeks. The desire to see her tiny boys was breaking her heart.

"Am I doing the right thing?" she said and sniffled.

"I guess so," her mother said, "but that doesn't make it any easier."

The delivery nurse came over and wiped Sandy's face with a cool cloth.

"You're a tough little trouper," she said. "You've been hauling around a lot of baby."

"Everything looks good," Dr. Berman said, joining the nurse. "Nothing came out that wasn't supposed to. In a few minutes, they'll send you up to a room."

"Where are the babies?" Sandy asked.

"In the nursery."

"What are they calling them?"

Dr. Berman looked at Sandy with kind eyes.

"Do you want to see them?"

"No." Sandy shook her head. "I'm just curious how they're going to tell them apart."

"One is 'Baby Jones,' and the other is 'Baby Smith,' " Dr. Berman said. "Sounds boring, doesn't it?"

Exhausted, Sandy closed her eyes and tried to let her mind go blank. An orderly rolled her to a regular hospital room, where she was transferred to the bed. Linda was there, looking at her with obvious respect in her eyes. Sandy's mother tucked the clean white sheet under Sandy's chin. Sandy gratefully closed her eyes and slept.

When she woke up, the morning sun was fighting its way through the blinds that covered the single window in the room. Another hospital bed between Sandy and the bathroom was empty. Her mother was lying in a recliner beside the bed with her eyes closed. In the split second between sleep and consciousness, everything that had happened over the past twenty-four hours rushed back into Sandy's mind.

She'd delivered twin boys.

There was a cup of water on a hospital

tray beside the bed. Sandy reached for the cup and slowly raised it to her lips. Few drinks had ever tasted so good. She took another sip and licked her lips. The door of the room opened, and Linda came in. She'd changed clothes from the previous night. She saw Sandy's mother asleep in the chair and put her finger to her lips. Linda walked quietly over to the bed and kissed Sandy on the forehead. She leaned over close to Sandy's ear.

"I've changed my mind. You're the most unselfish person on the planet."

Sandy smiled. There was a light knock on the door. Sandy's mother stirred and opened her eyes.

"Come in," Linda said.

It was Mrs. Longwell. Another woman Sandy had seen a few times at the adoption agency was with her.

"Do you feel like having visitors?" Mrs. Longwell asked.

"Yes."

Sandy introduced her mother. The other woman with Mrs. Longwell was named Mrs. Baker.

"You were right about the twins," Mrs. Longwell said. "I won't be as quick to doubt a woman who thinks she's going to have multiples in the future."

"How are they doing?" Sandy asked.

"Fine. I stopped by the nursery. They're going to spend a few extra days in the hospital to make sure they're eating and eliminating as they should. Their lungs are fine, which is a concern for smaller infants, especially boys."

"Do they look like me?" Sandy asked. "Their father is a redhead."

"They're newborn babies," Mrs. Longwell said. "There's nothing to stop you from taking a look if that's what —"

"No, I can't put myself through that."

"I understand," Mrs. Longwell said. "I have some good news about the father. He's agreed to sign the surrender papers."

Sandy closed her eyes in relief.

"The papers were delivered via courier to his lawyer's office in Rutland. I called this morning, and the father is going to come by the office today to sign."

"What day is it?"

"Friday," Mrs. Longwell said.

"I guess they'll let him out of school," Sandy said. "Anyway, once he signs I'll do it too. I just want him to go first."

"I understand, but it's a good idea to take care of it as soon as possible. The prospective parents are on their way to the hospital. As you know, they'll take the babies home even if the ten days haven't run out. As you requested, neither of the couples knows their child is a twin."

"And the babies aren't identical, right?"

Mrs. Longwell looked at Mrs. Baker, who smiled.

"They are, without question, fraternal twins," Mrs. Baker said.

"Okay." Sandy looked at her mother. "Mama, what am I forgetting to ask?"

Sandy's mother hadn't brushed her hair and looked a bit disheveled.

"Have you ever taken a baby away from the adoptive parents because the mother's consent was revoked?" she asked.

"Yes, but we try as hard as we can to keep that from happening. It's very traumatic for all parties. I've told Sandy many times that she doesn't have to place the babies for adoption unless she's convinced it's the best thing to do. Is that right, dear?"

"Yes, but I thought my heart was going to break when I didn't get to see the babies last night in the delivery room."

"Second thoughts on the adoption?"

"No, I need to follow through on what I've decided. Mama, are you still okay with that?"

Her mother didn't respond. Mrs. Longwell took out a large envelope and handed it to Sandy.

"The surrender papers are in here. We went over them together a few weeks ago, but I want to leave them with you. Check everything and write down any questions. And remember, you have the right to have a lawyer review them."

Sandy put the envelope on a small night-stand beside the bed.

"When will you be back?" her mother asked.

"Probably tomorrow. I want to be able to confirm that the birth father has signed everything."

"Thanks," Sandy said.

"You did great," Mrs. Longwell said, patting Sandy on the hand.

The two women left.

"Would you like a cup of coffee?" Linda asked Sandy's mother.

"Yes, thanks."

When Linda left the room, Sandy turned to her mother.

"Why did you ask Mrs. Longwell that question about the mother taking back her consent to the adoption?"

The sad look Sandy had seen in her mother's eyes the previous night returned.

"It's so painful to think that my first two grandsons are going to slip out of my life forever before I get to know them."

"I saw you staring at them in the delivery room."

"I couldn't see much. They were busy cleaning them up."

"Did either one of them look like Ben or Jack?"

Her mother got a faraway look in her eyes.

"The second one reminded me of you and Jack. There wasn't much difference between the two of you for the first few months. Ben has always looked more like your daddy."

"And the first one?"

"I didn't see him as clearly. I was still in shock about the fact that there were two."

Sandy's image of the babies in the delivery room was so fleeting that she couldn't slow it down to get a better look.

"Did you go by the nursery?" she asked.

"Linda did, but I didn't think it would be right for me to see them without you."

"What did Linda say?"

"That Baby Jones and Baby Smith looked like tiny, shriveled-up old men."

Sandy reached out and squeezed her mother's hand.

"I want to see them," her mother said.

"You do?" Sandy asked in surprise.

"Very much."

The resistance Sandy had built up

231

crumbled in an instant.

"Me too."

Now that the decision had been made, Sandy sat up and moved her legs toward the edge of the bed.

"Wait, Dr. Berman hasn't come by to say that you can get up."

"But I feel okay."

"No," her mother said emphatically.

Suddenly feeling light-headed, Sandy didn't argue. She laid her head back on the pillow and tried to relax; however, her heart didn't get the message. It was beating out of her chest.

It was over an hour before Dr. Berman came to the room. Sandy's mother and Linda were watching a cooking show on TV. Dr. Berman examined Sandy.

"You look good, but I wouldn't have expected anything else. Your vital signs are stable, and I wish every one of my patients had blood pressure as rock-solid as yours." She made a notation in the chart. "Of course, it helps to be eighteen years old and in great physical condition."

"Can I get out of bed?" Sandy asked.

"Yes, but not until the nurse removes the catheter. There's no use dragging that around with you if you can make it to the bathroom on your own. I want to keep you on the IV for the rest of the day. If you have a good day and night, I'll discharge you tomorrow."

"I'm going to see the babies," Sandy said.

Dr. Berman raised her eyebrows.

"Having second thoughts about the adoption?"

Sandy glanced at her mother. "I'm trying not to, but I have to see them, even if it's only to say good-bye."

"You've got to weigh the risks," the doctor said, sitting on the edge of the bed. "When you were in labor and delivery, I told you to trust your instincts. Now you should listen more to your head than your heart. Your instincts will drive you down a path I'm not sure you're ready to follow."

It was the most direct Dr. Berman had been about the adoption process.

"I know," Sandy said. "Mrs. Longwell came by earlier. I told her to come back tomorrow so I can sign the release papers. My mind is made up."

"Do you want me to begin the medicine that will stop your milk production?"

"Yes."

"Are you sure?"

"Yes," Sandy repeated.

"Okay, I'll send in a nurse. See you in the

morning."

Dr. Berman left.

"Does the adoption agency cover her charges?" Sandy's mother asked. "Your father didn't mention anything about paying a deductible."

"I don't know," Sandy said. "Mrs. Longwell took care of that stuff."

"Don't you think she has a conflict of interest?" Sandy's mother turned to Linda.

"Careful, Julie," Linda replied. "What the doctor told Sandy about following her head and not her heart applies to you too."

Sandy remembered Mrs. Longwell's comment that paternal grandmothers sometimes tried to step in and short-circuit an adoption. Undoubtedly, the same thing happened with maternal grandmothers. A nurse removed the catheter, then stayed until Sandy demonstrated her ability to walk to the bathroom.

"It's harder to move my legs than I thought," Sandy said as she slowly returned to the bed. "Maybe I should use a wheelchair to go to the nursery."

"I'll find one," her mother said, quickly leaving the room.

After she left, Sandy and Linda looked at each other.

"I don't think she was prepared for how

she would feel when the babies arrived," Linda said. "She called your father in the middle of the night, and they were on the phone for a long time."

"Did you hear her side of the conversation?"

"No, she asked me to leave so they could talk in private."

"I can't imagine what they said. At first, Daddy wanted me to get an abortion. Since then he's been okay with the idea of adoption. I think he's just been waiting for this to end so our lives can get back to normal. There's no way he wants to take on the responsibility of two infants."

"Your father is bullheaded, but your mother knows how to get what she wants."

"Yes, but this isn't her decision. It's mine."

Sandy's mother returned with the wheelchair and rolled it to the side of the bed.

"The nursery is just around the corner," she said brightly.

Sandy eased out of bed and into the wheelchair. Her mother flipped down the footrests and put on her slippers.

"We're off," her mother said. "Linda, are you coming with us?"

"Yes, I think I should supervise this visit."

FIFTEEN

The first person they encountered was a woman with an infant in her arms being wheeled back to her room. The woman, a beautiful smile on her face, was nuzzling the baby and talking softly to it. Sandy swallowed. They went around a corner into a different hallway. On the left was a row of patient rooms. To the right, there was a long window that extended from the floor to the ceiling. Through the window, Sandy could see several rows of clear plastic bassinets. Workers wearing masks were moving about. On the front of each bassinet was either a blue or a pink card that recorded the baby's last name, gender, date and time of birth, birth weight, mother's name and room number, and the baby's pediatrician. There were at least thirty babies in the nursery.

"Where were the twins when you came to see them in the night?" Sandy's mother asked Linda.

"One was at the far end, and the other one was in the middle."

Sandy's mother pushed the wheelchair down the hall. As she did, Sandy let her eyes scan the crowd of infants.

"Stop!" she said. "There's one of them. In the back row."

Her mother stopped the wheelchair.

"She's right," Linda said. "It's Baby Smith."

Sandy stood up and put her face close to the glass. In the third row was a baby boy smaller than those surrounding him.

"Can you see the card?" her mother asked. "I left my glasses in the room."

Linda read the information on the card, which listed a fictitious name and room number for the mother. All the other data was correct. The pediatrician was listed as Dr. Fletchall. The baby was wrapped tightly in a white blanket and lying on his side. His eyes were closed.

Sandy drank in every detail.

There was a hint of blondish fuzz on the baby's head. He had a perfectly shaped nose and lips that were slightly pouty. His left cheek had a healthy rose color. As she watched, a female worker came over and patted him on the back while she talked to another woman. Seeing the worker have physical contact with the baby made Sandy's heart climb into her throat.

"Try to get the nurse's attention," her mother said. "She can bring him up to the glass for a closer look."

"Mama," Sandy said, "this is killing me. Let him sleep."

"I want to see him."

"Julie." Linda put her hand on her sister's shoulder. "Please don't push Sandy on this. It's not fair."

Sandy's mother turned to Linda, her eyes flashing.

"You've never been a mother!"

"And you're the grandmother," Linda answered testily. "Sandy is the mother."

Sandy's mother tapped on the glass. The woman patting the baby didn't hear and turned away before responding. Sandy started rolling the wheelchair forward.

"You're being ridiculous," Sandy's mother said to Linda.

"No, you're out of line," her sister shot back.

Sandy spun the wheelchair around.

"If you don't stop, I'm going to scream!" she said with as much force as she could muster. "We're going to see them from the hallway. That's it. Why are you trying to ruin this for me?"

Tight-lipped, her mother didn't answer. Linda looked into the nursery.

"There he is," Linda said. "Just ahead in the second row. They had him there last night."

Sandy repositioned the wheelchair, rolled forward a few feet, and stood up. Baby Jones was closer to the window. He was wrapped snuggly in a white blanket as well and lying on his side. Sandy sucked in her breath.

"He's a redhead," she gasped. "Just like Brad."

There was no mistaking the color of the hair on the baby's head. He, too, was smaller than the babies beside him, but his features were perfectly proportioned. His mouth was slightly open. While they watched, he screwed up his face for a second, then relaxed.

"Did you see that?" Sandy whispered.

The worker who had been patting the back of Baby Smith noticed the three women on the other side of the glass and started walking toward them. She pointed at Baby Jones's bassinet and made a hand signal asking if they wanted her to bring him closer. Sandy quickly shook her head from side to side, then glanced at her mother, who was staring stoically in front of her. The attendant gave them a puzzled look and turned away. Sandy continued to stare at the baby, whose similarity to Brad didn't make her love him less. When her brain couldn't absorb another detail, she sat down in the wheelchair.

"I'm done," she said.

Sandy turned the wheelchair around and started going in the opposite direction. Her mother and Linda silently followed. When she was level with Baby Smith, Sandy suddenly stopped and turned the wheelchair toward the window. She'd not given him as much attention as his brother. She stood in front of the glass and created an internal photo album of every detail she could record. While she watched, the baby didn't move a millimeter. He was a sound sleeper. She turned to her mother.

"I'm going back to my room. You can stay if you like, and even ask one of the nurses to bring the babies closer. I won't mind. But for me, that would be more than I can handle."

"I'll stay by myself," her mother said.

"And I'll go with Sandy," Linda replied.

Sandy let Linda roll her down the hall. They turned the corner. Numb, Sandy didn't notice anything or anybody. Linda held the wheelchair steady while she stood up. Sandy slowly eased herself into the bed and lay down, turning her head to the side to stare at the wall. Linda left the room. Sandy had shed unnumbered tears over the past eight months, but today the fountains were dry. It wasn't long until her mother returned and sat in the chair beside the bed.

"I had a long talk with your daddy last night," she said.

Sandy waited, dreading what was coming next.

"I already knew one of the babies looked like you and the other favored Brad. I suspected as much in the delivery room, and Linda confirmed it last night when she came back from the nursery. Since you're determined to send the twins to separate homes, I thought we might consider taking the younger one."

Her mother paused. Sandy found herself holding her breath.

"Your daddy and I could raise him and let you be involved as much as you wanted to. Years ago it wasn't unusual for grandparents to take a primary role in a child's life, especially when families lived close to one another. My mother spent a lot of time with her paternal grandmother. She went to her house every day after school and stayed until suppertime. It wouldn't be necessary for us to adopt the baby. He'd still be yours.

After you graduate from college, we could see how things worked out. Of course, when you get married, you would create a home of your own for him." Her mother turned toward Sandy, her eyes imploring. "I'd like to take both babies, but I know that's not practical. I made my choice based on appearance. It would be easier to incorporate a child into the family if he looked like you and Jack. We'd all have to sacrifice, but it would be worth it. What do you think?"

Sandy took a deep breath and exhaled before she spoke.

"I think you already love your grandsons, and it's going to hurt like crazy to let them go."

"Will you consider it?" her mother pleaded.

Sandy had never heard her mother use that tone of voice when addressing her. She hesitated.

"What exactly did Daddy say?"

"Oh, he talked in circles. Remember, it was the middle of the night. But he'll come around eventually."

The two women were silent for a moment.

"Are you willing to discuss whether this is a good idea with Mrs. Longwell?" Sandy asked.

"It's none of her business," her mother

said crisply. "She has an agenda."

"Mama, she works for an adoption agency. It's her job to find homes for babies. And I went to her for help, not the other way around."

"You'd still be letting her place one baby for adoption. Mrs. Longwell wasn't sure there would be two babies until last night."

"I'm not sure it's a good idea."

The door of the room opened and Linda walked in, then stopped in her tracks.

"Should I go for another walk outside?" she asked. "It's a gorgeous spring day."

"No," Sandy's mother said. "Whether you're here or not isn't going to make any difference."

Tension hung in the air for the rest of the morning. Shortly after lunch, the door opened. Mrs. Longwell and Mrs. Baker returned.

"You're looking better already," Mrs. Longwell said to Sandy.

"I'm weaker than I thought, but Dr. Berman said I should be able to go home tomorrow."

"That's good news," Mrs. Longwell said. "And I have some great news. I just confirmed that Brad signed the surrender papers around ten this morning. They are going to be sent by overnight mail to my office."

Sandy glanced at the envelope Mrs. Longwell had brought by earlier in the day. It was in the same place Sandy had put it when the caseworker left.

"I haven't opened the envelope," Sandy said. "I'm sure it's the same thing you went over with me at your office."

"It is. Are you ready to move forward?"

Sandy looked at her mother, whose face appeared slightly flushed.

"My mother has a question," Sandy said.

Mrs. Longwell shifted her gaze to Sandy's mother.

"I talked to my husband last night about keeping one of the babies," Sandy's mother said slowly. "Sandy and I have discussed it but haven't reached a decision."

While her mother spoke, Sandy watched Mrs. Longwell's face. The caseworker showed no sign of shock or disappointment.

"What do you think?" Sandy blurted out.

Mrs. Longwell put her hands together in front of her for a moment. It almost looked like she was praying.

"Whether there is one baby or two, the decision to surrender parental rights is very difficult, not just for the birth mother, but for every member of her family. I've been doing this for a long time, and questioning an adoption decision after a baby is born is perfectly understandable."

The calm way Mrs. Longwell spoke released some of the tension in the room.

"My feelings caught me off guard," Sandy's mother said.

"Based on the time I've spent with Sandy, I'm not surprised her mother would consider restructuring her life to raise a grandchild. Which one of the babies are you considering?"

"The younger one," Sandy's mother said.

"Stronger family resemblance." Mrs. Longwell nodded, glancing at Mrs. Baker. "We saw that immediately."

"Even as a newborn, the older boy looks like Brad," Sandy said.

The women sat in silence for a few awkward moments.

"Where are the prospective parents?" Sandy asked.

"One couple is already in Atlanta. They've checked into a hotel and are waiting for me to call them. The other couple is flying in this afternoon. Because you requested a closed adoption, my plan was to keep them away from the hospital until you've checked out."

Sandy thought about the blond-haired

woman from South Carolina. She wanted that woman to have a baby and suspected she and her airline-pilot husband were already in the city.

"Would my number one couple still get a baby?" she asked.

"Yes."

Sandy imagined the woman standing in front of the tree in her front yard holding Baby Jones.

"No," she said, almost to herself.

"What?" her mother asked.

"Something's not right."

Her mother gave her a puzzled look. Sandy looked at Mrs. Longwell.

"My number one choice needs to have Baby Smith."

"What are you talking about?" her mother asked.

Sandy sat up straighter in bed. An unexplainable confidence entered her.

"The first couple I selected is supposed to raise the younger baby. If we're going to take a baby home, it should be Baby Jones."

"That doesn't make any sense," her mother replied. "He's the one who looks like Brad. It would be hard to look at the baby every day and be reminded of what his father did to you."

"Don't ask me to explain it, Mama,"

Sandy said. "But something inside me knows it would be wrong for us to keep the blond-haired baby."

Sandy's mother turned to Linda.

"Does this make any sense to you?"

"It doesn't make sense to me for you and Bob to take either one of these babies home to Rutland. You already have a beautiful family, and there's no reason why you should add the responsibility of an infant at this point in your lives when there are childless couples who desperately want just one baby. More important, I think Sandy should do what she believes is best for these children. She's the one who thought she was going to have twins. And whether it's fate or God, I believe she's been given the right to make this choice."

Sandy looked at her mother.

"Do we need to talk about taking home Baby Jones?"

"No," her mother sighed.

"Then I'm ready to sign the papers," Sandy said to Mrs. Longwell. "For both babies."

Sandy wanted to have her mother's approval. But that might not be possible, at least not now. She reached for the envelope, opened it, and turned to the signature page.

"Not so fast," Mrs. Longwell said. "Read

each sheet and put your initials at the bottom. You'll sign two sets. One for us, the other for you to keep."

While Sandy was reading the first page, her mother left the room. Linda followed her.

"Are you pushing your mother too hard?" Mrs. Longwell asked when the door closed.

Sandy glanced up. "I can't do anything else. I hope she'll be okay when we're at home and her life gets back to normal."

"Don't be surprised if she goes through a period of grief. You will feel the loss too. It's better if you can support each other in that process."

All Sandy wanted to do was sign the documents. Once the decision had finally been made, she didn't want any more confusion or distractions to come against her. She skimmed as fast as she dared and signed. Mrs. Baker notarized her signature. Sandy was relieved that it was done.

"Do you want us to wait with you until your mother comes back?" Mrs. Longwell asked.

"No."

"You're aware of your right to change your mind within the next ten days," Mrs. Longwell said. "All that is outlined in the papers I'm leaving with you."

"I'd only do that if Brad changes his mind."

The door to the room opened. It was a nurse coming to check her vital signs.

"Then we'll be on our way," Mrs. Longwell said. "Call if you have any questions."

After the two women left and the nurse finished her duties, Sandy rested her head against the pillow and closed her eyes. She felt empty. Not bad. Just drained. Forty-five minutes later her mother and Linda returned. Without saying a word, her mother came over to the bed and kissed Sandy on the forehead.

"After I calmed down, Linda and I had a good talk," her mother said.

Sandy looked at Linda, who nodded her head.

"I'm sure I'll have second thoughts later," Sandy's mother said, "but for now I see why placing the babies for adoption in good homes is probably the best thing to do."

"Mrs. Longwell said both of us would grieve," Sandy replied. "And I want us to help each other, not be mad."

"You sound more like a parent than I do."

"I learned most of what I know from you."

"Maybe," her mother replied. "But you've matured by years instead of months since you came to Atlanta."

The three women spent the rest of the afternoon peacefully. Sandy wanted to have another peek at the twins but wasn't sure if it was a good idea for her mother to join her. When supper arrived, it was an unappetizing piece of brown meat and tasteless mashed potatoes. "Linda and I need food too," her mother said. "I'll get something from the salad place we saw when we went out earlier."

"I'll go," Linda said. "You're not familiar with the city."

"It's only three blocks from the hospital," Sandy's mother said. "I can handle that. And I know exactly what Sandy would like to eat."

"Okay," Linda said.

After Sandy's mother left, Linda sat in the chair beside the bed and started reading a book. Sandy watched her for a moment. Linda glanced up and saw her.

"Do you want to see the babies?" Linda asked.

"Yes, but not while Mama is here."

"We have at least twenty minutes before she comes back."

This time Sandy leaned on Linda's arm and walked around the corner to the nursery. The babies had been moved again, and Baby Jones was in the second row. He was lying on his other side.

"He looks just as perfect from this angle," Linda said.

Sandy nodded as she studied his face. While she watched, he wiggled slightly and one of his hands came into view. Sandy gasped at the sight of the tiny fingers. A few moments later, a nursery worker picked him and took him out of the room.

"Probably going to supper," Linda said.

Sandy tried to shake off the anxiety she felt as the baby disappeared. She continued down the hallway. Baby Smith was now in the front row, which meant Sandy was less than three feet from him. He, too, was asleep, but she had a chance to observe every twitch of his face. Sandy watched the blanket rise and fall with each breath.

"He's a miracle," Sandy said.

Linda didn't respond but stayed by her side. Sandy was transfixed.

"Better head back to the room," Linda said.

"But we just got here."

"No, the twenty minutes is almost up, and I think you should be in bed when your mother returns with the food."

Sandy put her fingers to her lips, then touched them to the glass in a good-bye kiss. After one last lingering look, she turned away.

When she did, she saw an older woman who looked vaguely familiar at the end of the hall. The woman's hair was pulled back in a bun, and she was wearing a blue-print dress. She glanced sideways at Sandy, who gasped and grabbed Linda's arm. The woman stepped around the corner out of sight.

"What is it?" Linda asked. "Are you feeling okay?"

Sandy stared down the hallway.

"Quick! Try to catch that old woman who was at the end of the hallway. Tell her I want to talk to her."

Linda gave Sandy a strange look.

"What old woman? I didn't see anybody."

"Just go. She can't be far away. She's wearing a blue-print dress and has her hair in a bun. I'll wait here."

Sandy leaned against the nursery glass as Linda walked rapidly down the hallway and disappeared. In less than a minute, her aunt returned.

"Where is she?" Sandy asked.

"I couldn't find an old woman," Linda said. "Maybe she got on the elevator. Why did you want to talk to her?"

Sandy glanced over her shoulder at the

nursery. Baby Smith was still in his bassinet. She turned to Linda.

"Do you really believe I'm doing the right thing letting the babies be adopted?"

"I've always thought that."

"And it's okay to place them with different families?"

"If that's what you want to do. I can see how that would make two families happy. Why are you asking me this now?"

"Okay." Sandy took a deep breath and exhaled. "There's nothing else I can do."

"What in the world are you talking about?"

Sandy reached out and took hold of Linda's arm.

"I'm ready to go back to my room."

"Do you need to ask the doctor for some medicine for anxiety?"

"No. I'm fine now."

Sandy's mother returned ten minutes later.

"I brought you a Cobb salad," she said.

The fresh salad tasted good. To Sandy's relief, Linda didn't bring up the incident with the old woman.

The following morning Sandy walked to the bathroom without any trouble, then took a shower and washed her hair. Her mother, after another night in the recliner beside the bed, looked even more haggard. Linda arrived while Sandy was finishing a bowl of oatmeal with raisins. Dr. Berman came into the room and performed a quick exam.

"Ready to leave?" she asked.

"Yes," Sandy said with finality.

"I'll prepare the discharge order. Are you going to follow up with me or a doctor in your hometown?"

"I'm going to spend two more weeks with Linda so I can finish school. The principal is allowing me to do a home-study program."

"Good. Call my office and schedule an appointment the first of the week. I'd like to see you at least one more time."

"Okay. And thanks for everything."

Dr. Berman left. Sandy's mother took a sip of coffee and put the cup on the tray.

"I'm going to take a last trip to the nursery," she said. "Do you want to come with me?"

"No," Sandy said. "I've said my good-byes."

"May I join you?" Linda asked.

"Yes. I'd like some company."

They were gone about thirty minutes. When they returned, Sandy could tell her mother had been crying. For Julie Lincoln, the first steps on the path of grief were wet with tears.

"Let me see what you have to wear home," her mother said, wiping her eyes with a tissue.

"There aren't a lot of —" Sandy started, then stopped when Linda shook her head.

Sandy's mother laid out her clothes and helped pack her suitcase just as she did when Sandy went to summer camp. A nurse came into the room, went over warning signs for problems, and handed Sandy a packet of information. She wheeled Sandy to the front door of the hospital where Linda was waiting with the car. As they drove away from the hospital, Sandy felt a wrenching pain deep in her heart. She turned around and saw the hospital disappear behind a row of buildings. Sandy knew the sharp ache was the cry of her spirit as she was separated from the two baby boys she'd never see again. She closed her eyes until the pain subsided.

Whatever the future held, part of her would remain forever with the sons she'd borne.

■ ■ ■ ■

PART TWO

■ ■ ■ ■

Sixteen

Santa Clarita, California, 2008

The Santa Clarita courthouse on West Valencia Boulevard in Los Angeles County was familiar territory to Dustin Abernathy. He usually entered the building as an attorney, not as a defendant forced to be there. It was cool in the air-conditioned courtroom, but Dusty was perspiring beneath his dark-gray suit as he waited for his case to be called. He ran his fingers through his reddish-brown hair and leaned over to Melissa Burkholder, the lawyer representing him.

"Are you sure we shouldn't offer another grand a month in alimony and extend it to twelve months? It's not that much money in the big scheme of things."

Melissa tapped the folder on her lap with a pen.

"Adultery may not be grounds to deny spousal support in California, but when I

259

show the judge that Farina is living with Nathaniel Cameron in his big house in Malibu and driving an $80,000 car he gave her, I don't think the judge is going to find a legal basis for ongoing need. That will save you a ton of cash."

"But she didn't have any earnings during our marriage."

"Which lasted a total of 854 days before you split up. Come on, Dusty, we were in complete agreement on our strategy when we went over this stuff at my office last week. If you hadn't followed Farina from the spa to Cameron's house, we never would have known what she was doing. You connected the dots."

Dusty glanced over at Farina, who was sitting beside her lawyer. Hadley Bingham was a senior partner with a prestigious firm in Beverly Hills. Farina's benefactor, Nathaniel Cameron, had to be paying the bill for such high-priced legal talent. Melissa was a battle-tested divorce attorney who wasn't afraid of a legal knife fight. However, most of her skirmishes were fought against storefront lawyers who handled so many divorce cases they had trouble keeping the names of their clients straight. Today, she would face off against an attorney who represented a handful of multimillionaires at a time.

Dusty's predicament was the result of his failure to insist on a prenuptial agreement with Farina in the first place. He'd been burned financially by Sharon, his first wife; and when he started dating again, his buddies at the law firm warned him not to tie the knot without a loose string attached to a prenup. Idealistic and in love, Dusty called his friends cynics, and he took the tall, black-haired Farina to St. Croix for a barefoot wedding as the surf rolled over their toes. Within a year and a half, the couple was spending most of their time arguing. They tried a few months of marriage counseling, but it exposed more problems than it solved. Then Dusty came home one Friday night after a three-day trip to Sacramento and found a note telling him that the marriage was over. Farina had moved out. She changed her cell phone number and instructed her mother not to tell Dusty where she was. The divorce petition landed on his desk thirty days later.

Judge Harriett Wilcher, a woman in her late forties, entered the courtroom. Everyone stood.

"Be seated," the judge said. "Madam Clerk, please call the first case on the afternoon calendar."

"*Abernathy v. Abernathy,*" the court clerk said in a nasally voice.

"Let's do this," Melissa said to Dusty.

They walked up to the counsel table. Dusty sat slightly hunched over as the lawyers went through the preliminary formalities. He avoided looking in Farina's direction.

"Proceed with your first witness," the judge said to Bingham.

The lawyer motioned to Farina.

"Plaintiff calls Farina Abernathy."

Farina walked to the witness stand like a model on the runway. Even now, Dusty had to admit she cut a classy swath across the room. However, Farina was Exhibit A to the old saying that beauty is only skin-deep. Push one of her multiple hot buttons and scalding steam escaped. Her lawyer smoothly brought out the basic testimony establishing that the marriage was irretrievably broken and that Farina met the prima facie requirements for spousal support.

"Were there any children from the marriage?" Bingham asked.

"One," Farina answered.

Dusty's eyes opened wider. He'd told Melissa this issue might come up, but he was surprised Farina wanted to go there.

"A year into the marriage I conceived, and

Dusty insisted I have an abortion," Farina said.

"Insisted? Please explain that for the court."

Farina turned toward Judge Wilcher. As she moved her head, Farina's steely gray eyes met Dusty's for a split second and shot a glint of hate in his direction.

"Dusty was belligerent and aggressive when he drank. I've looked it up online, and the way he treated me when he was drunk would be considered emotional abuse —"

"Objection," Melissa said, quickly standing up. "First, the witness isn't competent to offer expert psychological testimony. Second, the answer is nonresponsive to the question."

"Sustained. The witness will answer the question without offering a legal or medical opinion."

"I wanted to be a mother," Farina continued, "but Dusty didn't want to be a father. When he found out that I was pregnant, we had a big fight. He'd been drinking all day and started yelling at me and broke a glass. I was terrified, and he forced me to go to the women's clinic on San Jacinto Boulevard for the abortion."

"Who drove to the women's clinic?"

"Dusty."

"Was he intoxicated while driving?"

"Objection on the same grounds," Melissa interjected.

"Sustained."

"How many drinks had he consumed?" Bingham asked.

"I'm not sure, but enough to make him mean. I was afraid not to do what he said."

"Did Mr. Abernathy physically threaten you?"

Every muscle in Dusty's body tensed.

"Not exactly," Farina answered. "But I was scared because he would yell and throw things. When that started happening, I tried to get out of his way. That day I didn't have a choice. If I hadn't done what he wanted, I'm sure I would have been hurt."

"Objection to speculation," Melissa said.

"Sustained as to the witness's last statement," the judge said.

"Please continue," Bingham said.

"I don't remember much about the trip home. I was in a lot of pain."

Farina's recollection of the termination of the pregnancy was only partially right. First, it was an accident that'd she become pregnant at all. However, when the home pregnancy test came back positive, the first thing Farina did was pour a stiff drink. Dusty was drinking a beer in their entertainment room when she hysterically broke the news. At first, the idea of being a father sounded exciting to Dusty, but Farina immediately ramped up a heated argument. After the dust settled, their discussion resulted in a rare instance of agreement when they decided abortion was the best option. They drove to the clinic in stony silence. Farina had had a previous abortion when she was in her early twenties and knew what she was getting into. Dusty was confident his version of the facts would come across as more credible than Farina's.

Bingham moved into the financial area and introduced the joint tax returns the couple filed during their marriage. Dusty wondered how his annual income compared to Bingham's. Lawyers like Dusty who worked on contingency cases often made more than attorneys who billed by the hour, even at Beverly Hills rates.

"What was your average annual income for the three years prior to your marriage to Mr. Abernathy?" Bingham asked.

"Thirty-five thousand dollars. Clerical jobs in advertising agencies don't pay very well."

"Did you continue to work during the marriage?"

"No, Dusty wanted me to be there when

he got home from work."

Dusty couldn't keep from smiling. Farina was thrilled that he'd set her free from the workplace grind. She had no trouble filling her day with self-centered opportunities to pamper her body and occupy her frivolous mind.

Bingham finished his direct examination without any effort at preemptive damage control about Farina's relationship with Nathaniel Cameron. Melissa stood up. Dusty saw Farina's eyes widen. He knew his estranged wife was scared.

"Ms. Abernathy, are you currently living in Malibu?"

"Yes."

"Do you live there on a full-time basis?"

"Yes."

Dusty relaxed. Proof that Farina was cohabiting and receiving substantial support would demolish any claim for spousal support.

"How many people are in the household?"

"Four."

"Who are they?"

"Myself, Nathaniel Cameron, the housekeeper, and a chef."

"The housekeeper and chef live in the residence?"

"Yes."

"So you don't have to do any cooking or cleaning?"

"No." Farina gave Melissa a puzzled look.

"Does Mr. Cameron furnish you a car to drive?"

"I can use the red Mercedes if I need to."

"Anytime you need it?"

"Pretty much. He drives the black Mercedes."

"When did you first start staying with Mr. Cameron?"

"Do you mean in Malibu or in New York City?"

Melissa raised her eyebrows. "You also lived with him in New York?"

"Yes, for about a year when I dropped out of college. He was working at Presbyterian Hospital in Manhattan, and he offered to let me stay with him at his apartment while I tried to land a modeling job."

"Mr. Cameron worked at a hospital?"

"Yes, he's a pediatric neurosurgeon. He's semiretired now."

"So, when he moved to Malibu, you continued your relationship, is that correct?"

"Of course."

Dusty's mouth dropped open. He could see that Melissa was also shocked.

"Natty is my uncle," Farina continued.

267

"Or half uncle, I guess. He and my mother have the same father but different mothers. I hadn't seen him for several years, but he was nice enough to let me stay with him when he found out that Dusty and I were splitting up. I didn't want to go to my mother's house because Dusty knows where she lives and would harass me. He doesn't know my uncle, so it was a safe place for me to live until the divorce was finalized."

Dusty glanced at Bingham, who had a bemused expression on his face. Melissa returned to the table and picked up some financial records. She avoided eye contact with Dusty. She faced Farina.

"Ms. Abernathy, besides enjoying the amenities of your uncle's house, is there anything preventing you from returning to work in the advertising field?"

"I've been looking for a job because I can't stay with Natty forever. I've submitted over a hundred résumés and had a few interviews but haven't gotten any offers. Dusty isn't giving me any financial help, and I don't have the money to get my own place closer to town where most of the jobs are."

Farina had been well coached and played Melissa like a fish on a hook. Information that could have been brought out on direct examination had much greater impact when spoken on cross-examination. Dusty wrote a figure on a legal pad in front of him and circled it. When Melissa finished and sat down, he slid it over to her. She grimaced and nodded.

"Your Honor," Melissa said, standing up. "Would you allow me a few minutes to consult with opposing counsel?"

"You've had several months to talk to Mr. Bingham. Why should I let you do it now?"

"To see if we can narrow down the issues," Melissa answered.

"I'd welcome the opportunity to address that as well," Bingham said amiably.

"Very well," the judge said. "But when you ask for a few minutes, that's all I'm going to give you."

The judge left the bench. Bingham and Melissa met in the space between the two tables. Dusty moved closer so he could listen.

"What would your client accept for spousal support?" Melissa asked.

Bingham had a legal pad in his hand and held it out so Melissa could see it but Dusty couldn't. Dusty saw Melissa swallow.

"That's a lot," she said.

"I have a strong case, and you haven't heard all of it."

Melissa showed Bingham the figure Dusty had written.

"I appear in this courtroom a lot, and I've never seen Judge Wilcher award this much," she said to Bingham.

"Then maybe we can set a new record," Bingham responded coolly.

The older lawyer stepped over and spoke to Farina for a moment. When he returned he showed Melissa a new number. She turned the pad so Dusty could see it. Dusty winced.

"That's as low as we'll go," Bingham said. "Otherwise, we'll let the judge decide."

"What's that other number?" Dusty asked, pointing to a figure below the amount for spousal support.

"My attorney fees," Bingham answered.

Dusty swallowed. Bingham definitely made more per year than he did.

The judge returned. Dusty stared at the table while Bingham and Melissa recited the general terms of the divorce agreement into the record. The judge looked out at the courtroom.

"I'll grant the divorce and accept the settlement as in the best interests of the parties. The attorneys will file a consent order and formal agreement within ten days."

Dusty and Melissa left the courtroom in a hurry. Out of the corner of his eye, Dusty could see Farina give Bingham a hug.

"That was a massacre," Dusty said as soon as he and Melissa were in the hallway.

"You were the one who put me on to Cameron —" Melissa began defensively.

"Don't go there," Dusty cut in. "I'm not blaming you. I should have had a prenup. But it's going to be peanut-butter sandwiches with an occasional night out for cheap Chinese food until I can get Farina off the payroll."

It was a thirty-minute drive from the courthouse to Dusty's office. The law firm of Jenkins and Lyons, P.C., was located in a modern, three-story building at the corner of a busy intersection. Dusty had clerked for the firm the summer after his second year in law school at Northwestern and received a job offer upon graduation. Five years later he became a partner; however, at Jenkins and Lyons partnership status didn't change the fact that orders issued by the two senior partners were obeyed with minimal opportunity for debate. Dusty parked in his designated spot and rode the elevator to the third floor.

"Mr. Lyons wants to see you," the receptionist said as soon as Dusty walked through the double doors. "He's in conference room three."

Dusty walked down the hallway to one of the firm's five conference rooms. Seated at the head of the table was fifty-five-year-old Fred Lyons, a bear of a man with a reputation for mauling the other side of a lawsuit into submission. Also present was Mike Gelwicks, a senior associate; and Bruce Mack, a first-year lawyer who barely knew his way to the courthouse.

"Where've you been?" Lyons barked when Dusty came into the room.

"In court. I didn't have a meeting with you on my calendar."

"That's because I scheduled it an hour ago."

Turning to Mike, Lyons said, "Show Dusty what we've got. Put it on the screen."

Mike hit a few buttons on his computer and a list of names appeared.

"These are the Dexadopamine clients in Georgia we've signed up with in the past three months," the associate said.

Lyons turned to Dusty. "Do you know what this means?"

"A lot of Dexadopamine was sold by nutritional supplement stores in the Southeast, and our TV ad is working."

"Yes. There are truckloads of rednecks with livers that are going to go haywire in the next twelve to twenty-four months. With this many cases, we're going to run into problems obtaining leave of court to appear as out-of-state counsel."

Dusty replied, "We'll get local attorneys who —"

"Will take a big bite out of our revenue."

Not sure what Lyons had in mind, Dusty waited.

"Is your Illinois law license still current?" Lyons continued.

"Yes."

"Bruce tells me there is reciprocity between Illinois and Georgia without a waiting period for a lawyer with your experience."

"You want me to apply for admission to the Georgia bar?" Dusty asked.

"And move to Atlanta to manage the cases for the next three or four years. I know you've split with your wife, so there's nothing holding you here."

Dusty looked at Mike and Bruce. They both had shocked expressions on their faces at the latest revelation of what a lawyer's life at Jenkins and Lyons could be like.

"Can we talk in private?" Dusty asked the senior partner.

"Out," the senior lawyer barked at the other two men, who hurriedly left the room.

As soon as they were gone, Lyons spoke. "Dusty, it will be worth your while. Jenkins and I will double your partnership percentage on the revenue generated by the Georgia cases. All you'll have to do is work the Dexadopamine files. If you pick up a few other cases, it will be gravy. Your caseload here will be redistributed, and we'll protect your work credit at time and a half when the cases go to trial or settle. People who took a lot of this Dexa stuff will die within the next year or so, and the number of new claims will dry up. Once you've wrapped up everything in Georgia, you can come back here and work with Adam."

Adam Valaoras was the best of the next generation of trial lawyers in the firm. Working on his cases was the closest thing the firm offered to a guaranteed income.

"When do I need to decide?" Dusty asked.

"How long do you need?"

Dusty glanced down at his watch, then looked back up at Lyons.

"That's enough time. I'll do it."

Lyons grinned. "Excellent. You've got to be a risk taker to make it as a plaintiff's lawyer."

SEVENTEEN

Sandy Lincoln glanced at the old-fashioned clock on the rear wall of the classroom. The clock was a holdover from years before when Sandy had sat in the same room and listened to Mrs. Brooks speculate on why Harper Lee never published a second novel.

Sandy finished reviewing her lesson plans for AP English and turned off her laptop. After almost three decades as a teacher, she'd refined the way she taught high school English to a level of excellence that resulted in student teachers from the nearby community college begging to be assigned to her classroom. Sandy slid the computer into a brightly colored tote bag. A slender black girl with short hair stuck her head through the open door.

"Ms. Lincoln, could I talk to you for a minute on the way to cheerleading practice?"

"Sure, Candace. Let's talk as we walk."

275

Sandy slipped the tote bag over her shoulder and joined the student in the hallway. They walked rapidly toward the gym. Even at fifty-one, Sandy didn't have any trouble keeping up with the long-legged girl. Today Candace wanted to ask Sandy's advice about the topic of a research paper in her AP American history class.

"There should be a manageable amount of information available about influential women who lived during Reconstruction," Sandy said after Candace laid out her idea. "Too often students pick a topic that's so broad it's hard to develop a thesis and effectively support it."

"Would you be willing to look at my first draft?" Candace asked.

"No," Sandy replied.

Candace glanced at her in surprise.

"I'd be willing to look at your second draft."

"Okay," Candace sighed.

They walked down a short flight of steps to the lower level of the school.

"How are you feeling?" Sandy asked. "I don't want you to have another hamstring injury this year."

"A lot better. It's amazing how much difference the stretching exercises make. I can almost lean backward and touch my hands to the floor before starting a backflip."

Cheerleading had changed a lot since Sandy and her teammates clapped their hands, turned a few cartwheels, and yelled catchy cheers. Candace and the varsity cheerleaders were gymnasts who practiced on thick foam pads to minimize the possibility of injury and dancers who performed choreographed routines that lasted several minutes. A lot of the people who came to the football stadium on Friday night wanted to see the cheerleaders as much as the team on the field. To them, the football game was a backdrop to the artistry on the sidelines.

They entered the gym. Sandy had coached the varsity cheerleaders at Rutland High for so long that the children of some of the girls on her first squad had attended a junior camp the previous summer. Several girls were already stretching and loosening up. Candace skipped ahead to the locker room so she could change into her practice uniform. Sandy laid her tote bag on one of the bleachers and went into the basketball coach's office. A corner of the office was her designated space. It contained a small filing cabinet, a rack of instructional DVDs, and a gold-plated whistle one of her squads had given her when the team won a state championship in their classification.

John Bestwick, the basketball coach, was sitting behind his desk with his feet propped up and reading a magazine. John had played guard on a small college team. The brown-haired coach with an infectious smile wasn't very tall, but he'd been very quick on the dribble and had a slashing move to the basket. He'd even been able to dunk a basketball if he got a running start. John's ability to dunk ended about the same time as his marriage. Not long after his divorce, he accepted the job at Rutland. As was the case with more than a few eligible males in Rutland within five years of Sandy's age, rumors flew about the possibility of romance between her and the coach. The fact that they shared an office for a few minutes a day added fuel to the fire. From Sandy's point of view, there wasn't even a spark.

"Don't barge in on me like that, Sandy," the coach said, tossing the magazine on his desk. "You know Dr. Vale is always lurking around wanting to catch me goofing off."

"Are you goofing off?"

John pointed at the magazine.

"Professional research."

Sandy leaned closer. The magazine was a special edition about the upcoming college basketball season.

"Are you coaching a college team on the

side?" she asked. "If you have that much free time, you need to teach another section of tenth-grade remedial math."

"No, but Jeff Ayers has a shot at a college scholarship, and his parents are expecting me to advise him. I want him to join an up-and-coming program."

Sandy took her whistle from its hook and draped it over her neck.

"You're always thinking about your players first. I apologize."

"Thanks." John grinned. "I'm glad I've made such a good impression. Hey, when basketball season rolls around, are your girls going to do another hip-hop thing like the one they performed last year? It really got the guys fired up."

"We'll have something special," Sandy promised. "Dede Simms is going to help choreograph the dance routines for basketball season. You know how talented she is. Don't worry, we'll do our part in getting a crowd out to cheer the team."

"Do that and I'll buy you a steak dinner at Aaron's."

"A gift card would be nice," Sandy said with a smile.

Fending off Coach Bestwick was easier than grading a multiple-choice grammar test. Sandy could relax around him because he never pushed too hard. Other men who'd pursued her didn't take rejection so cordially.

Sandy returned to the gym. There were twelve varsity cheerleaders and eight girls on the junior varsity squad. This year two members of the varsity squad were Hispanic and two were black. Rutland's ethnic mix had changed dramatically over the past twenty-five years. When Sandy was a student, there were black and white students with a rare additional minority. Due to a large influx of men and women from Mexico, Guatemala, Costa Rica, Honduras, and other parts of Central America, there was a rapidly growing group of Hispanic students. Some of the new immigrant students excelled in school; others struggled. For Sandy, the change gave her fresh opportunities to speak Spanish.

Sandy blew her whistle. The girls quickly gathered in a semicircle and sat at her feet.

"Who's missing?" Sandy asked.

"Meredith," one girl piped up.

The gym door opened, and a petite brunette with a large pack strapped to her back entered the room.

"Sorry, Ms. Lincoln," the captain of the squad called out. "I was helping Billy Wilson with a chemistry problem —"

"I don't want to hear it," Sandy said, holding up her hand. "You know what time practice starts. After you change and loosen up, do five wind sprints."

"Billy Wilson is thick as a brick," a girl sitting close to the front whispered in a voice loud enough for everyone to hear. "He doesn't know the difference between the symbols for carbon and oxygen."

"We're not here to discuss Billy Wilson's knowledge of chemistry," Sandy said. "Break into groups of four and finish stretching. I want every muscle and tendon in your bodies loose and ready. We're going to wow them this week with a synchronized tumbling routine."

The girls chatted while they got ready. The camaraderie among the group was fairly solid. To discourage cliques, Sandy made the girls spend a lot of time on team-building activities. The fact that they competed as a group, not as individuals, helped. And Sandy had a zero-tolerance policy for cattiness. If Sandy caught a whiff of gossip between teammates, the offending party had to apologize to the individual and then to the whole squad. Sandy's zeal in this area was reinforced by a written pledge signed by every girl who made the team.

Sandy drew up the new routine on a large

whiteboard. Meredith finished her wind sprints and trotted over to her.

"I apologize for being late," she said, huffing and puffing. "I was tutoring Billy so we could go out Friday night after the game."

Billy Wilson was a running back on the football team. He came from a well-to-do family and seemed like a decent young man. But Sandy didn't trust him with Meredith.

"Where are you going?"

"A party at his parents' lake house."

"Meredith —" Sandy started.

"Mr. and Mrs. Banneker are going to chaperone," Meredith added. "Billy's parents are going to be out of town and couldn't do it."

Whenever Sandy heard about students going to a party at the lake, it was hard not to react.

Meredith studied the diagrams. The girls on the team were identified by their initials. Meredith pointed to the lines and arrows that laid out the final, climactic sequence of stunts.

"Do you think Alita can do this?" she asked, referring to one of the Hispanic girls.

"I want to give her a chance."

Sandy called the girls together and went over the routine with the entire group. Meredith and Candace demonstrated the different stunts. It had been years since Sandy had put on gym clothes. It was better for the girls to learn the moves from their peers than wonder if Ms. Lincoln was going to attempt a handstand and end up in a crumpled heap on the floor.

An hour and a half later, the girls were on their way to learning the routine. The most shaky spot was the sequence Sandy gave to Alita, a junior with short dark hair, black eyes, and a compact, muscular build. Alita's strength was her weakness. She emphasized power over grace when she needed to combine the two in equal measure. Sandy pulled her to the side.

"Hold your hand like this," Sandy said, demonstrating. "And let your body unfold like a flower, not pop open like a knife."

"I saw the way Meredith did it," Alita replied. "I'll get it right."

Alita moved away and went through the sequence again while Sandy watched.

"That's better," Sandy said.

After practice was over, Sandy rolled the whiteboard back into a corner of the gym while the girls folded up the mats. When she returned to the office, Coach Bestwick was gone, but he'd left her a note taped to the wall beside the hook where she kept her whistle.

Blow three loud whistles if you ever decide to let me buy you a steak, and I'll pick you up at six-thirty.

Maria Alverez wants to see you. I told her to wait beside the main entrance.

— Coach B.

Sandy took the note from the wall and put it in her purse. Maria was a sixteen-year-old girl from Mexico who'd arrived at the school two years earlier. Sandy had been drawn to the shy, withdrawn student during orientation and offered to tutor her in English. It soon became clear that Maria was going to need extra help, and she was placed in remedial classes where the slower pace proved helpful. This semester Maria was in three regular classrooms and on track to successfully complete her junior year.

Even though Sandy was no longer tutoring her, Maria would occasionally come to Sandy's class when the school day ended. She would sit quietly in a desk by the windows while Sandy worked on her lesson plans or graded papers. Maria didn't necessarily want to talk; she simply wanted to be with her. Sandy suspected the young girl's home life was probably chaotic and the classroom served as a refuge.

Just inside the main entrance to the school

a small bench was bolted to the floor. When Sandy turned onto the hallway, she saw Maria, her long black hair in a ponytail, sitting on the bench with her head down. A tattered book bag lay on the floor at her feet.

"Hello, Maria," Sandy called out.

Maria looked up but didn't respond. Sandy sat down beside her on the bench.

"Coach Bestwick said you wanted to see me."

"Yes." Maria nodded, her head still drooping. "I have a big problem."

Maria spoke with a strong accent, but her English had been getting better and better. Sandy waited, but the girl didn't say anything else.

"Does it have to do with Ms. Ranford's class?" Sandy asked, suspecting where the difficulty might lie. "Math is a hard subject, but she can give you worksheets to go over with a student who is a volunteer tutor. If you need help finding a tutor, I can set it up."

Maria picked up her backpack. Reaching inside, she took out a folder and handed it to Sandy. Inside was a sheaf of papers from the math class. There were red marks indicating mistakes, but overall Maria's scores were okay.

"This looks great," Sandy said. "You

shouldn't be worried. You should be proud of yourself."

Sandy handed the folder back to Maria, who continued to sit with her head down.

"Do you have a ride home?" Sandy asked.

"Rosalita is going to pick me up on her way home from work."

Rosalita, Maria's older cousin, worked at a chicken-processing plant. Sandy checked her watch.

"Stay here until she comes. Once you leave the building, the door will lock behind you and you can't get back in."

Maria looked up at Sandy with pathos in her eyes. A single tear escaped from the girl's right eye and ran down her brown cheek. The tear fell from her face and landed near a rip in her jeans. Sandy put her arm around Maria's shoulders.

"Maria, what's wrong?"

Maria buried her head in her hands and began to cry. The crying quickly turned to sobs. Sandy rested her hand on Maria's heaving back and waited. The sobs turned to sniffles. Sandy placed several tissues into Maria's right hand. The girl wiped her eyes and blew her nose. Mystified, Sandy asked her question again, this time in Spanish. Maria put her hand on her stomach.

"Bebé," she said.

286

Sandy's mouth dropped open.

"You're pregnant?"

"Sí."

EIGHTEEN

Rosalita arrived before Sandy could get much information from Maria, so they agreed to meet early the next morning to talk with Carol Ramsey, one of the school counselors. Sandy and Maria walked out of the building together.

"Don't be late," Sandy said. "Meet me here at seven-thirty. Okay?"

"Yes. I will be there. Thank you."

Rosalita's little green car belched smoke as it left the parking lot. There were so many things working against Maria. A pregnancy compounded everything.

Sandy returned to her classroom and looked up Carol's cell phone number in the faculty directory. She didn't know the young counselor very well, but Dr. Vale had made it clear during fall orientation that all serious student issues needed to be funneled into the counseling office. Sandy left Carol a voice message asking her to call as soon as possible.

Sandy left the school and drove toward the center of town. She passed Lincoln Insurance Services, the business started by her father. The agency had grown significantly since her brother Ben took over. Ben was a natural salesman and had opened branch offices in two nearby towns, Kernersville and Tryon. He'd increased revenue so much that he'd paid off his father twice as fast as required by their buyout agreement. The last payment was made a few months before Sandy's father died of a heart attack. Her mother now lived in a retirement community in Sarasota.

Sandy's house was a compact yellow cottage at the end of a short dead-end street. Her property was adjacent to a small park. The park was within walking distance of several residential areas and had become a popular destination for families with children. A hedgerow planted by a previous owner served as a buffer between Sandy's house and the park; however, she could still enjoy the sounds of children playing in the late afternoon when she sat on her screened porch. The backyard was surrounded by a low wooden fence.

Sandy was thinking about Maria as she pulled into her driveway. Her dog, Nelson, was trying to push his nose between the spaces in the fence.

"I'll be back in ten minutes," she called out to the curly-haired animal.

Sandy unlocked a side door that opened into the kitchen. She placed her tote bag on a round table and poured a glass of purified water from a container in the refrigerator. The floor plan of the house reminded her of Linda's home in Atlanta and was one reason Sandy had bought it. The master bedroom and a tidy guest room were upstairs. The third bedroom was downstairs. Currently it was a computer center, lesson-planning room, and craft area where Sandy created a scrapbook for each year's cheerleading squad. The popularity of the scrapbooks increased with the passage of time, and former cheerleaders who returned for high school reunions loved to gather around the photographs and relive teenage memories.

Sandy changed into exercise clothes. No one who saw Ms. Lincoln walking her dog could call her a slouch. In the fall, Sandy wore stylish workout pants with matching tops. Winter brought out jackets with coordinated hats. Whatever the season, Sandy's wardrobe reflected the orderliness passed down from her mother, and she dressed in a way she hoped would inspire her female students to treat themselves with respect.

She took Nelson's leash from its hook by the door and grabbed the Labrador/standard poodle mix by the collar. The tight curls covering Nelson's body were a clue that he was more poodle than Labrador.

The dog sniffed the ground for a moment before pointing his nose up the street. Within a few steps, he settled in beside her. It was four blocks to the church Sandy attended with her family. She remained a faithful member. A sign in front of the church announced the sermon topic for the coming Sunday: "Don't Be Late for Your Funeral." Reverend Peterson used catchy but sometimes corny titles in an effort to draw a crowd.

Nelson had the awareness of a Seeing Eye dog of the flow of traffic and waited without being told at street corners until it was safe to cross. Sandy did some of her best thinking and praying on walks. Today she thought back many years to Angelica. After the Hispanic girl moved back to Monterrey, she and Sandy had corresponded for a few months, but when Sandy wrote about the birth of the twins, Angelica never replied. Sandy suspected her friend didn't want to be reminded of the loss of her own baby.

Sandy passed rows of small businesses and shops and turned left in front of the county courthouse. Many people she encountered nodded in greeting. Few knew or remembered her past. After three decades, the community had moved on, and if the subject of Sandy's teenage pregnancy came up, longtime residents focused on the positive influence of her life since then, not the disgrace of a long-ago mistake.

Recent gossip focused on whether the notoriously picky Ms. Lincoln would ever meet a man who could convince her to marry him. Sandy had seriously dated a man in college and fallen in love with him. He'd visited Rutland, and everyone in her family liked him. Her boyfriend's parents welcomed Sandy with open arms. A few months before graduation, Sandy was on pins and needles in expectation of an imminent marriage proposal. One Saturday night her boyfriend took her to dinner at their favorite restaurant and, instead of giving her a ring, told her he wasn't ready for a long-term commitment. Shocked, Sandy asked if that meant a delay. He told her no — it meant the relationship was over. Burned twice by men, Sandy resolved not to be hurt again. The best way to do that was to avoid getting too close to one.

Sandy and Nelson reached the local veterinary practice. The dog looked to the side and sniffed the air. He didn't like going to the vet. He strained against the leash and picked up the pace until they passed the facility.

Sandy's cell phone buzzed. It was Carol Ramsey.

"Hi, Carol. Thanks for returning my call. I just met with a student who has a serious problem you should know about." Sandy told her about Maria. "Would you be able to meet with her at seven-thirty in the morning?"

"I have a meeting out of the office on my calendar, but I'll get in touch with the other person tonight and reschedule. A situation like Maria's has to take priority."

"Thanks. See you then."

Sandy's walking route for the day was a giant rectangle. She and Nelson reached the edge of the business district, then walked down a slight hill toward the elementary school Sandy attended as a child. Beyond that, they entered an older residential area with large trees whose roots caused the sidewalk to crack and buckle.

As she walked, Sandy prayed for Maria Alverez. Times had changed in Rutland since high school girls were automatically expelled for getting pregnant. It wasn't unheard of for a pregnant student to attend classes. Eyebrows went up when a young woman graduated in a gown that couldn't conceal a growing baby, but a new generation had ushered in more relaxed societal attitudes. Sandy suspected none of that was going to help Maria. Her challenges went deeper than the negative opinions of women at the hair salon.

Sandy's favorite residential street in Rutland was an avenue lined on both sides with massive oaks. The large, older houses, with differing architectural styles, occupied spacious lots and exuded character. Locals called the street "Millionaires' Row." Owners included doctors, lawyers, businesspeople, and old-money families. Ben and Betsy had looked at a house at the end of the row when it came on the market but decided to buy a newer home that required less upkeep. On a teacher's salary, all Sandy could do was enjoy the free view from the curb.

At the end of the street, she was only a few blocks from the park near her home. The park was deserted when she cut through it. Nelson's tongue was hanging out of his mouth with thirst, and he buried his face in his water bowl as soon as they were home. Sandy slipped his leash over a hook on the kitchen wall as the phone rang. It was Jessica.

"How close did I time it?" Jessica asked. "From the time I saw you, I guessed you would walk through the door in another eight minutes."

"Where did you see me?"

"I drove past you and Nelson going the opposite direction when you were on Millionaires' Row. I waved, but you seemed deep in thought."

"Yeah, I found out today that a Hispanic girl I tutored a couple of years ago is pregnant."

"How old is she?"

"Barely sixteen. She cried like a baby when she told me the news."

"Who's the daddy?"

"I didn't get a chance to ask. Carol Ramsey, the new counselor at the school, and I are going to meet with her in the morning."

"Why bring in the counselor so quickly? It sounds like the girl trusts you."

"That's the new procedure. Dr. Vale made it clear at teacher orientation in the fall that when serious personal issues involving students come up, one of the counselors needs to take the lead."

"And you don't want to use Stanley Lapp?"

"Right. He's not equipped to work with a shy, pregnant teenager. I can tell Carol a little about the student's background and hope she does the right thing."

Sandy could hear the TV in the background at her friend's house.

"Have you fixed supper?" Jessica asked.

Sandy looked at the cold stove. She didn't have a meal in mind, but she had leftovers in the refrigerator.

"Not yet. I may warm up —"

"No, you're not. Get in your car and come over. It will take you exactly eight minutes if you don't get stuck at the red light on Poplar Avenue. Rick is having dinner with his boss, and I'm here alone. I've got the makings of the best salad you've ever seen, but it will be a work of art if your hands get involved. All I need to complete it is Roquefort cheese. You can pick some up for me at the store."

"I'll change and be on my way."

"Change? That outfit you had on when I saw you walking a few minutes ago was nicer than what I wore to the dentist's office this morning. Of course, if I had your figure, any clothes would look better on me."

"You look great, and remember, you've had three children," Sandy said.

"And I'm glad I did, but that's not helping me fight the bulges that seem to pop out in all the wrong places."

NINETEEN

Jeremy Lane placed a new photograph on the credenza in his office. In the picture his wife, Leanne, and their two children were standing barefoot in a mountain stream. Leanne was looking down at the children, who were squealing with delight as the chilly water rushed over their feet and crashed against their ankles. Ten-year-old Chloe's sandy hair hung to her shoulders. Five-year-old Zach's wide-open mouth revealed several missing teeth. Leanne's face, framed by dark hair, showed a mother's delight in the presence of happy children.

Jeremy positioned the photo beside a more formal family portrait of Jeremy and Zach wearing identical blue sport coats and Leanne and Chloe in matching dresses. It was a corny photo, but that only made Jeremy like it more. A grainy picture of Jeremy as a little boy in front of his parents' home near Charleston was propped on the corner of his desk.

The phone buzzed. It was Deb Bridges, his secretary/legal assistant.

"Have you checked your e-mail?" Deb asked.

"No, I haven't even turned on the computer yet."

"I'm not trying to ruin your coffee, but you need to see what came in from the lawyers on the other side of the Grosvenor case."

Jeremy sat in the burgundy leather chair that had been a gift from his mother when he left the district attorney's office to open his own practice. He swiveled to the side and turned on his computer. He scrolled down to the subject line, *Grosvenor v. Alcott Business Systems, et al.,* and opened the file. He'd been electronically served with a motion to compel discovery. A hearing on the motion was set in Fulton County Superior Court in downtown Atlanta. Jeremy quickly read the motion. Deb came to the office door and leaned against the doorframe. The auburn-haired secretary was in her midforties. A pair of half-frame reading glasses hung from a chain around her neck.

"Did you read this?" Jeremy asked.

"Every word."

"This is bogus. We filed answers to all the

interrogatories and requests for production of documents last week."

"But you didn't give them what they really wanted — details about the termination of Mr. Grosvenor's consulting contract with the company in Virginia."

"If they want that information, they're going to have to go to Virginia and take depositions. When that happens, the CFO of the Virginia company is going to hurt them."

"Or so you hope."

"Oh, he'll hurt them. I just want that information to come out after I depose Alcott's regulatory compliance officer and get him nailed down on the record." Jeremy looked up from his computer. "Prepare a notice to take the deposition of Gregory Sexton, the compliance officer. Set it for the afternoon of the hearing on their motion in Atlanta. If they refuse to make him available, I'll file a countermotion to compel his appearance and ask the judge to hear it at the same time as the motion to compel."

"Sounds like you're going to war."

"I knew that going in." Jeremy turned back to the computer screen. "But what Alcott did to Mr. Grosvenor was wrong, and if I can survive summary judgment and get this case in front of a jury, there's a chance for a decent verdict."

The lawyers on the other side of the Grosvenor case fired their legal missiles from ninety miles away in a fancy office tower in Atlanta. The advent of computer legal research, with its virtually unlimited resources, had leveled the battlefield between big-city lawyers and small-town practitioners. A lawyer like Jeremy, who knew the right questions to ask the search engine, could compete with any law firm in the country.

A half-empty cup of black coffee grew cold as Jeremy checked and reviewed the appellate decisions cited in the motion to compel. Only one case gave him concern, and the problem it raised for his position made him shake his head. This was going to take some serious digging. The phone buzzed again.

"Did you forget your appointment with Larry Bishop?" Deb asked.

Jeremy glanced at his watch.

"Yes. Call the Blackwater and tell Bobby to be on the lookout for a gray-haired man in his early sixties who's not from Tryon."

Jeremy grabbed his jacket from a small closet in the corner of the office and quickly checked his appearance in the mirror on the back of the closet door. His sandy hair was slightly darker than his daughter Chloe's, but they had matching blue eyes. At five foot nine inches tall, Jeremy still had the sinewy strength that had made him a successful wrestler in high school. Leanne jokingly held his hand tight when they went for walks on the beach because she didn't want a bikini-clad female to get the idea he might be available.

"I'll be back by eleven for the conference call in the Dobbins case," he said to Deb as he passed her desk.

"I'm typing the memo right now," she replied. "It'll be on your desk waiting for you."

Jeremy's office was on the ground floor of a two-story office building located two blocks from the courthouse. Other tenants in the building included a two-person accounting firm, an investment adviser, a real-estate lawyer who spent most of his time in the courthouse deed room, and a child psychologist. Jeremy and the accounting firm occupied the prime spaces on the ground level. When he had a deposition involving multiple parties or lawyers, the accountants let Jeremy use their conference room.

Jeremy stepped into the crisp air of the late fall morning. The Blackwater Coffee

Shop was several blocks away on South Avenue, the main street through the center of town. Tryon wasn't large enough to attract a national coffee franchise, so Bobby Miller, the owner of a sandwich shop, created his own. Skeptics doubted local residents would pay several dollars for a flavored cup of coffee, but Bobby had proved them wrong, and the Blackwater did a brisk business.

Jeremy opened the door of the shop and saw Larry Bishop sitting in a corner chair reading the *Wall Street Journal.* A cup of coffee and a thin pastry were on a small round table in front of him. Like Jeremy's father, Bishop was a Vietnam War veteran who had served in the air force and went on to become a pilot with a major U.S. airline. The two men rode the wave of high salaries for commercial pilots to their highest point before deregulation and airline bankruptcies eroded the wage scale so that many pilots were paid like glorified bus drivers. Jeremy shook the distinguished-looking man's hand.

"Sorry I'm late," Jeremy said. "I was caught up in some research on a big case."

"No problem," Bishop replied in a rich Charleston accent. "The owner set me up with a cup of Blue Mountain java and this

303

flaky bit of sweet stuff. He's got a great concept going here. Did you mention our conversation about trying to franchise this place in other small towns? I can think of several spots where it would take off."

Since his retirement, Larry Bishop had been a successful business investor.

"Yes." Jeremy waved to Bobby, who was behind the counter, and called out, "The arabica, please."

"Was he interested in expanding?" Bishop asked.

"He told me that if his son comes back to work for him after college, he'll consider it. Bobby doesn't want business to cut into his deer-hunting time. His sandwich shop was popular, but he didn't want the hassle of running two businesses at once so he shut it down."

The owner brought over Jeremy's coffee and handed it to him. It was black as a moonless midnight.

Since Jeremy's father's death from a stroke three years earlier, Bishop had made a point of stopping to see Jeremy every time he was near Tryon. Today he was on his way to Atlanta to play golf and had landed his small private plane at the tiny county airport that was not much more than a strip of asphalt in an empty field. The airport manager loaned Bishop a car so he could drive into town to see Jeremy.

"How was your flight?" Jeremy asked.

"Clear and smooth. The avionics on my new plane are topnotch. It practically flies itself."

Jeremy took a sip of the coffee. It was strong and bitter.

"Kip and I saw your mother last weekend," Bishop continued. "We went out to eat at a new place on Sullivan's Island not far from the condominiums we bought last year. The condos have been renting great. Your mother's unit is cash-flowing with extra to spare."

"Leanne and I want to take the kids there during the off-season this winter."

"You'll like it. Oh, and your mother had her latest houseguest in tow. The poor girl thought boiled shrimp were a delicacy. She must have eaten two dozen."

Jeremy's mother had been providing temporary housing for unmarried pregnant girls since Jeremy's younger sister left home for college. Most of the girls were referrals from a local crisis pregnancy center, but several churches were aware that Ruth Lane had a furnished efficiency apartment over the two-car garage beside her home.

"How old was the girl?" Jeremy asked.

"I've not talked to Mom about her."

"Sixteen, but she looked thirteen," Bishop said, shaking his head. "The girls your mother takes in look younger and younger."

"Cara's mother was barely seventeen when she was born," Jeremy said, referring to his younger sister, who was also adopted. He took another sip of coffee. "Did my mom mention that Cara is interested in finding her birth mother?"

Bishop, who was about to pick up his pastry, left it on the plate.

"No, she didn't. What's going on with that? You have the best mother on the planet. Why in the world would Cara want to run off and try to find someone who didn't want to keep her in the first place?"

"Don't be too hard on her. She's just curious. Before she did anything, she talked it over with Mom and reassured her of how she felt. And you nailed one of the reasons Cara gave me when we talked about it. She wants to know why her mother didn't, or couldn't, keep her."

Bishop grunted. "She doesn't have to look far. Based on the girls your mother takes in, it's easy to see why sixteen-year-old girls don't keep babies. And your dad treated Cara like a princess. I doubt she's secretly related to European royalty."

306

"You're probably right, but she's got the itch. I think losing Dad so suddenly is part of it too. Mom and I are concerned she'll be hurt, but Cara is an adult. She'll be twenty-six in February."

"Are you helping her?"

"Not much. Since she was placed by an adoption agency in Virginia, I checked the Virginia open-records statute and gave her the number of an outfit that helps connect adoptees with their birth parents. I'm not sure if she's called them, but I think she will."

Bishop ate a bite of pastry and took a sip of coffee.

"Have you thought about trying to find your mother?"

"No." Jeremy shook his head. "I think it's more of a girl thing. I'm not curious about facts that don't have any current relevance."

"You sound like a lawyer."

Jeremy smiled. "When I look at Chloe's blond hair and blue eyes, I know where they came from. She's exhibit A from my gene pool. Where I got the genes in the first place doesn't really interest me."

The two men stayed in the coffee shop chatting for another thirty minutes. After Jeremy checked his watch a second time, Bishop stood up.

"I get the message. I'm retired, but you're just getting started and need to get back to work." He leaned forward and pointed to the owner of the shop. "Work on Bobby. If we can franchise this place, there will be an equity stake for you as a finder's fee. We'll start with three locations, double that every year for five years, then sell out."

"I'll see what I can do. Thanks for stopping by. It means a lot."

Bishop shook Jeremy's hand and patted him on the back.

"Your dad would be proud of you."

"Mom says he is."

"Oh yeah," Bishop said with a wave of his hand. "She talks about heaven like it's in the next room. That's one area I leave to her and Kip. They huddle together and discuss the Bible and pray. Sometimes I think they're praying for me."

Jeremy smiled. "That makes three of us."

TWENTY

Sandy stood near the front entrance to the school waiting for Maria. It was 7:40 a.m., and Maria was ten minutes late. A puff of black smoke announced the arrival of Rosalita's car. She pulled to the curb, and Maria got out. The girl looked to the right and left as she walked toward Sandy.

"Are you okay?" Sandy asked.

"No. I had a fight with my father. He did not want me to come to school, so I ran to Rosalita's house. She brought me."

"Why didn't he want you to come to school?" Sandy asked as she held the door open.

"The baby," Maria replied cryptically.

Sandy didn't ask a follow-up question. The story, as bad as it might be, would come out soon enough. It shouldn't happen in a school hallway.

Carol Ramsey's office was in a suite close to the school's main office. The Rutland school system employed three counselors: two at the high school and a third who split time between the high school and the local middle school. Carol's door was cracked open, and the dark-haired, slightly overweight guidance counselor was sitting at her desk when Sandy tapped lightly.

"Come in," Carol said, glancing up.

Carol was in her second year at the school. Unmarried, she provided students with academic advice and help with college placement issues, but her passion was supportive counseling services. Earlier in the year she'd shared in a faculty meeting that the personal problems she'd faced as a student had motivated her to help those going through similar challenges. She stood up to greet Sandy and Maria, who sat across from the counselor's desk. Carol held a pen in her left hand and clicked it open and shut a couple of times.

"Before we get started, I need to ask Maria a few questions," she said. "Do you feel comfortable talking to me in English?"

"Yes, my English is better."

"Good. If I say something you don't understand, will you let me know?"

"Yes."

"Do you want Ms. Lincoln to leave the room while we talk?"

Maria gave the counselor a startled look.

"Do you want Ms. Lincoln to leave?" Carol repeated.

"Why would I want her to leave?"

"You have a right to keep our conversation private from anybody else. Do you know what I mean by private conversation?"

"Private conversation?"

Sandy translated the phrase into Spanish. Maria nodded.

"I understand. I want Ms. Lincoln to stay. She has been very nice to me."

"Okay. Let me ask some background questions."

Sandy listened while Carol obtained basic information from Maria. The young girl was two months past her sixteenth birthday.

"Who do you live with?"

"It used to be my father, me, my stepmother, and my two little brothers, Desi and Felipe. My stepmother took Desi and Felipe back to Mexico six months ago. When they tried to come back to the United States, they were stopped at the border, so my father is trying to get enough money to get them here. He started letting other men stay with us. They pay him money for a place to sleep."

"Where is your real mother?"

"She died when I was six years old. She

311

was killed by the drug men in our town. They shot guns at a man who was walking in the road. My mother was standing in front of our house and a bullet hit her. She died that day."

"Did you see this happen?" Carol asked, her eyes wide.

"Yes. I ran over to her." Maria held up her right hand. "Her blood was on this hand. After that I did not talk for a long time and would not leave the house to go to school."

Sandy didn't know this personal information. It helped her understand why Maria was so behind educationally when she first arrived in Rutland.

"How many men are staying in the house with you and your father?"

Maria shrugged. "It changes. Sometimes four, sometimes six to eight."

"Why does it change?"

"People, they come and they go. They ask my father about it and he says yes or no."

"Does Rosalita stay in your trailer?" Sandy asked.

"No, she lives near us. She has three children."

"Who is Rosalita?" Carol asked Sandy.

"Her older cousin who works at one of the chicken plants."

"I sleep at her trailer a lot," Maria added.

"Why?" Carol asked.

Maria shook her head.

"Please, it's important," Carol said.

Maria looked at Sandy.

"Tell her," Sandy said.

"No," Maria said, to Sandy's surprise.

Carol didn't seem upset.

"Do you have your own room at Rosalita's trailer?"

"No, I stay with Carla. She is the oldest girl."

"Do you have your own room at your father's trailer?"

"Not now; I sleep on a cot in the kitchen."

"The kitchen?"

"Yes. I put a sheet up." Maria paused. "But it's not so good."

"What are the names of the men who pay money to your father to stay at your trailer?"

"Julio, Emilio, Juan, Carlos. Bernardo, he moved out last week."

"Do they drink alcohol?"

Maria looked at Sandy, who translated.

"Yes," Maria said. "Beer. And tequila."

"When do they drink beer and tequila?"

Maria touched her fingers as she spoke. "Monday, Tuesday, Wednesday, Thursday, Friday, Saturday, Sunday."

"Every day of the week?"

"Sometimes, but always on Friday and Saturday. That is when they have money."

"Do they use drugs?"

"I don't know. I do not see that."

"Do they ever get in fights?"

"Yes. I run to Rosalita's house."

"Has anyone ever hit you?"

Maria hesitated again. "No."

"Where does your father work?"

"Pet Home. He works at night."

Pet Home was a local factory that made ornate houses for cats and dogs.

"It is better when he is at home," Maria continued.

"Why is it better?"

"Because he makes the men act better."

"When he is not there, they act bad?"

Maria nodded.

Carol then asked Maria a series of questions about her classes at school and social interaction with other students. The girl kept to herself and had few close friends. Carol paused and made a few notes.

"Maria, why did you come to see me today?" she asked.

"Ms. Lincoln talked to me yesterday and told me to come."

"After you told her you were pregnant?"

Tears welled up in Maria's eyes.

"Yes."

"How do you know you are pregnant?"

"Rosalita told me." Maria wiped her eyes.

"How did she know?"

"The little paper turned blue. That means there is a baby."

"You took a home pregnancy test?"

Maria looked at Sandy, who translated the question.

"Yes," Maria said. "Rosalita bought the test at the store."

"I think you should go to the county health department for a second test," Carol said.

"What?" Maria responded.

Sandy explained, and Maria nodded.

"Yes, second test, okay," she said.

"Can she do that without her father's permission?" Sandy asked.

"If she wants to."

Carol glanced at the screen of the computer on her desk.

"How about eleven o'clock this morning? Come here after your third-period class, and I'll take you to see a nurse. Okay?"

"Yes."

Carol made another note on her form.

"How did you get pregnant?" she asked.

Maria looked puzzled. "Don't you know?"

"Yes," Carol replied patiently. "Did you want to get pregnant?"

"No."

"Who is the man who made you pregnant?"

Maria shook her head.

"You don't want to tell me?"

"No."

"Why not?"

Maria didn't answer.

"Is it a boy who goes to the school?"

"No."

"Did the man make you be with him?"

Maria didn't respond.

"Is it someone who lives at the house?"

Maria didn't answer. Carol glanced down at her notes.

"Was it Emilio?"

Maria didn't answer.

"Was it Carlos?"

No response.

"Was it Bernardo, who moved out? Did your father make him leave?"

"Please," Maria said as she turned to Sandy. "Do I have to tell?"

Before Sandy could respond, Carol spoke.

"Would you be willing to talk to the police?"

"The police?" Maria said in alarm. "What have I done wrong?"

"Nothing," Sandy and Carol said simultaneously.

"But the man who made you pregnant did something wrong," Carol said. "And he should be punished."

A look of panic crossed Maria's face. Sandy wanted to ask Carol to not push too hard but kept her mouth shut.

"We'll talk more when we go to the nurse." Carol looked at her watch. "It's almost time for first period."

"Will you go with me to see the doctor?" Maria asked Sandy.

"No, I have to teach a class. Ms. Ramsey will take care of you. But come see me before you leave school this afternoon."

Sandy held the door open for Maria so she could leave.

"Ms. Lincoln, could you stay for a minute?" Carol asked.

"Sure."

Carol straightened her glasses.

"There's obviously something bad going on at that trailer, and I have a legal duty to inquire," she said as soon as Maria was gone. "I'm concerned she might be exposed to ongoing abuse. What do you know about the situation?"

"Nothing much. I didn't know about her mother's murder until this morning, and I wasn't aware she was in an all-male household. She's never talked to me about personal matters until now."

"Why did she seek you out?"

"I tutored her in English when she first came to the school, and I think she feels safe with me."

"Does she know what you went through when you were a high school student?"

Sandy raised her eyebrows in surprise. "You mean my teenage pregnancy?"

"Yes."

"I seriously doubt Maria knows about that."

Carol tapped her pen against the papers on her desk.

"It doesn't look like she's very far along, which will give her options. I wanted to ask about that, but it may be better for the nurse at the health department to bring that up."

"Options? Won't you have to involve her father in that discussion?"

"What if he's the reason for the problem?"

A sick feeling hit Sandy in the pit of her stomach. She remembered Maria's statement that she and her father had a fight that morning.

"It's okay that Maria comes by your classroom from time to time for a supportive chat," Carol continued. "However, let me take over as her counselor. That's

318

why I'm here."

"Okay," Sandy replied numbly.

Shortly before third period began, Sandy glanced out the window of her classroom and saw Carol and Maria walking across the parking lot. Sandy's heart ached for Maria, and she offered up a quick, silent prayer for the young girl.

"Ms. Lincoln, I couldn't understand what you wanted us to do for homework," a female student said, interrupting Sandy's thoughts.

Sandy turned around. Daphne Boatwright, a short girl with light-brown hair and a pixie nose, was standing in front of Sandy's desk.

"What part?" Sandy replied. "I gave you ten vocabulary words to look up and use each one in an original sentence. Then you're to pick one of the words and include it in a one-hundred-word paragraph about a topic you selected."

"Oh, we didn't have to use all ten words in the same paragraph?"

"No," Sandy replied patiently. "It would be difficult to write a coherent paragraph that contained *declaim, cauterize, disjunctive,* and *nonsectarian.*"

After the class ended, Sandy kept looking

out the window. She knew it was unlikely that Carol and Maria would return within an hour, but she couldn't stop checking. The bell rang, and the students filed out of the room. Sandy put away her teaching materials and entered the bustling hallway.

The school cafeteria had been completely remodeled since Sandy was a student and now offered a much more diverse selection of food. A salad was no longer three or four pieces of wilted lettuce garnished with strips of shredded carrot, a barely ripe slice of tomato, and a dollop of runny ranch dressing. Now there was a self-service salad bar with more than twenty options. After getting her food, Sandy took her tray to the corner of the room reserved for faculty.

"Join us," said Kelli Bollinger, the dark-haired head of the foreign language department. Kelli taught Spanish and had been at the school for almost ten years.

Sandy placed her tray on the table between Kelli and Patty Crutchfield, a biology teacher who coached the girls' track team.

"How is this week's routine shaping up?" Kelli asked after Sandy sat down. "I heard Meredith talking about it after class. She seems excited about it."

"It has energy," Sandy said, spearing a

peach slice with her fork.

"Push them hard," Patty added. "Especially Tameka. I want you to get her heart rate into the training zone and stay there."

"She pushes herself and the other girls," Sandy replied. "She has springs for legs."

"Which is why she's going to compete for a conference title in the 400-meter intermediate hurdles."

While they were talking, Sandy saw Carol come into the cafeteria. She tried to catch the counselor's eye, but Carol didn't look in her direction. Patty finished and left Sandy alone with Kelli.

"Have you had much contact with Carol Ramsey?" Sandy asked in a low voice.

"A little. Why?"

"I took a student to see her for counseling this morning."

"She cares about the kids," Kelli replied. "But she's territorial, very territorial."

"That's what I picked up on," Sandy said, nodding. "The student trusts me, and I felt like Carol wanted to cut me out of the loop."

"Counseling is her area of expertise." Kelli shrugged. "How would you feel if she barged into your classroom and started lecturing on Emily Dickinson's fixation with death?"

"You know about that?"

"Remember, English is my native language." Kelli smiled. "And I saw the title of the paper Meredith was writing for your class."

Carol emerged from the food line and joined a table of younger teachers.

"You're right," Sandy said. "I can't assume I know the best way to help a student in trouble."

"But you're one of the people I'd want my daughter to talk to if she was in a mess and didn't feel comfortable coming to me about it."

"You're sweet." Sandy smiled. "But Cathy never got within a hundred yards of serious trouble. How is she doing in college?"

Instead of going to the faculty lounge during her free period, Sandy stayed in her classroom to grade papers. Hearing footsteps, she glanced up and saw Maria standing in the doorway. The Hispanic girl looked forlorn and alone.

"Come in, come in," Sandy said, putting down her red pen. "I'm glad to see you."

Maria sat in a student desk across from Sandy.

"How was your visit to the health department?"

"Okay."

"Did they give you another pregnancy test?"

"It was yes. The woman who talked to me said seven or eight weeks."

Sandy had a sudden flashback to Dr. Braselton's office.

"Just getting started," Sandy said, as much to herself as to Maria.

"Ms. Ramsey is going to take me to see a doctor in Atlanta," Maria continued. "We go there next Tuesday."

"Atlanta?" Sandy asked in surprise. "There are at least three doctors in Rutland who take care of pregnant women."

"Ms. Ramsey says the doctor in Atlanta will not cost any money."

"Oh," Sandy said, then had an idea. "Does your father have health insurance that pays for you to go to the doctor through his work?"

Maria opened her backpack and took out a brown leather wallet with the stitching coming loose. She handed Sandy a ragged yellow card.

"Yes," Sandy said. "This proves that you have health insurance and can probably see a doctor in Rutland. Atlanta is a long way to travel for prenatal care."

"Prenatal care?" Maria asked slowly.

"A doctor to help until the baby is born."

Sandy handed the insurance card back to Maria.

"Did you show Ms. Ramsey this card?"

"No, she didn't ask me for it."

"I think you should let Ms. Ramsey see the card and tell her you'd like to see a doctor in Rutland."

"Okay."

Maria sat silently. Sandy wished she could open the teenage girl's mind, climb inside, and help her sort out her thoughts.

"Is there anything else you want to talk to me about?" Sandy asked.

"Ms. Ramsey says a woman from the police is going to ask me questions. Do I have to talk to the police if I do not want to?"

Sandy was on shaky ground. She suspected Maria had the right to remain silent, but to do so might not be in the girl's best interest.

"Why are you afraid to talk to the police?"

"I want to stay in school here."

The great unspoken threat of illegal immigration status hanging over the heads of many Hispanic students was now out in the open.

"I see," Sandy said. "Does your father have a green card?"

"Yes."

"Then what are you worried about —"

Sandy stopped at the realization that Maria's fear of the police might not be limited to deportation of herself and other family members. Something worse might be lurking in the darkness.

"The police probably can't make you talk to them," Sandy said slowly. "But it might be good if you do."

Maria covered her face with her hands for a moment.

"I don't want to."

"When does Ms. Ramsey want you to talk to the police?"

"I don't know. Please tell her I can't do it."

"Let me see if I can find out some answers for you."

Maria brightened a little bit. She glanced around the room.

"Can I stay here until the end of school?"

"Aren't you supposed to be in your sixth-period class?"

"Yes, but I cannot think about my schoolwork right now."

Sandy didn't have the heart to make the girl walk in late to class and then waste her time staring out the window.

"Okay, but just this once. You can't do this again."

"Thank you." Maria smiled shyly. "I feel happy and safe when I am in your room."

Sandy gave her a kind look. "I like to be with you too."

TWENTY-ONE

Sandy spent much of her late-afternoon walk with Nelson praying for and thinking about Maria. The girl was still on Sandy's mind later when she pulled into Ben and Betsy's driveway.

Her brother and his wife may not have bought a house on Millionaires' Row, but the residence they purchased was far from a shanty. The large brick home was on a cul-de-sac in the middle of a tract of land that fanned out behind the house for more than five hundred feet. A wooded area was filled with wildlife: squirrels, raccoons, owls, pileated woodpeckers, and deer. When Sandy spent the night, she enjoyed getting up early in the morning to drink coffee in the sunroom as deer grazed at the edge of the woods.

Sandy, Ben, and Jack Lincoln dutifully trudged through life with a strong sense of perfectionism inherited from their mother.

Betsy married into the Lincoln family but didn't adopt the same attitude toward life. Wisps of her brown hair were often out of place, and it wasn't uncommon for a guest to have to move a partially read magazine or section of the newspaper from a chair before sitting down. The casual clutter of the house made Sandy's mother's jaw clench when she came to visit. Betsy didn't seem to notice, or if she did, to care.

Sandy rang the doorbell. Within seconds she heard the deep-throated bark of Ben's dog, Ginger, a female Rottweiler with a huge head. Ben opened the door. He resembled their father in the prime of life before old age zapped his vitality.

"Come in so Ginger can sniff you," Ben said. "You could have brought Nelson."

Sandy entered the foyer. The dog sneezed on her foot.

"The last time I brought Nelson for a play date he was traumatized for the next twenty-four hours," she said. "Ginger can knock him over with one paw and hold him down on the floor while eating a bowl of dog food."

Finished with her inspection of Sandy, Ginger trotted over to a huge plaid dog bed and lay down. Her mouth opened in a massive yawn.

"Betsy is in the kitchen," Ben said.

Sandy followed Ben through a wood-paneled den and into a large formal dining room. The shiny table in the dining room was covered with piles of used clothes.

"What's going on?" Sandy asked.

"Those are going to Mexico. Betsy is sorting through everything that's been donated. There are bags of shoes in the garage. A group from the church is going to take everything when they leave on a mission trip in a couple of weeks."

Ben and Betsy attended a large nondenominational church. Sandy occasionally visited the church, especially when her nephews were in a play or music program.

The kitchen was beyond the dining room. Betsy, wearing an aqua-colored cotton top that was partially tucked into her jeans, stood at the stove with her back to them. She was barefoot. Her toenails were painted bright red.

"Sandy, help!" she said, glancing over her shoulder. "I feel like I'm making stone soup and no one has brought anything except the stone and a handful of turnips."

Sandy joined her at the stove. There was a wonderful aroma rising from the pot.

"It smells great. Is that a chicken stock?"

"Yes, but taste it."

Betsy handed a spoon to Sandy, who took a sip and licked her lips.

"Add a few twists of white pepper and a dash or two of Tabasco sauce. It's a good base; it just needs some kick."

"You do it," Betsy said, stepping away from the stove. "I don't want to ruin it."

Sandy knew her way around Betsy's kitchen. She found the ingredients in a cupboard, added them to the pot, and stirred.

"Try it now," she said to Betsy, who was brewing iced tea.

Betsy dipped her spoon in the pot and lifted it to her lips. A smile creased her face, making her green eyes shine.

"That's sublime. We'll eat as soon as the corn bread comes out of the oven."

Betsy was from south Alabama and made the best corn bread on the planet. She baked it in miniature pans that yielded a dainty loaf for each person. Her corn bread was fluffy with a hint of sweetness. Mayonnaise was one of her secret ingredients.

"That's why I invited you over," Ben said to Sandy from a chair in the breakfast nook where he was reading the local paper. "It's the only way I'm guaranteed corn bread for supper."

"You get it every time the boys come

home," Betsy said.

"Which isn't enough," Ben answered.

"What do you hear from them?" Sandy asked.

"Mark gets up at six every morning to beat the worst of Atlanta rush-hour traffic on his way to work," Betsy said. "Robbie has trouble getting out of bed in time for a ten o'clock class."

"His time will come," Ben said.

They ate in the breakfast nook. Sandy's youngest brother, Jack, lived in Chicago with his wife and two teenage daughters. Sandy and Ben had always been close, and since Sandy didn't have a husband, Ben had slipped into the role of trusted male adviser. Betsy didn't seem to mind sharing her husband with his older sister.

"The pepper and Tabasco really helped the soup," Betsy said after she ate a couple of bites.

"But the corn bread is what makes the meal," Ben said, cutting his second loaf in two. "Baby, you're the reason God gave us cornmeal to eat."

"Speaking of babies, a pregnant student sought me out yesterday," Sandy said before swallowing a spoonful of soup.

"How old is she?" Betsy asked.

"Barely sixteen. She's from a Hispanic

family and won't identify the father of the child. Her mother was murdered in Mexico when she was just a little girl."

"How horrible! What are you going to do to help her?"

"I'm not sure. And I'm concerned she might not get the best advice from one of the counselors at the school. I took her to the woman and got the feeling she wanted to cut me out of the loop."

"Take it up with Dr. Vale," Ben said.

Sandy shook her head. "I'm not sure that's a good idea. When he spoke to the faculty at the beginning of the year, he made it clear that the counselors are the ones to help students with serious personal problems. But this student has legal issues too. The police want to talk to her about the circumstances surrounding the pregnancy. She doesn't want to say anything, and I'm not sure that's what she ought to do. Do you think she should talk to an attorney?"

Ben spread a thick pat of butter on a piece of corn bread.

"Any lawyer would say yes," he said, "but that's self-serving. You could take her in to see Ralph Hartness."

"He writes wills," Betsy interjected. "What would he know about pregnant teenage girls?"

Ben took a bite of corn bread and chewed thoughtfully for a moment.

"I've met a sharp young lawyer in Tryon. I wrote a life insurance policy for him several years ago when he was in the district attorney's office. Since then, he's gone out on his own and seems to be doing well. He's increased the amount of his insurance twice since he first took it out."

"Does he have a specialty?" Sandy asked.

"I'm not sure, but he goes to court, and somebody as young as he is should still remember how to do research. Betsy's right. Ralph Hartness probably never cracks a law book."

"I like the idea of meeting with someone who isn't in Rutland," Sandy said. "But I'm not sure how I'll get the girl to Tryon."

"In your car," Ben said, dipping his spoon in his soup bowl.

"And don't worry about getting in trouble with the school administration," Betsy added. "You've been at the school forever, and everyone in Rutland thinks you're fantastic. I don't think Dr. Vale would cross you."

Sandy laughed. "I wish that were true, but the key to survival in the school system is learning how to not rock the boat. I teach my English classes, work hard with the cheerleaders, and tutor a few Spanish-speaking students. In those areas I'm bulletproof. Step outside of my bubble, and I could get my hand slapped, or worse."

"I wouldn't want to take you on in a fight," Ben said. "Do you remember the time you almost broke my arm when we were arm wrestling?"

"That story gets taller every time you tell it," Sandy replied with a smile. "What's the name of the lawyer in Tryon? My student needs an answer fast."

"Jeremy Lane. If you like, I could call him for you tomorrow."

"What would you tell him?"

"Just some background about you and your student. That way he could decide before you get in your car and drive to Tryon whether he may be able to help."

"Let him do it," Betsy said. "If it weren't for you, Ben wouldn't know his right foot from his left."

"I would have figured it out eventually," Ben protested.

"But the color coding helped," Sandy said. "Remember?"

"Yes," Ben responded dutifully, "blue is left and red is right."

It was Spirit Week at the school, and the

hallways were decorated with banners and posters. Based on her years of seniority as a teacher, Sandy didn't have homeroom responsibilities. There was a knock on the doorframe. It was Carol Ramsey.

"Come in," Sandy said.

"Good morning," Carol replied. "I noticed Maria Alverez sitting in your classroom yesterday afternoon. Didn't she have a class?"

"Yes."

"Why did she come to see you?"

Sandy couldn't dodge a direct question.

"She mentioned that you took her to the health department and wanted her to see an ob-gyn in Atlanta. Did you know she's covered by her father's health insurance policy at work?"

"Really?"

"Yes, she showed me the card."

"What did you say to her?" Carol asked.

"I mostly listened."

Carol nodded. "Please keep it that way. I don't want her to receive inconsistent advice."

"I'm not trying to do your job," Sandy replied evenly. "I have plenty of responsibilities of my own."

"I'm sure you do. The police department is going to send out a bilingual female officer to talk to Maria sometime this week. I haven't scheduled an appointment with the clinic in Atlanta."

"But why go all the way to Atlanta for prenatal care?" Sandy couldn't resist expressing her opinion. "Won't one of the local ob-gyn doctors accept her as a patient? As a juvenile, she should qualify for Medicaid if the pregnancy isn't covered on her father's health insurance at work."

Carol looked directly at Sandy.

"The doctor in Atlanta is on the staff of a women's health clinic. I think Maria should know about all her options."

"An abortion clinic?" Sandy felt the blood drain from her face.

"Is one of at least three options Maria should consider. The women's health clinic provides information about resources available for single women who want to raise a child, abortion for those who aren't ready for motherhood, and adoption."

"Are you going to tell her father about this?"

"It's not necessary at this point. The parental notification requirement isn't triggered until a woman decides to exercise her reproductive rights. I'm surprised you didn't know that. The clinic is a well-respected facility that meets all the state regulatory requirements."

Sandy didn't like the way Carol was lecturing her. The bell rang, signaling the end of homeroom. In a minute students would start streaming into the classroom.

"Don't forget your commitment to let me do my job," Carol said. "That means keeping your interaction with Maria inside the proper boundaries. I have Dr. Vale's full support."

Sandy wanted to ask if Carol had told Dr. Vale she was going to transport a sixteen-year-old student to an abortion clinic in Atlanta without her parent's consent.

Carol left the room. Sandy stared after her, but her mind was filled with the image of Maria, confused and dazed, sitting in a chair as a group of people bombarded her with advice and recommendations that included the death of her unborn baby.

That evening Sandy warmed up a bowl of Betsy's soup. It tasted even better the second day. Her cell phone rang. It was Ben.

"I talked with Jeremy Lane," Ben said. "He said he'd be glad to meet with you and your student. It turns out his mother helps teenage girls who are pregnant, so he's sympathetic."

Sandy told Ben about her conversation

with Carol Ramsey.

"That hacks me off," Ben said with an edge in his voice. "You know a lot more than —"

"I'm not trying to get you on my side," Sandy interrupted. "I know you support me, but I haven't had a chance to think through what I should do, and I didn't see Maria today at school."

"Do you know where she lives?"

"The trailer park off Haggler Road."

"That's a rough place. Don't walk around out there in the dark calling her name."

"I won't. I'll wait to see if she's at school tomorrow."

"Good. I'll send you a text with Jeremy Lane's contact information."

Sandy spent a troubled night thinking about Maria. It especially bothered her that the Hispanic girl lacked a supportive family surrounding her. There was no Aunt Linda willing to take her into her home or a wise adoption caseworker like Mrs. Longwell to guide her. Sandy had no idea about Maria's religious or cultural views concerning adoption or abortion. After an hour of tossing and turning, Sandy fell asleep to restless dreams.

When she arrived at school in the morning, she poured herself a cup of coffee in the faculty lounge and headed down the hallway to her classroom. When she turned the corner near her room, she saw Maria leaning against a locker by her door. Sandy hurried toward her.

"Are you okay?" she asked.

Maria shook her head. Her hair was disheveled, her clothes wrinkled.

"Do you want to talk?"

"Yes."

Sandy unlocked the door. There was no way she was going to turn the girl away. As soon as they were inside, Sandy closed the door and locked it. Maria sat down in a chair opposite Sandy's desk.

"What happened?" Sandy asked.

"The police came to our trailer last night. They took my father and the other men to the jail. I ran over to Rosalita's and stayed with her."

"Why did they arrest your father?"

"I don't know. He showed them his green card, but it did not help. If he does not go to work, he will lose his job."

Sandy thought about Carol's comment that a criminal violation may have occurred. She leaned forward.

"The police may be asking all the men in the house questions to see which one made you pregnant."

Maria looked puzzled, so Sandy switched to Spanish.

"Yes, I understand. But why would they take away my father?"

A small wave of relief washed over Sandy. She explained in Spanish why Maria's father had also been arrested. Maria's face paled. She stood up and began to speak rapidly.

"I have to go and tell them. Will you take me? Rosalita is at work."

Sandy hesitated. She could ask Carol Ramsey to transport Maria to the jail. Another possibility would be to find a teacher who didn't have to teach first period to cover for Sandy.

"Let's see if Ms. Ramsey can take you," Sandy suggested.

"No, I want you to go with me," Maria said, shaking her head.

"I have to teach my classes," Sandy said patiently. "This is something Ms. Ramsey can do for you. It's her job."

"What if they don't let my father go?"

"Then I'll find a lawyer to represent him."

Maria seemed to relax a little bit. They went to the counseling offices.

"Wait here," Sandy said.

She left Maria in the hallway and went to

Carol's office. It was empty. Sandy turned away and almost ran into Carol. Sandy quickly explained what had happened.

"Are you behind the arrests?" Sandy asked when she finished.

"I reported what I thought necessary, but I didn't tell the police what to do. I thought an officer was going to interview Maria later this week."

"She wants to try to get her father released immediately."

"Then I'll take her to the jail," Carol responded without hesitation. "And if the arrests are related to my report, maybe I can find out what happened."

Sandy thought about the lawyer Ben had contacted. It might not be necessary to see him.

"Okay."

She and Carol walked to the entrance of the school together.

"Ms. Ramsey is going to take you to the jail to find out about your father," Sandy said to Maria.

"I'm glad to help," Carol said. "I'll be back in a minute."

"And I have to teach my class," Sandy said. She glanced over her shoulder as Carol moved out of earshot. "Come see me later," she whispered to Maria.

Sandy returned to her classroom. A few minutes later, she saw Maria and Carol leave the campus. They didn't return until shortly before lunchtime. When Sandy entered the cafeteria, she noticed that Carol was sitting alone. Sandy hurriedly went over to her.

"Can we eat together?" Sandy asked.

Carol seemed irritated by the request.

"Yeah, but I'll be here for only a few more minutes."

Sandy quickly selected her food and returned to the table.

"What happened at the jail?" she asked. "Did the police release Maria's father?"

"For now. It turns out they went to the trailer looking for the man named Bernardo. When he wasn't there, they arrested everyone to see if they could get information about his whereabouts."

"Why were they looking for Bernardo?"

"I don't know. The detective said it was part of an 'ongoing investigation.' It didn't have anything to with Maria."

"Did she meet with an officer?"

"Yes." Carol looked at Sandy. "And after this morning, I have serious doubts that Maria is competent."

"Competent?"

"To make decisions in her own best interests. We tried to communicate with her in English and Spanish. Neither worked, so I'm going to have her evaluated."

"You think she may be mentally incompetent?" Sandy asked, trying to digest Carol's statement.

"It's something I have to consider, given my observations." Carol took a bite of her salad. "And you're not helping me."

"What do you mean?"

"Talking to her behind my back. Maria needs to open up with me, but she won't as long as you're manipulating her."

Sandy felt like she'd been slapped in the face. It took her a moment to regain her composure.

"I brought her to your office this morning," she said. "Was that manipulation?"

"You came in accusing me of causing the arrest of her father. It was an obvious attempt to turn her against me."

Sandy felt her face flush. She started to challenge Carol but realized if she did, the conversation could quickly deteriorate even further. At that moment three other teachers sat down at the table, and Carol left. Sandy continued to pick at her food for a few minutes, then took her tray to the dirty-dishes window.

Turning away from the window, Sandy

made a decision. Maria deserved help beyond what was available through Carol Ramsey. Taking out her cell phone, she offered up a quick prayer, then dialed the phone number for attorney Jeremy Lane.

TWENTY-TWO

"Lane Law Offices," a woman answered the phone.

"This is Sandy Lincoln. My brother Ben is an insurance agent with an office in Tryon. He contacted Mr. Lane yesterday about a situation involving a pregnant high school student."

"Yes," the woman replied. "Mr. Lane mentioned you to me before he left for court. Would you like to schedule an appointment?"

"Yes."

"Can you make it around five-thirty? I assume it will need to be late in the afternoon."

"Today?"

"Yes."

Sandy hesitated. Maria's issues weren't going to wait. A five-thirty appointment would give Sandy time to finish cheerleading practice and drive from Rutland to Tryon.

"Let me check with the student and get back to you."

"Fine. I'll mark it tentative. Do you need directions to the office?"

"What's the street address?"

Sandy was familiar with the street. She wrote the number on a pad she kept in the car.

The call ended. To transport Maria to Tryon for a meeting with a lawyer would be considered a declaration of war by Carol Ramsey; however, the counselor had fired the first shot over a bowl of lettuce with Italian dressing.

Her jaw set, Sandy returned to her classroom. She logged on to the school system and found out where Maria would be during fifth period. No one was in the room, so Sandy left the teacher a note asking her to send Maria to see Sandy as soon as her class ended.

At the end of fifth period, Sandy's students filed out of the room. Sixth period would start shortly. Several early arriving students dragged themselves into the room and slumped down in chairs. Sixth-period grammar and composition was Sandy's most challenging class. The students were tired at the end of the day and considered the subject matter a form of waterboarding torture. Maria appeared in the doorway. Sandy quickly ushered her into the hallway.

"I know your father got out of jail," she said quickly in Spanish. "But I still think it would be a good idea for you to talk to a lawyer yourself. I'd like to take you to meet with one this afternoon. We'd leave the school about five o'clock. I'm not sure when we'd be back."

"How will I get home? Rosalita won't be able to pick me up."

"That's not a problem. I'll take you."

"And I do not have any money to pay a lawyer."

"I'll take care of it."

Maria, her eyes big, looked at Sandy.

"Ms. Lincoln, why are you doing this for me?"

"Because you're worth every minute of time and every dollar of money. Come to the gym where the cheerleaders practice around four-thirty."

"Is Ms. Ramsey going with us?"

"No," Sandy replied. "And don't mention it to her if you see her before then."

Even as she listened to her words, Sandy felt herself cringe on the inside. It was the sort of statement that made sense in context but if repeated later would sound horrible.

"Now, get to class," Sandy said.

Maria disappeared into a large group of students moving down the hall. Sandy went into her classroom. Two football players were teasing a skinny boy with a pointed nose. One of the football players had made a fake nose out of paper and put it on his own face.

"Lonny," Sandy said to the boy with the paper nose on his face. "Give me examples of sentences illustrating the difference between a gerund and a present participle using the verb *fake*."

"I don't know any," the boy replied, snatching the nose from his face.

"That's going to earn you an F for this class period and a note from me to Coach Hampton about running extra wind sprints this afternoon."

"How about you, Bruce?" Sandy pointed to the other player. "Are you up to date on the distinction between a gerund and a present participle?"

"A gerund is a verb ending in 'ing' that's used as a noun," Bruce replied. "A present participle is a verb ending in 'ing' that's used as either a main verb or an adjective. 'Faking wears at a teacher's patience.' In that sentence, *faking* is a gerund. 'The football player is faking if he claims it wasn't a stupid move to make a paper nose in English class.' In that sentence, *faking* is a present participle used as the main verb in conjunction with *is*."

Bruce Lowell had a shot at receiving a college scholarship to play football at an Ivy League school. He was on track to be one of the valedictorians for the senior class.

"That's right," Sandy said.

"And I'd be faking if I didn't admit that I made the paper nose," Bruce continued. "If Lonny is going to be punished, I should be too."

"Okay," Sandy said. "You got it. Anything else you want to say?"

Bruce leaned forward to the skinny student and whispered in his ear. The boy nodded without turning around.

"Did that correct the problem?" Sandy asked the boy, who gave her a look that pleaded for her to move on. "Open your composition books to page 124."

Sandy confirmed the appointment with Jeremy Lane's assistant. Several times during cheerleading practice, she thought about Maria and grew nervous. She tried to push the jittery feeling down inside and focus on the girls on the practice mats. Time dragged by. At 4:30 p.m. sharp, Sandy blew her whistle.

"That's it for today," she said. "We're in good shape for tomorrow night's game."

As the cheerleaders left, Sandy saw Maria slip into the gym. Sandy waved to her.

"I'll be right back."

After Sandy went to the coaching office to hang up her whistle, she and Maria walked out of the building together.

"Is Tryon far away?" Maria asked as they got in the car.

"About twenty minutes if traffic isn't bad."

Sandy turned out of the school parking lot and onto the two-lane highway that connected Rutland with Tryon. Maria sat with her hands folded in her lap.

"Have you had any morning sickness?" Sandy asked.

"A little."

"And how is your heart feeling?" Sandy touched her chest.

"My heart?"

"Your emotions. Your feelings."

"My heart does not know what to feel. My mind does not know what to think."

Sandy nodded. Maria's English was rudimentary, but her thought processes gave no indication that she was mentally incompetent. Carol Ramsey's allegation about in-

350

competency had no chance for success.

They left Rutland. The rolling countryside was dotted with cattle farms and soybean fields.

"Maria, let me tell you one reason why I want to help you," Sandy said.

Maria shifted in the seat and listened as Sandy told about her own pregnancy. The Hispanic girl's eyes widened as the story unfolded.

"Where are your baby boys now?" Maria asked after Sandy told about their birth.

"It was a closed adoption," Sandy said in Spanish. "That means the records are locked up and can't be opened unless everybody wants to do so. The adoption society in Atlanta would have contacted me if one of the boys ever tried to find me." Sandy counted for a moment. "They would be thirty-three years old now."

Maria silently stared out the window. They reached the outskirts of Tryon.

"It won't be long now," Sandy said. "Remember, everything you tell the lawyer is secret, so you can be honest with him."

"Will he tell my father?"

"Not if you don't want him to."

Sandy parked on the street in front of the building. It was 5:35 p.m. A neatly lettered white sign with dark-blue letters over the door read Jeremy Lane, Trial Lawyer.

Sandy and Maria entered a compact but nicely furnished reception area.

"Ms. Lincoln?" a middle-aged woman with half-frame glasses on her nose asked.

"Yes," Sandy answered.

"I'm Deb Bridges. I'll let Mr. Lane know you're here."

Sandy had been to see a lawyer only a couple of times: once when she bought her house in Rutland and a second time when she made a will splitting her property between Ben and Jack upon her death. Maria sat on a short leather sofa and ran her finger over the pliable material.

"It's nice, isn't it?" Sandy asked.

"Yes."

"Ms. Lincoln?"

Sandy stood up and faced a handsome man in his thirties with blond hair and blue eyes. She suspected Jeremy Lane would have an immediate edge with the female members of a jury.

"Yes," Sandy said. "And this is Maria Alverez."

"Hello, Maria." Jeremy looked the girl directly in the eyes. "Thanks for coming to see me."

Maria smiled shyly.

"Let's talk in my office."

They entered a well-furnished office with diplomas and certificates on one wall and paintings of rural scenes on the others.

"Please sit down," Jeremy said.

Sandy and Maria sat beside each other across from the lawyer.

"How can I help you?" he asked.

Sandy provided a brief background of what had happened so far. Jeremy listened and made notes using the keyboard of his computer.

"Before we go any further, I'd like a bit of background information from Maria," he said. "Are you okay with that?"

"Yes," she said.

"And if I ask any questions you don't understand, please let me know, and I'll try to do better."

Maria nodded. Sandy already liked the gentle approach the lawyer was taking with Maria. Using simple questions, he began drawing out information about Maria and her family. While Maria talked, Sandy's eyes wandered around the office. Several of the paintings looked like original watercolors, and there was a row of family photographs on a credenza. The lawyer had a nice-looking wife and two children. His daughter resembled him, and his son had reddish-brown hair.

"How have you been feeling?" Jeremy asked Maria.

"Scared. I don't know what's going to happen to me."

Jeremy nodded. "And physically?"

"Okay." Maria shrugged. "I feel a little bit sick when I wake up in the morning. But it goes away after I eat."

Jeremy began asking Maria more specific questions about the circumstances of her pregnancy.

"Is one of the men who lives in the trailer the father of your baby?" Jeremy asked.

"Yes."

Sandy sat up straight in her chair.

"Which one?" Jeremy asked in a soft voice.

"Emilio."

Sandy held her breath.

"Are you sure it's Emilio?"

Maria nodded. "It happened while my father was at work."

"Does your father know?"

"Yes. He told me not to tell anyone."

"Why are you telling me?"

Maria looked at Sandy. "Ms. Lincoln told me I could tell you anything and you would keep it secret."

"Why was Emilio living with your family?"

"My father knows his father in Mexico.

They are from the same village."

"How old is Emilio?"

"About thirty years old."

"Okay, and did he force you to be with him?"

"Yes. The men had been drinking beer and needed to buy more beer. They went to the store and left Emilio with me. That is when it happened. Emilio said if I told anyone, he would kill me."

Sandy felt her skin crawl.

"Does your father know this?"

"Yes."

"Is Emilio still living at your house?"

"Not every day. If he is there, I stay with Rosalita. My father is afraid of Emilio. Everyone is afraid of him."

"Have you talked to your father about the baby?"

"Yes. He thinks I should have a doctor take it out while it is little, and it won't hurt me very much. If the baby is gone, Emilio will not be mad."

"What do you want to do?" Jeremy asked.

"I do not know."

"Maria, what Emilio did to you was very, very wrong," Jeremy said in a calm voice. "Some people believe that makes it okay to end the pregnancy. Other people think it's better to let the baby live because it's not the baby's fault that it's inside you. Do you understand?"

"Yes, I think about this too," Maria said, keeping her head bowed.

Sandy's already high level of compassion for Maria increased. The girl's decision was even more difficult than her own.

"Can you translate for me now?" Jeremy asked Sandy. "I want to explain her rights, and it might be clearer that way."

"I'll try."

Jeremy turned to Maria. "The decision of what to do about your pregnancy is up to you. No one can make you keep the baby, end the pregnancy, or allow the baby to be adopted. It doesn't matter that you're barely sixteen years old and unmarried. You will make that choice, not your father, not Emilio, not Ms. Ramsey, not Ms. Lincoln."

Sandy explained and Maria nodded.

"The law requires proof of parental notification before a minor can have an abortion and a twenty-four-hour waiting period between scheduling the procedure and performing it."

"Notice, not consent?" Sandy asked.

"Right. The parent can't stop the child but has a right to be told. Tell her that."

Sandy translated.

"Emilio could get in trouble with the

police because he forced you to be with him. It's up to you to decide if you want to tell the police what happened. If you do, Emilio will be arrested and may be sent to jail."

Maria looked puzzled and Sandy explained.

"Because my father told me not to tell anybody, I would not talk to the police," Maria said.

"Police?"

Sandy told him what she knew about the arrests and interrogation of the men who lived in the trailer.

"So none of the arrests were related to Maria?"

"Right, but an officer still tried to interview her."

Jeremy looked at Maria. "You decide if you want to talk to the police or not."

Maria nodded.

"Carol Ramsey was there during the attempted questioning," Sandy said. "She told me Maria refused to cooperate and mentioned the possibility of having Maria declared mentally incompetent. What do you think about that?"

"It's a clever tactic," Jeremy replied.

"Clever tactic?"

"Yes. If a juvenile court judge ruled Maria

incompetent, a guardian would have input into what happens to the baby. The appointment of a guardian doesn't mean Maria would lose all her rights, but it would raise the question of whether she can make a decision in her own best interests. The fact that the pregnancy is the result of rape would be a factor to be considered in support of terminating the pregnancy."

"There's no reason for a guardian," Sandy said. "You can see for yourself that Maria is competent."

"What you and I think is irrelevant. A psychologist and/or psychiatrist would evaluate her and render an opinion to the judge. Their assessments would probably dictate the result."

"Could Carol suggest who would do the evaluations?"

"Yes."

Sandy's confidence that Carol's opinion about Maria's competency wasn't a serious threat was shaken.

"I'm not sure I can translate all that," she said.

"I think we've given Maria enough to think about today. That part will be relevant only if an incompetency petition is filed."

Maria looked from Jeremy to Sandy.

"What?" she asked.

"Tell her we're talking about things that haven't happened but might," Jeremy replied. "If there are other problems, you and Ms. Lincoln can come back to see me."

Sandy translated.

"Okay," Maria said.

"Do you have any other questions?"

"No." Maria shook her head.

"How about you?" Jeremy asked Sandy.

"What's the fee for your services today?" Sandy reached for her purse. "I appreciate you seeing us on such short notice. I brought my checkbook so you won't have to send me a bill."

Jeremy raised his hand. "Nothing. If my mother were here, she'd send me to my room without supper if I charged a fee. She does a lot of volunteer work with pregnant teenage girls. Compared to her sacrifices, this is minor."

"Thanks. Ben mentioned that," Sandy said.

"And don't hesitant to call me if something else comes up. Especially if the counselor at the school files a petition to declare Maria incompetent."

Everyone stood, and Sandy stepped forward to shake Jeremy's hand. When she did, she saw a framed photo on the corner of his desk. Something about the picture looked vaguely familiar. She turned her head to look, and Jeremy followed her eyes.

"My childhood home in Charleston," he said, handing the photo to Sandy. "That's me as a little boy standing in the front yard."

Sandy felt the office spin around. It was the house in the picture she'd looked at in Mrs. Longwell's office. There was no doubt about it. Sandy's hand trembled slightly as she returned the photograph to him.

"Very nice," she managed. "Charleston is a beautiful old city."

"My mother still lives there. Did Ben mention to you that I'm an adoptee?"

"Uh, no."

"It's another reason why I'm willing to help you and Maria. I don't know anything about my birth mother, but I'm glad she made the decision to give me life."

Sandy nodded numbly and looked at the pictures on the credenza.

"And those are your children?" she asked.

"Yes, Chloe is ten and Zach is five."

Jeremy pointed to the photo taken in the rushing stream.

"That's my wife, Leanne, and the children during a vacation in the mountains last summer."

"May I see it?" Sandy asked, her voice a little shaky.

Jeremy handed the picture to Sandy, who devoured the images with her eyes and seared every nuance into her mind.

"Your son has reddish-brown hair."

"Yes, we're not sure where that came from. There aren't any redheads in Leanne's background."

Up close, Sandy could see the influence of Brad Donnelly's gene pool in the little boy's features. The girl looked like a Lincoln. Sandy put her hand on the lawyer's desk to steady herself.

"Are you okay?" Jeremy asked.

"Uh, yes. It's been a long, emotional day. And I need to get Maria home."

She handed the photo to Jeremy, who returned it to its place. He took two business cards from a brass holder on his desk and handed one to Maria and the other to Sandy.

"Keep these and call me if you have questions."

Sandy clutched the card and stared at Jeremy. Memories of the fair-haired newborn in the infant nursery of the hospital in Atlanta flooded her thoughts. To see the finished product staggered her.

"Anything else today?" Jeremy asked with a slightly puzzled expression on his face.

Sandy's mind screamed that she had

thousands and thousands of questions. She tore her gaze away from Jeremy.

"No, thanks again for meeting with us."

"I'll see you out since Deb probably locked the door."

As he led them from his office, Sandy had a chance to see the back of Jeremy's head and his broad shoulders. The young lawyer walked with the confident step of a man who knew where he was going in life. Sandy's emotions boiled to the surface. She dabbed her sleeve against her eyes as Jeremy unlocked the door and held it open for them.

She hurried past, hoping he couldn't see the tears that were now streaming down her cheeks.

TWENTY-THREE

Sandy grabbed a handful of tissues from a small pack beside her seat. Maria stared at her. Sandy didn't speak as she dried her eyes. She adjusted the rearview mirror so she could see her face. Her eyes were red, but what struck her was how much of her could be seen in Jeremy Lane. It made her wonder why she'd not suspected who he was even before she saw the picture on his desk. Her eyes flooded again. The magnitude of what had just happened was enough to make her heart burst.

"I'm sorry," she said through her sniffles to Maria.

"Did I do or say something bad?" Maria asked with a worried look.

"No, no." Sandy reached out and patted Maria's leg. "It's not you. It's me."

Sandy started the car and backed out of the parking spot. Jeremy came out of the building, saw them, and waved. Sandy fought an impulse to jump out of the car, tell him who she was, and collapse in his arms. Instead, she waved weakly, hoping there was enough distance that he couldn't see her tearstained face. As she drove away from the office, she saw Jeremy get in a white SUV.

Oh Lord, what is going on? she said to herself.

Maria continued to stare at her.

"Do you need to drink some water?" Maria asked.

"Yes," Sandy said. "That's a good idea."

Sandy pulled into a convenience store.

"Pick out whatever you'd like," she said to Maria. "I'll pay for it."

Sandy went into the restroom and inspected herself in the mirror. She was a mess. She splashed cold water on her face. Standing in front of the drink cooler, her mind went back to the long-ago day when she'd stopped at the gas station between Rutland and Atlanta and encountered the strange woman who told her about the twins. Seeing Jeremy grown up and safe made more tears come. Sandy didn't know where the other twin might be, but if the woman's warning was true, Sandy had done her part to keep them safe. She opened the cooler and grabbed a water. Maria was waiting for her at the cash register with a bottle of fruit juice in her hand.

"Good choice," Sandy said.

They left Tryon and rode in silence as Sandy went over in her mind what she'd seen in Jeremy's office. Every time she thought about the family photos on the credenza, her tears returned.

She had two grandchildren!

No children are perfect, but the two youngsters looked as perfectly normal as possible. Sandy held them with invisible arms and kissed them with imaginary kisses. Maria continued to sit calmly with her hands in her lap, looking out the car window.

"Maria," Sandy said.

The girl turned toward her. Sandy spoke in Spanish.

"You'll never know who the baby inside you might become if you don't give him or her a chance to be born."

Maria knit her eyebrows together for a moment.

"Do you understand what I mean?" Sandy asked.

"I think so."

Sandy started to explain but didn't. She'd planted a seed. There would be time later to water it.

■ ■ ■ ■

It was dusk when Sandy turned into Maria's trailer park. She passed rows of mobile homes. Most were in need of repair; a few didn't look fit for human habitation.

"That's our trailer." Maria pointed to one that had three pickup trucks parked in front of it.

"Is your father home?" Sandy asked.

"No, and Emilio is there. Please don't stop," Maria said anxiously. "Rosalita lives over there. I'll stay with her tonight."

Farther down the row, Sandy saw a smaller trailer with Rosalita's car parked in front.

"Are you going to tell your father about the meeting with the lawyer?" Sandy asked.

"Is it wrong not to tell him?"

Sandy had never advised a student to keep a secret from her parents.

"If you think it might put you in danger from Emilio, I don't think you should tell him. At least not now."

Maria nodded. "I will talk to Rosalita."

"Can you trust her to keep a secret?"

"Yes. We talk about everything."

"Okay. Ask her what she thinks about letting the baby be adopted by a couple who wants a child very much."

Maria opened the door of the car.

"Thank you for taking me today," she said.

"You're welcome."

"I'm sorry you are so sad."

"No," Sandy said and shook her head. "Those tears came from another place. I'll see you tomorrow."

Maria turned away. Sandy waited until the door of the trailer opened and the girl went inside. When Sandy passed Maria's trailer on her way out, there were two rough-looking men standing on the narrow front stoop drinking beer. They watched Sandy pass.

With Maria out of the car, Sandy gave full rein to thoughts about Jeremy and his family. Questions rose so rapidly in her mind that she didn't have time to come up with possible answers. After arriving home, she fed Nelson then turned on her computer and searched for "Jeremy Lane Attorney." The first few hits provided little more than Jeremy's business address and phone number. When she found one that included personal information, the first item that popped up made her stop and stare at the screen.

"Born April 5, 1975, Atlanta, GA."

Seeing the concrete information made Sandy feel light-headed. She'd not doubted who he was. The photo of him as a little boy in front of the house in Charleston settled that. But seeing his date and place of birth in black-and-white was like reading the news on a giant billboard. He'd gone to college at Furman University in Greenville, where he received a BA, magna cum laude, in English.

She smiled. "That's my boy."

He attended law school at the University of South Carolina and had been a member of the Georgia bar for eight years. She continued to search, but to her disappointment nothing else turned up. She turned off the computer and sat back in her chair, completely drained. She'd been on an intense emotional high, and it was time to come down for a rest.

She brewed a pot of hot tea and relaxed in her favorite reading chair in the living room. Nelson lay at her feet. Sandy considered calling her mother, Jessica, and Ben to share her amazing discovery; however, she knew it wasn't the right time. Also, she enjoyed privately hugging her newfound knowledge close to her heart. Sandy took a sip of tea and looked down at Nelson. He was a safe confidant.

"Nelson, let me tell you what happened today," she began.

■ ■ ■ ■

The following day was football Friday. Normally, Sandy ran through the evening's cheerleading routine in her mind while she drank her morning coffee. Not today. The wonder of her encounter with her son flooded her kitchen with brightness. Still dressed in her pajamas, Sandy slowly stirred her coffee as she sat at the kitchen table. She was proud of the kind and gentle way Jeremy had treated Maria. Her cell phone beeped. It was Ben.

"Ready for tonight?" her brother asked.

"I think so." Sandy tried to make her voice sound normal. "We're doing a tumbling routine."

"Betsy and I are looking forward to it. Do you have any plans after the game?"

"I left it open in case some students invite me to join them."

Rutland was small-town enough that students would go out to eat pizza after a game and occasionally asked their favorite teachers to tag along for part of the evening.

"If that doesn't work out, Betsy and I are going to have some folks over to the house. Nothing fancy."

"Who's going to be there?" Sandy asked.

"You sound like the boys. Is there anyone you're trying to avoid?"

"No."

"Oh, did you get in touch with the lawyer in Tryon?"

Sandy swallowed. "Yes. The student and I met with him late yesterday afternoon."

"Nice guy, isn't he?"

"Yes."

"Did you hire him?"

"Not yet. He told us what we needed to know at this point."

"Did he tell you to stop helping the girl?"

"That didn't come up. We spent all our time focusing on the student and her situation." Sandy paused. "And a little bit about Mr. Lane's family."

"Yeah, he's got a couple of cute kids and a pretty wife. I delivered a disability policy to their home not long ago because she had some questions, and Jeremy wanted me to answer them in person."

"Where do they live?" Sandy asked, trying to sound casual.

"On the south side of town. The house is nice but nothing fancy. I think they chose the area because it has the best elementary school in town. Also, you know how hard it can be starting up any new business."

"I think he'll do well."

"No doubt. Listen, I've got to run to a breakfast meeting with a client. Remember the invitation for tonight."

Sandy went through the day resisting the wild urge to get on the school intercom to proclaim that she'd met her son! During third period, she noticed a young man in her class with a slight resemblance to Jeremy. Sandy gave him a big smile as he passed her desk. After the room cleared of students, Maria slipped in.

"Are you feeling better?" the student asked.

"Yes," Sandy said. "But don't worry about me. Did you talk to Rosalita about the meeting with the lawyer?"

"Yes. My father came over to her house, and I asked him about adoption. He does not like that idea."

"Why not?"

"The baby would go to a stranger we do not know and might not be taken care of."

Sandy frowned. Maria's father was being hypocritical. If he'd cared more for his own daughter, he would have shown a higher level of concern about letting a group of unsupervised men live in the trailer with her.

"What did Rosalita think?"

"She is like me and does not know."

Two other female students entered the room to see Sandy.

"Thanks for stopping by," Sandy said to Maria. "We'll talk later."

Maria left, and the students pulled papers from their backpacks.

"Ms. Lincoln, we have questions about the comments you made on our papers," one of the girls said.

"Let me see what I wrote," Sandy said.

Only a portion of Sandy's mind was present with the students. The rest of it was with her newly discovered family twenty minutes away.

Like the football team, the cheerleaders assembled for a Friday night pregame meal. Of course, the two groups didn't meet in the same place. Putting the girls and boys together would have created a major distraction that neither Sandy nor Coach Hampton wanted.

The cheerleaders met in the banquet room of a restaurant where the local Rotary Club met each Thursday. The booster club paid for the meal. Sandy, wearing a gray sweater and red woolen slacks, arrived at 5:30 p.m. Several of the girls were already there. Dick Dressler, the owner of the restaurant, greeted her at the door.

"Thanks for hosting us," Sandy said.

"Glad to do it. Do you think we have a chance against Butler County? They have a running back who may go to Georgia next year. He's a real brute."

"I don't know, but the cheerleaders are going to perform a tumbling routine that really pops."

The rotund man wiped his forehead with a dish towel. "Sandy, you could get more out of our team than Coach Hampton. He's too predictable. Always runs on first and second down and ends up with third and long. High school quarterbacks can't be consistent enough to convert in those types of situations. To have a chance tonight, we're going to have to score, and score in bunches."

"Bruce Lowell should be able to get open tonight," Sandy said. "I made sure he ran extra wind sprints yesterday."

"You did?" Dressler looked surprised.

"Yes, he had a disciplinary issue in my class, and I passed along a note to Coach Hampton. Watch Lonny Mitchell too. He should be able to get to the line a fraction of a step sooner from his outside-linebacker spot."

Dressler smiled. "I like the sound of that.

Bruce can flat read a defense and find a crease. Lonny, on the other hand —"

"Can create havoc in the blocking scheme even if he doesn't get to the ball carrier. That enables Scott Nash to come in from his middle linebacker position and clean up the play."

Dressler swore under his breath. "Sandy, you are all over it."

"I've been watching Rutland County football games for over thirty years," she said. "You can't help but pick up a bit of knowledge by osmosis."

More girls entered the restaurant. Within a few minutes, the entire team had arrived. They stood in a large circle, and Sandy called on Meredith to offer a prayer for the meal. When she said "Amen," the room erupted in noisy chatter as the girls made their way around the salad bar. Sandy sat at a table with Alita and another Hispanic girl.

"How do you feel about the routine?" Sandy asked Alita.

"I'm nervous. I don't want to mess up."

"You won't. You were perfect during practice yesterday."

"Not really. You weren't watching one time, and I got out of sync. Cindy cornered me later and told me if I wasn't going to nail it, I shouldn't be front and center."

Sandy glanced over at Cindy Garrett, a smug, talented junior who expected to be named captain the following year. However, if she didn't improve her ability to encourage, not criticize, that wouldn't happen. Sandy leaned closer to Alita.

"Let's talk you through it."

Alita listened and nodded her head as Sandy began to give a step-by-step summary of the routine.

"I need to remember to really arch my back at that part," Alita said. "That sets me up for the next move."

"Right. Remember to be as beautiful as you are strong."

"The word is out among the Hispanic students at school that Alita has a big role tonight," the other Hispanic girl said. "Everyone is going to be watching and yelling as soon as she starts."

"Then feed off that energy," Sandy said. "It makes me have chill bumps just thinking about it."

Sandy always asked one of the girls to prepare a brief talk for the group. Most of the students hated it. Some came up with creative excuses to try to get out of it, but Sandy wouldn't budge. She knew public speaking was a fear that had to be faced head-on.

"Candace, please come up," Sandy said. "We're ready to hear from you."

The slender black girl walked to a wooden podium and faced her peers. Taking out a sheet of paper, she cleared her throat and began speaking in Spanish. Sandy's mouth dropped open. Candace's Spanish accent had a north Georgia lilt, but her meaning was clear to those who had taken Spanish III. She was celebrating the participation of the Hispanic girls on the cheerleading squad. Sandy, who was sitting at the front of the room, turned her chair to the side so she could see the reaction of the team. Those who didn't speak Spanish had puzzled looks on their faces. Two of the Hispanic girls were wiping away tears. Cindy Garrett looked pale. After three minutes, Candace stopped and repeated her message in English with a few additional lines thrown in at the end.

"I appreciate what Ms. Lincoln has taught us about accepting people from other cultures and encouraging them. The cheerleading squad is a team, not just a group of individuals, and I think what we've experienced together is something I'm going to carry with me the rest of my life. Oh, and Coach Lincoln didn't ask me to talk about this. Now, let's go out and do our part to beat Butler County!"

The Hispanic and black girls stood and clapped as Candace left the podium. When they stood up, the rest of the squad followed. Sandy smiled. It was a statement that needed to be made, and Candace was qualified to make it. Sandy went up to the podium. She resisted the urge to emphasize Candace's remarks. Instead, she went through a few housekeeping details. When she finished, the girls gathered in a circle, put their hands in the middle, and yelled, "RHS!"

They drove in a caravan to the football stadium. The bleachers on the home side could accommodate almost two thousand people, and the stands would be full. Football on Friday night trumped everything except weddings and funerals. The visitor's side could hold about five hundred fans. Because Butler County was having a good year, a lot of people would make the hourlong drive to Rutland for the game.

The home team was at the far end of the field going through their pregame drills. Rutland High's squad had been mediocre for years, but Sandy didn't blame the coaching. Some of the best athletes at the school opted to play soccer, and the soccer team was always at the top of the conference.

As she watched the players loosen up, Sandy wondered what sports Jeremy Lane had played in school. The lawyer had a compact muscular build. She felt a pang of loss that she'd never seen him in action.

Sandy placed a folding chair on the track surface in front of where the girls would line up. The cheerleaders were still in the girls' locker room using every spare second to fine-tune makeup that couldn't be seen beyond the first few rows of the bleachers. Elementary-school-age children ran up and down the track, chasing one another and playing catch with miniature footballs. More and more people began filing into the stadium. Several people stopped to chat with Sandy on the way to their seats.

One couple that came over to her was Barb and Bob Dortch. Two of their daughters had been on the varsity cheerleading squad. The girls were grown and gone from Rutland, but the Dortchs still came to all the home football games. Bob owned a local car dealership. Barb was wearing a sweater identical to Sandy's.

"Don't tell me where you got that!" Barb laughed, holding her sleeve next to Sandy's arm. "Just don't say you bought it on sale. I paid full price at Neal's."

"John Neal doubled his money with us,"

Sandy replied. "But it looks better on you than it does on me."

"Shut up," Barb replied. "What do you think, Bob?"

Bob Dortch, a blond-haired man with a slightly red face, pretended to inspect them.

"Both of you look better than ninety percent of the women in their thirties coming to this game."

Barb patted her husband on the arm.

"You can have peanuts and popcorn during the game."

Sandy suddenly had a thought.

"Bob, do you rent cars?"

"I sure do. I can put you in a sweet lease. The trade-in on your car would cover the down payment, and I could finagle a great rate."

"No, I meant rent a car for a day."

"Oh, we have a few loaners for regular customers to the service department."

"Could I rent one of those tomorrow? I need to run over to Tryon."

Bob hesitated. "Saturday is a very busy time for service. I'm not sure —"

Barb punched him in the arm. "Honey, let her drive one of the demos you keep complaining about. You told me at supper that you have four or five of them sitting on the lot begging for someone to take them off your hands."

"It would only be for part of a day," Sandy said. "I'd be glad to pay whatever you think is fair as a daily rate."

"Fair is nothing," Barb said emphatically before her husband could speak. "I can't count the number of times you brought the girls home from practice when Bob and I were working late at the dealership. And you'd never let me pay you a penny."

"She's right," Bob said. "Come by anytime after seven-thirty in the morning, and I'll set you up. Putting another fifty miles on one of those vehicles isn't going to affect the value."

"Are you sure?" Sandy asked.

"He's sure," Barb answered. "Come on, Bob. What do you want first, popcorn or peanuts? I'm buying, with your money, of course."

Sandy watched the Dortchs move toward the concession stand. It had been a spur-of-the-moment idea. Jeremy had seen Sandy's car when she took Maria to his office, and if she wanted to catch a glimpse of her grandchildren, she'd need another vehicle to do so. She felt a mixture of fear and excitement. She looked toward the south end zone as the cheerleading squad came onto the field holding a giant paper banner.

A few seconds later, the football team came tearing through it.

It proved to be a long night for fans of Rutland High football. The running back from Butler County had the strength of a Hereford bull. On most plays it took three defenders to bring him down. On the bright side, Bruce Lowell caught a touchdown pass in the fourth quarter, but that only made the score 48–12.

The cheerleaders' performance went off without a hitch. Because the game was so lousy, the fans gave the girls their undivided attention. Alita popped off her part of the routine perfectly, and the Hispanic contingent in the stands went wild. Sandy rewarded her with a big smile and hand clap. Toward the end of the fourth quarter, Candace trotted over to Sandy.

"Some of us are going to Pizza Town after the game. Would like to come along?"

"Sure."

Sandy told Ben and Betsy of her plans.

"We'll do it again after the Oakboro game," Ben said. "That should be a celebration. We can always count on Oakboro for a win."

The students bounced back from the loss more quickly than the adults. By the time the waitress brought soft drinks to the large round table, the girls were laughing and watching the door for members of the football team to arrive. The boys came in wearing practiced frowns, but in a few minutes they were cutting up and making jokes.

"Thanks, Ms. Lincoln," Bruce Lowell said when he came up to the table. "If I hadn't gotten in some extra speed work this week, I don't think I could have gotten a step on the Butler County defensive back."

"That was the backup DB," another football player replied. "My brother in eighth grade could have gotten a step on him."

"No, number 84 was a starter."

"Bruce is right," Sandy said. "I noticed 84 during the introductions because he was so tall."

"He was at least six foot five," Bruce replied. "And he ran like a Thomson's gazelle."

Bruce moved away.

"What do you think about Bruce?" Meredith whispered to Sandy. "Do you think he's phony?"

"His brain isn't phony," Sandy answered. "Are you attracted to him? I thought you liked Billy Wilson."

"That didn't work out," Meredith said with a shrug. "I told him I just wanted to be friends."

"How did he take it?"

"Not too well, but he'll still want help with chemistry."

"Does Bruce know you're interested in him?"

"No."

"He's probably not smart enough to figure that out on his own," Sandy said. "Very few men are able to do that."

"I may get Candace to talk to him. They have a couple of classes together. She thinks Bruce is more my type than Billy."

Sandy agreed with Candace but didn't say so. She didn't stay long at the restaurant. Acceptance of the invitation included a willingness not to overstay her welcome. Several of the girls hugged her when she got up to leave after eating a single piece of pizza. Bruce struck a pose as if catching a pass when she walked by. Sandy laughed. As she unlocked her car, she thought that her life might have been different if Brad Donnelly had been more like Bruce Lowell. A smart, witty football player was the kind of boy Sandy needed. But then she thought about Jeremy Lane — he was the result of a distinct moment in time between two unique people.

Bad situations can turn out good.

TWENTY-FOUR

The following morning Sandy arrived at the car dealership shortly after eight o'clock. Bob Dortch was sitting in the glass-walled office he occupied on the showroom floor. He came out to greet her.

"Could a mechanic change the oil in my car while I'm gone?" she asked.

"Sure. We'll run a twenty-one-point inspection."

Sandy started to protest but kept her mouth shut. She couldn't quibble when she was getting a free car.

"I have a nice ride for you," Bob said.

Sandy followed him to the used-car lot on the side of the building.

"There it is," he said, pointing to a shiny blue sedan.

"It looks like my car," Sandy blurted out.

"I thought you liked your car," Bob said, giving her a puzzled look. "At least that's what you told me when you bought it."

"No, it isn't that," Sandy replied frantically, trying to find a way to explain her need for a different vehicle. She quickly scanned the lot. "I was hoping to use a pickup truck. You know the big plant nursery in Tryon?"

"Yeah, Barrett's."

"I may buy some plants to put out in the yard at my house. A truck would be perfect for that."

"This time of year?"

"Fall is a great time to plant certain types of bushes."

"Okay," Bob answered slowly. "Let me show you what I've got."

They walked to another row of vehicles. Two trucks were parked beside each other, one white, one gray. The white truck had heavily tinted windows.

"The white one would be perfect," Sandy said. "I'll be sure to bring it back clean."

"Are you sure that's what you want?"

"Yes."

"All right," he said and shrugged. "Wait here, and I'll get the keys."

The truck had been cleaned up, but it's impossible to wash away the scrapes and dents that are a work truck's badges of honor.

"This isn't a fancy demo," Bob said when

he returned. "And it's a straight shift."

"No problem. I drove a VW Beetle in high school and college. I enjoyed shifting gears."

"A Beetle had a more forgiving gearbox. Do you want me to back it out for you?"

"No, no."

Sandy got inside. Bob stepped back. Sandy rolled the window down by turning a handle.

"I haven't used one of these in a while," she said.

"It's solid with no frills. Reverse is all the way up on the left."

"I got it," Sandy said.

She pushed in the clutch, pressed on the gas, and started the engine. The truck roared to life. She quickly lifted her foot from the gas pedal.

"Strong engine," she said.

"Remember. All the way up on the left," Bob repeated. "Ease it out."

Sandy grabbed the shifter in the floorboard and pushed it toward the top left. She slowly let out the clutch. Nothing happened.

"You have to gun it a little bit to shift it into reverse," Bob said.

Sandy revved the engine and pushed the shifter up harder. The gears growled in protest but moved into place.

"Sorry," she said, smiling weakly.

"That's how it works," Bob said. "Back it out nice and easy."

Sandy gently let out the clutch and softly pressed the gas pedal. The truck shuddered for a moment, then started moving. Sandy turned the steering wheel and backed up. She stopped and moved the shifter into first gear. She leaned her head out the window.

"Thanks, Bob. Pray for me!"

"I am," Bob replied. "And I may call Barb and ask her to pray too. Be careful."

"I will."

Sandy let out the clutch and lurched forward. Bob jumped back. She reached the road in front of the car lot without slowing down and shot out into the street. It was early on Saturday morning, and fortunately the roadway was deserted. She pushed in the clutch and revved the engine as she shifted into second gear. The truck shuddered as the gear engaged. Sandy glanced in the rearview mirror as Bob Dortch, his mouth gaping open, watched her.

By the time she reached the outskirts of Tryon, Sandy was doing a better job of shifting gears. On the seat was her tote bag. Instead of student papers, lesson plans, and her laptop computer, it contained a camera and a notebook. Upon arriving in Tryon, Sandy stopped at the same convenience store where she'd bought water earlier in the week and went inside.

"Do you have a local phone book?" she asked a female clerk.

The woman reached under the counter and pulled out a thin, tattered book.

"You're welcome to look, but it's a couple of years old."

"Thanks."

Sandy opened the book to the page where "Lane" would be found. There were two people in Tryon with the last name Lane. "Ronald Lane" lived on Westerly Way, and "Jeremy Lane" lived on Saxony Lane. Sandy wrote down the street number and returned the phone book to the clerk.

"How do I get to Saxony Lane?" she asked.

The clerk gave her a puzzled look. "I have no idea. I moved here from Alabama about six weeks ago."

"Okay."

Sandy was sure someone at Barrett's Nursery would be familiar with the area. She pulled into the gravel parking lot. The nursery had a broad selection of bushes, and Sandy selected a pair of dwarf yaupon hollies from the open-air display. She put the plastic pots on a little cart and took them into a barnlike structure. A man in blue overalls was checking out another customer. Sandy waited until he finished and then set her hollies on the counter.

"Those are nice ones," the man said. "We just got them in."

"I've bought plants here before and have always been satisfied," Sandy replied.

"You look familiar. I'm Danny Barrett."

Sandy started to introduce herself but stopped. She smiled instead.

"Nice to meet you," Sandy said. "I need to go to Saxony Lane from here. Can you help me?"

"Sure. Let me ring these up."

Sandy paid in cash. Barrett tore a narrow sheet of paper from a large roll beside the cash register and took a pen from behind his left ear. He sketched a quick map. The route involved several turns.

"Who are you going to see?" he asked. "I may be able to tell you exactly where to go."

Barrett looked directly into Sandy's eyes. She couldn't think of a way to gracefully avoid the question.

"Jeremy Lane," she said as fast as she could.

"The lawyer." Barrett nodded. "We delivered a bunch of stuff to him earlier this year."

Barrett marked a spot on the road with a big *X*.

"He lives about here in a brick house with white shutters. It's landscaped real nice. His wife likes to work in the yard."

He handed Sandy the paper.

"Thanks," she said, turning away.

"Don't forget your hollies," Barrett said. "Once you pay for something, it's yours. Do you need help carrying them to your car?"

"No, thank you."

Sandy cradled the pots in her arms and left the building. She put the bushes in the back of the truck.

"Do you want me to tie those in so they don't roll around?" a voice said.

Sandy jumped. It was Barrett. He'd followed her out of the store.

"Uh, that would be nice," she said.

Barrett left and returned a minute later with a piece of twine that he wrapped around the pots and tied off to the truck bed.

"That should hold them," he said.

Sandy drove slowly out of the lot. She fought the notion that Danny Barrett had gone inside and phoned Jeremy to let him know a woman in a white pickup truck was on her way to his house.

With each turn Sandy's heart began beating faster. When she saw the sign for Saxony Lane, she paused and took a deep breath. She drove slowly down the street. A boy on a bicycle approached her. The boy was wearing a helmet, and Sandy stared intently at him. Then she remembered that Zach was only five years old and wouldn't be riding a bike alone on the street. The boy on the bike was at least twice Zack's age.

Sandy drove another hundred yards before seeing Jeremy's house. Barrett had been right. It was red brick with white shutters and a beautiful yard of green grass. The garage doors were open, and Sandy could see two vehicles, a silver minivan and Jeremy's white SUV. It was 9:15 a.m., and no one was in sight. She continued past the house. Glancing back, she saw that the backyard was fenced in with a wooden privacy fence. Rising over the top of the fence was a large play set with a crow's nest on top.

Sandy drove on down the road and turned around in a cul-de-sac. When Jeremy's house came into view the second time, she saw the young lawyer standing at the entrance to the garage. He was wearing a black golf shirt and blue jeans. A moment later, a girl wearing a soccer uniform joined him. A small boy also wearing jeans and a white shirt came into view. Chloe and Zach. Sandy pulled to the side of the street beneath a large oak tree. Actually seeing the children, even from a distance, made her heart feel like it was about to explode.

Jeremy and the children disappeared from view, but less than a minute later the silver minivan backed down the driveway. Sandy could see Leanne in the passenger seat. Sandy followed the van, being careful to maintain several car lengths' separation. She also put on sunglasses in case Jeremy looked in the rearview mirror. Jeremy and his family left the neighborhood and headed toward town. The absurdity of what she was doing hit Sandy. Was she turning into a stalker who spent all her free time spying on the Lane family? Wouldn't it be more honest to contact Jeremy, tell him who she was, and respectfully ask if he had an interest in getting to know her? While these thoughts swirled through her head, the minivan turned right into the parking lot of one of Tryon's two elementary schools. Families were milling about. Girls in soccer uniforms were walking in small groups toward a sports field where soccer nets were set up. Sandy slowed down and watched as Jeremy pulled into a parking space. Chloe hopped out of the car. She was wearing high-top blue socks and soccer shoes. Jeremy and Leanne followed carrying portable chairs. Zach ran ahead to the field. Chloe started talking to some other girls.

There was a large playground with swing sets, slides, and monkey bars at the rear of the school. From the playground area, Sandy would be able to watch the soccer game from a safe distance. She parked the truck near the playground. Jeremy and Leanne placed their chairs along the sidelines. Using the telephoto lens on her camera, Sandy snapped a few photos. The girls were warming up on the field. Chloe's team was in front of the goal nearest Sandy, so she had a good view. Warm-ups consisted of the girls kicking balls to one another. After the coaches called the teams together, a referee blew a whistle, and the game began.

Chloe was playing midfielder. Twice she kept the opposing team from kicking the ball into her team's end of the field. Then she intercepted a pass and started running toward the goal. Sandy expected her to pass off to one of the forwards, but Chloe executed a nifty move around a defender, stopped in front of the goalie, and kicked the ball into the net with her left foot. Sandy's mouth dropped open. It was an amazing shot for a ten-year-old. Chloe had frozen the goalie. The opposing team's coach yelled at his goalie and gestured with his hands. Jeremy and Leanne were standing up and cheering. Chloe's coach called her over to the sidelines, gave her a high five, and directed her to a place on the bench.

After the momentary excitement the game was a typical soccer stalemate. Even with young players, it isn't easy to score. When the referee whistled the end of the first half, the score was 1–0. During halftime, Chloe ran over to her parents. Sandy took more pictures. The second half started with Chloe playing striker. The other coach saw the shift and directed one of his players to shadow Chloe at all times. That made it hard for Chloe to get the ball. Several minutes passed before she had a chance. She dribbled toward the goal, then stopped so suddenly that the defender stumbled. Chloe kicked the ball to a teammate who was at the other end of an undefended net. The girl tapped the ball in for a goal.

"Yes!" Sandy exclaimed. "Beautiful assist."

Sandy wasn't a big soccer fan, but she was enjoying this game immensely. Zach divided his time between sitting on the grass next to his mother and running up and down the sidelines. Sandy saw him say something to Leanne, then he turned and ran in Sandy's direction. Her heart leaped into her throat. He came closer. Sandy couldn't take her eyes off him. The little boy had Brad Donnelly's hair and eyes, but there was someone else's influence in his mouth and the shape of his head. He reached the playground and began swinging on a swing. Sandy was surprised at how high he went as he pumped his sturdy little legs. Sandy reached for her camera and took some wonderful pictures. Jeremy and Leanne were focused on the soccer game. The other team scored a goal after Chloe whiffed on an attempt to kick the ball away from an offensive player, who kicked it over the goalie's head into the net.

Zach stopped swinging and trotted over to the monkey bars. He was barely tall enough to climb up to a row of horizontal bars. He grabbed hold of the top bar and swung out into space. He reached forward with his right hand and grabbed the next bar. The camera clicked rapidly as Sandy took more pictures. Zach released his left hand so it could join his right hand and twisted his body slightly to bridge the gap. Suspended in space, he swung his feet forward. Sandy snapped another photo. Suddenly Zach lost his grip with his right hand and tumbled to the ground, landing on his left shoulder.

"No!" Sandy cried, covering her mouth with her hand.

Zach rolled over and cried out in pain. He grabbed his shoulder with his right hand. His parents were on their feet cheering as Chloe's team tried to keep their opponent from scoring the tying goal. Zach tried to stand up but collapsed, crying, on the ground. Sandy dropped the camera on the seat and desperately looked around. No one was paying attention to the little boy. Sandy reached for the handle of the door to get out but then had another idea. She hit the center of the steering wheel and sounded the truck's horn. Pressing down on it again, she sounded a long blast. Leanne looked in the direction of the playground and grabbed Jeremy by the arm. He began running rapidly toward the playground, with Leanne trailing behind him. Sandy turned on the truck's engine and backed out of the parking space. As she put the truck into gear, she looked in the rearview mirror and saw Jeremy gingerly helping Zach to his feet.

Leanne, who still hadn't reached the playground, glanced at the truck, then arrived at the monkey bars where she fell on her knees in front of Zach, who leaned his head against her.

Shaking, Sandy left the parking lot. There was no doubt Zach was hurt, but she couldn't tell how serious it might be. She drove a few blocks from the school and pulled into the empty parking area for a dentist's office. She wondered if she should have jumped out of the truck to help the little boy, but she'd been frozen by indecision. Turning off the truck's engine, she leaned her head against the steering wheel to collect her thoughts and feelings.

By blowing the horn, she'd got Jeremy's and Leanne's attention. That was the best thing to do. If she'd dashed onto the scene, Zach would have been frightened by a stranger running up to him. Sandy lifted her head and saw the silver minivan pass by with its hazard lights flashing. The local hospital wasn't far away. That's where they had to be taking Zach.

Sandy wanted to go to the hospital but knew she shouldn't. Her heart ached for Zach. Her trip to Tryon had been so much more than she could have hoped for until the little boy took his tumble. She exited the parking lot. As she passed the town limits for Tryon, Sandy was praying for Zach.

After unloading the bushes at her house and sweeping out the truck bed, Sandy pulled smoothly into Bob Dortch's car lot and backed the truck into the space where it had been earlier in the day. Bob walked across the pavement toward her.

"After four hours of shifting gears, you're an expert who has to show off what she can do," he said.

Sandy handed him the keys and smiled.

"It was rough at first, but it came back to me. Thanks for letting me borrow the truck. I bought a couple of bushes at Barrett's."

"I'm glad that place isn't in Rutland," Bob said. "Barb never spends less than $200 every time we go over there."

"Maybe I'll invite her the next time I make a trip."

"Not in one of my trucks! She'll spend $500 if she has a truck to haul stuff back in." Bob motioned toward the service department. "Your car is ready. We changed the oil. Everything else checked out fine."

"Great."

"Lenny has your keys and invoice for the service."

Alone in her house, Sandy felt the ache of separation from Jeremy and his family. It was a new sensation, and Sandy wasn't sure how to handle it. After eating a sandwich, she called the hospital in Tryon.

"Is Zach Lane a patient?" she asked the woman who answered the patient information number. "He fell off the monkey bars at the elementary school a couple of hours ago."

The woman was silent for a moment.

"No," she replied. "He was treated in the emergency room and sent home."

"Okay, thanks," Sandy said with relief.

Knowing that Zach wasn't seriously injured, Sandy was able to enjoy downloading the photographs she'd taken. Some of the pictures were fuzzy due to her distance from the subjects, but she had quite a few that turned out nicely.

The photos of Zach at the playground were the clearest of all. Sandy suspected he was a wide-open little boy who kept his mother on edge. She leaned forward and looked at Jeremy. Even though he was an adult, in Sandy's mind he was still part child. The gap between the infant nursery in Atlanta and the house in Tryon was too broad for Sandy to leap over in forty-eight hours. She printed out several photos. A knock at her kitchen door interrupted her.

"Sorry I didn't call before dropping in," Jessica said. "But I went by to see Mrs. Jackson, and she wanted me to give you something."

Mildred Jackson was a woman in her early eighties who'd been the librarian at the middle school Sandy and Jessica attended. The girls had thought she was old then. Jessica handed Sandy a small linen napkin.

"She made this on the little loom she set up in the sunroom off her kitchen."

Sandy fingered the closely woven fabric.

"It's just like her to take up a new hobby at eighty-two. She said she was going to make something for me the last time I stopped by. Come in for a few minutes."

Jessica paused at the door long enough to scratch Nelson's head. Sandy put on a pot of water to brew some tea. The women sat at Sandy's kitchen table.

"How is your pregnant student doing?" Jessica asked.

"I'm doing more than I should to help her."

"What do you mean?"

Sandy shared with Jessica what she'd told Ben.

"Yesterday I drove her to Tryon so she could meet with a lawyer who could explain her legal rights to her."

"Tryon?"

"Yes, it was somebody Ben suggested."

"Who?"

A lump suddenly rose in Sandy's throat.

"Jeremy Lane," she said, trying to sound casual. "He's in his thirties. Very smart and compassionate. He has a beautiful family of his own."

"You met his family?"

"No, but he had pictures of them on his credenza," Sandy replied awkwardly.

The teapot whistled and rescued Sandy. While she brewed the tea, Jessica went to the bathroom. Sandy poured the tea into cups. Jessica liked her tea sweet, so Sandy added an extra spoonful of sugar.

"Sandy," Jessica said when she returned. "Who is this?"

Jessica had a photograph of the Lane family in her hand. Sandy dropped the teapot on the stove so abruptly that tea sloshed out onto the burner and hissed.

"Where did you —" Sandy asked.

"The printer on your computer was beeping, and I checked to see if something was

wrong. This was lying beside the monitor
—"

"I know." Sandy leaned back against the kitchen counter and closed her eyes for a moment. "That's Jeremy Lane's family."

"Why do you have pictures of his family at a soccer game?"

"Jeremy Lane is my son."

Jessica took a few steps forward and collapsed into a chair.

"How?" Jessica mumbled.

The women sat down, and Sandy told her the story. Jessica started to cry. Sandy got up to get her some tissues.

"Does your mother know?"

"No. I haven't told any of my family." Sandy paused. "I wasn't ready to tell you but didn't have much choice after you snooped around my computer and found the pictures."

"That was an accident."

"And you're closer to me than a sister. I don't mind you being the first to know."

Jessica reached across the table and squeezed Sandy's hand.

"Does Jeremy have any idea?"

"How could he? If I'd not seen the Charleston house in his parents' file years ago, I wouldn't have made the connection. But once I realized the truth, there's no denying the family resemblance."

Jessica put on her reading glasses and studied the picture.

"It's hard to tell at this distance, but he looks like Jack, and you, of course. His daughter is a Lincoln, but the little boy —"

"Favors Brad Donnelly."

"Yes." Jessica nodded.

"It was strange seeing Brad in miniature, but Zach also picked up a lot from his mom."

Jessica shook her head. Suddenly she sat upright.

"Does Jeremy know he has a twin?"

"I doubt it," Sandy replied. "The adoption agency placed the boys with families on opposite sides of the country and sealed the records."

"And I won't breathe a word to anyone about this, not even Rick." Jessica looked again at the picture. "When are you going to tell Jeremy who you are?"

"Do you think I should?" Sandy asked. "Most of the time it's the child who tries to find the birth mother. He may not want to meet me. The woman who raised him sounds like an amazing woman."

Jessica sipped tea while Sandy told her about Jeremy's adopted mom.

"That tells me you made a good choice at

the adoption agency," Jessica said. "And it's not like Jeremy is a sixteen-year-old boy who wants to run away from home and find his birth mother. At thirty-three, he has his own life and family and can relate to you as an adult. He should be thrilled to find you, and it's neat that you've ended up living so close together. I think it's meant to be."

Sandy smiled. "I had an urge to hug him and kiss his cheeks as if he were a little boy."

"That makes sense to me. Your last memory of him was in a bassinet in a hospital nursery. But you'll move past that."

"Yeah, and I need to think this over from every angle before doing anything. I don't want to be selfish."

"It would be selfish if you barged in and tried to push his mother out of the way. Tell Jeremy the truth and let him set the boundaries for your relationship with his family. That wouldn't be your responsibility."

Sandy got a faraway look in her eyes.

"When I saw his children, I thought my heart would come out of my throat," she said. "Maybe it was suppressed maternal instinct, but I've never felt that way or thought I could."

"You'll be a wonderful grandmother."

"But what if Jeremy doesn't want to have anything to do with me? In his mind, I abandoned him."

"If he feels that way after he hears your story, he's not the outstanding young man you think he is."

"And if he wants to meet his father?"

Jessica raised her eyebrows. "That's something I hadn't considered. Do you even know where Brad is? He's never been back for a reunion."

"Jimmy Caldwell pulled me aside when he was in town for Coach Cochran's retirement party and told me Brad was living near Pittsburgh and working as a salesman for a chemical company. He'd been married a couple of times and was recently divorced."

"Any children?"

"Jimmy wasn't sure."

"You didn't tell me about that."

"Did you really want to know?"

"No," Jessica admitted. "My mother prayed for Brad when we were in school together, but I never did. I guess I'm still mad at him for how he treated you."

"If you could see Jeremy and his family, you'd believe it worked out for good."

Jessica pointed to the photo.

"Do you have any more pictures? I'd love to see them."

Sandy brightened up. "Wait here."

Sharing the photos with Jessica was more fun than Sandy could have imagined. They pored over every detail. Sandy told her about Zach's fall and the trip to the hospital emergency room.

"Ouch," Jessica said. "I bet he broke his collarbone. There's not much they can do about that except put the arm in a sling and send him home. The good news is that he'll heal in no time."

"How can I find out the details?" Sandy asked. "I was surprised the hospital told me anything at all."

Jessica thought for a moment.

"Does Melissa Henry still teach kindergarten in Tryon?"

"I think so."

"Maybe she could tell you."

"But how would I ask her? I mean, she would want to know how I know Zach and why I'm interested."

"Yeah." Jessica nodded. "That wouldn't work."

The women continued to look at photographs and speculate about life in the Lane household. Jessica checked her watch.

"I'd better get going. Rick is going to think I've taken up weaving with Mrs. Jackson. I'm sorry I barged in like this, but to be able to share this with you is" — Jessica

paused as tears returned to her eyes —
"beyond words."

Sandy leaned forward and gave her friend
a hug.

"It's made it more special for me to bring
you into my new little world. It would be
lonesome to look at the pictures by myself."

Jessica touched her purse.

"You've always been willing to look at
every new batch of photos of my grandchildren without complaining."

The two women walked to the door together. Jessica put her hand on the door-
knob and turned around.

"Sandy, you deserve something good like
this to happen to you. And I'll do anything
I can to help. Anything."

TWENTY-FIVE

As usual, Sandy went to church on Sunday. Although she was surrounded by the other members of the congregation, she had a private worship service of thanksgiving to God for bringing Jeremy into her life. After the benediction, she went to lunch at a local restaurant with three women from her Sunday school class. Sandy was the youngest member of the group, two of whom were widows. The third was married to a man who often went fishing or hunting on Sunday.

"Sandy, you sure are quiet today," one woman said when there was a lull in the conversation at the table. "Is everything okay?"

"Yes. I'm just listening."

"No you weren't," another said. "You've been sitting there daydreaming about a new beau."

"That would be worth hearing about," the

third woman said.

"Sorry to disappoint you," Sandy said, "but nothing's changed in that part of my life."

"Well, something exciting is going on with you," the second woman insisted. "I can feel it."

Alarmed that she was so transparent, Sandy laughed nervously.

"I promise, if I pick up a boyfriend on the side of the road, this group will be among the first to know about it."

"That will be a lucky boy," the first woman said.

"Oh, did you hear about Bess Gibbs?" the third woman asked, perking up. "She met a fellow. They've gone out to eat four times in the past three weeks."

The conversation veered away from Sandy. As soon as she could politely do so, she excused herself.

Monday morning Sandy's normal routine was hectic enough that she didn't have time to daydream. After her third-period students left the classroom, Carol Ramsey entered.

"Sandy, please come with me," the counselor said.

"Can't do it right now. I have an honors composition class that is going to be here in the next ten minutes. I have a planning period immediately after lunch. Maybe we can —"

"Dr. Vale is sending someone to take your next class for you."

Sandy's mouth went dry.

"Does this have to do with Maria Alverez?"

"Should it?" Carol answered coldly.

"Who's going to be my sub?" Sandy asked, trying to regain her composure.

Coach Bestwick appeared at Carol's shoulder.

"Hello, Ms. Lincoln," the basketball coach said cheerily. "Dr. Vale ordered me to help a group of functionally illiterate kids learn about the finer points of English composition."

Sandy didn't smile. She handed John a folder.

"Here's an in-class writing assignment. There are four topics based on their outside reading assignments. Tell each student to choose one and then write a three-hundred-word essay with at least five paragraphs."

"Do I have to read these things?"

"No, that's my job."

Sandy and Carol left the room. The counselor stared straight ahead as they walked side by side. Instead of going to Carol's of-

fice, they went into the administrative suite.
Dr. Vale's secretary looked up.

"Go in. He's waiting for you," she said.

Everything was happening so fast. As she
followed Carol into the principal's office,
anger boiled up in Sandy. She clenched her
teeth.

Russell Vale was a former history teacher
who preferred staff meetings to the classroom. The thin, balding man was a few
years younger than Sandy and had been
recruited to Rutland High by the chairman
of the local school board. He never addressed a teacher by his or her first name.

"Ms. Lincoln," Dr. Vale said, rising from
his chair behind a glass-topped desk.
"Thanks for coming in on such short notice.
Have a seat."

Sandy nodded and sat down. Carol
scooted her chair a few inches away from
Sandy before she sat.

"Ms. Ramsey has been keeping me abreast
of the situation with Maria Alverez," Dr.
Vale began. "It's a serious matter."

Sandy didn't say anything, and the administrator cleared his throat.

"Would you agree that counseling a pregnant student is within the purview of Ms.
Ramsey's duties at the school?" he asked.

"Yes."

"And do you recall my comments about this during fall orientation?"

"Yes, but if a student —" Sandy began.

Dr. Vale held up a bony finger to silence her.

"Don't jump to any conclusions," Dr. Vale said. "A student certainly has the right to talk to any teacher. It's up to that teacher to keep the relationship within the proper boundaries. I'm here to help you know where those boundaries lie in this situation."

Dr. Vale opened the top drawer of his desk and took out a business card. He leaned forward and placed it on the edge of the desk in front of Sandy. It read, "Jeremy Lane, Attorney at Law."

Sandy swallowed.

"Ms. Ramsey took this card from the student at a meeting earlier today. I interviewed the girl, and she informed me that you took her to see Mr. Lane at his office in Tryon on Friday. Is that true?"

"Yes. We left after the school day."

"Was this meeting scheduled at the request of the student or did you initiate it?"

"I made the appointment. Given the totality of the circumstances, it seemed appropriate for the student to have access to independent legal advice."

"Why did you think that was necessary?"

Sandy looked at Carol. "Ms. Ramsey mentioned that she may try to have Maria declared legally incompetent. That's a drastic step."

Dr. Vale pursed his lips together for a moment before he spoke.

"Did Mr. Lane tell you and the student that a judge would make that determination after reviewing the facts and evidence?"

"Yes."

"And that a guardian ad litem would be appointed by the judge to advocate for the student's best interest?"

"No. He mentioned a guardian would be appointed if she were found incompetent."

Dr. Vale tapped his desk with a writing pen several times.

"Did you also take the student to see Mr. Lane because of your opposition to a woman's right to terminate an unplanned and unwanted pregnancy?"

Sandy felt her face flush. "My ideas and beliefs didn't come up."

"Have you been trying to influence the student's decision?"

Sandy tried to remember every conversation with Maria. They'd talked about options, and Sandy had encouraged her to think about the unborn baby as a person.

"I'm not forcing myself or my beliefs on

Maria, but I share openly with her when she seeks me out."

"And you're perfectly free to be supportive of her during this difficult time." Dr. Vale's eyes became steely. "But when it comes to providing counseling and specific advice, you are to defer to Ms. Ramsey. We have a responsibility to furnish professional help, and I'm going to make sure that's what the student receives."

"I will maintain a proper professional relationship with Maria," Sandy said testily. "After thirty years of teaching, I have a good grasp of my role."

"Would you agree that part of that role is following the policies of the administration of this school?"

"Yes."

"Good." Dr. Vale nodded and turned to Carol. "I think we're on the same page here."

"I don't," Carol replied. "I'm concerned that Ms. Lincoln will continue to undermine my work with the student."

"That's not what I'm hearing," Dr. Vale said.

Carol looked stone-faced but kept her mouth shut.

"Thanks to both of you," Dr. Vale said, standing to his feet. "I'd rather have tension between staff members because they care about students than deal with apathy among those who don't. Please return to your duties."

As they left the office, Sandy could tell Carol was upset. The meeting had gone better than Sandy expected.

Carol stopped and spoke, her words clipped. "I'm going to be watching your involvement in this situation closely, and I won't hesitate to bring Dr. Vale back into it if you get out of line."

Sandy put her hands on her hips. "Carol, I'm not looking for a fight, but I'm not a stranger to schoolhouse power plays either. Hopefully both of us will act in the student's best interests, and there won't be any other problems between us."

Sandy knew her words were both conciliatory and threating. In dealing with people like Carol Ramsey, it was often best to make things ambiguous. Carol spun around and walked toward her office. Sandy returned to the classroom.

The students were leaning over their desks, dutifully writing. John Bestwick was doodling on a sheet of paper.

"Thanks," Sandy said softly. "I can take over from here."

John wrote something on the sheet of

paper and slid it toward her: *Are you in trouble?*

"At the edge of it," Sandy whispered. "My heart wants to overrule my head."

John wrote again: *You have a good heart.*

"Thank you." Sandy smiled gratefully.

Toward the end of the school day, Sandy looked out the window and saw Carol and Maria walking across the parking lot. Sandy was in the middle of her lecture and stopped in midsentence to watch. Several students saw her and turned in their seats.

"Uh, and the painting on the wall in the living room in the story is one example of symbolism," Sandy continued. "Who can tell me another?"

Maria got into Carol's car.

"I know," a girl in the front of the class said.

Sandy turned toward the girl.

"Yes, Chrissie."

"The dog represents the boy escaping from the family farm and venturing into the wider world. The dog's death on the road shows how dangerous that world can be."

"Excellent."

Carol's car left the parking lot. Sandy worried that the counselor was taking Maria to the women's clinic in Atlanta.

"The world is a dangerous place," Sandy

added. "Very dangerous."

Sandy had trouble focusing during cheer-leading practice. Fortunately, she'd prepared the routine months earlier and at the beginning of practice handed out diagrams and descriptions that explained each member's role. During the second run-through, Candace took a scary spill after a series of backward flips.

"Are you okay?" Sandy rushed over as Candace slowly got to her feet.

"I twisted my ankle," she replied, rubbing the side of her left foot.

"Take it easy the rest of the day, and if it's sore tomorrow, tape it up before practice."

When Sandy left the gym at the end of practice, Maria was sitting on the floor in the hallway. She looked up when Sandy approached.

"What happened today?" Sandy asked. "I saw you leave the school with Ms. Ramsey during sixth period."

"She wanted to see my father. She took a paper for him to sign."

"What kind of paper?"

"I'm not sure. She asked me to leave the room while she talked to him."

"You went with her to your trailer?"

"Yes."

"How good is your father's English?"

"He can speak some, but he can't read much at all."

Sandy thought for a moment. "Was it a parental consent or notification form for you to have an abortion?"

"I don't understand what you mean."

Sandy repeated the question in Spanish.

"I don't know," Maria replied.

"Did you hear her say anything to him about you not being able to make your own decisions?"

"No."

"Did she leave a copy of the paper with your father?"

"No."

Several options raced through Sandy's mind.

"And she told me that I am going to see the doctor in Atlanta on Wednesday," Maria said. "We're going to meet at the school at seven-thirty in the morning."

"Is she going to take you to the women's clinic where you went the other day?"

"I think so. She called the doctor's office and said we would be there at eleven o'clock."

"Do you know the reason for the appointment?" Sandy asked, her heart sinking.

"Ms. Ramsey told me the doctor would

talk to me."

"Do you want me to ask the lawyer to help you?" Sandy asked. "He could talk to Ms. Ramsey for you."

"What would he say?"

"He would find out what she is trying to get you to do and explain it to you in a way you can understand."

"Can you talk to her for me?" Maria asked, her eyes pleading. "And you can tell me what she says in Spanish."

"No," Sandy replied. "My job is to teach, not be a counselor."

Maria looked confused. Sandy felt frustrated.

"I'll get in touch with the lawyer and see what he thinks," Sandy said.

It was too late in the day to call, but early the next morning Sandy phoned Jeremy Lane's office. Deb put her on hold for so long that Sandy thought she may have forgotten about her.

"Sorry for the wait," Deb said. "Mr. Lane was on a conference call and had to finish. He can meet with you briefly if you can be here at 4:45 p.m."

"Today?"

"Yes."

Sandy would have to cut cheerleading

practice short.

"I'll take it," she said.

When the call ended, Sandy felt a mixture of apprehension and excitement — apprehension for the serious decisions facing Maria, but excitement at the opportunity to be in the same room with Jeremy Lane. Sandy went to Maria's second-period class and summoned her into the hallway to tell her.

To avoid shortchanging the cheerleading squad, Sandy asked Meredith's mother to chaperone practice after Sandy left. She was a former cheerleader and popular with the other girls.

"They've rehearsed the routine," Sandy said when it was time for Maria and her to leave. "Let them practice basic cheers. The girls have several new ones they've come up with."

During the drive to Tryon, Sandy felt she was on a mission to save a baby's life and a teenage girl's conscience. They arrived at Jeremy's office a couple of minutes early. As they approached the entrance to the building, the door opened and a woman and a young boy came out.

It was Leanne and Zach.

Zach had his right arm in a sling decorated with superhero action figures. Leanne was wearing jeans, a lightweight tan sweater, and running shoes. They walked slowly toward Sandy and Maria. Zach had a cute nose and a surprising number of freckles. Up close, Sandy could see that the freckles came from Leanne.

"Your daddy is right," Sandy heard Leanne say to the little boy, who was pouting. "You can't play flag football until we're sure your bone is better."

They came face-to-face. Zach opened his mouth, and Sandy saw a missing tooth on the bottom.

"Will it be okay next week?" the little boy asked.

"No," Leanne said as they passed by Sandy and Maria.

Sandy turned and watched them continue down the sidewalk. Perhaps sensing her eyes on him, Zach looked over his shoulder and their eyes met. He gave her a puzzled look and pulled on his mother's sleeve. Sandy spun around and walked quickly toward the front door of office. She and Maria went inside.

"Hi," Deb said. "Have a seat, and I'll let Mr. Lane know you're here."

Deb spoke into a phone receiver and listened for a moment.

"It'll be a few minutes," she said.

Southern Living, one of Sandy's favorite magazines, was on a coffee table in front of the chair where she was sitting, but she didn't touch it.

"Was that Mr. Lane's wife and son leaving the office?" she asked.

"Did the little boy have his arm in a sling?"

"Yes."

"That's his son, Zach."

"I saw his picture on the credenza when we came in the other day. What happened to him?"

"Fell at a playground on Saturday and fractured his collarbone. It hurts, but he'll heal quickly."

"How old is he?"

"Five and a half."

"Is he in school? I know some of the kindergarten teachers in Tryon."

"He goes to a private kindergarten that's run by the church they attend."

"Which church is that?"

"Grace Fellowship. It's on the west side of town not far from the lumberyard. I go there too. You ought to visit one Sunday."

"I might do that," Sandy said, choosing her words carefully. "If I decide to go, could I call and let you know I'm coming?"

"Sure."

Deb took a card from a little rack on the

edge of her desk, wrote a phone number on it, and handed it to Sandy.

"That's my cell number on the back. Call me, and I'll meet you out front."

Sandy slipped the card into her purse.

"Thanks."

"How long have you lived in Rutland?" Deb asked.

"Except for college and a short stint teaching in Floyd County, I've been there my entire life. My father started Lincoln Insurance Services many years ago."

"That's right." Deb nodded. "Your brother Ben has been in to see Jeremy several times. There's a family resemblance."

"You think so?" Sandy swallowed. "My younger brother and I look a lot alike. Ben favors my father."

At that moment Jeremy walked out. If Deb really had an eye for common family traits, a glance at Jeremy and Sandy in the same room would be a dead giveaway.

"Hey," Jeremy said in a harried voice, then turned to his assistant. "Deb, if I get a call from Jerome Ennsworth on the Norton matter, interrupt me."

"Will do."

Sandy and Maria followed Jeremy into his office. Sandy's eyes immediately went to the credenza. The same photos were in the same places. She stole another glance at them before she sat down.

"Thanks so much for seeing us again on short notice," she began.

"Deb filled me in on the reason you wanted the appointment. Do you have the parental notification form?"

"I'm not one hundred percent sure that's what it was. The counselor didn't give Maria or her father a copy, and her father wouldn't have been able to understand what he was signing without a translator. The only people in the trailer at the time were Maria, Ms. Ramsey, and Maria's father."

"Did you hear what the counselor said to your father about the form?" Jeremy asked Maria.

"No. She told me to leave the room, and she talked to him."

"Leave the room?"

"Yes, so I went to the back bedroom and closed the door."

"Does your father understand English?"

"Enough to get by on his job. When we go shopping, he tells me to do the talking."

"What did he say about the paper after the counselor left?"

"Nothing. He got mad at me."

"Why did he get mad at you?"

"He is mad that I am pregnant."

Jeremy turned to Sandy. "Did you ask the counselor for a copy of the form?"

"No, the school principal called me into his office yesterday and made it clear I'm not supposed to give Maria any advice. He and Ms. Ramsey found out that I'd brought her to see you. I have to be careful."

"Okay," Jeremy said. "And I understand Maria has an appointment scheduled with an abortion clinic in Atlanta."

"I think so," Sandy replied.

"You don't know?"

Sandy felt her face flush.

"No, but why else would she take Maria to a doctor in Atlanta after getting her father to sign a form?"

"It makes sense, but it would be better if we knew for sure."

Jeremy pulled the lobe of his right ear with his right hand for a moment. Sandy opened her eyes in surprise. It was a gesture she and her brothers made when faced with a tough dilemma.

"This doesn't change anything I told you last week," he said to Maria. "The decision to keep, abort, or allow your baby to be adopted is up to you. Do you understand?"

Maria looked at Sandy, who translated for her.

"Yes." Maria nodded.

"What do you want to do?"

Maria looked at Sandy before she answered. Sandy held her breath.

"I do not want to kill the baby," Maria said simply. "Ms. Lincoln said to me that a baby has the right to be born and find out what kind of person it is going to be. I think this is true."

"Do you feel that way even though you did not want to get pregnant and were forced to be with the man who is the father?"

"I think so."

Jeremy typed something on his computer and sat back in his chair.

"Do you want to go to a women's health clinic in Atlanta where you may be pressured to terminate the pregnancy?"

"I don't understand," Maria said.

Sandy translated the question.

"I don't want to go to that place," Maria said after Sandy finished.

"Then the easiest way to put a stop to it would be for me to write a letter as your lawyer notifying the school system that you have made a choice not to terminate your pregnancy and warning the school officials not to seek to influence your decision." Jeremy turned to Sandy. "Translate that for her, please."

Sandy took a minute to explain Jeremy's suggestion.

"Yes, write the letter," Maria said.

Jeremy checked his watch. "I'll have Deb prepare an abbreviated attorney-client agreement while I compose a letter to the school. I'll need the full names of the counselor and principal and the address of the school."

Sandy gave him the information.

"You can wait in the reception area," Jeremy said.

This time there was no small talk. Deb's fingers flew across the keyboard. Once she stopped and spoke to Jeremy on the phone, but Sandy couldn't hear what was said.

"He's ready for you," she said.

Jeremy had two sheets of paper on the front of his desk.

"This is the attorney-client agreement," he said, pointing to one. "No fees are going to be charged, but it states that Maria wants me to act on her behalf in communicating with the school about her pregnancy."

"Can she sign this even though she's a minor?"

"Yes."

Sandy read the document out loud to Maria in English and translated it into Spanish.

"Do you want me to do this for you?" Jeremy asked Maria when Sandy finished.

"Yes," Maria said.

"Then sign here," he said. "Ms. Lincoln, you can be a witness to both our signatures."

When they finished, Jeremy handed Sandy the letter. It was addressed to both Dr. Vale and Carol Ramsey.

"What is *Bellotti v. Baird* 443 U.S. 622 (1979)?" Sandy asked after she read a sentence in the middle paragraph.

"A case that affirms a woman's right to obtain an abortion, even if she's a minor."

"Why mention that case?"

"Because the Court made it clear that the decision of whether or not to have an abortion is the prerogative of the mother, even if she's a minor. That means no one — including parents, counselors, doctors, et cetera — can pressure a young woman to have an abortion."

"Or not have one?"

"Correct. It applies both ways. The Court's purpose in the case was to protect the rights of the mother."

"But not the baby."

"That's an ongoing battle that's being fought in state legislatures and the courts all the time. None of that will affect Maria. Her situation is fairly straightforward. Once

Dr. Vale gets this letter, he'll contact the school board's attorney for an opinion, and I suspect the lawyer will tell him to back off."

Brian Winston represented the school board. Winston was part politician, part lawyer. Sandy occasionally saw him in the stands at football games eating a hot dog. She couldn't see him eager to start a legal war.

"Do you think you should prepare separate letters for Dr. Vale and Carol Ramsey?"

"It's not necessary," Jeremy said. "Both letters would say the same thing and end up in the principal's office. I've included a sentence that Maria is fully competent to exercise her reproductive rights."

"Okay."

"There's one other thing," Jeremy said. "How am I going to deliver the letter to the school before the counselor takes Maria to the clinic in Atlanta in the morning? I can't mail it, and it's too late in the day to have it sent via courier. We could fax it, but that won't guarantee personal notice."

Sandy swallowed. "You want me to take it?"

"Do you have another suggestion?"

"What if I lose my job?"

"You'll have a lawsuit for wrongful termination."

"I don't want a lawsuit. I want to teach my students."

"I understand, but there's nothing I can do to protect you in advance." Jeremy paused. "I could try to locate an off-duty sheriff's deputy who could go to Rutland in the morning to deliver the letter."

"Yes," Sandy replied immediately. "I'll be glad to pay. And it would make it more official."

Jeremy nodded. "Okay, I think that's the best way to go."

He picked up the phone and asked Deb to get in touch with the sheriff's office to find out if a deputy about to finish his shift was interested in making some easy money the following morning.

"We'll wait in here until we find out if someone is available," Jeremy said to her.

Sandy relaxed. There was no place she'd rather be than hanging out in Jeremy Lane's office.

"I saw your wife and son when they were leaving your office today," she said. "He had his arm in a sling."

"Yeah, he broke his collarbone in a fall at a playground this past weekend. Fear isn't in his vocabulary."

"Were you the same when you were a boy?"

"No, I've always been one to think things through. I'll take a risk, but not until I've considered the consequences."

"That's the way my brothers are," Sandy answered.

"Tell me about your family," Jeremy said.

Sandy felt herself blush. "Uh, you know my brother Ben. He's married with two grown sons. We have a younger brother, Jack, who lives near Chicago with his family. My father is deceased and my mother lives in Sarasota."

"No children of your own?" Jeremy asked.

Sandy bit her lower lip.

"My students are my kids," she said evasively.

"I had a teacher in the tenth grade like that." Jeremy didn't seem to notice. "I've kept up with her over the years. Do a lot of your students stay in touch?"

Sandy thought about the hundreds of Christmas cards, wedding announcements, and birth notices she received each year.

"Yes. The mailbox in front of my house doesn't have room for junk mail."

"That must be satisfying."

The phone on Jeremy's desk buzzed, and he picked it up.

"Excellent," he said after a few seconds, then hung up. "An off-duty deputy is going to deliver the letter first thing in the morning. He's on his way here now to pick it up."

"How much will he charge?" Sandy asked.

"He'll let me know."

Sandy reached into her purse and handed Jeremy one of her personal cards.

"Send me the bill."

Jeremy took the card and placed it beside his computer keyboard.

"Promise me you'll send the bill," Sandy repeated.

"You sound like my mother," Jeremy said with a smile. "I'm old enough to make decisions like that on my own."

Jeremy's use of the word *mother,* even though directed at her in jest, hit Sandy like a punch in the stomach. She hoped her face didn't reveal what she felt inside.

"Okay," she said weakly.

Jeremy stood. "Let me know how things go tomorrow. I have a hearing at ten-thirty, but I should be back before lunch, and I'm in the office all afternoon."

Jeremy extended his hand to Maria, who lightly shook it. He then reached out to Sandy. She stared at his right hand for a split second before taking it. It felt strong and smooth. She held it slightly longer than politeness dictated.

"Thanks again for seeing us on such short notice," she said, backing toward the door. "I'll call you tomorrow, and if you're not here, I'll leave a message with Deb."

Sandy and Maria went into the reception area.

"Any chance I'll see you Sunday?" Deb asked as Sandy passed by her desk.

"I'm not sure," Sandy replied. "But I'll definitely call tomorrow about Maria."

In the car, Sandy glanced over at Maria and felt guilty that she was thinking more about Jeremy and his family than the girl with the immediate crisis.

"Is there anything you want to ask me that you didn't say in front of the lawyer?" she said.

"No, but it is hard not to worry." Maria sighed. "This is like a long trip. I think about one thing, another thing, and back again to the beginning."

Sandy remembered her own pregnancy. If her mind had been a map of the United States, she would have driven to California and back several times over.

"I understand," she said. "When I was pregnant my mother told me to take it a day at a time."

Sandy drove Maria to Rosalita's trailer. A

dark-haired girl who looked to be about eight years old opened the door. Rosalita came outside and walked down the steps. Maria disappeared into the trailer. Rosalita lingered. Sandy lowered the car window.

"Thanks for helping Maria," Rosalita said to Sandy in Spanish. "She looks up to you."

"I want to be there for her."

Rosalita looked back over her shoulder at the door, which remained closed.

"Maria told you about Emilio, didn't she?" she asked.

"Yes, when we were with the lawyer the first time."

"He left with another man this morning," Rosalita said. "A friend told me they were going to Texas."

"To stay?"

"Who knows?" Rosalita shrugged. "But at least he's gone."

"Good."

"Yes. They say Emilio killed a man in Mexico."

Sandy involuntarily shivered.

"My husband drives a truck," Rosalita continued. "He's gone all week and comes home on the weekends. He bought a gun that I keep on top of the refrigerator. If Emilio tried to hurt Maria, I would shoot him."

"You should call the police and let them handle it," Sandy said. "You have little children in the house."

"Do you think the police will come here fast enough if I call them?"

"I hope so."

Rosalita smiled wryly. "It's not the same for us when we call for help. I told Maria to come stay with me if she's ever afraid."

"Have you talked to Maria about her baby?"

"Yes, I'd like to help her if she decides to keep the baby, but I have my hands full. I have three children of my own."

"You're doing a lot for her already. Taking her to school when she can't ride the bus, letting her stay here if things aren't good at her house."

"I do what I can." Rosalita rested her hand on the car door for a moment. "A lot of people do not like us being here and wish we would leave. You're different."

"I believe in doing what's right no matter what other people think. And I just want the best for Maria and her baby."

Rosalita nodded and stepped away from the car.

TWENTY-SIX

The following morning Sandy put on a business outfit. If she was called into Dr. Vale's office or to an emergency meeting of the school board, she wanted to look as professional as possible. She'd selected a pale-blue suit with a cream-colored blouse. When she inspected herself in the full-length mirror on her bathroom door, she pulled on her right earlobe and thought about Jeremy. Genetic tendencies surfaced in some of the most unexpected ways.

When she arrived at the school, a sheriff's car from Tryon was parked in front of the building. Sandy didn't know whether to sit in her car until the deputy left or go inside and face what awaited her. Deciding not to delay the inevitable, she slung her tote bag over her shoulder and marched toward the building.

"Good morning, Sandy. You look nice," a male voice to her left said.

It was John Bestwick, who jogged a couple of steps until he was beside her.

"Does the outfit have anything to do with the meeting you had in Dr. Vale's office the other day?"

"It might. I want to be prepared for anything."

The basketball coach held the door open for her.

"Don't forget what I wrote the other day about your heart," he said. "Stay sweet even if the people around you turn sour."

"Thanks," Sandy said gratefully.

She glanced toward the school office. There was no sign of a deputy, Dr. Vale, or Carol Ramsey. The principal was probably on the campus, but it was still early for Carol to be at school.

Not having homeroom responsibilities gave Sandy a few extra minutes each morning. Usually she stopped by the faculty lounge for a fresh cup of coffee. Sandy opened the door to a room full of silence. There was the usual collection of educators with coffee cups in their hands, and the sheriff's deputy. The deputy's back was to Sandy, who could see the principal reading a sheet of paper. She started to back out of the room, but the principal looked up and saw her. She froze like a student caught roaming the halls without a pass.

"Ms. Lincoln, go to my office," the principal ordered. "I'll see you there."

Everyone in the faculty lounge stared at Sandy as she turned around. She could only imagine the hubbub that would erupt as soon as Dr. Vale left the room. She walked slowly down the hall. In a few seconds, she heard a door close behind her and glanced over her shoulder. It was the deputy sheriff. He casually took out his cell phone and started tapping the screen. To him this was nothing more than an easy moonlighting opportunity.

Sandy reached the administrative offices and went inside. The school secretary wasn't in yet. Sandy was too nervous to sit so she paced back and forth. In a few moments, Dr. Vale appeared. He walked past her into his office without speaking. She followed. The principal tossed the letter onto his desk.

"Ms. Lincoln, please sit down."

Sandy sat in the same chair she'd used at the previous meeting. Dr. Vale stood beside his desk and leaned against it.

"I'll be brief," the administrator said. "Did you take Maria Alverez to meet with the lawyer who sent this letter?"

"Yes. She was concerned —"

Dr. Vale held up his hand. "This is not a

formal inquiry. I'll send the letter to the school board's attorney and refer your involvement in this matter to the personnel committee. You can return to your classroom."

Sandy was already in trouble and wasn't going to leave the office without making sure the counselor was on notice to cancel the trip to Atlanta.

"Will you give Ms. Ramsey a copy?"

"Yes," Dr. Vale replied curtly.

"Thank you."

Sandy left. When she reached the hallway she took a breath. She wasn't sure how long it had been since her last one. One of the doors at the main entrance opened, and Carol came in. She saw Sandy, and a smug expression crept across her face. Sandy looked at her with pity. This wasn't about beating Carol; it was about helping Maria do the right thing.

"Good morning, Sandy," Carol said as she passed by.

"Hey, Carol."

Sandy doubted Carol would be as stoic as Dr. Vale when she read the letter. Students passed by her classroom door on their way to homeroom. Sandy called Jeremy's office. No one answered, so she left a message.

"Please let me know if there's anything

else I should do," Sandy said as she ended the call. "Thanks again for your help."

The rest of the day passed uneventfully. During first and second periods, Sandy frequently looked out the window at Carol's car. It didn't move. By the time second period was over, she knew there was no way Carol and Maria could make it to Atlanta in time for an 11:00 a.m. appointment at the women's clinic. In between each class, Sandy expected Maria to show up, but the Hispanic girl never appeared. Even though Maria had been spared a trip to the abortion clinic in Atlanta, a cloud hung over Sandy's head.

At cheerleading practice, the satisfaction Sandy usually experienced working with the girls was absent.

"Ms. Lincoln, are you feeling okay?" Candace asked toward the end of practice.

"Yes, just distracted by a personal matter. Thanks for asking."

At eight-thirty that evening, her cell phone beeped. It was from an unknown caller.

"Hello," Sandy said.

"Ms. Lincoln, it's Maria."

"Are you okay?" Sandy asked quickly.

"I went to Atlanta with Ms. Ramsey."

"Atlanta?" Sandy asked in shock. "Why? The reason the lawyer wrote the letter to

Ms. Ramsey and Dr. Vale was to stop the trip."

"That's not what Ms. Ramsey told me. She said the appointment had been scheduled with the doctor, and it would be wrong not to go."

"When did you leave school? I saw Ms. Ramsey's car in the parking lot all day."

"A woman named Ms. Sullivan drove us."

Maria was so easily influenced by any authority figure.

"What happened at the doctor's office?"

Maria spoke in Spanish. "A woman talked to me about keeping the baby, letting someone else raise it, or having it taken out of my body while it is not a real baby. A nurse showed me a movie about girls who had done each one of those things and how they felt about it. The movie was in Spanish. Then the doctor talked to me. He spoke Spanish too. He said having the baby taken out of my body would hurt less now than if I waited until it's bigger."

Maria stopped. Sandy's heart sank. The most likely reason why Maria was so late getting back to Rutland would be the recovery time following an abortion.

"Did you let him take out —" she started.

"No," Maria replied. "He wanted to, but I told him my mother was dead, and I needed to talk to you."

"Thank God." Sandy sighed with relief. "Was Ms. Ramsey there when you said that to the doctor?"

"Yes."

"What did she say?"

"Nothing. She stayed to talk to the doctor after a nurse took me into another room where she examined me to see how I was doing. The nurse said I was very healthy."

"That's good. Why were you so late getting home?"

"After I saw the doctor, we went to another place. It was a big office building. I sat in a chair and waited for Ms. Ramsey and Ms. Sullivan for over two hours."

"Why did you go there?"

"I don't know. But I sat and sat. When we left there were many, many cars on the road. I did not know there were that many cars in the whole world."

"Rush-hour traffic doubles the time to get back to Rutland."

"Ms. Ramsey and Ms. Sullivan talked a lot on the phone. I was in the backseat and couldn't understand because they turned on the radio and spoke very fast." Maria paused. "I want you to be with me. Rosalita has to take care of her children."

"Be with you? What do you mean?"

"If I decide to let the doctor take out the baby."

Sandy was shocked by the request. Whether Dr. Vale liked it or not, Sandy was going to tell Maria what she thought.

"Maria, I don't believe you should let the doctor take out the baby. Even though it's very tiny right now, it has everything necessary to grow up into a person who can live in this world. All it needs is a safe place to be for the next seven months. Remember what we talked about with Mr. Lane?"

"But the people at the doctor's office explained to me that it's different because I did not want to be with Emilio. He made me be with him in that way and now I have this big problem."

"That's true," Sandy said, then stopped. "Maria, I'd rather talk about this with you when we can look in each other's eyes. Does that make sense to you?"

"I think so."

"Did Ms. Ramsey say anything to you about going back to Atlanta?"

"Yes, but I don't know when."

"Okay. Please come to my classroom when you have a few minutes tomorrow, and we'll set a time to get together. Will you do that?"

"Yes."

Dusty Abernathy's office in Atlanta was located north of the city near the intersection of I-75 and I-285. Clients suffering from liver damage caused by Dexadopamine didn't want to fight their way into the center of the city to meet with a lawyer. The building had three disabled-parking spots close to the entrance, with wide doors inside the office to facilitate wheelchair access. The wisdom of Fred Lyons's decision to open a satellite branch in the Southeast had been validated by an increasing number of new clients and resulting income. The money that ended up in Dusty's bank account didn't remove the sting of paying significant spousal support to Farina, but it made the pain more bearable.

Dusty lived in a rented townhome overlooking the Chattahoochee River about ten minutes from the office. The cost of the townhome was a third of the rent for a comparable place in Los Angeles. There were scores of restaurants close by, and Dusty had joined a golf club where he'd lowered his handicap three shots. After growing up near San Francisco and attending college and law school in Chicago,

Dusty found Atlanta a manageable, medium-sized city.

However, running a solo law office was a culture shock. Dusty regularly talked with the lawyers at Jenkins and Lyons, but a conference call wasn't the same as multiple contacts with fellow attorneys throughout the workday. The eerie quiet made him uneasy, and he missed the frenetic, noisy, argumentative environment of L.A.

Dusty hired a secretary and paralegal the week after being admitted to the Georgia bar. The secretary lasted a month. The Southern accent Dusty found charming during the interview hid a serious lack of basic grammar skills that needed more remedial work than he was willing to provide. His new paralegal, Valerie Sanders, was a great find. Valerie had good administrative skills, but her most valuable asset was the ability to establish great rapport with clients. Sick people who found a listening ear when they called the office made fewer demands on Dusty, leaving him free to focus on moving their cases through the legal system to a lucrative conclusion. After Dusty terminated the first secretary, Valerie contacted a woman she knew from a former firm who jumped at the opportunity to earn an extra $10,000 per year, even though she knew the job wasn't permanent. Cynthia Campbell was a fast word processor familiar with the peculiar quirks of Georgia litigation practice.

It was a clear, crisp morning. Dusty got out of his expensive sports car and looked up as a military cargo jet from nearby Dobbins Air Reserve Base flew over. The first time he saw a C-5 Galaxy overhead, he did a double take at the size of the massive airfreighter that crept slowly across the sky. Inside the office, he hung his sport coat on a hook behind the door and listened to the messages on his voice mail.

"Hey, brother," his sister, Lydia, said. "George and I are going to be coming through Atlanta from D.C. in a couple of weeks and thought we might spend the night with you on our way to the Gulf. Don't worry; we're going to board Buddy. Give me a call or send me an e-mail."

Lydia was eighteen months younger than Dusty. Her delivery had been tough on Dusty's mother, and after she was born, their parents decided not to have any more children. The siblings bore little resemblance to each other. Lydia was fair-haired, with her father's Roman nose and brown eyes, and her mother's small frame. Dusty had none of those characteristics. When new acquaintances commented on the lack of common family traits for the siblings, their parents laughed and chalked it up to a large German and English gene pool.

Lydia's husband, George, was a bureaucrat with the U.S. Department of Commerce, and in Dusty's opinion, a government leech. However, Dusty would put up with George for a day to see his sister. Buddy was the couple's Jack Russell terrier. Any shoe left on the floor in a house visited by the dog was treated as a surrogate rat and fair game for vigorous chewing. Dusty sent a short e-mail to his sister asking for more specific information about the visit.

There were three messages from existing clients and an inquiry about Dexadopamine from a potential new one. Dusty wrote down the man's name and number and put a star beside it. It was too early to call, but at 8:30 a.m. sharp he would try to reach the prospective client. Injured people who wanted to hire a lawyer often went down a list calling multiple attorneys and leaving messages for them all. The first lawyer to return the call had a good shot at getting the case. A call back before 9:00 a.m. showed the injured person that Dusty came to work early. The fifth message in his voice mail was from Shania Dawkins.

"Hey, Dusty. Good morning. I could have left a message on your cell, but I thought it would be nice for you to hear a friendly voice on your office machine. Dinner was great the other night, and I hope to see you again soon."

Shania was from Gainesville, Florida. Unlike the fired secretary, her Southern accent wasn't a smoke screen for grammatical ignorance. She had a graduate degree from Georgetown and worked for a global non-profit organization that focused on women's rights nationally and internationally. The spunky young woman with dark curly hair had been in as many countries as Dusty had courtrooms. They met at a social event sponsored by the golf club and had gone out to dinner several times since. Dusty enjoyed talking with Shania as much as any woman he'd ever met. She had the ability to combine logic with emotion in a way that would have made her a terrific trial lawyer; however, she'd decided to use her skills to organize and lobby for women subjected to everything from household slavery and polygamy in third-world countries to denial of equal pay and reproductive freedom in Western societies. Shania's goal in life was to do as much good as she could regardless of financial reward. Dusty wanted to help people too, but he liked to get paid to do it.

Dusty logged on to his computer. He pulled up a new case he'd taken a few weeks earlier and began reading medical records obtained by Valerie. The human liver can fail for many reasons or for no known reason at all. A key aspect of every Dexadopamine case was linkage between a person's use of the supplement and a quantifiable decline in liver function without any other intervening causes. Dusty could interpret lab reports with the expertise of a hepatologist.

When the clock reached 8:30 a.m., he called the potential client. The man sleepily answered the phone, and they set an appointment for the following afternoon. Cynthia buzzed his office.

"Dusty, are you in there?"

"I've been here since seven."

"You sure are quiet."

"Lab reports have a way of keeping a lid on my excitement level."

"Maybe this will excite you," Cynthia replied. "Shania Dawkins is on line 3."

Dusty pushed the button.

"Thanks for the message," he said. "I enjoyed dinner too."

"Great. Do you have a minute? I have something important to talk to you about."

"Sure."

"It's something I'd like us to do together."

Dusty sat up straighter in his chair. He knew Shania liked him, but he was surprised she'd been thinking of ways to spend more time with him.

"Yes."

"What is your firm's policy on pro bono work?"

"Uh, most of our pro bono work is used up on the contingency cases we lose."

"This isn't a contingency case. It has to do with coercion of a mentally challenged, pregnant girl by a right-wing high school teacher."

Dusty hesitated. Pleasing Shania might be worth a legal detour without monetary compensation.

TWENTY-SEVEN

As soon as first period ended, Sandy went to her car and called Jeremy's office.

"Deb, this is Sandy Lincoln. Is Jeremy available?"

"No, but he should be here any second. Would you like to leave him a voice mail?"

"Uh, could you put me on hold and let me wait? I'm between classes and need to talk to him."

Sandy tried to relax. She'd not seen either Dr. Vale or Carol when she arrived at the school that morning, but she knew discussions and meetings about her involvement with Maria were taking place all over Rutland.

"Hello," Jeremy said when he came on the line. "I got your message about delivery of the letter. What's been the response?"

"The counselor ignored it. She took Maria to the women's clinic in Atlanta anyway."

Sandy told him what she'd learned

from Maria.

"That's not totally unexpected," Jeremy said when she finished. "I knew this might happen."

"You did?" Sandy asked in surprise. "I thought they'd have to obey your letter."

"The letter put the administration on notice of Maria's right to decide what she wants to do about the pregnancy at the time I met with her. Under the law, the choice is still hers. From what you're saying, she made a voluntary decision to go to the clinic. The letter has authority so long as it reflects Maria's current state of mind. The issue at this point is whether, considering all the facts and circumstances, the counselor exerted improper influence on Maria."

"She told Maria it would be wrong to cancel the appointment. That's not true."

"But does that constitute coercion?"

"Who are you representing here?" Sandy shot back.

Jeremy was silent for a moment.

"Ms. Lincoln, you asked me to advise Maria about her legal rights. That's what I'm trying to do. You're a teacher, but you're also a woman who cares about this girl. When I talked to Maria in my office, I tried to educate her about her options in a way that emphasized the life of the child within her. There's value in letting the principal and counselor know someone is watching the situation and prepared to respond on her behalf."

Sandy was confused.

"This isn't how I thought it would work. I just want her to do the right thing."

"I know you do, but the real battle for this baby will be fought in Maria's mind."

"She's so easily swayed."

"Yet neither of us thinks she needs a guardian."

Sandy wasn't sure exactly what she thought about Jeremy Lane as a lawyer. He seemed to be talking in circles. She checked her watch.

"What should I do next?"

"Continue to find out everything you can. And ask Maria if she wants me to write another letter."

"Another letter?" Sandy asked in shock. "The first one didn't do any good."

"With Maria's permission, I'll notify them to advise me of any contact they have with her."

Sandy checked her watch again.

"Look, I've got to get to class. I'll mention the possibility of another letter to Maria, but it sounds like a waste of time."

"I understand. I'm not trying to force

myself into the situation."

"I know," Sandy said quickly. "Sorry for venting."

"It's okay. You care."

Care or not, Jeremy had kept his cool when she didn't. Sandy returned to her classroom.

Shortly before first lunch period ended, Maria came by as Sandy was finishing up with another student.

"How are you?" Sandy asked as soon as she and Maria were alone.

"I felt a little sick this morning, but I didn't throw up."

"Good. Have you talked with Ms. Ramsey?"

"No, but she usually finds me in the afternoon."

Sandy told Maria about her conversation with Jeremy Lane.

"He can write another letter to Dr. Vale and Ms. Ramsey," Sandy said, "but it won't do any good unless you make Ms. Ramsey obey the letter."

Maria glanced down at the floor for a moment.

"It's hard for me. When I talk to you I feel one way, but I feel another way when I talk to her."

In Maria's presence Sandy didn't have the heart to scold her. The pregnant student was a sixteen-year-old girl with a limited education and deprived cultural background. Everyone in her world was a dominant authority figure.

"I'm not mad at you," Sandy reassured her in a soft voice. "But I think it would be a good idea if you talk to Mr. Lane and me before making any big decisions. I'm here for you anytime, day or night. You know that, don't you?"

Maria nodded. "Yes."

"And Mr. Lane can give you advice about the law."

"Sometimes he uses words I don't understand, but I act like I do."

"Tell me when that happens. Do you want him to write a second letter?"

Maria hesitated. "No, I want him to talk to you, then you can talk to me."

"That will only work if you let me know what Ms. Ramsey says," Sandy responded patiently. "Will you do that?"

"Yes."

"Okay, I'll let Mr. Lane know."

During her lunch break, Sandy didn't go to the cafeteria but closed the door of her classroom and called Jeremy's office. He wasn't in.

"You can give me a detailed message if you like," Deb said. "We talked about Maria this morning after he spoke with you."

Sandy hesitated; however, Jeremy seemed to rely on his assistant. She told Deb about her conversation with Maria.

"Got it," Deb said when she finished. "We'll try to make that work. All of us want to avoid what happened to the woman in Florida who filed a lawsuit against a doctor and his clinic for a forced abortion."

"Forced abortion?"

"Sounds like something from China, doesn't it? The woman told the doctor to stop at the very beginning of the procedure, but he didn't. He ended up perforating her uterus and pulling out part of her intestines while workers at the clinic held her down. He claimed it was a busy day, and he didn't have time to argue with her since she'd already signed consent papers."

Sandy's stomach turned over. She definitely wouldn't be eating any lunch.

"We can't let anything like that happen to Maria," she said numbly.

When the call ended Sandy leaned back in her chair. She knew the statistics. Since *Roe v. Wade* millions of babies had died — a large percentage of an entire generation wiped out. And countless women were dealing with nagging questions, lingering regrets, physical trauma, and crushing psychological problems.

The horror of what had happened to Angelica came back with fresh pain. Angelica's trip to the emergency room to treat her uncontrolled bleeding, although not as terrible as the injuries suffered by the woman in Florida, was nevertheless hurt piled upon hurt.

Thinking about Angelica, Sandy's determination to help Maria, regardless of the personal consequences to herself, stiffened. Maria was one among the millions of young pregnant women in America, but she was the one in Sandy's basket. If Maria wanted to give her baby a chance at life, Sandy would do everything she could to help make that happen.

During her afternoon walk with Nelson, Sandy heard a car horn beep behind her. Jessica pulled over to the curb and lowered the passenger window of her car. Sandy leaned in the window.

"Get in, and we'll sit here for a minute," Jessica said. "I have to hear the latest. It's all I've been thinking about."

Sandy tied Nelson to a nearby tree.

"It's been a roller-coaster ride," Sandy said, "but not because of Jeremy. It has to do with the pregnant girl I'm trying to help."

"I'm praying for her, but I can't get Jeremy out of my mind. Have you seen him again?"

"Yes."

Sandy told her about the second trip to the lawyer's office, including the encounter with Leanne and Zach.

"I'm glad Zach is going to be okay," Jessica said. "I thought it might be a collarbone fracture from the way you described the fall."

"I can't wait for you to meet them."

"When is that going to happen?" Jessica asked impatiently. "Life isn't supposed to be a masquerade ball. Eventually you're going to have to take off the mask and let Jeremy know who you are."

"I know." Sandy sighed. "Right now I can stay in touch with him because of the pregnant student. At some point that's going to end."

"Have you decided how to break the news that you're his mother? It has to be in person."

"Are you sure? If he isn't excited about it, then he'll be trapped into pretending he is. I did some research on the Internet, and most birth mothers and adoptees begin with a long-distance communication to find out if the other person is interested in knowing about their birth history."

"That might be true if he were living in Alaska and you'd never seen each other. But people on the east side of Rutland buy groceries in Tryon. You're practically next-door neighbors. Think about all the places he could have gone after graduating from law school."

"I have," Sandy admitted.

"Well, if you don't do something, maybe I will. He needs to hear from you — sooner rather than later."

Sandy's hands suddenly started perspiring. She rubbed her palms together.

"It makes me nervous to think about it."

"You wouldn't be normal if it didn't. Take along a few photos of your family to show him. Do you still have that picture of us in your mother's kitchen about a month before your babies were born?"

"Are you serious? I looked like a giant human basketball."

Jessica patted her on the arm.

"A cute basketball. I have a copy if you don't. The sweet expression on your face still makes me smile. When he sees that, he'll know you didn't resent carrying him around for nine months."

"I just don't know when and how to tell him."

"If you don't act soon, I'm going to put on an old-fashioned print dress, mysteriously show up in Jeremy's life someday in the near future, and tell him about you. Then I'll disappear, just like the woman you met years ago at the gas station."

"I don't think you could pull that off." Sandy laughed.

"Don't dare me," Jessica replied. "Remember when I jumped out of the maple tree in your backyard on a dare?"

"And sprained your ankle so badly you had to use crutches for a week."

Jessica drove away, and Sandy continued her walk past the street where the Donnelly family formerly lived. In addition to curiosity about his father, Jeremy was sure to have questions about "Baby Smith." The existence of a twin brother might cause Jeremy to launch his own search, and as a lawyer, he'd likely be successful. The thought that she might someday be reunited with both her sons sent a tingle down Sandy's spine, followed immediately by a shudder as she remembered the old woman's warning. Unlike Jessica's idle threat, the woman's words retained their power after thirty-three years.

Trying to explain to Jeremy why she'd separated him from his brother at birth would be hard. Asking him not to find his brother would be impossible. As she turned the corner toward home, Sandy considered another possibility — not telling Jeremy he had a brother at all.

The following morning Sandy was in the teachers' lounge pouring a cup of coffee when Kelli Bollinger came over to her.

"That's a cute skirt," Kelli said. "Where did you get it?"

"On sale at Blake's," Sandy replied.

"I like their clothes, but I never find anything there I can afford." Kelli leaned in closer. "How is the situation going with the pregnant student? I heard a police officer served papers on Dr. Vale."

Before Sandy could respond, the door opened and a tall, young deputy sheriff wearing a Rutland County uniform entered.

"Is Ms. Sandra Lincoln here?" the deputy asked in an official-sounding voice.

Sandy swallowed and raised her hand like a student with little chance of knowing the answer to a difficult question.

"That's me," she said.

"This is for you," the deputy announced, handing her a thick envelope.

"What is it?" Sandy asked.

"You'll need to open it to find out," the deputy replied. "I'm just serving the papers."

"Uh, thank you."

The deputy left. Sandy stared at the envelope. There was a return label in the top-left corner — Jenkins & Lyons, with an address in Atlanta. She turned to Kelli.

"I guess I have to open this, don't I?"

"Yes, but not in here. Find someplace private."

Sandy left the lounge. As she walked down the hall, coffee sloshed out of the cup and a few drops splattered the front of her skirt. When she reached her room, a student from her third-period class was waiting for her with a paper in her hand. Sandy could see the red ink almost dripping from where she'd corrected the student's work.

"Not now, Gloria," Sandy said. "Try to get to class a couple of minutes early, and I'll explain my comments."

"But I want to work on revisions during my second-period study hall," the student protested. "You said today was the last chance we had to make changes."

Sandy thrust out her hand. "Give it to me."

As quickly and efficiently as she could,

Sandy explained to Gloria that it isn't a good idea to have two topic sentences in the same paragraph and why it's important for there to be agreement between a sentence's subject and verb.

"Turn this paragraph into two and check the sentences I marked for subject-verb agreement problems," she said. "That's what this symbol means."

"Oh," Gloria replied. "I missed the day when you explained the abbreviations. That helps a lot."

As soon as Gloria left, Sandy ripped open the envelope. Printed at the top was *In the United States District Court for the Northern District of Georgia.* Beneath the heading were the words *In Re: Sandra H. Lincoln,* followed by *Motion for Temporary Restraining Order.*

Sandy read as fast as she could. The general intent of the motion quickly became clear. Someone had hired a lawyer in Atlanta to file a legal action in federal court claiming that Sandy had violated Maria's civil rights by wrongfully interfering with her reproductive freedom. The motion also alleged that Maria was mentally incompetent and needed a court-appointed guardian. This claim was followed by a reference to a related petition that was being filed in the juvenile court in Rutland seeking appointment of a guardian. The motion asked that Sandy be ordered not to communicate with Maria or else face a citation for contempt of court. The papers were signed by a lawyer named Dustin Abernathy, a member of the Georgia, Illinois, and California bars.

The motion itself was merely the first part of the paperwork. Attached was a *Notice of Hearing* for the following week at the Richard B. Russell Federal Building in Atlanta. Sandy blanched at the thought of being forced to drive to Atlanta to appear in front of a federal judge. Following the notice was a ten-page brief that set out facts about Sandy's involvement with Maria and several pages of legal arguments in support of the motion. Sandy saw a reference to a women's rights organization and turned back to the first page of the motion. The organization was mentioned in one of the opening paragraphs and appeared to be responsible for hiring the lawyer.

Students started coming in for first-period class. Sandy folded up the paperwork and slipped it into her tote bag. Fifteen minutes later, while the students worked on a class assignment, she glanced down at the bag. She wanted to read the papers again but knew she had classroom responsibilities. When the class ended, she didn't have time to sneak away and inform Jeremy of the latest development before another group of students arrived.

It wasn't until her lunch break that Sandy could leave the building. Sitting in her car, she unfolded the motion and phoned Jeremy's office. Deb Bridges answered.

"Is Jeremy available?" Sandy asked. "It's an emergency."

While she waited on hold, Sandy felt like such a nuisance. She'd initially contacted Jeremy for a onetime appointment to help Maria know her rights. Since then, the situation had snowballed. And now, with service of the motion and reference to an incompetency proceeding, the snowball had the makings of an avalanche.

"What's the latest?" Jeremy asked when he picked up the call.

"A lot," Sandy replied.

After she read the first few paragraphs of the motion, she paused for a moment and Jeremy spoke.

"Maria mentioned going someplace in Atlanta with the counselor after the appointment at the women's clinic, didn't she?"

"Yes, she had to wait on Carol and the woman named Ms. Sullivan for a couple of hours at an office building."

"My guess is they stopped by the head-quarters of the organization mentioned in the pleadings. What does the motion say in the prayer?"

"The prayer?"

"The request for relief that appears above the lawyer's signature on the last page. It should begin with something like 'Where-fore, the Court is hereby requested to, et cetera.' "

Sandy turned to the final page of the motion.

"Yes," she said. "Here it is."

She read the language to Jeremy.

"When is the notice of hearing on the motion?" he asked.

"Next Wednesday morning at ten-thirty at the Richard B. Russell Building."

"Hold on," Jeremy said.

Sandy waited.

"I can do it if we're back here by four o'clock. I have a hearing on a motion for summary judgment that can't be post-poned."

"You're going to help me?"

"Of course. But this case may go way beyond a fight over who gets to talk to Ma-ria."

"What do you mean?"

"When a women's outfit like this gets

involved in litigation, it's often because the leaders of the group want to obtain a legal precedent that can be used to advance their goals in other situations, locally and nationally. Who's the judge assigned to hear the case? It should be listed someplace on the notice of hearing."

Sandy read the sheet.

"I don't see a name. It just gives the number of the courtroom."

"Turn to the first page and see if there are initials beside the case number."

"Yes, it says *WST.*"

"That's the judge. His name is Wendell S. Tompkins."

"Do you know him?"

"I've only appeared in front of him one time, but I know his reputation."

Sandy swallowed. "Good or bad."

"Not good. There may have been some judge-shopping going on when the motion was filed."

"Judge-shopping?"

"It's hard to pull off, but sometimes a party to a lawsuit will try to get a case assigned to a judge who will be more likely to rule in their favor. Because federal judges are appointed for life and don't have to answer to anyone, they can be notoriously unpredictable. Judge Tompkins has a history of stretching the limits of judicial power. And that's exactly what this motion is trying to do."

Sandy's head was spinning.

"What am I supposed to do?" she asked.

"Scan and e-mail a copy of the papers you received to me. Deb will send you a contract so I can represent you. Once we're set, I'll file a notice of appearance with the court and notify opposing counsel. The preliminary hearing next week is the first volley in the war, not the last shot. I'll be planning for all contingencies."

"What kind of contingencies?"

"That will be part of my research. But at this point the motion isn't seeking money damages. The goal is to obtain a court order and dare you to violate it."

Sandy thought about the resolve she'd felt the previous night. It seemed less rock-solid.

"Since there's no order in place, you can still communicate with Maria," Jeremy said. "The motion also mentioned a juvenile court action in Rutland. If that's been filed, it will be served on Maria and her father. Get me a copy of that as soon as you can too."

"Okay. This sounds so complicated. What are you going to charge me?"

"An hourly rate will be set out in the

contract, but I'll waive any deposit. I'll continue to help Maria on a pro bono basis."

Sandy swallowed. Her convictions were about to cost her real dollars.

"If my suspicion proves correct that the women's group wants to obtain a broad legal precedent, there may be national prolife advocacy groups willing to get involved to counter those efforts."

Jeremy was looking far down the road. Sandy wasn't sure what she might face when she left her car and returned to the school building.

"How soon can you get me a copy of the papers you received?" Jeremy asked.

"Uh, I can send them from the computer in the basketball coach's office. It's on the school network, of course, but it's in a private location."

"Is there a rule against using the school computers for personal use?"

"Yes, but it's only applied if there's an abuse of the system."

"Use your judgment. I'll be in touch."

The call ended. Sandy checked the time. If she hurried, she could get to John Bestwick's office and send the information before her next class started.

TWENTY-EIGHT

Sandy walked rapidly down the hallway. She barely acknowledged greetings from students who passed by. She crossed the basketball court. The office door was closed. Coach Bestwick often left the campus to eat lunch with boosters of the basketball team. Sandy threw open the door and charged in.

"Huh, what?"

A startled John Bestwick dropped his feet from his desk to the floor.

"Sorry," Sandy said, stopping in her tracks. "I thought you'd probably be at lunch. I didn't mean to barge in on you."

"It's okay," John replied, wiping his eyes. "I subbed for Mr. Gaston's sociology class this morning and almost put myself to sleep."

Sandy turned around to leave.

"Hold on. You had a reason for coming. Don't let me stop you."

Sandy squeezed the papers in her hand.

"It's personal. I need to use the scanner."

"Something to do with the deputy sheriff coming by to see you this morning in the faculty lounge?"

"You heard about that?"

John pushed away from the desk.

"Sandy, first, a deputy sheriff from Tryon serves papers on Dr. Vale. Now, a local constable calls on you. Some people claim the incidents are related. Others claim they aren't. The most logical guess is divorce papers; however, unless you secretly got married in Vegas and didn't invite me to the wedding, I'm going to toss that rumor to the side."

Sandy managed a slight smile. John stood up.

"Just don't turn me in for taking a short nap. I worked until ten o'clock last night."

"Your secret is safe with me."

"And yours with me." John's face became serious. "I'm not going to pry into your business, but if there's anything I can do to help, let me know. In the meantime, I'm going to defend your honor to the max."

"Thanks," Sandy said gratefully.

As soon as the coach left, Sandy logged on to the computer and placed the papers she'd received on the scanner. After they were sent to Jeremy, she returned to her classroom where a dull roar of conversation greeted her. Sandy clapped her hands together and cleared her throat.

"Turn to page 287 in your literature books."

Sandy was uneasy the rest of the day. The notoriety caused by the deputy in the teachers' lounge was similar to the reactions from others she had experienced when her pregnancy became common knowledge. There were questions on every face she encountered. Knowing it's impossible to control a rumor mill, Sandy kept her mouth shut. Efforts to stop the mill often gave it greater power. At cheerleading practice she tried to act normal, and as practice progressed the girls slipped into familiar patterns.

During her afternoon walk several cars seemed to slow down as they passed by, and Sandy had to push away thoughts of paranoia. Later, she logged on to her computer and printed off the attorney-client contract sent by Jeremy. She stared, bug-eyed, at the hourly billing rate. Legal representation could end up costing her the price of a car at Bob Dortch's auto lot. Sandy had counted the emotional and professional cost of helping Maria. Now she had to face the financial cost. She checked her bank account. Most of her savings, accumulated in small increments over the years, was tied up in investments recommended by Ben. She'd have to ask him for advice on which ones to sell. Before getting more depressed, she signed the contract and sent it back to Jeremy. She was in too deep to back out now.

While eating supper, her cell phone beeped. It was Ben.

"Hey, brother," she said.

"When were you going to call me?" Ben asked.

"What did you hear?"

"That a sheriff's deputy served you with legal papers this morning at the high school. Three people called to let me know about it and ask what was going on. Does this have anything to do with the pregnant student you're helping?"

"Yes, and I'm sorry I didn't let you know," Sandy said. "I was thinking about you when I checked my bank account earlier."

"Your bank account?"

"Yes. I'm going to have to hire Jeremy Lane to represent me."

Sandy quickly told Ben what had happened, but he wasn't satisfied with a condensed version. He made her read several paragraphs of the motion and the brief.

"The newspaper is going to find out about this," he said when she finished. "You need to decide what you're going to say when a reporter calls."

Sandy hadn't considered the possibility of media interest.

"And I'm not just talking about the Rutland paper," Ben continued. "This is the sort of thing that newspapers all over the country might pick up. The women's organization in Atlanta probably has a publicity angle it wants to work."

"I hadn't thought about reporters. I guess I'll tell anyone who calls to speak to Jeremy."

"I'm not sure that's a good idea." Ben paused. "He's a sharp young lawyer for a town like Tryon, but you're going to need an attorney who's used to playing on a bigger stage."

"He mentioned the possibility of getting help from national pro-life groups."

"You can't count on that. I'm going to make some calls and try to find a lawyer with more experience to protect you."

"Thanks, but I want to stay with Jeremy."

"Why? You barely know him."

Sandy paused and took a deep breath.

"Because he's my son."

It wasn't the way Sandy wanted to tell Ben

about Jeremy, but her brother deserved to know the truth. There was nothing but silence on the other end of the phone.

"How do you know?" Ben asked after a few moments.

"Is Betsy there? I'd like both of you to hear this at the same time."

"I'll tell her to pick up on the phone in the kitchen."

Sandy waited for a minute until her sister-in-law came on the line.

"Hi, Sandy. What's up?"

When Sandy repeated her news about Jeremy, she heard Betsy gasp. Sandy told them about the first meeting in Jeremy's office and the photograph on the corner of his desk.

"And you're sure it's the same house?" Ben asked.

"No doubt about it. And Jeremy mentioned that one reason he was willing to help my student is because he's an adoptee. Think about it. Doesn't he look like Jack?"

"Maybe a little."

"And when I researched him on the Internet, I found out that he was born in Atlanta on April 5, 1975. That's the day the twins were born."

"Sandy, this is amazing," Betsy said. "When are you going to tell him?"

"I don't know, but I'm going to have to do it soon."

"Who else knows?" Betsy asked.

"Only Jessica. She found out by accident the other day when she came by the house and saw a photograph of Jeremy's family beside my computer."

"You're going to have to tell Mama too," Ben said. "And Jack."

"I know, I know," Sandy said, "but I barely have my head around the situation myself. Then all this came up with the lawsuit. I need to think about helping the student, but I'm distracted by Jeremy and his family." Sandy paused. "Betsy, he has the cutest kids, a little girl and a boy. She looks like a Lincoln. The little boy favors Jeremy's birth father."

"Sandy, you're a grandmother!" Betsy exclaimed.

"Yes, and I'm desperate to give them a hug."

"Hold on to something else for a minute," Ben said. "We still need to figure out what you need to do about an attorney. This personal connection makes it less appropriate for Jeremy to represent you. Your lawyer needs to be focused on the case, not learning about his mother."

There was logic to Ben's point.

"You may be right," Sandy admitted. "Let me think about it. Jeremy said the hearing next week is just a preliminary matter, the first shot in a bigger battle. Maybe I can decide after that."

"I'm not going to wait," Ben said. "Tomorrow morning I'm going to start making some phone calls. I've had some recent dealings with a lawyer at a big firm in Atlanta who may be able to give me a recommendation. You need a constitutional lawyer with experience in that area."

"A son and two grandchildren!" Betsy cut in.

"And he has a lovely wife," Sandy said. "Ben, you've met her."

"Yes," Ben sighed. "Leanne Lane is an attractive woman who seems to love her husband and kids. She asked several good questions when I met with them about their insurance plan."

"Smart too," Betsy said. "Sandy, with you in the children's bloodline, the kids are probably geniuses."

"Okay, ladies," Ben said. "Is there any thing else we need to talk about?"

"Yes," Betsy responded immedia "When can I come over and see the p Jessica saw? Do you have any others

"Tomorrow," Sandy replied. "

bunch of pictures the other day when I followed them around in Tryon."

"You spied on them?" Ben asked.

"Yes, and I'm glad I did," Sandy shot back.

"Me too," Betsy said. "Call me when you get in from your walk tomorrow afternoon and I'll be right over. This is so exciting!"

The following morning Maria came by Sandy's classroom before first period. She was holding some papers in her hand.

"Come in," Sandy said. "I think I know what you have."

"A man from the police gave this to my father."

Sandy took the papers from Maria and read them. It was a petition filed in juvenile court in Rutland claiming that Maria was mentally incompetent and needed a guardian appointed as soon as possible.

"What does it mean?" Maria asked. "Rosalita and I couldn't understand it."

Sandy explained in Spanish about the ~tion. Maria looked even more puzzled.

b~ English is not perfect, but it's getting ~and better. And I'm passing all my

matio~ot the point. I'll send this information~

Mr. Lane, the lawyer. He already

knows about it and is willing to help you for free."

"What should I tell my father? After the policeman came to our trailer, my father told me this is causing too much trouble for our family and that I should stop listening to you."

"He blames me?"

"I told him you are trying to help, but he didn't believe me. He said you just want me to do what you want me to do."

"Do you feel that way?" Sandy asked, realizing it would be a question that would come up at some point in the lawsuit filed against her.

"A little bit."

"How can I help without making you feel like I'm trying to make you do something?"

Maria didn't answer. Instead, a tear rolled down her cheek. Sandy dropped the legal papers on the desk and wrapped the girl in her arms. Maria buried her head in Sandy's shoulder and cried. After a couple of minutes passed, Sandy glanced up at the clock in the rear of the classroom. Students would start arriving shortly. She gently separated herself from Maria. The girl wiped her eyes with the back of her hand.

"My shoulder is here anytime you need it," Sandy said softly.

"Thank you." Maria sniffled. "That is what I need the most."

"Have you heard from Ms. Ramsey?" Sandy asked.

"I go to her office later this morning."

"What time?"

"Second period. She gave Ms. Harrison a note taking me out of class."

Sandy bit her lip. She wanted to tell Maria before she left not to keep the appointment with Carol, but she didn't.

As soon as Sandy's class was in their seats, she gave them an assignment and hurriedly walked to Coach Bestwick's office. Five minutes later the petition was scanned and on its way to Jeremy.

During her lunch period, Sandy felt multiple eyes following her down the line at the salad bar. When she sat with some fellow teachers, the conversation around the table stopped. Several women greeted her, but no one asked her any questions. She ate her salad in silence. The other people at the table drifted away, leaving her alone with Kelli Bollinger.

"I think people are afraid that if they're seen with you, some of the taint will rub off," Kelli said.

"That's understandable. It's never smart

to take on the administration in public education."

"Unless you're doing the right thing."

"Any advice?" Sandy asked.

"I realize you can't tell me anything that Maria has shared with you in confidence, but you have support among the staff."

"Is that why the other teachers left the table as soon as they could?"

"Everyone knows you have a good head on your shoulders and wouldn't do anything improper or unprofessional." Kelli leaned forward. "And no one on the faculty has as much support in the general community as you do. I mean, every woman who's been a cheerleader during the past twenty-five years would rally for you if asked to do so. And they'd make their husbands join them."

"This isn't going to be a popularity contest with women carrying signs in front of the school," Sandy replied. "It's moved into the court system. I've had to hire a lawyer."

Kelli's eyes grew big. "Then you may need to take your crowd to the courtroom."

Sandy hadn't thought about turning the lawsuit into a public spectacle. Images of former students carrying signs outside the federal courtroom in Atlanta flashed through her mind.

"That's something I need to mention to

my lawyer," Sandy replied. "My head's still spinning about what's happened."

"And I can pray for you," Kelli said.

"Please do, but more for Maria than me. She's scared and confused."

Right there, sitting at the table, Kelli started praying in Spanish. Her eyes were open, and no one nearby realized what she was doing. But Sandy understood. Hearing prayers for herself and Maria rolling off Kelli's lips made tears come to Sandy's eyes.

"That was beautiful," Sandy said in Spanish when Kelli finished. "I've spoken Spanish almost my whole life but never in prayer. I know God understands every language, but in some strange way, it makes sense to pray for Maria in Spanish."

"Spanish is a language of the heart." Kelli smiled, touching her chest. "And the desire of your heart is to help this girl."

Kelli got up from the table.

"Call me if you need me," she said. "I mean it."

As she watched Kelli walk away, the isolation Sandy had felt minutes before was gone. Instead, phrases the Spanish teacher sent heavenward stayed with her.

TWENTY-NINE

Maria stopped by Sandy's classroom at the end of day and told her Carol Ramsey had canceled the appointment with her.

"Did she set another time?" Sandy asked.

"No. She sent a note to my teacher telling me not to come. That's all."

"Okay," Sandy said, relieved. "Mr. Lane has a copy of the papers you and your father received. I'll let you know what he says about them."

Maria seemed on the verge of saying something else. Sandy waited. The girl wrung her hands together.

"What is it, Maria?" Sandy asked.

Maria hesitated, then shook her head. "No."

Maria didn't need another hug. It seemed a new problem had appeared in the girl's world. Sandy wanted to ask about it but held back.

"If you want to talk later, call my cell

phone," Sandy said. "Do you still have the number?"

"Yes."

While on her afternoon walk Sandy's phone rang. It was an unfamiliar number without a caller ID, and she suspected it was Maria calling from a borrowed phone. She switched Nelson's leash to her other hand and answered the call.

"Hello."

"Ms. Lincoln, it's Jeremy Lane. Is this a good time to talk?"

"Yes, I'm walking my dog. Did you receive the attorney-client contract and the legal papers served on Maria and her father?"

"Yes, and this afternoon I did some preliminary investigation into both matters. I think the women's group has two goals. First, to create a strong judicial precedent making it illegal for public educators to influence pregnant students not to have an abortion. Second, to expand the use of state guardianship laws to authorize third-party control of a pregnant teenager's reproductive choices."

"That's horrible."

"Good."

"What?"

"I want to frame the other side's position

484

to sound shocking, horrible, terrible, and any similar adjective. This type of case will likely be as much a media battle as a legal one."

"I don't want a media battle, but both Ben and a teacher at the school told me the same thing. I just want to protect Maria and her baby."

"It's not always possible to control the boundaries of a legal fight. I'm preparing a sheet of talking points for you to use if you're contacted by the press. The summary I gave you a minute ago will be on that list."

Sandy couldn't imagine herself standing in front of a bank of microphones.

"I'm not sure I'm prepared for this."

"You aren't. No one is. This is way beyond my comfort zone as a lawyer, but after I read the motion, something rose up inside me. I talked to my mother about it last night, and she believes strongly that I'm supposed to help you and Maria."

"You told her about me?"

"I didn't give her your name, of course, but I told her what you were facing. She's been more of a zealot about this issue than I have."

"That makes sense."

"What? I didn't catch that."

"That's good." Sandy thought about Ben's

concerns regarding Jeremy's inexperience. "Do you still think it would be a good idea to bring in outside help, especially if all this media stuff might happen?"

"Maybe, but the lawyer representing the women's organization is similar to me. He's a plaintiff's lawyer who specializes in cases against drug companies. He doesn't have a background in constitutional litigation, and I suspect he took the case because someone he knew asked him to. I talked to him briefly. He's been told you're a domineering, right-wing authority figure trying to force a mentally limited pregnant teenager with poor English skills to have a baby that is the result of a rape or incest."

"That sounds bad too."

"He's doing the same thing I am. Are you prepared to hear a news reporter repeat that about you as if it were true?"

"No."

"There is a way to keep that from happening."

"What is it?"

"Agree to cut off all contact with Maria now. We would enter into a consent order similar to the type used in cases of domestic abuse. You'd be prohibited from being around Maria or communicating with her in any way. If you did, you'd be subject to contempt of court."

"I'm not going to agree to that."

"I knew you wouldn't, but I had to let you know it was an option."

"Then what's next?"

"Does Maria want me to represent her in the petition to have her declared incompetent?"

Sandy told him about her conversation with Maria.

"I need to meet with Maria and her father," Jeremy said. "And it might be better if you're not present or serving as the translator."

"Why?"

"Because it will weaken the argument that you're manipulating the situation."

"Okay," Sandy said. "I felt pressured not to say much to Maria when I talked to her earlier today. There's a Spanish teacher at the school who knows what's going on. She's served as a translator on medical mission trips for doctors. Her accent and vocabulary are top-notch."

"I'm not sure it's a good idea to use a teacher from your school. Let me think about it."

"For a domineering, authoritarian teacher, I don't have much say in what happens, do I?"

"Because you aren't."

Sandy and Nelson reached the end of her driveway. Betsy's car was parked beside the fence. Betsy got out and started walking to her. She stopped when she saw that Sandy was on the phone. Sandy lowered the phone to her side.

"It's him," she said in a low voice to Betsy.

Betsy nodded. Sandy returned the phone to her ear and drew closer to Betsy.

"Excuse me," Jeremy said. "I missed that."

"Uh, I'm home now, and I was talking to Ben's wife."

Betsy, a big smile on her face, pointed to herself and then the phone. Sandy shook her head. She wasn't going to let Betsy talk to Jeremy.

"Okay," Jeremy said. "I'll send you an e-mail attachment with suggestions for your comments if you're contacted by a reporter."

"Can't I just refer them to you?"

"You can, but it's more powerful when a person who's been sued speaks on her own behalf instead of hiding behind her lawyer."

"And you're not worried I'll say something that can be used against us in court?"

"A little bit, but what you've done shouldn't be illegal in America."

The call ended.

"I just wanted to hear his voice," Betsy said. "Was he giving you advice about the lawsuit?"

"Yes."

"I told Ben not to waste his time trying to find another lawyer. Nothing could be more powerful than an adopted son defending his birth mother who's helping a pregnant teenager choose life for her child. Jeremy standing in the middle of the courtroom is exhibit A of the potential God has put in each human being. How dramatic!"

"Yeah," Sandy sighed. "Everyone is telling me there is going to be plenty of drama in my life for a while. Come inside and I'll show you the pictures."

Betsy stayed for over an hour. Her enthusiasm helped restore Sandy's excitement.

"I'd better get going," Betsy said, looking at the clock on the microwave. "I'm not cooking supper for Ben, but the least I can do is be there when he gets home to take me out to dinner. Do you want to join us?"

"No, thanks. I need some alone time."

Betsy gave Sandy a hug.

"And don't worry about the money to pay Jeremy. I told Ben I'm going to organize a Sandy Lincoln Defense Fund. You won't have to do anything. I'll handle the publicity, set up the events, and collect the donations."

Sandy shook her head. "No."

"Why not? Ben said the legal fees in a case like this could be thousands and thousands of dollars. That burden shouldn't fall on you. Don't worry. Everything will be done tastefully."

"Give me a few days to think it over," Sandy said reluctantly.

"All right, but don't let your pride get in the way of letting other people help you."

After Betsy left, Sandy checked her computer. There was an e-mail from Jeremy with an attachment containing the talking points he'd mentioned. Sandy printed out the information and read over it while eating. The comments were well-worded, but instead of admiring Jeremy's writing skills, Sandy cringed at the thought of having to deliver them to an anonymous crowd. Like many teachers, Sandy could talk all day in front of students, but change the audience to adults and her hands became clammy. She slid the papers to the side of the table and focused on the remaining lettuce in her bowl.

To Sandy's relief, the next few days passed by without a whiff of media interest in the lawsuit filed against her. Maria came by Sandy's classroom and told her that she and her father were going to meet with Jeremy on Thursday afternoon in Rutland.

"We go to the courthouse on Thursday. Mr. Lane said they have rooms where lawyers can talk to people."

Sandy had seen the conference rooms when she'd paid her property taxes.

"Is Mr. Lane going to have a translator there?"

"Yes, a woman who works at the court building. I wish you could do it, but I know it would make my father mad."

Later that day Sandy received a text message from Jeremy asking her to call him. Deb Bridges answered the phone.

"Yes, Jeremy was wondering if he could meet with you on Thursday after he finishes with Maria and her father. He needs to go over some things with you about the hearing. He suggested your brother's office in Rutland."

"I'll check with Ben, but I'm sure that won't be a problem."

That evening Sandy phoned Ben at home to ask him about the use of his office.

"I have a client meeting at five-thirty. You

can use Paul's office or our conference room."

Sandy heard Betsy call out something in the background.

"Betsy wants to know if you've thought any more about her offer to help raise money for your legal defense," Ben said.

"Not yet. But I'll let her know soon."

"Okay. I'll see you on Thursday."

Before she went to bed, Sandy logged on to her computer. Dr. Vale had sent her an e-mail informing her that the personnel committee for the school board was going to review her conduct at its next scheduled meeting in three weeks. Sandy sent Jeremy a copy of the e-mail. It was one more item of worry she had to take to bed.

On Thursday, Sandy wrapped up cheerleading practice at 4:50 p.m. It was an away football game, and the girls were going to do a dance routine they'd performed the previous year. Sandy incorporated a few minor changes to make it fresh.

It was less than a five-minute drive from the school to Ben's office. Sandy checked her appearance in the mirror in the girls' locker room before she left. She'd carefully selected a conservative outfit that was more businesslike than stylish. One question she had for Jeremy was how she should dress for the hearing in Atlanta.

When she arrived at Ben's office, the only cars in the parking lot belonged to her brother and his administrative assistant, Mary Walker. Jeremy's white SUV wasn't in sight. Sandy went inside.

"Hey, Mary," she said.

"Hi, Sandy. We're going to the game tomorrow night. Did you know Harry's younger brother moved to Foster County last year? He took a job with the Farmers Home Administration, so we're going to meet him at the game."

"Come down to the sidelines and say hello. There won't be a lot of friendly faces in that crowd. They stick the visitors at the end of the stands on the home side of the field."

Mary shut down her computer and picked up her purse.

"Gotta go. See you tomorrow."

After Mary left, Sandy tried to sit still, but she kept getting up every couple of minutes to walk around. Finally, the front door opened. It was Jeremy. He was wearing a dark-blue suit with a white shirt and maroon tie. His hair was slightly disheveled. He had a folder in his hand.

"Sorry to keep you waiting," he said. "It's

been a hectic day."

"How was your meeting with Maria and her father?"

"Tough. Dustin Abernathy talked to Maria's father before I got to him. He tracked him down where he works and spoke to him on the phone through a translator."

"Can he do that?"

"Yes, her father isn't an adverse party to the petition. In fact, he'd normally be the court's first choice for guardian. Abernathy told Maria's father that the easiest way to make the problem go away would be for Maria to have an abortion. Her father already believed that, so the lawyer didn't have much convincing to do."

"What did Maria say today?"

"Not much. When her father is there, she's much less willing to open up."

"So they didn't hire you to represent her?"

"No." Jeremy shook his head. "Even after I explained that I would help them for free."

"Who'll protect her?" Sandy asked with concern.

"If she doesn't hire a lawyer, a guardian ad litem will be appointed by the court to act as an advocate on her behalf during the proceeding."

"Dr. Vale mentioned that the other day."

"I checked with the juvenile court clerk,

and the guardian ad litem program in Rutland is staffed by non-attorney volunteers."

"If you get the list of names, pass it along to me. I probably know some of them."

"Good idea."

At that moment Ben came into the room and shook Jeremy's hand. Sandy watched Ben as he closely inspected Jeremy. Ben turned to her.

"You can meet in my conference room," he said.

Jeremy and Sandy followed Ben down a short hallway. The walls of the conference room were decorated with Auburn football photos and framed paraphernalia.

"All this is a holdover from my father's days," Ben said. "Whenever he was in town, he always checked to make sure I hadn't redecorated. He was disappointed when I wanted to go to Georgia, but he changed his mind when I received a scholarship and he didn't have to pay any tuition bills."

"I can ignore the decor." Jeremy smiled.

"I'll be down the hall if you need me," Ben said. "I'm sure you have a lot to talk about."

Ben looked at Sandy and winked as he left the room. Sandy's heart started pounding. Jeremy laid the folder on the table and took off his jacket. He sat at the head of the table with Sandy to his left.

"Okay," he said, slipping a legal pad covered with notes from the folder. "I've done more research that will help me prepare you for the hearing next week."

Sandy coughed nervously and cleared her throat.

"Jeremy, before we get started, there's something I need to ask you."

THIRTY

"There'll be plenty of time for your questions later," Jeremy said. "I'll probably answer some of them in my presentation."

"I'm one hundred percent sure my question isn't in your notes."

"Okay." Jeremy placed the legal pad on the table. "I'm listening."

Sandy took a deep breath.

"Have you ever been curious about your birth mother?"

"Every adoptee thinks about that." Jeremy shrugged. "My younger sister recently took the first steps to try to locate her birth mother. The record of my adoption was sealed by the court at the request of my mother, so I assume she didn't want to be found."

"Does that bother you?"

"I suppose she had her reasons. I was born a year or so after the Supreme Court decided *Roe v. Wade* and could have been legally aborted. I'm obviously glad my mother didn't take that step and thankful for my parents who raised me." Jeremy gave Sandy a curious look. "The hearing in front of Judge Tompkins isn't going to focus on the merits of adoption. It's about your free-speech rights and Maria's access to different perspectives on her reproductive choices."

"If you had a chance to meet your birth mother, would you want to do it?"

"I'm really not sure. What does this have to do with you and Maria?"

"Nothing. It has to do with you and me."

"What are you driving at?" Jeremy asked, then paused and opened his eyes wider. "You don't think that you're my mother, do you?"

"I don't think so. I know so."

Jeremy's mouth dropped open. He stared at Sandy for a moment.

"That's not possible."

Sandy took a deep breath.

"Do you want to know why I believe you're my son?"

A skeptical look crossed Jeremy's face, and he leaned back in his chair.

"I'm listening."

"Shortly before my senior year at Rutland High, I got pregnant. My boyfriend played wide receiver on the football team. I decided not to have an abortion and moved in with an aunt in Atlanta. She took me to an adoption agency that allowed me to pursue a closed adoption with input in the selection of the adoptive parents. I reviewed at least a hundred files with the names and addresses removed. One day my caseworker left the room, and I saw a photo sticking out of a file. I peeked at the picture and saw a woman standing beside a large palmetto tree in front of a brick house with a cream-colored convertible parked in the driveway."

"What kind of convertible?" Jeremy asked, sitting up straighter in his chair.

"It was a Chevrolet with South Carolina license plates. The woman had short blond hair and was wearing a yellow blouse and green skirt. After I looked at the photo, I slipped it back into the file. Later that day, my caseworker gave me the information, without the picture, and I found out that the woman worked part-time at a florist shop and was married to an airline pilot. When I saw the picture of you as a little boy in front of the same house, I realized who you are."

Jeremy's face grew pale. Now that she'd opened the floodgate of information, Sandy felt stronger.

"I've never forgotten one sentence your mother wrote as part of the application process to the adoption agency: 'I believe Jesus will send us the child he wants us to love as he loves us.' It was such a heartfelt statement of faith and desire to love a child the way he should be loved. I was just a teenager, but her words touched me deeply, and I knew this was the woman to raise my baby." Sandy smiled. "It also helped that she had blond hair and blue eyes like me. I wanted the baby to fit in with the family based on appearance too."

Jeremy was now looking at her with a mixture of bewilderment and wonder.

"And there's nothing I want from you," Sandy said, then stopped. "No, I didn't say that right. I'd love to get to know you and your beautiful family, but I don't want to intrude or force my way into a relationship. You have a mother, and your children have a grandmother. I'll leave it completely up to you to decide what, if any, contact we should have."

Jeremy glanced down at his legal pad.

"You're right. None of this was in my notes. Do you mind if I ask you a few specific questions? I'm having trouble absorbing this."

"Go ahead."

"Where was I born and how much did I weigh?"

"You were born on April 5, 1975, at Piedmont Hospital in Atlanta. You weighed four pounds, ten ounces and were called Baby Smith."

Jeremy nodded. "My mother still has the card that was taped to my bassinet in the hospital nursery. Why was I so tiny?"

Sandy gulped. From the moment the conversation started, her intent was to finesse her way around the issue of a brother, but it was an impossible goal. Sooner or later, the truth would come out.

"Because you are a fraternal twin. Somewhere, you have an older brother who weighed five pounds, two ounces."

Jeremy put his head in his hands and leaned his elbows on the table. Sandy didn't know if he was upset or holding his head up because his brain had suddenly gotten heavy with new information. After a few moments, Jeremy raised his head.

"Do you have any idea where he is?"

"No. The records were sealed by the court, and I've never requested they be opened."

"And my birth father?"

"His name is Brad Donnelly. The last I heard he was living in Pennsylvania. I've not had any contact with him since high school. It was a very hurtful situation for me, but if you want to track him down, I'll help any way I can. Zach looks a little bit like him."

Jeremy looked down at his hands, then at Sandy's fingers.

"Our hands look similar."

Sandy held out her hands. "I hadn't noticed, but you're right. Also, the way you touch your right ear with your right hand when you're thinking is something my brothers and I do."

"When you were in my office the other day, you mentioned another brother who lives in Chicago?"

"Yes, Jack. You look a lot like him."

"Do you have a picture of him?"

"Ben does in his office."

"I'd like to see it."

Sandy left the conference room. She felt like she'd stepped off a spaceship onto a new planet. She went down the hallway. Ben's door was cracked open. Sandy knocked.

"Come in," he said.

"I thought you had someone coming in for an appointment," Sandy said.

"He rescheduled. How's it going?"

"Good, I think. I told him who I am, and

he wants to see a picture of Jack."

Ben picked up a photo of himself and Jack taken several years earlier at the beach.

"Would it be okay if I take it to my nephew myself?"

Sandy smiled. "He's ours, not just mine."

The three of them spent the next hour without ever discussing the hearing in front of Judge Tompkins. Jeremy got more and more excited and animated. There was so much to talk about that the conversation veered wildly. Sandy shed a few tears, but laughter quickly banished them. Finally, Jeremy looked at his watch.

"I have to get going," he said. "I'm going to be up late tonight talking to Leanne."

"When will you tell your mother?" Sandy asked.

"I want to do it the right way," Jeremy replied thoughtfully. "That will require some planning."

"Whatever you decide, I'd like for you to give her a letter from me if you think it's a good idea," Sandy said. "I want to thank her."

"That's a great idea."

They all stood up. Jeremy leaned forward and hugged Sandy. Her arms hung limply at her sides for a moment, then she reached up and embraced him. He kissed her lightly on the cheek as he let her go.

"Is that okay?" he asked.

All Sandy could do was nod. Ben and Jeremy shook hands, then the three of them walked together to the front door of the office.

"I'll call you tomorrow to talk about our legal matters," Jeremy said to Sandy. "We can discuss the hearing over the phone."

"I need to leave for a football game at five-thirty," Sandy replied.

"Then I'll call around four."

Jeremy left. Ben took his cell phone from his pocket.

"Betsy called me four times in the past hour. Do you think I should call her back?"

"Only if you ever want to eat another bite of corn bread in your life."

"And you'd better come to supper with us. She's going to ask so many questions I can't answer that I'm going to end up in big trouble."

"Okay."

"We'll get a table in the back at Dressler's place. It shouldn't be too crowded on a Thursday night."

Sandy stood beside Ben while he locked the front door of the office.

"What do you think about Jeremy?" she asked.

"He's an impressive young man. I'd say young, but he's only fourteen years younger than I am."

"How is Mama going to react to the news?"

"Awkwardly at first. She's going to remember how embarrassed she was when you turned up pregnant. It's going to take her awhile to get her head around the fact that she now has a thirty-three-year-old grandson and two great-grandchildren in her life. She's going to feel really, really old."

Sandy laughed. Ben looked down at her and smiled.

"But what I'm going to enjoy the most is the happiness I hope this brings to you. You haven't spent your life feeling sorry for yourself, but you're no stranger to disappointment. I pray things work out so you can have a good relationship with Jeremy and his family."

"Me too."

Betsy was so excited she barely ate any of her supper.

"Box it up," she told the waiter when it was time to pay for the meal.

After the waiter left, Ben leaned forward. "And then Jeremy gave Sandy a big hug. He finished it off with a kiss on the cheek."

"How sweet." Betsy sighed. "He sounds like such a doll."

"I wouldn't use that word," Ben replied. "At least in front of anyone except the three of us."

"Sandy knows what I mean," Betsy said. "It takes a real man to show affection to his mother. I have to stick my cheek out like a highway billboard for Robbie to know it's time to give me a little peck before he leaves the house for another couple of months."

When she got home, Sandy called Jessica to share the news. Her friend went into the bathroom and closed the door so Rick couldn't hear her side of the conversation.

"When can I tell him?" Jessica asked when Sandy paused for a moment.

"Not until I talk to my mother. Okay?"

"I'll try. The only secrets I remember ever keeping from him were the appointment I had with the diet doctor who wanted me to drink that awful mixture of grass and leaves, and the consultation with the plastic surgeon when my eyes started to sag."

"A girl has a right to keep a few bits of information to herself. It won't be much longer before I break the news to my mother, but I'm all talked out for tonight. Part of me wants to tell her in person. I think that's what Jeremy will probably do with his mother."

"You're his mother."

"Yes, but I'm not going to start calling his mother his 'adopted mother.' She's the one who raised him and influenced who he is today. I'll be satisfied if he calls me Sandy."

"How about the grandkids?"

"You know how that works. They'll come up with their own name for me, and I'll love it."

After she hung up the phone, Sandy went out to the porch at the rear of her house and listened to the night noises. During the summer, the evening chorus could be deafening, but with the arrival of cooler weather, it became quieter. Sandy sat in a rocking chair, closed her eyes, and let her imagination about the future fly free.

The following day she floated through her time at school with a slightly goofy grin on her face. At lunchtime she turned around and almost bumped into Carol at the end of the salad line.

"Hi, Carol," Sandy blurted out before she could stop herself.

Carol gave her a strange look and kept walking. Sandy didn't care whether she looked foolish or not.

At 4:00 p.m., she was sitting in her kitchen

drinking a cup of tea and waiting for Jeremy's call. Her phone beeped, and she answered. It was Jeremy.

"Hey, Sandy," he began. "It's been an interesting twenty-four hours."

"Tell me."

"I waited until the kids were in bed to break the news to Leanne. She remembered seeing you come to the office with Maria the other day and wanted me to ask you a strange question. Were you in Tryon when my son, Zach, broke his collarbone in a fall at the elementary school last weekend? There was a woman in a pickup truck who blew the horn to let us know something had happened and then drove off. I know it's an odd thing to ask, but —"

"That was me," Sandy said. "I drove over to Tryon to see where you lived and hoped I'd get a chance to see your family. As soon as Zach fell I wanted to jump out and run over to him, but I realized a stranger would frighten him, so I honked the horn to get your attention instead. I called the hospital later in the day to make sure he was okay."

"Leanne was right."

"I wasn't trying to be a stalker, but I guess that's what I was doing. I apologize."

"I understand."

"And please tell Leanne my reasoning.

I've been in a partial state of shock for the past two weeks. At times I'm not sure I've been thinking straight."

"How could you? Looking back, I can remember you giving me a few odd looks when we were talking about the pictures in my office, but I didn't think anything of it."

"I memorized every detail of those pictures."

"One of the first things I want to do is put together a photo album for you that will include pictures from my childhood up through the present. Leanne started working on it today."

Sandy felt overwhelmed. "That would be wonderful."

"Leanne and I are going to wait to introduce you to the kids until after I talk with my mom. I need to do that in person, which can't happen for a couple of weeks. In the meantime, it would be nice if you could pull together some background information about yourself, including photos and a letter I can take when I go to see her in Charleston."

"Of course."

Jeremy was silent for a moment.

"I really enjoyed meeting you," he said. "I haven't been able to stop thinking about it."

Sandy felt like she'd received a huge hug.

"It means the world for you to say that," she said. "This has been such a vulnerable time for me. And I agree with your suggestion about waiting on any contact with the children. But would it be okay if I visited your church on Sunday? Deb invited me, so I could come as her guest. Maybe I could meet Leanne before or after the service and talk to you for a minute."

"That would work. The kids will be in children's church and won't be with us until we pick them up. It would be easy to squeeze in a few minutes."

"Are you sure?"

"Yes, I miss you already. We have so much catching up to do."

Sandy felt her heart do another flip.

"Deb gave me her cell phone number," she said. "I'll give her a call. See you then."

"Sandy," Jeremy said before she could hang up the phone.

"What?"

"We're not finished. We need to talk about the hearing next week."

"Sorry. It's been a fight to keep focused on that."

Forty-five minutes later, Sandy had a better idea of the purpose for the hearing and what she'd be expected to say. The burden of proof would be on the women's organization to prove the need for immediate action by the judge. Jeremy's response would largely depend on the evidence presented by the other attorney. He and Sandy would rehearse her testimony some more during the drive to Atlanta for the hearing.

While she got ready to leave for the football game, Sandy glanced at herself in the bathroom mirror. The slightly goofy smile she'd worn to school was still on her face.

And she didn't want it to leave.

THIRTY-ONE

Sunday morning Sandy woke up at first light and immediately knew it would be impossible to go back to sleep. It was several hours before she needed to leave for Tryon, so to fill the time she took Nelson for a post-dawn walk. The temperature was brisk and the streets deserted. A morning walk wasn't part of Nelson's routine, and he excitedly pulled on the leash when they started off. Sandy sipped coffee from a travel mug. Slung over her shoulder was her camera.

Sandy took a route that passed her childhood home. The people who owned it now had maintained the outside of the house, but the yard was a shadow of its past manicured brilliance. It was a clear morning, and the fresh sun beautifully illuminated the residence. Sandy took several photos for Jeremy. The backyard was empty. Sandy had given the Victorian playhouse to Jessica when her older daughter turned four.

It was better for the playhouse to be used by a child than endure a lonely wait for Sandy's daughter who would never come.

Several blocks away, Sandy turned down a street she rarely visited and stopped in front of the single-story brick ranch house that had been the Donnelly home. The house was no longer a source of pain. Finding Jeremy had removed the remaining hurt from her heart. She snapped a few photos.

At home, she began selecting pictures to include in Jeremy's album. She decided to keep it simple and not overwhelm him. She picked out one or two pictures a year from her childhood until her senior year in high school. There weren't many photos from her pregnancy, so she added most of them, including the one with Jessica in the kitchen.

The only pictures of Brad were in their high school yearbook. As a football star and first baseman on the baseball team, he figured prominently. Sandy had her share of coverage from the fall term. After that, she disappeared as if snatched from the earth.

Butterflies fluttered in Sandy's stomach during the twenty-minute drive to Tryon. She was looking forward to seeing Jeremy and meeting Leanne but was anxious she might say or do the wrong thing. The church parking lot was crowded. Sandy had put on a blue dress and a lightweight white sweater. A necklace around her neck was complemented by matching earrings. She saw people wearing jeans and felt over-dressed. When she reached the church entrance there was no sign of Deb Bridges or Jeremy and his family.

"Good morning," said a male voice behind her. "What brings you all the way over here?"

Sandy turned around. It was John Bestwick.

"Uh, meeting a friend," Sandy replied. "I didn't know you attended this church."

"Just started a few months ago. A guy I know from college goes here with his family and invited me. There's been a big change in my life since then, but I guess you haven't noticed."

Sandy remembered the kind note John wrote when she returned from her first meeting with Dr. Vale.

"Maybe a little," she said.

"When was the last time you heard me lose my temper with a player and cuss him out?"

"Never."

John pointed to his head. "But there was plenty of that going on in here."

Deb came up to them, and Sandy introduced them.

"If you have any influence with Sandy, put
in a good word for me," John said to Deb.
"I've been trying to buy her a steak dinner
for months."

John entered the church.

"He seems like a nice guy," Deb said after
John left. "And he seems very interested in
you."

Sandy noticed that Deb wasn't wearing a
wedding band.

"Don't let that keep you from getting to
know him. He's the boys' basketball coach
at Rutland High. If he offers to buy you a
steak dinner, let him do it."

They went into the sanctuary. It was a
long, rectangular metal building.

"Where do Jeremy and his family sit?"
Sandy asked.

"Usually in the back on the left."

"Then let's sit on the right."

"I thought we'd worship together."

"Not today," Sandy said firmly.

The sanctuary started to fill up. Sandy
kept glancing over her shoulder until she
saw Jeremy and Leanne enter the room.
Jeremy was looking around and their eyes
met. He smiled and waved before whisper-
ing something to Leanne, who looked

intently in her direction and nodded slightly. Jeremy and Leanne continued up the aisle and sat on the left side of the sanctuary. Sandy could see Leanne lean in close to Jeremy and start talking.

"There're Jeremy and Leanne," Deb said, nudging Sandy.

"Yes, I saw them come in."

The service reminded Sandy of Ben and Betsy's church. She could see John Bestwick's head close to the front of the room. It warmed Sandy's heart that the basketball coach was connecting with something other than the squeak of shoes in a high school gym. The songs were new to Sandy. Deb sang boisterously and didn't seem to notice that Sandy held back.

The sermon topic for the day was taken from the story of the prodigal son. The pastor, a man named Mark, was in his early forties and seemed comfortable in his role as a speaker. He read the famous passage from Luke's Gospel, then focused on the need for every person to have the perspective of the father who wanted the son to return home without recrimination. Sandy was grateful that her son wasn't a prodigal.

At the conclusion of the message, the congregation was encouraged to divide into groups of four or five and pray for the prodigals in their families. An older couple in front of Deb and Sandy turned around, and the four of them became an instant small group. Deb prayed for a sister, an uncle, and a woman she'd known for more than twenty years who'd recently turned away from God. The older couple added a few more names to the list. While the wife prayed, Sandy racked her brain to come up with someone to mention. When the couple finished, Sandy sat in awkward silence for a moment, then prayed for her nephew Robbie. She wasn't sure Robbie qualified as a prodigal; he just liked to sleep late on Sunday mornings and went to church only when visiting his parents in Rutland. But as she mentioned his name, Sandy knew that Betsy would appreciate the prayer.

The end of the service left Sandy with a logistical dilemma. How was she going to separate from Deb so she could spend private time with Jeremy and Leanne?

"What did you think?" Deb asked. "Isn't Pastor Mark a good speaker?"

"Yes."

Sandy saw Jeremy and Leanne moving toward them.

"Go ahead," Sandy said to Deb. "I'm fine on my own."

"I thought we could go to lunch," Deb

replied. "There's a cute spot with scrumptious sandwiches not far from the church. It's the sort of place I think you'd enjoy."

"Uh, I'm sure I would, but I wasn't going to —" Sandy stopped as Jeremy came up to her.

He leaned over and gave her a hug. Deb's eyes widened. Leanne extended her hand to Sandy.

"Jeremy hasn't stopped talking about you since he got home on Thursday," Leanne said.

A big grin on his face, Jeremy turned to Deb, who was gawking at Leanne.

"Deb, you may as well find out now, since it will come up at the office soon enough. Sandy is my birth mother."

Deb took a step back, then looked at Jeremy and Sandy in quick succession.

"Wow!"

Jeremy leaned over so his face was beside Sandy's.

"Does that help?"

Deb stared at them for a few seconds.

"Yeah, it's uncanny." She nodded. "How in the world did you figure it out?"

"I'll fill you in later," Jeremy said. "I wanted Sandy to meet Leanne before we pick up the kids. I'm not going to say anything to them until I talk to my mom.

So I'd ask you to keep a lid on this too. If I didn't think you could, I wouldn't tell you."

"Sure," Deb said, glancing at Sandy again. "Amazing."

Deb moved away but looked over her shoulder twice before she'd gone ten feet. Sandy turned to Leanne.

"I know this is a shock," Sandy said. "And I hope Jeremy told you that I don't want to disrupt your family or cause any problems. It was so unexpected, and I wasn't sure —"

Sandy saw tears come into Leanne's eyes and stopped. Jeremy put his arm around Leanne.

"What is it?" he asked.

Leanne wiped away the tears with her hand.

"I suddenly thought how I'd feel if I had to go through my life without seeing Zach until he was a grown man."

Within seconds, tears were streaming down Sandy's cheeks. Leanne stepped forward and hugged Sandy as tightly as a best friend. Sandy felt Jeremy's hand on her shoulder. She and Leanne parted. Leanne, her eyes red, looked in Sandy's face.

"I don't know you, but I hope you feel what is in my heart for you."

"I do." Sandy managed a small smile. "I feel like the prodigal mother who has come home to open arms and a big feast."

"But you didn't do anything wrong," Jeremy quickly cut in.

"She knows what I mean," Sandy said, keeping her eyes on Leanne. "I walked away from my babies. And now one of them has been brought back to me."

Leanne briefly hugged Sandy again. Jeremy had a confused look on his face.

"Don't worry, honey." Leanne patted Jeremy on the arm. "You're a smart lawyer, but you're not supposed to understand everything a woman thinks and feels."

"Obviously."

Leanne took a packet of tissues from her purse and offered one to Sandy. They both blew their noses and laughed.

"What's funny?" Jeremy asked, bewildered.

"We need to get the kids," Leanne said. "Chloe is going to wonder why her mommy has been crying. Jeremy, what are you going to tell her?"

"That she should know because she'll be a woman someday."

They walked out of the sanctuary together. The sun was shining, and the air had the comfortable cool that only autumn provides.

"There's not much time for us to talk now," Leanne said to Sandy, "but there's one question I have to ask you. Why did you send the boys to different families?"

Sandy didn't feel threatened by Leanne.

"I thought it was the right thing to do. Someday I'll tell you the whole story."

Leanne took both Sandy's hands in hers and peered into her eyes.

"I think having two mothers-in-law is going to be a blessing."

Sandy wasn't sure if she drove her car back to Rutland or if it flew a few inches above the pavement. When she got home, she knew it was time to call her mother. Linda was visiting in Florida for a few weeks. That way Sandy could tell both women at the same time. Her mother answered the phone.

"Hey, Mama," Sandy said. "Where are you?"

"In my bedroom. Why?"

"Would you please ask Linda to pick up the phone in the kitchen? I have something important to tell both of you, and I don't want to repeat it."

"Are you sick?"

"No, no, I'm fine."

Sandy heard her mother call Linda's name.

"This had better be important," Linda said when she came on the line. "I'm near the end of a good book and want to find out what happened."

"This is better than fiction," Sandy replied. "I have some exciting news. I've met one of my sons."

The two women's initial reaction was total silence.

"Say that again," her mother said after a few seconds passed.

"I've found the younger of the twins. He's a lawyer in Tryon named Jeremy Lane."

"Are you positive it's him?" her mother asked. "How can you be sure?"

Sandy repeated her story. When she mentioned the card on Baby Smith's bassinet in the infant nursery at the hospital, Linda interrupted her.

"I remember that card. I never told you, but I took a picture of the cards on both bassinets. The photos are in a box in the guestroom closet at my house."

"Jeremy's mother has the original. When he asked why his birth weight was so low, I told him he had a fraternal twin."

"How did he take that news?" her mother asked.

"So far, he's not seemed that interested." Sandy paused. "He really wants to get to know me."

"Did he ask about his father?"

"Yes, but only to find out who he was. If he wants to track down Brad, I won't try to discourage him."

"I would," Linda grunted.

"I know why you're saying that," Sandy replied. "But when you meet Jeremy and see his family, the negative things of the past will seem unimportant."

"Do you have pictures of him?" her mother asked.

"Yes. I'll e-mail some to you later. Oh, and I haven't told Jack yet, but I'll try to call him this afternoon. Other than Ben and Betsy, the only person who knows is Jessica. She was over here the other day and saw some photos lying around. There was no hiding the truth from her."

Sandy heard someone blow her nose.

"Are you okay?"

"That's me, crying like a baby myself," Linda said. "All the memories of those months we spent together hit me like a flood. It was one of the happiest times of my life. And to think about seeing one of the boys is unbelievable."

"Maybe I could ride back to Georgia with Linda and we could all get together," Sandy's mother said.

"I think that would be a great idea," Sandy said. "Let me mention it to Jeremy and see what he thinks. I'm trying to let him set the pace for the relationship."

"Good idea," her mother said.

"Maybe, but you've ruined the rest of my afternoon," Linda said. "There's no way I can get back into my book."

When the call ended, Sandy waited a few minutes, then phoned Jack. After listening to her story, he asked so many questions that Sandy finally had to suggest that he send an e-mail so she could make an effort to find out everything he wanted to know about Jeremy.

Monday morning Maria came to Sandy's classroom before first period started. The Hispanic girl looked tired.

"I'm staying with Rosalita for a few days," Maria said. "My father is very mad at me because I have not had the abortion."

"Will he bother you at Rosalita's trailer? It's so close by."

"No. He wants me to be there. If I am going to have a baby, he wants me to take care of it myself."

Sandy switched to Spanish. "What do you want to do about the legal papers filed against you to have you declared mentally incompetent?"

"I want Mr. Lane to help me," Maria replied.

"Are you sure?"

"Yes."

"And you won't change your mind?"

Sandy didn't want to be hard on Maria, but she felt it necessary to make sure the girl had really made a firm decision.

"Rosalita and I talked about it. She believes I need to have someone I can trust helping me. Will you let him know? He told me I needed to sign a paper so he can be my lawyer."

Satisfied, Sandy said, "I'll call him today."

During the short break between first and second periods, Sandy went to her car and phoned Jeremy's office.

"Lane Law Offices," Deb said.

"Hi, Deb. This is Sandy Lincoln. Is Jeremy —"

"Sandy," Deb interrupted. "This is so incredible. After seeing you and Jeremy together at the church, I can totally see the family resemblance. I was looking at the pictures in Jeremy's office this morning. Chloe looks even more like you than he does. Send me a cute photo of yourself, and I'll have it framed to put on his credenza. It will be a fun surprise."

"Thanks, but I'm already working on an album for him. If he wants a picture for his office, I'm sure he'll let me know. I'm trying to avoid surprising him any more than I already have."

"There's no use being too coy. This is huge. I tried to corner Jeremy this morning, but he dashed in here for five minutes, then left for the courthouse. Did you enjoy meeting Leanne? She's a sweetheart."

"Yes, very much."

"She's more serious than Jeremy. He has a big playful streak that he doesn't show much as a lawyer, but it comes out when he's with his kids. You'll see it eventually. Oh, I assume you're going to ride together to the hearing in Atlanta on Wednesday."

"Yes, we talked about it the other day. He'll prep me some more during the drive."

"This must be so exciting for you. Do you have any other children?"

"Did Jeremy tell you he has a fraternal twin?"

Deb screamed so loud that Sandy had to hold the phone away from her ear.

"Sorry about that," Deb said. "It's a good thing I'm here by myself. This is like something from a movie. Have you met him?"

"No, and I don't know where he is."

"I'm sure tracking him down will be one

of Jeremy's priorities."

"Maybe." Sandy frowned. "Listen, I'm in between classes and have to go, but I talked to Maria Alverez this morning, and she wants Jeremy to represent her in the juvenile court case. Can you ask Jeremy to send me an attorney-client contract for Maria to sign?"

"Of course; he had one in the file when he met with her and her father in Rutland on Thursday" — Deb paused — "the day he found out about you. I know it was intensely personal, but I wish I could have been there. Was he skeptical at first? Did he cry?"

"No tears from him. And it wasn't too hard to convince him."

"How did you do it?"

"I think the key was when I told him how much he weighed when he was born."

"That's so perfect. Who else would know that after thirty-three years but a mother?"

Sandy heard some muffled talking, then Deb came back on the line.

"I've got to go," Deb said. "A client came in to pick up some papers."

"Okay. Don't forget the papers for Maria."

"I'll send the contract within an hour."

■ ■ ■ ■

Sandy had submitted a request for a vacation day as soon as she found out about the hearing in Atlanta. When she stopped by the teachers' lounge on her way to the cafeteria for lunch, there was a sealed envelope in her school mailbox. Inside was an approval for paid time off; however, at the top of the page was typed "Carol Ramsey." Sandy suspected her letter had been sent to Carol. She put the envelope in Carol's box, which turned out to be empty.

Sandy wasn't surprised that Carol would be at the hearing. Who else would claim that Sandy had been intimidating Maria? However, it didn't make being on opposite sides of the courtroom from a coworker any easier. Before going to the cafeteria, Sandy went by the school office. Dr. Vale's secretary, a young woman who didn't look much older than some of the students in Sandy's classes, was sitting at her desk.

"The approval for Carol Ramsey's request for a vacation day on Wednesday was in my box," Sandy said. "I put it in hers. Did she turn mine in to the office?"

"I haven't seen it," the woman said. "Are you sure you sent one in?"

"Yes," Sandy replied patiently. "You weren't at your desk, so I gave it to Ms. Falls. She was filling in for you."

"I can check with Dr. Vale, but you should probably put in another request. I can't be responsible for things that aren't given directly to me."

Sandy clenched her teeth.

"I'll be right back."

Returning to her classroom, she printed out a copy of the request with the date at the top and marched down the hall. When she entered the office, Dr. Vale was standing beside his assistant's desk.

"Here she is," the secretary said.

"Ms. Lincoln," Dr. Vale said, "it's school policy to file requests for vacation days at least five business days in advance."

"Which is why I gave this to Ms. Falls last week," Sandy replied, handing him the request. "Check the date at the top. Apparently it wasn't delivered to you in a timely manner."

"Do you have proof of delivery?" the principal asked.

"Do you have a Bible handy?"

"Why?" Dr. Vale gave Sandy a blank look.

"So I can swear on the Bible that I delivered the request more than five business days in advance."

"Make arrangements for your own substitute," Dr. Vale answered curtly. "And in the future, give any requests for days off directly to me."

"I'll do that."

Fuming, Sandy left the office. Never in her teaching career had she faced overt harassment from the school administration. She took a couple of deep breaths to calm herself. Dr. Vale was probably catching heat from the school board about two of his staff squaring off in a legal proceeding that would bring negative publicity to Rutland High.

After lunch, Sandy went by the teachers' lounge. There was an envelope in her box. It was approval for her vacation request signed and dated the previous day by Mr. Blankenship, the assistant principal.

Bureaucratic foul-ups could drive a person crazy.

THIRTY-TWO

Tuesday morning Maria signed the contract hiring Jeremy as her lawyer. Sandy took it to Coach Bestwick's office to scan and send to Jeremy. The basketball coach was sitting at his desk reading when she entered.

"Sorry, something else," she said holding up the sheet of paper.

John scooted away from his desk.

"Go ahead."

When Sandy placed the contract on the printer and pressed the Scan button, she saw a devotional book and an open Bible on John's desk.

"You're reading the Bible?" she asked.

"Yeah, I'm trying to get in thirty minutes a day. That's still less time than I spend running and lifting weights."

"I'm impressed."

"I've been making some changes. I even contacted my ex-wife last week and apologized for being such a jerk during the final year of our marriage. She didn't know what to think."

Sandy didn't know the details of the divorce.

"Is she remarried?"

"Yes, but I needed to do it anyway. A few days ago, I called my daughter Fay, you know, the one who just started a new job in Jacksonville. She'd heard from her mother and asked me a bunch of questions. She ended up telling me she loved me. That hasn't happened in years. I feel like the prodigal father who came home."

Sandy removed the contract from the machine.

"I know what you mean," she said.

John Bestwick's words were still in Sandy's mind when she left school after cheerleading practice. Instead of going straight home, she pulled into the parking lot for her church. Margie Little, the church secretary, was there. The two women had known each other for decades.

"Reverend Peterson is at the hospital visiting Bill Woods," Margie said when Sandy came in.

"What's wrong with Bill?"

"Gallbladder. They thought it might be

something more serious, so the news was a relief."

"I didn't come by to see Reverend Peterson," Sandy said. "I just wanted to spend a few minutes in the sanctuary."

"Go ahead," Margie said and waved her hand. "I won't be finished here for at least half an hour. Take your time."

The deserted sanctuary was as still and quiet as a secluded pond on a windless day. Sandy walked down the center aisle but didn't stop at the pew where she usually sat. Instead, she headed toward the spot where she'd sat with her family the night of the special Christmas Eve service.

Sitting down, Sandy closed her eyes and folded her hands across the body that had been full of new life that long-ago night. Now she knew one of the tiny, hidden babies was a strong, grown-up man — Sandy smiled — who was no longer able to kick her bladder in the middle of the night so she had to crawl out of bed and go to the bathroom.

Everyone is a prodigal in their own unique way, Sandy thought. She knew she'd come reluctantly to the church on Christmas Eve as an unmarried, pregnant teenager and been embraced by the welcoming arms of a loving heavenly Father. She was a prodigal who came home and experienced God's peace and forgiveness. The ensuing years had proven the change genuine. She took a few minutes to silently express her gratitude.

But Sandy sensed the need for something more. God knew every hidden whisper of her heart, but she wanted to receive a tangible token to carry with her on the next stage of her journey. She rested her fingers lightly on the top of the pew in front of her for a few moments.

And knew what to ask for.

Sandy bowed her head and prayed that she, like her heavenly Father, would open loving, unselfish arms to the people God brought into her life — Maria, Jeremy, his family, the cheerleaders, and others not yet known. Sandy didn't have a traditional family, but she could hold out her arms as wide as God's grace allowed. It was a vivid picture, something she could hold on to in the days and years to come.

Grateful again, she slipped out of the pew.

Sandy had arranged to meet Jeremy in the parking lot at Ben's office early in the morning to leave for Atlanta. The lot was empty when she arrived. She sat quietly in her car as she waited. Jeremy's white SUV came around the corner.

"Sorry I'm a few minutes late," Jeremy said when Sandy got in his vehicle. "Chloe had an upset stomach last night, and I didn't get a lot of sleep."

"What's wrong with her?"

"Probably too much pizza and ice cream at a friend's birthday party. By this morning she felt better than I did, so Leanne sent her to school. Where is the best place to get a cup of coffee in Rutland? I need a second jolt."

Sandy directed him to a coffee shop with a drive-through window.

"Do you want anything?" he asked.

"No, thanks."

They left Rutland and headed down the familiar road to Atlanta. Sandy thought about the drive she took in her VW when Jeremy was an unborn child.

"I had a long conversation with the lawyer on the other side of the case," Jeremy said, taking a sip of coffee.

"You did?" Sandy asked in surprise.

"Yeah, sometimes it's a good idea to talk to opposing counsel before a case gets going and emotions start to run high. That's especially true when dealing with an unfamiliar attorney. I wanted to show him a bit of Southern hospitality. I think I caught him off guard, and he opened up more than he might have if he'd had time to think about it. He's only been in Atlanta for about a year. Most of Dusty's trial experience has been in Los Angeles."

"Dusty?"

"That's what he goes by. We're about the same age. I'll call him Mr. Abernathy in front of the judge."

"If you talked to him about Southern hospitality, won't that make him think he can run all over you?"

"If he tries," Jeremy said with a steely glint in his eye, "it would be a serious mistake."

"Did you find out why he took the case?"

"A friend asked him to. My guess is that his 'friend' is a woman he's interested in who supports or volunteers for the organization he's representing."

"Anything else?"

"Dusty isn't married and doesn't have any children."

"You asked him about that?"

"Yeah, I told him a little bit about my family and asked about his. I even mentioned that I'm an adoptee who's glad my mother didn't abort me."

"You didn't tell him who I am, did you?"

"No, but he needed to know that I have a high level of personal interest in this case. I also wanted to find out how hard-core he was about abortion rights. He thinks a woman's right to end a pregnancy should be protected from restrictions."

"Even late term?"

"We didn't get into specifics." Jeremy looked in the rearview mirror. "And I told him you were a nice lady who was trying to help a student."

"Did you say nice older lady?"

"I might have." Jeremy smiled.

"You didn't!"

"No, but I said you're a well-respected teacher who is not going to come across in court as a fanatic crackpot."

"Why tell him that?"

"So he'll have questions in his mind about whether his client is telling him the truth about you. Believe me, if he's got any skill as a trial lawyer, he'll size you up in a couple of minutes."

"What's he going to do after he sizes me up?"

"Try to cut you up."

"Then now would be a good time for you to tell me how to keep that from happening. And don't go easy on me."

"Okay," Jeremy said. "What will you say when Dusty accuses you of trying to force your religious beliefs on Maria?"

Sandy thought for a moment.

"There's so much I could say in answering a question like that."

She told him about the night she started to take a sleeping pill but couldn't bring herself to risk harming the tiny life within her.

"That's a powerful story," Jeremy said quietly when she finished. "You want to protect an unborn child because you're a mother. It's your essence. You don't need a religious or political reason to do what is as natural for you as breathing."

Sandy felt her emotions rising. She stared out the passenger window.

"It must have broken your heart to —" Jeremy began.

"Please," Sandy said. "Don't make me go there."

"I'm sorry," Jeremy responded. "I was thinking out loud. You did the right thing placing me for adoption. I believe that. But everything you're saying makes me appreciate you more."

"That's not helping either," Sandy said as she took a pack of tissues from her purse. She wiped her eyes and blew her nose. "I'm going to have to redo my makeup before we get to the courthouse."

They rode without speaking for several

miles. Sandy wasn't sure what was in Jeremy's mind. She was clawing her way out of raw feelings from old wounds that were still sensitive.

"I need to practice answering questions," she said when she'd regained her composure. "Let's try again."

Jeremy repositioned his hands on the steering wheel.

"Okay, but don't hesitate to use what you just told me in an answer."

"Which part?"

"How you can't stand the thought of an unborn baby being harmed."

"I'm not sure I can do that without crying."

"Genuine tears aren't a bad thing in court, but I think you're going to have your game face on."

"How can you be so sure?"

Jeremy smiled. "Because I'm the same way. I can be a softy in private, but when something important is on the line, I'm serious and focused."

"I hope you're right."

Sandy told him some of the things she knew about fetal development, beginning with what she'd learned during her first few days at Linda's house.

"I look forward to meeting your aunt," he

said. "And adding a scientific reason for your belief helps." Jeremy switched lanes to pass a car. "Also, don't hesitate to use an answer as a chance to give a little speech. Dusty will try to make you sound like a bigoted member of a conservative religious group. You can use a question like that to explain to the judge that you have strongly held beliefs yet understand your role as a public school teacher with almost thirty years of experience. That way, you admit what is true but put it in the context of your professional obligation to Maria. A student has a right to know about her options and then make up her own mind. You can give the judge examples of conversations you've had with Maria and what you told her."

"Am I allowed to do that? Isn't that what they call hearsay?"

"No, it would be hearsay if you testify to what Maria said to you."

"I'm not sure I remember what I've told her."

Jeremy glanced at her. "You're a woman. You remember plenty, especially about something as emotionally charged as this."

Sandy had to admit she could recall a lot of details about the times she and Maria had talked since the first afternoon on the bench near the school entrance.

"Okay, but I don't want to get too carried away."

"Let the judge set the limits. His opinion is the only one that matters."

"Won't you be questioning me first?"

"Not necessarily. I suspect Dusty will call you for purposes of cross-examination during the presentation of his evidence. Remember, there's nothing wrong with pausing for a second or two before responding. That will give you a chance to collect your thoughts so you say what you want to, not what he's trying to coerce from you. There's nothing more frustrating to a lawyer than repeatedly failing to make a witness look bad."

Sandy was less confident than Jeremy that she was going to be such a dynamite witness.

Jeremy continued.

"I'll be hitting hard on the point that you were exercising free-speech rights on a controversial topic about which sincere people have different opinions. A primary purpose of the free-speech provision of the First Amendment is to create a society where ideas can be expressed without governmental restriction."

"That makes sense."

"Unfortunately, the free-speech clause

isn't as strong a weapon as some of us would like it to be, especially when it comes to speech that is linked to religion. You can tell the judge that your pro-life opinions are based on science, but we can't deny that your faith plays a big role in what you believe. And when religious free speech comes into conflict with the prohibition against governmental establishment of religion, religious speech often loses."

"How am I establishing religion?"

"You're a schoolteacher, a paid government employee. Remember, that's the angle I think the women's organization wants to exploit. Schools are a huge battleground in the abortion fight because that's where teenage girls are influenced."

"Did you talk to the other lawyer about that?"

"No, it would have made him shift into advocacy mode. My purpose in calling him was to create a little bit of personal rapport with him as a fellow attorney."

"You were manipulating him."

Jeremy smiled. "In a friendly, Southern sort of way."

They approached the gas station where Sandy had encountered the old woman who told her she was going to have twins. The structure had been remodeled and the name changed several times. There were rows of shiny new pumps out front.

"I need gas," Jeremy said as he turned into the parking lot.

"This place has been here for a long time," Sandy said.

She got out of the car and looked around. No strange old women seemed to be lurking in the shadows.

"Do you want anything?" she asked.

"No, thanks."

While Jeremy filled up the gas tank, Sandy went inside and tried to reconstruct her makeup in the restroom.

"You look great," Jeremy said when she returned to the car.

"I appreciate the compliment, but I'd rather you not say anything else that will make me cry."

"I'll do my best to avoid sensitive topics." Jeremy grinned. "If we don't hit any traffic problems, we'll be a half hour early for the hearing."

"That will be thirty minutes for me to get more and more nervous."

They pulled away from the pumps.

"It's impossible not to be nervous, but you know what you've done and what you haven't done."

"Can we practice some more?" Sandy

asked. "It helps keep me from thinking about how scared I'm going to be."

Until they reached the outskirts of Atlanta, Jeremy pretended he was Dusty Abernathy. Several times Sandy stumbled, and Jeremy gently corrected her. Twice she used a question as an excuse to give a longer explanation of her motivation for helping Maria. The second time, Jeremy laughed.

"Lawyers on TV control witnesses a lot better than in real life. If a witness said what you just said to me, I'd be tempted to crawl back to the counsel table and wait to fight another day." Jeremy paused. "The real wild card is what Judge Tompkins wants to hear. There won't be a jury, so his opinion is the only one that matters. If he asks questions, turn in your chair so you can make eye contact with him when you answer. The judge would rather hear what you have to say than the words Dusty and I try to put in your mouth."

The Richard B. Russell Federal Building came into view. The white structure, named after a longtime Georgia senator, dominated a city block. Jeremy drove into a parking deck.

"I didn't realize the courthouse was this big," Sandy said. "Do you know where to go when we get inside?"

"It's more than a courthouse. It's a big government complex, but I have a pretty good idea how to find the courtroom. If you have a gun in your purse, leave it in the car."

"I'm relying on my lawyer to take care of me," Sandy replied.

They entered the building and passed through a security checkpoint. Jeremy found the correct elevators. Sandy's mouth was dry, and she could feel her heart beating in her chest.

"I'm already terrified," she whispered as the elevator climbed higher. "My heart can't beat this fast for thirty minutes."

"It won't," Jeremy answered, checking his watch. "Once the hearing starts, your adrenaline should kick in and calm you down."

"Are you sure?"

"Yes."

Sandy took a deep breath as they got off the elevator. Jeremy led the way down a hallway. The courtroom was empty.

"This is a courtroom?" Sandy asked. "It's not very big."

"There are several big, fancy courtrooms, but there's no need to hold a hearing on a motion in one of them."

"We're going to be sitting close together,

aren't we?" Sandy eyed the counsel tables beside each other and the small seating area.

"Yes. Now that you know the layout, do you want to wait here or go downstairs to the snack bar?"

"Go downstairs. Waiting here will make me more tense."

The snack bar was on the ground level of the building. Sandy bought a banana.

"Did your heart slow down?" he asked.

"Back to normal, for now. Are you nervous?"

Jeremy smiled. "I don't think that's the right word to describe how I feel. There's always a mixture of excitement and anticipation of a fight before I go into court."

Sandy nibbled her banana. They were at a table for two in the corner of the snack bar. Jeremy had his back to the door. Sandy looked up and saw Carol Ramsey enter. Beside her was an attractive young woman with dark curly hair. Bringing up the rear was a handsome man, somewhat taller than Jeremy, in his early thirties. He was wearing a dark-gray suit and had wavy, reddish-brown hair. He held the door open for the woman with curly hair.

"Don't turn around, but there's Carol Ramsey," Sandy whispered to Jeremy. "She's wearing dark slacks and a white blouse."

Jeremy immediately glanced over his shoulder.

"And that's probably Dusty Abernathy with her," he said. "Do you know the other woman?"

"No."

"Then she's the representative from the women's group."

Before Sandy could say anything else, Jeremy got up and headed toward the threesome. She was amazed at Jeremy's boldness. He walked up to the other lawyer and introduced himself, and they shook hands. Carol looked as uncomfortable as Sandy would have if unexpectedly confronted by someone she knew was about to attack her. The other lawyer seemed relaxed as he and Jeremy talked. There was something vaguely familiar about his eyes and the shape of his mouth. He tilted his head slightly to the side and ran his right hand through his hair.

Suddenly, Sandy's mouth went dry.

The other lawyer reminded her of Brad Donnelly. Sandy closed her eyes and shook her head to drive the insane thought from her mind. Finding Jeremy had so unsettled her that she wasn't thinking straight. She didn't want to go through life inspecting strangers in grocery stores and airports, always wondering if one of them was her other son. Jeremy returned with the other lawyer in tow.

"Sandy," Jeremy said, "this is Dusty Abernathy."

Up close, the similarity to Brad was stronger than from across the room. Carol and the other woman were paying for something at the cash register. Sandy stood up.

"Hello," she said, trying to sound self-assured.

Dusty took Sandy's hand in hers and firmly shook it.

"Nice to meet you," he said. "We'll talk more when we go upstairs to the courtroom."

"That's why I'm here," she replied. "To tell the truth about what's going on with Maria Alverez."

"The time for that is later," Jeremy cut in. "I just wanted Dusty to meet you and see for himself that you don't have horns or fangs."

"Only when someone threatens one of my students," Sandy found herself saying.

Dusty glanced sideways at Jeremy, then turned and left. As soon as he was out of earshot, Jeremy leaned in close to Sandy.

"Why did you say that?" he asked sharply. "It sounded like you wanted to pick a fight with him."

"He had the kind of cocky look on his face that I don't tolerate in male students. It ticked me off."

"Well, I hope you're going to keep your cool when you're on the witness stand. Abernathy is going to try to bait you. You just made things harder on yourself."

"You were right about one thing," Sandy replied.

"What?"

"When my adrenaline kicked in, I didn't feel nervous."

"You should save that for later and use it to help you stay calm, not get feisty. Let's get out of here."

Sandy took a last big bite of banana and dropped the peel in a trash can.

"I'm not sorry," she said as they waited for the elevator. "But if he's in there bragging to Carol and the other woman that he's going to make me look foolish on the witness stand, he's in for a rude awakening."

Jeremy gave Sandy a puzzled look.

"What happened to my sweet little schoolteacher mother?"

"I guess some of the excitement and anticipation you feel when you're about to fight in court is in me too."

THIRTY-THREE

A court reporter was setting up her equipment in the small courtroom. Jeremy gave her his card.

"When will the judge get here?" Sandy asked him.

"Not until it's time to start. The parties wait for the judge, not the other way around."

They sat at one of the two tables set up for lawyers and their clients. Jeremy opened his briefcase and gave Sandy a blank legal pad.

"Write down anything that pops into your mind as you listen to the testimony and argument. You may catch something I miss."

Sandy sat with her ankles crossed beneath the table. Jeremy was busy organizing papers from his file. Sandy saw her name on the outside of the folder. Jeremy opened his laptop computer.

"What are those?" she asked, pointing to

a stack of papers.

"Court decisions relevant to the issues. I want to have the full text available in case the judge has a question."

"Won't the judge have a computer?"

"Yes, but some judges like to see the papers. I'm not sure about Judge Tompkins."

The back door of the courtroom opened. Dusty led Carol and the other woman into the courtroom. Carol avoided looking at Sandy. Like Jeremy, Dusty immediately busied himself with preparation. A door to the side of the bench opened, and an older man with white hair and wearing a black judicial robe strode into the room. Jeremy and Dusty jumped to their feet. Sandy followed them. The judge sat down and looked at the court reporter.

"Are you ready?" he asked her.

"Yes, sir."

"On the record," the judge said without any preamble. "This is the hearing on a motion for a temporary restraining order in the matter of Sandra H. Lincoln. Proceed for the petitioner."

Dusty stepped out from behind the table.

"Your Honor, I'm Dustin Abernathy, and I represent the petitioner in this matter. Would it be helpful to the court if I summarized our theory of the case before presenting any evidence?"

"Are you going to tell me anything that's not in your motion and brief?"

"Not at this point."

The judge narrowed his eyes. "I studied the file before I came in here, and I assume you're prepared to present proof of egregious conduct by Ms. Lincoln sufficient to justify your claim for relief. Prior restraints against free speech, even against government employees, are granted only upon a showing of immediate and eminent threat to a fundamental right."

Sandy saw Jeremy tap one of the court decisions he'd copied.

"Yes, Your Honor," Dusty said. "And it's my client's position that such conduct has occurred in this case, thus justifying immediate action because of the time-sensitive nature of the rights being impacted."

"Proceed," the judge said.

"Ms. Carol Ramsey. Come forward and be sworn."

Carol walked up to the witness stand and stood beside it.

"Judge, would you like to swear in all the witnesses at once?" Dusty asked.

"Yes," the judge said. "Everyone who may testify in this matter, please stand and raise your right hand."

Sandy stood up, as did the attractive curly-haired woman. The judge administered the oath.

Sandy said, "I do," in a loud, clear voice.

Once Carol was seated in the witness stand, Dusty said, "Ms. Ramsey, please tell the court your name and profession."

As Sandy listened to Carol provide background information, she found herself feeling sorry for her rather than angry. It was clear that Carol became a high school counselor because she wanted to help students navigate an often difficult time in their lives. But when Carol mentioned Maria, Sandy bristled. Good intentions don't trump bad actions.

"What is your understanding of the student's relationship with Ms. Lincoln?" Dusty asked.

"Objection," Jeremy said, standing up. "This is speculation unless a proper foundation is laid for an opinion."

"Granted," the judge replied. "Lay a foundation."

"Did you and Ms. Lincoln discuss her interaction with Maria Alverez on several occasions?"

"Yes."

"How many meetings did you observe

between Ms. Lincoln and Maria?"

"Several."

"What did Ms. Lincoln say to you about her relationship with Maria during those meetings?"

Sandy was poised to write any lies or errors on the legal pad, but Carol's summaries of their conversations and the meetings with Maria were fairly accurate. She even knew the dates and times they got together, which made Sandy a bit nervous. If asked that type of specific information, Sandy wouldn't be able to answer.

"On how many occasions did you hear Ms. Lincoln seek to influence and coerce the student's exercise of her right to reproductive freedom?"

Sandy leaned forward.

"Maria told me of several instances. The first occurred on —"

"Objection," Jeremy said. "That would be hearsay."

"Granted."

Sandy remembered what Jeremy told her in the car.

"Did Ms. Lincoln deny making coercive statements to Maria?" Dusty asked.

"No."

Sandy quickly jotted down on her legal pad: *We never talked about what I told Maria*

— Carol doesn't know about any so-called coercive statements.

"What change did you see in Maria's behavior as a result of her interaction with Ms. Lincoln?"

"Objection," Jeremy said. "That is speculative."

"Granted," the judge said. "Mr. Abernathy, this hearing may not have the formality of a jury trial, but the rules of evidence still apply. Lay a foundation for this line of testimony."

"Yes, sir."

So far, Sandy was pleased with the way the judge was approaching the case.

"Was there a correlation between Maria's statements to you and her interaction with Ms. Lincoln?"

"Yes."

To Sandy's amazement, Carol seemed to know most of the dates and times Maria had stopped by Sandy's classroom to talk. Referring to a notebook, Carol created a time line.

"What did you observe about Maria's mental status as this situation progressed and Ms. Lincoln's involvement persisted?"

"She was very afraid."

Sandy made another note: *Maria was afraid of Emilio and her father, not me.*

By this point, Carol was talking about the first meeting with Dr. Vale. Carol's opinion about the meeting with Dr. Vale wasn't surprising. She portrayed Sandy as pretending to acquiesce to the principal while intending to maintain her influence with Maria.

"Ms. Lincoln actually increased her attempts to coerce Maria after that meeting," Carol said.

Carol gave another summary of Sandy's meetings with Maria and the letter from Jeremy. A copy of the letter was placed into evidence without objection. Sandy was impressed by Carol's performance. Dustin Abernathy had obviously spent more time choreographing her testimony than Jeremy had spent with Sandy. The judge granted most of Jeremy's objections, but that didn't seem to have any effect in derailing the testimony.

"After the second trip to the women's health center in Atlanta, it was obvious to me that Maria needed legal help to protect her rights. That's when I met with Ms. Dawkins."

"Has there been any change in Ms. Lincoln's activity with Maria since the motion was filed early last week?"

"No. She has continued to do what she's

been doing all along."

Carol then described the incident when Maria broke down in tears in Sandy's classroom. Sandy's mouth dropped open. She rapidly wrote on her legal pad: *There must be a camera in my classroom.* She slid the pad over so Jeremy could see it. He nodded. Carol spun the weeping episode as an example of Sandy's harshness toward Maria by claiming that Sandy drove the student to tears. As the testimony dragged on, Sandy started to squirm in her chair. Every time she thought Carol was almost finished, Dusty started down another line of questioning designed to cast Sandy in the most negative light possible. If she didn't know what was in her heart and mind, Sandy would have questioned her own motives and actions. Finally, the lawyer paused for a moment. Sandy glanced over and watched him review his notes one last time.

"That's all I have from this witness at the present time," he said.

Jeremy stood up. Sandy sat up straighter in her chair in anticipation of what was about to happen.

"Mr. Abernathy," the judge said. "Who else are you going to call to testify in support of your motion?"

"I intend to call Ms. Lincoln for purposes

of cross-examination as well as Ms. Shania Dawkins, the regional director for the petitioner."

"Where is the student?"

"In school, Your Honor."

The judge looked down from the bench at Dusty.

"Don't you think it would helpful to hear from the party whose rights are in issue today?"

"Normally, it would. However, there is a petition filed in juvenile court in Rutland alleging that Ms. Alverez is mentally incompetent."

"Who filed that petition?"

"I did. The goal is to appoint a guardian who can assist Ms. Alverez in making the best decision about her pregnancy."

"Has there been a hearing on that petition?"

"No, sir. But given the student's mental limitations, her testimony would not be probative on the issues before the court. She is easily influenced and swayed by whoever happens to be talking to her at the moment."

Sandy grunted in agreement.

"And she barely speaks English," Dusty finished.

"I assume you've interviewed Ms. Alverez

as the foundation for making that representation to the court," the judge said.

"Uh, no, sir. I'm relying on Ms. Ramsey's evaluation. You heard her qualifications at the beginning of her testimony and —"

"I'm charged with deciding this important issue," the judge interrupted. "When I'm the trier of fact, I want all potentially relevant evidence before me. You can call any witnesses you like, but I'm not going to consider granting your motion until I have an opportunity to hear from and observe Ms. Alverez for myself. If needed, I'll bring in a translator."

Sandy saw Dusty swallow.

"May I have a moment with my clients?" he asked.

"Yes."

Dusty huddled with Carol and Ms. Dawkins. Sandy leaned over to Jeremy.

"What's going to happen?" she whispered.

"He's going to ask for a continuance."

"You mean, we'll have to come back and do this —"

Before Sandy could complete her question, Dusty spoke.

"Your Honor, we request a continuance of the hearing so we can bring Ms. Alverez before you. Because of the time-sensitive nature of the issue, we ask the court to reschedule the hearing as soon as practicable."

"Granted," the judge said. "I'll instruct the clerk to place this matter back on a hearing calendar within ten days."

The judge left the courtroom. Jeremy began stacking up his papers and putting them in his briefcase. He closed his laptop. Sandy was dazed.

"Ready?" he asked her.

As they left the courtroom, Dusty, Carol, and Dawkins followed them. Jeremy held the door open for Sandy, then allowed the others to pass by. They ended up in a silent cluster in front of the elevators. The elevator door opened. Sandy wanted to wait, but Jeremy stepped forward and held the door open so everyone could get on. Sandy ended up standing between Jeremy and Dusty. She cut her eyes from side to side. The two men seemed relaxed and unaffected by what had happened in the courtroom. Sandy's stomach was twisted into a massive knot. As they neared the ground floor, Dustin turned to Carol and Dawkins.

"Shania, I'll call you later," he said. "Thanks for giving Carol a ride back to the center."

When the elevator door opened, Sandy breathed a sigh of relief. Carol and Shania turned right; Dusty, Jeremy, and Sandy turned left.

"Are you in the parking deck?" Jeremy asked the other lawyer.

"Yes. Shania parked in a surface lot."

"Do you have time for lunch?" Jeremy asked. "I don't have to be back in Tryon until four."

Sandy almost fainted.

"Yeah, I thought we'd be spending more time with Judge Tompkins."

Speechless, Sandy fell back half a step. Jeremy and Dusty moved closer together.

"There's a nice lunch spot that's between here and my office. It isn't out of the way for you either."

"Sandy, is that okay with you?" Jeremy asked, glancing over his shoulder.

"I guess so," she managed. "But I'm not very hungry."

Jeremy and Dusty continued to chat as they walked. Sandy stared at the back of their heads. Dusty was taller and leaner than Jeremy. Sandy decided her initial impression that Dusty resembled Brad Donnelly was the product of an overactive imagination. They reached the elevator for the parking deck.

"I'm on level three," Jeremy said.

"I'm on four."

"I'll wait for you. What are you driving?"

"A black BMW."

When Jeremy and Sandy got off the elevator and the doors closed, she immediately turned to him.

"Why in the world did you ask him about eating lunch? Don't you realize how uncomfortable this is going to be for me?"

"I'd like to get to know him," Jeremy replied patiently. "Lawyers on opposite sides of cases usually don't take it personally. As soon as the judge leaves the room, they stop fighting. If they didn't, it would dramatically increase the incidence of ulcers."

"What about my ulcers?"

"Do you have ulcers?"

"No."

"Look, I know this isn't what you wanted, but while we were in the elevator, I felt an inner nudge from the Lord to reach out to this guy. When that happens, I try to obey it."

Sandy bit her lower lip. It was hard to argue with someone who claimed to be following God. She remembered her recent prayer at the church.

"What am I supposed to say at lunch?" she asked.

"Nothing unless you want to. We're not going to talk about the case. If he brings it up, I'll change the subject."

They got into Jeremy's vehicle. He backed out of the parking space and stopped to wait. "Jesus said to love your enemies," he added.

"I love Carol Ramsey," Sandy sniffed, "but that doesn't mean I want to have lunch with her. At least not now."

A black BMW whizzed around the corner and honked its horn. As the car passed by, Sandy saw Dusty wave his hand. They moved forward.

"Is this our first argument?" Jeremy asked.

"No," Sandy replied. "An argument implies a discussion. You delivered an ultimatum."

"Okay." Jeremy smiled. "Complain to Leanne. She'll sympathize with you. I've dragged her into awkward social situations several times because I thought it was the right thing to do."

"How did that work out?"

"Sometimes good, other times not so good."

They left the parking deck and merged onto the expressway. Dusty drove fast, and they zipped in and out of traffic. He started to leave them behind. Jeremy accelerated.

"Who's going to represent you if you get a speeding ticket?" Sandy asked, gripping the armrest on the door.

Before Jeremy could answer, Dusty changed two lanes of traffic and took an exit ramp on the right. Jeremy tried to follow. The sound of a loud horn made Sandy jump. A large truck had switched lanes and was within inches of the passenger side of the vehicle. Jeremy jerked the steering wheel to the left, braked sharply, then cut over onto the exit ramp, just missing a row of safety barrels. Sandy, who had been holding her breath, exhaled.

"That was exciting," Jeremy said, shaking his head.

"No, we could have been killed!"

They reached the top of the ramp and rolled to a stop. Dusty was waiting at a traffic light that was red.

"Sorry," Jeremy said, glancing over at Sandy. "That was a close call. I should have thought more about your safety than keeping up with Dusty. I forgot to ask for his cell phone number and didn't want to lose him."

"Don't drive like that, no matter the situation," Sandy fumed. "And your concern shouldn't be for me. You have a wife and two children who need you."

The light turned green, and Dusty turned left onto the street. He accelerated quickly.

Jeremy held back. They made it safely through two intersections, then Dusty turned right into a restaurant parking lot. He was waiting for them at the entrance to the restaurant and held the door open for Sandy, who walked past without looking at him. A hostess seated them at a table next to a window that offered a view of the parking lot on the other side of the building.

"I had a little trouble keeping up with you," Jeremy said as soon as they were seated.

"The exit snuck up on me," Dusty replied casually as he read the menu. "The Reuben sandwich here is the best I've had in Atlanta."

"Sounds good to me," Jeremy said. "That's one of my favorites."

Sandy loved Reuben sandwiches too, but she kept staring at the menu. A young waiter brought them water.

"I looked at your firm's website," Jeremy said to Dusty. "Did you move here from California?"

"Yeah, I've been with Jenkins and Lyons in L.A. since law school. The firm developed a niche in liver damage suits against a big health supplement manufacturer. There are enough claims in Georgia to justify an on-site presence for a couple of years, so I volunteered."

"I can imagine how the volunteer thing came down."

"No, I had a say in it. I needed a change in scenery."

The waiter returned to take their order. The two men looked at Sandy.

"The Reuben," she said, "with a side of fresh fruit."

"Same for me," Jeremy said.

"Make that three," Dusty added.

The waiter left.

"At least we all agree about one thing," Dusty said with a smile.

Sandy didn't respond. Jeremy took a sip of water.

"Did you grow up in California?" he asked.

"Yeah. My father was a computer designer, and my mother worked at a school."

"Was she a teacher?"

"A speech therapist."

Sandy's mind flashed back to Linda's kitchen and a folder from the adoption agency about a similar couple in California.

"She died from a brain aneurysm when I was fifteen," Dusty continued.

A sharp sadness cut through Sandy's heart. Dusty turned to Jeremy.

"I looked at your website and saw that you

used to be an assistant DA. Did you prosecute a lot of moonshiners?"

"No, that's a federal offense. But I had this one case involving a guy who thought he was making —"

Sandy didn't listen as Jeremy told a war story. The folder at the agency had identified the adoptive father as a computer engineer, which sounded a lot like a computer designer. And how many computer designers in California were married to speech therapists? She stared as hard as she could at her water glass, but her eyes kept darting to Dusty. He bore a passing resemblance to Brad, but it wasn't as striking as Jeremy's similarity to Sandy and her brother Jack. Dusty's hair had a hint of red, but the nose and mouth weren't right, and his chin was shaped differently.

Jeremy finished a story that left the two men laughing. The waiter brought their food. The sandwiches were made with corned beef, sauerkraut, Swiss cheese, and Russian dressing, all piled high between slices of dark rye bread.

"The owner claims they make the bread in the back," Dusty said. "If this isn't any good, there's a fast-food place you can go to on the other side of the expressway."

Jeremy took a big bite, chewed for a moment, and shook his head.

"Is there a problem?" Dusty asked.

Jeremy swallowed. "No, it's probably the best Reuben that's ever passed my lips. It's impossible to find something like this in Tryon."

Sandy nibbled the corner of her sandwich. They ate in silence for a few minutes. Sandy took a drink of water and looked at Dusty.

"Are you adopted?" she asked.

Dusty had his sandwich halfway to his mouth. He stopped and gave her a surprised look.

"No," he said.

"Are you sure?"

Dusty returned his sandwich to the plate.

"Yes. And I have the birth certificate and baby pictures to prove it."

Jeremy coughed into his hand. "Sandy, I told you and Dusty that I'm an adoptee. Maybe that's what you're remembering."

Sandy gave Jeremy an incredulous look.

"I think I can keep that information sorted out in my mind," she said.

Dusty looked at Jeremy and rolled his eyes. The way he did it reminded Sandy of an identical gesture she'd seen Brad do many times.

"Talking about adoption reminds me of maybe the strangest case I handled when I was in the DA's office," Jeremy said, obviously trying to change the subject. "It involved a grown woman who legally adopted her elderly stepfather after her mother passed away and then tried to collect on a life insurance policy as the only surviving heir when the old man fell down a flight of stairs and died."

Jeremy launched into another story, leaving Sandy with questions racing through her head. She wanted to find out Dusty's date of birth and ask whether any of the early pictures he mentioned included shots of his pregnant mother. She excused herself and went to the restroom. While washing her hands, she looked at herself in the mirror. She didn't see anything of herself in Dustin Abernathy.

Also in the back of Sandy's mind was the warning she'd received from the old woman at the gas station. Everything the woman told her had come true. Now, the boys were grown men whose contact with each other was a ticking time bomb. Sandy thought about the close call on the expressway on the drive to the restaurant and shuddered. For Jeremy to continue to interact with Dusty was daring death. When she got back to the two men, her focus returned to the table.

"Jeremy, I'm ready to leave," she said firmly.

"I'm almost done," Jeremy replied, turning back to Dusty. "And it turned out that the woman's boyfriend was the one who pushed the man down the stairs. They'd gotten into an argument over who would get the transmission from an old pickup truck parked in the front yard. If the boyfriend hadn't confessed, we never would have figured out what happened."

"I've never handled any criminal cases," Dusty said, shaking his head. "Why is it that so many people open their mouths and convict themselves? Don't they realize the risk? I mean, is it that hard to understand a Miranda warning?"

"I think it's something God puts in each person," Jeremy replied. "People have an innate desire to tell someone when they've done something wrong. Maybe not immediately, but most folks eventually want to clear their conscience."

"I don't know," Dusty remarked and pulled on his right earlobe with his right hand.

Sandy stared at Dusty's ear.

"There's no other explanation," Jeremy said. "If people were only interested in self-preservation, they'd shut up and wait for a lawyer. I've never studied the psychology of guilt, or whether the medical community admits such a thing exists, but I know how powerful it is in real life."

Sandy caught Jeremy's eye and tilted her head toward the door.

"A couple more bites," Jeremy responded. "I don't want to feel guilty for leaving any of this sandwich uneaten on the plate."

Sandy had no choice but to wait. The two men cleaned their plates, then had a brief argument over who would pick up the tab.

"I selected the restaurant," Dusty said, grabbing the bill from the waiter as soon as he approached the table. "If I'm ever in Tryon, you can pay."

"I was going to call you about that later, but I'll mention it now," Jeremy said. "The judge thought you should meet Maria for yourself. I agree. You'll discover that she comes across as a normal Hispanic teenager learning English as a second language. If you still think she's incompetent after meeting her, proceed with the motion and the incompetency action in juvenile court."

"She'll need to be psychologically evaluated in the juvenile court action."

"I'm sure the juvenile court judge will order a battery of psychological tests if we reach that point. How many lawyers would grant you access like this to their client on such short notice?"

Dusty studied Jeremy for a moment. Sandy wanted to speak but knew Jeremy would be furious if she stepped in now.

"Are you talking about a deposition?" Dusty asked.

"You can start with a conversation, then decide if you want to depose her. All I ask is that everything be set up on the same day."

"Okay, let's check our calendars and pick a date as soon as possible. I'd like to talk to her first and reserve the right to depose her the same day if I choose to do so."

"That's fine. Either way, you'll want to have a translator present."

"Do you know any translators who work regularly with the courts?"

"Yes, I'll send you a couple of names."

They stood up from the table.

"You're pretty confident about this girl's mental capacity, aren't you?" Dusty said as they walked toward the door.

"I've spent enough time with Maria to form an opinion."

Once outside, Jeremy and Dusty shook hands. Dusty faced Sandy, who wanted to turn and run.

"Thanks for being a good sport and joining us for lunch," he said. "Lawyers are like professional wrestlers. They bluster in the ring, but once the lights are off and the crowd goes home, they go out and eat a Reuben together."

Dusty got in his car. Jeremy and Sandy walked together across the parking lot. As soon as they were seated in Jeremy's SUV, Sandy spoke.

"Do you know who Dusty is?"

Thirty-Four

"I assume you're going to say Dustin Abernathy is my twin brother," Jeremy replied.

"When did you figure it out?" she asked in surprise.

"I didn't. But it was a reasonable guess based on the fact that you asked him if he was adopted, to which he replied without hesitation, 'No.' "

"I remember his parents' folder at the adoption agency. The father was a computer engineer, and the mother was a speech therapist. They lived on the West Coast."

"Any pictures?"

"No, that only happened with your mother."

Jeremy turned out of the parking lot onto the busy street.

"There are thousands and thousands of computer engineers and designers on the West Coast, which includes California, Oregon, and Washington."

"I know U.S. geography." Sandy sniffed. "And he looks like Brad Donnelly. When I show you the pictures from my high school yearbook, you'll see the similarity."

Jeremy shook his head. "But he said he wasn't adopted. Who raises a child today and doesn't let him know?"

"It's possible."

"Maybe, but there's not much circumstantial evidence to prove it. Do you think meeting me has sensitized you to the possibility of finding my brother?"

"No. What's his birthday?" Sandy asked.

Jeremy sped down the ramp onto the expressway.

"Take the wheel," he said to Sandy, "while I try to find the answer."

"No, we've already had one close call. I'm not going to cause another one."

Jeremy took his phone from his pocket and braced the steering wheel with his knees while he entered information.

"That's not legal or safe," Sandy said, crossing her arms over her chest.

"No, but there's no place to pull over, and you want answers now."

Jeremy used his hands to change lanes, then continued to press keys.

"Okay, here it is," he said. "According to the website for Dusty's law firm in Los

Angeles, Dustin L. Abernathy, Esq., was born in Escondido, California, on April 15, 1975. He attended UCLA, then went to law school at Northwestern." Jeremy glanced sideways at Sandy. "We're the same age, but I assume you weren't in labor for ten days and didn't travel three thousand miles to a different hospital to deliver a second baby."

"That could be a mistake or they changed the records. And just because he has a birth certificate doesn't prove anything. They put the adoptive parents' names on it."

"Anything is possible, but in a court of law you just lost your maternity case on a motion for summary judgment." Jeremy returned his phone to the front pocket of his shirt and put both hands on the steering wheel. "Could you let me enjoy getting to know you without complicating everything?"

Sandy's face fell. The inside of the car was silent for several miles.

"It's okay," Jeremy said. "You've been under a lot of pressure today."

"I bet your mom in Charleston is always calm and poised." Sandy sighed. "She looked so at peace in the picture I saw."

"She keeps things in perspective," Jeremy said. "But I'm not trying to compare you to her. It's a lot more fun finally finding out who you are and discovering where some of my traits come from. For example, Leanne noticed the way both of us look at other people when talking to them."

"Like this?" Sandy looked at Jeremy, who glanced sideways at her.

"Yeah. It's intense and can put people off."

"I'm just paying attention."

"I know. But it can be interpreted as an attempt at intimidation."

"I do it because I'm a schoolteacher who has to use every trick in her bag to control a classroom."

"And I'm a lawyer who wants a witness to know I mean business when I stand up to ask questions. But that look is genetic, not learned."

Sandy relaxed a little bit. It made her feel good that Jeremy wasn't secretly criticizing her. They dropped the subject of Dusty Abernathy and spent the next thirty miles discussing inherited tendencies and common interests. Sandy discovered that not only did Jeremy like Reuben sandwiches, he also loved well-buttered popcorn.

"I'll go to a movie just to eat popcorn," Sandy said. "I'm careful about my diet most of the time, but don't tell me I can't have popcorn at the theater."

"Then we'll each get our own bucket,"

Jeremy replied.

As they left Atlanta behind, Sandy's confidence that Dusty might be "Baby Jones" weakened. She had to admit she'd jumped to a conclusion she wouldn't have considered at the time she met Jeremy. His pedigree was certain. Dusty's wasn't.

"Did you know they use coconut oil to cook popcorn at the theater?" Jeremy asked after a long silence.

"No."

"It gives it a flavor you can't duplicate at home."

"Are you craving popcorn right now?" Sandy responded.

"Yes."

When they reached Rutland, Jeremy asked, "Could we swing by your house? Not to go in. I'd just like to see the outside."

"Sure, and we can go inside if you have a few minutes. I don't have children at home. If it gets messy, there's no one to blame but me."

They reached the corner of Sandy's street.

"There's my church," she said. "My family went there when I was growing up."

Jeremy slowed down. The sermon topic for the following Sunday was "Leaving Without Cleaving — How to Stay Married Without Killing Each Other."

"Our minister is doing a series on marriage and family," Sandy said. "He tries to come up with catchy sermon titles. And since I'm not married, I might visit your church again if it's okay with you."

"Sure, and Deb will be thrilled. She'll treat you like a rock star."

When they turned down Sandy's street, Jeremy got a call on his phone. It was Deb. The lawyer on the other side of the case scheduled for four o'clock in Tryon was sick and the hearing was going to be postponed for two weeks.

"Postponements happen a lot, don't they?" Sandy asked.

"Yeah. I get all psyched up and then have to dial it down. But this will give me a chance to spend more time this afternoon with you."

Jeremy's words made Sandy feel warm inside.

"That's my house," she said when they reached the dead end, then quickly added, "Where's my car?"

"At your brother's office," Jeremy said. "I'll take you there next."

"I forgot. A lot has happened since we left this morning."

Nelson was in the backyard. He barked in warning at the strange vehicle. When he saw

Sandy, he wiggled his entire body.

"Someone is excited to see you," Jeremy said.

Sandy introduced Nelson to Jeremy, who rubbed the top of the dog's head.

"I got a dog for my fifth birthday," Jeremy said. "He lived until just before I graduated from high school. Nicky was a member of the family."

"Do you have a dog now?"

"No. Leanne and I have talked about it, but she's not an animal lover. Maybe when Chloe and Zach are old enough to help take care of a pet, we'll get one. My dog and I went everywhere together. Nicky loved the water, so as soon as it was warm enough each year, we spent a lot of time at the beach. He would attack the surf and try to bite the tops of the waves."

Sandy unlocked the kitchen door. Nelson trotted in, followed by Jeremy and Sandy. Jeremy looked around.

"This is nice," he said.

"Thanks. Would you like something to drink?"

"Water would be great."

Sandy poured a glass of ice water. On the corner of the kitchen table was a stack of photographs. Jeremy looked down at the top one.

"Is this you as a little girl?" he asked.

"Yes. I was five years old, and we took a family trip to Tybee Island. Ben was in diapers, which doesn't go very well with a week at the beach."

Jeremy picked up the photograph.

"You can look at those now," Sandy offered, "or wait until I make the scrapbook and surprise you."

"Are all these going to be in the scrapbook?"

"I'm not sure."

Jeremy sat down at the table with the photos. Sandy stood behind his shoulder. He picked up a picture of Sandy and Ben sitting in a porch swing at their maternal grandmother's house.

"Go ahead," she said. "I'll be back in a minute. These shoes are killing my feet."

Sandy went to her bedroom and changed into another outfit. When she returned to the kitchen, Jeremy was sitting at the table with his face buried in his hands.

"What's wrong?" Sandy asked in alarm.

Jeremy looked up. There were tears in his eyes. He pointed to a picture on the table. It was the photo of Sandy and Jessica in the kitchen taken a few weeks before the babies were born.

"When I saw you in that picture, it hit

me," he said. "You went through so much to bring me into this world."

Sandy tried to smile, but tears quickly filled her eyes too. Jeremy picked up the photo again and stared at it.

"It would have been so easy for you to end the pregnancy. But you didn't." Jeremy rubbed his eyes. "You gave everything you had for me, and there wasn't enough left to have your own family."

"That's not true. It just never worked out."

"I want to make it up to you," Jeremy persisted. "To love and respect you the way you deserve."

And with that Sandy lost it. She sat in a chair opposite Jeremy and sobbed. When she finally looked up through blurry eyes, she could barely make out his face.

"I'm sorry I made you cry," he said. "But I had to say that to you."

"It's the most wonderful thing anyone has ever said to me," Sandy managed through sniffles.

Jeremy touched the photo. "I'd love a copy of this picture, but I'm going to have to be careful no one else is around when I look at it."

All Sandy could do was nod. She watched as Jeremy went through a few more photographs. She wanted to provide a running commentary but was too emotionally fragile to speak. There would be time later for the stories behind the pictures. She dabbed her eyes with a tissue.

On the corner of the table was her high school yearbook. Sandy opened it to the page that contained Brad's senior football picture. He was wearing his uniform and kneeling on the grass with a football cradled in his right arm. She slid the yearbook across the table.

"This is your father. He was the star wide receiver on the football team our senior year."

Jeremy studied the photo for a moment.

"You're right," he said. "I can see some of him in Zach."

"And here's the class photo."

Sandy turned to a page she'd marked with a slip of paper. All the boys looked like they were wearing tuxedos. Sandy didn't like Brad's picture. He had an unpleasant smirk on his face.

"The way you and I look at people may be intimidating, but I like it better than his expression in that picture," Jeremy said.

"Yes."

"And I don't see a strong resemblance to Dusty Abernathy. The only similarity is the brownish-red wavy hair. The eyes, chin, and nose are all different."

Sandy wasn't going to argue. Not with a man who'd just pledged his love and respect to her. She pointed to the pile of photos.

"Are there any pictures you've seen that shouldn't be in the scrapbook?" she asked.

"No, but I want more."

"Let me exercise a bit of creative license," Sandy said with a smile. "The theme of this album is how you got here. Later, you can get copies of all the photos you want. My mother has a bunch at her house too."

"What did she say when you told her about me?" Jeremy asked.

Sandy told him about the phone call to Florida. They sat at the kitchen table and talked for over an hour. There seemed to be an unlimited amount of information to be discussed. Finally, Jeremy looked at his watch.

"I'd better get going. I have to pick up Chloe from soccer practice."

"She's a fantastic player."

"Yeah. Her two favorite things are soccer and reading."

When they reached Ben's office, Jeremy gave Sandy a hug and kiss on the cheek.

"I could get used to that," Sandy said, "but you've touched me much deeper in here." She pointed to her heart. "Thank you for wanting me in your life."

Jeremy took her hand and gave it a squeeze.

"Would it be okay if I gave you a kiss?" Sandy asked.

Jeremy lowered his face, and Sandy planted a firm kiss on his right cheek.

After Jeremy left, Sandy returned home. The familiar surroundings of the kitchen now seemed empty. Nelson lay in his favorite spot in the corner. Sandy looked at the dog.

"Once you have a family, it doesn't feel right unless you're all together."

The first thing Sandy did when she arrived at school the following day was look for a hidden surveillance camera. The ceiling area of her classroom was clear, so she began looking in more obscure places. She moved the ancient clock, checked in the area of the fire evacuation chart, and carefully inspected every inch of the blackboard. When she turned around, a male student in her first-period class was watching her with a puzzled look on his face.

"What is it, Curtis?" Sandy asked.

"I brought my paper by early. I have a dentist's appointment today. Did you lose something?"

"No."

Curtis handed her the assignment. As he turned to leave, Sandy looked over his shoulder into the hallway. There, unobtrusively stuck to the place where the ceiling met the top of the wall, was a black orb that concealed one of the cameras used to monitor student activity. The range of the camera must include the first few feet of her classroom. Sandy waved.

It took half of her first-period class for Sandy to reorient herself to her job as a teacher. She longed for the days when her greatest concerns had to do with managing her time and making sure a student with academic problems didn't slip through the cracks. After the third-period bell sounded, her classroom emptied. A few moments later, Maria appeared in her doorway. Sandy resisted the urge to shoo her away. Even if Maria left immediately, the camera still would have recorded a visit.

"Come in," Sandy said. "I need to tell you what happened yesterday."

Sandy spoke in Spanish. Maria listened without asking any questions until Sandy mentioned that the judge wanted her present at the rescheduled hearing.

"I don't know what to say to the judge."

"Mr. Lane and I will go over that with you. In the meantime, there's a chance the lawyer from Atlanta is going to come to Rutland next week to talk to you. Mr. Lane hopes that once the lawyer meets you, he will realize that you are able to make decisions about your pregnancy on your own."

"I saw Ms. Ramsey after first period," Maria said. "She wants me to come by her office before I leave school today. Why does she want to see me?"

"Probably to talk about the hearing."

"Do I have to go?"

"I can't tell you what to do," Sandy replied slowly. "If I suggest you don't talk to Ms. Ramsey, the lawyer in Atlanta will use that to make it seem like I'm making you stay away from her. That could get me in trouble." Maria shook her head. "And we need to stop talking in my classroom," Sandy added.

"Why?"

She explained to Maria about the surveillance camera. The Hispanic girl's eyes widened.

"Don't turn around now," Sandy said. "It might be better if we talk on the phone and arrange a place to meet that's not on school property. I'm going to get you a cell phone that allows me to buy a set number of

587

minutes. When you run out, I can add more. That way you can get in touch with me, and Rosalita too."

"Thank you," Maria said with obvious gratitude. "I won't waste the minutes."

After Maria left, Sandy felt a sense of relief but couldn't understand why. Nothing had been settled. Maybe it had to do with the fact that the process was getting clearer. The unknown is frightening. But Sandy had been inside a federal courtroom. She'd seen Judge Tompkins and met Dusty Abernathy. She'd heard Carol testify. And she knew in general terms what lay ahead.

When it was time for her lunch period, Sandy marched into the cafeteria without worrying whether she might encounter Carol. After going down the salad bar line, she sat with some teachers and entered into a conversation about plans for homecoming. The event was normally one of the highlights of Sandy's year. As a Rutland High graduate who still lived in the area and worked at the school, she was a natural focal point for homecoming activities. This year she hadn't done anything. She jotted a few notes to herself on a napkin and slipped it in her purse.

That afternoon on her way home, Sandy

bought a cheap cell phone for Maria and programmed both her home and cell numbers into speed dial. Then she drove to the trailer park to give the phone to Maria. The dirt road between the trailers was deserted. Still, the place made Sandy feel uneasy. She made sure the doors of her car were locked and didn't stop at Maria's trailer but continued to the one where Rosalita lived. If Maria wasn't there, Sandy would ask Rosalita to give the phone to her. Sandy walked up the steps to the door of the trailer and knocked. One of the older girls she'd seen previously cracked open the door. Sandy spoke in Spanish.

"Is Maria here?" she asked.

"No," the girl answered in English.

"How about your mother?" Sandy replied, also in English. "I'm Ms. Lincoln from the high school."

"She's taking care of the baby," the girl answered.

Sandy couldn't see anything inside the trailer. She took the phone from her purse.

"Can you ask your mother to give this cell phone to Maria?"

"I'll do it," the girl replied. "She's coming over to help fix supper."

"Okay. Tell Maria to call me as soon as she gets it. My number is marked in her directory with my name. Do you understand?"

"Yes." The girl nodded with a slightly disgusted expression on her face. "I know how a cell phone works."

Sandy heard a chain rattle as the door was locked. She slowly turned away. Something wasn't right about the way the girl acted.

As she left the trailer park, Sandy slowed down when she reached Maria's trailer. There were two pickup trucks and a beat-up car parked in front. Lights shone from two of the trailer's three windows. Sandy suddenly wanted to get away as fast as she could. She pressed down on the accelerator and left in a cloud of dust.

Early the next morning Sandy went to Maria's homeroom class. The students hadn't arrived. The homeroom teacher was a young woman named Ms. Randolph who taught algebra II, trigonometry, and calculus. Sandy told her she needed to see Maria and sat on the front row to wait. The large room was also used by the school chorus. In the back corner was the telltale black orb that concealed a camera.

"How is Maria?" Ms. Randolph asked.

"What do you know?" Sandy replied, not sure whether she could trust the young woman.

"I know she's pregnant and about the court cases. My boyfriend is a lawyer with the public defender's office. When I told him people were getting served with legal papers in the faculty lounge, he checked the records."

"Nothing has been resolved," Sandy replied.

"I'm sorry. I think it's terrible, and my boyfriend says this case could have an impact on teachers all over the country."

Before Sandy could respond, two members of the cheerleading squad entered the room. Seeing Sandy, they came over to her. While the three of them chatted, Sandy kept one eye on the door. The tardy bell sounded just as Maria came in. Sandy immediately escorted her into the hallway. There was another surveillance camera directly overhead.

"Did you get the phone?"

"Yes."

"I told Rosalita's daughter to tell you to call me to test it out," Sandy said.

"She didn't. But everyone was upset last night."

"Why?"

"Rosalita heard that Emilio has come back, and he's mad at Rosalita's husband."

"Why?"

"Something to do with money. Rosalita didn't tell me."

"Is Rosalita's husband on the road?"

"Yes, and he won't be back until the middle of next week."

Sandy's mind was whirring.

"Is it dangerous for you to be at your father's house?"

"I don't know. My father doesn't want Emilio to come there, but the lock on our door wouldn't keep him out. It's the same at Rosalita's house."

"Maybe someone should talk to the police."

"What good would that do?" Maria asked, shrugging her shoulders.

"I understand. Go to homeroom, and I'll talk to you later."

Sandy paced back and forth in the hall for the few minutes she had to wait until students streamed out on the way to their first-period classes. Returning to the choral room, she approached Ms. Randolph.

"I've been thinking. Could your boyfriend find out if there are criminal charges against someone?"

"Ted is a defense attorney, not a prosecutor, but I could ask him. What's the person's name?"

"Uh, Emilio. I don't know a last name,

but he's in his thirties. When he's in town he spends a lot of time at the trailer park where Maria lives. It's the one off Haggler Road."

"Without a last name, it may not be possible to find out anything. What do I say when he asks me why I want to know about this guy?"

"That I'm concerned about Maria, and Emilio is the big reason."

"Okay, I'll see what I can do."

"Thanks."

Sandy walked down the hallway to her classroom. The best way to remove Emilio as a possible threat to Maria and the other families in the trailer park would be his arrest. A criminal charge of statutory rape would be a straightforward way to do so. Sandy had sympathized with Maria's early reluctance to talk to the police, but the situation had changed.

Later that afternoon during cheerleading practice, Sandy received a text message from Jeremy:

Hearing in Atlanta rescheduled for next Wed. at 9:00 a.m. Sorry for the early morning time, but the judge set it. Dusty Abernathy is coming to Rutland on

Monday afternoon to meet Maria. Details to follow.

THIRTY-FIVE

Later that evening Sandy received a telephone call at home from an unfamiliar number.

"Sandy, this is Mimi Randolph. I talked to my boyfriend about Emilio. He couldn't find an arrest warrant for anyone with that name, but he talked to some of his contacts in the Hispanic community. Several people knew a man named Emilio. No one liked him."

"That's probably him."

"You didn't tell me this man's link to Maria," Mimi said, "but is he the father —"

"I can't say," Sandy replied quickly.

"You don't have to. But Ted said if Emilio raped Maria, then she's the one who has to take action against him."

Mimi's intuition was sharp.

"I'll let her know."

After the call ended, Sandy tried to reach Maria, but the girl didn't answer the phone.

Sandy felt frustrated. If Maria wasn't going to be available, the cell phone was a waste of money. Fifteen minutes later, Sandy's phone beeped. It was Maria.

"Why didn't you answer earlier?" Sandy asked.

"I was with my father and waited until I came to Rosalita's trailer to call you. It's better if we talk while I'm here."

"Okay. It just makes me worry when I can't reach you."

Sandy told Maria about her conversation with Ms. Randolph and the information obtained from the teacher's boyfriend.

"Would I have to go to the police station?" Maria asked. "I'm too scared to do that."

"Or an officer could meet with you somewhere else. That's what Ms. Ramsey was trying to set up a few weeks ago."

The phone was silent for a moment.

"I know my father would say no. He told me that every time I talk to someone, I make a bigger problem for myself and my family."

"Please think about it. I'd go with you to the police station if you want me to."

"I'm not sure."

Sandy then told her about the text message from Jeremy.

"This means you're going to have to do

some talking on Monday," Sandy said. "I'll try to get more details from Jeremy and let you know."

"Jeremy?"

"Mr. Lane, the lawyer. I'm going to see him on Sunday."

"I don't want to talk to the lawyer from Atlanta. I won't understand what he says."

"A translator will be there."

"That won't help. Mr. Lane uses big words I haven't learned, but I have you there to explain them to me. And he's trying to help me. This man wants to hurt me."

It was a simple but accurate description of Dusty Abernathy's job.

"I'll tell Mr. Lane to make sure you understand the questions," Sandy said. "Don't worry. He'll take care of you."

Friday night at the football game Sandy was buying a drink at the concession stand. A crowd was milling around in front of the booth. When she turned around, she bumped into Brian Winston, the school board's attorney. Their eyes met.

"Ms. Lincoln, please have your lawyer get in touch with me," Winston sputtered.

"Okay."

Winston moved away, knocking a woman off balance. The press of the crowd kept her from falling.

"Watch it!" the woman called out as Winston continued through the crowd.

Sandy returned to the sidelines. She'd told Maria to trust Jeremy and not worry. Now she was going to have to take her own advice.

The Rutland team was driving the ball steadily down the field. Someone touched Sandy on the arm. It was Jessica.

"What's the latest news about your thirty-three-year-old baby?" Jessica asked.

"More than I can squeeze into a few minutes."

"I'll take anything you can give me."

"I told him," Sandy said.

Jessica screamed, and several of the cheerleaders turned around. Sandy told Jessica about the meeting at Ben's office.

"I have goose bumps on top of goose bumps," Jessica replied, rubbing her arms.

Sandy started to mention Leanne but suddenly changed her mind.

"There's a big problem," Sandy said. "I'm afraid Jeremy has met his brother."

"What?" Jessica said in a loud voice that was fortunately drowned out by a roar from the stands as the Rutland quarterback completed a pass.

As Sandy told her about Dusty Abernathy,

Jessica's mouth dropped open in shock.

"I'm not one hundred percent sure, and Dusty denies being adopted," Sandy said. "But I wish you could see him. He has some of Brad's mannerisms."

"A mother's intuition is better than a lie detector test." Jessica reached into her purse and took out a piece of paper. "Tell me Dusty's full name again. I'll get online at home, find his picture, and let you know what I think."

Jessica scribbled down the information.

"Did you say anything to Jeremy about the old woman at the gas station?"

"No, he would really think I'm loony. He already believes I was imagining the similarity between Dusty and Brad Donnelly."

"How would he know anything about Brad?"

"I showed him some photos from our high school yearbook."

"Oh." Jessica paused. "If you let him look at my senior picture, there's no way he'll recognize me now."

At that moment, Rutland scored a touchdown. The cheerleaders sprang into action.

"Not a word about this to anyone," Sandy said into Jessica's ear.

Jessica raised her right index finger to her lips and nodded her head.

The game ended in a Rutland High School victory. Sandy turned down an invitation to go out with a group of students. At home, she logged on to the website for Jenkins and Lyons. She was reading about the firm when Jessica called.

"What is Jeremy thinking?" she said. "Dusty has Brad's eyes. Grab the yearbook for our senior year and turn to page thirty-four."

Sandy flipped open the yearbook. It was a candid photo of Brad standing in front of the school with a few of his friends. The way Brad stood, the shape of his head, and the expression on his face all looked very similar to Dusty Abernathy.

"Yeah," she said. "You're right. But for some reason, Jeremy didn't see it."

"You're going to have to tell him," Jessica replied.

"I already tried."

"Try again. And both of us should keep digging into Dusty's background to see what turns up. Did you know he's been married twice?"

"I think I read he was divorced."

"And he doesn't have any children. He has a younger sister who lives with her husband in Washington, D.C."

"How did you find out about that?"

"One of the genealogy groups I belong to. Family researchers post data about people that ends up in public forums."

"Do you know his sister's name?"

"Lydia Abernathy Duncan. I have her address and phone number."

"You got that from a genealogy site?"

"No, once I had her name, I used an address finder. Do you want to call her?"

Sandy paused. "Give it to me, but I doubt I'll contact her. What would I say? 'I recently met your brother, who claims he's not adopted, but I think he's my son.' She'd report me to the police as a cyberstalker."

Sandy jotted down the address and phone number.

"I'll keep digging," Jessica said. "You have to be a member of the genealogy group to access the information I found, but I'll print out copies of his family tree for you. His paternal grandfather was an actor who appeared in several films. I found a publicity picture, and Dusty doesn't look anything like him."

Sunday morning Sandy drove to the church in Tryon. She sat down beside Deb Bridges.

"Great to see you," Deb said, then leaned in closer. "I'm sorry the hearing in Atlanta had to be rescheduled. I know that's a big strain on you."

"Yeah. The judge wants to hear from Maria."

"Which makes sense to me." Deb reached into her purse and took out a breath mint. "Do you want one?"

"No, thanks."

"Jeremy likes the lawyer on the other side of the case."

"I know. We ate lunch together after the hearing."

"I bet that was awkward."

"Yes, but Jeremy is pretty strong-willed."

"Tell me about it." Deb made a face.

Sandy glanced over her shoulder and saw Jeremy and Leanne come in. Jeremy saw her and waved. He nudged Leanne, who smiled in greeting.

Sandy relaxed and enjoyed the service. After it was over, she and Deb made their way outside and found Jeremy and Leanne.

"Hey, Sandy," a male voice said when Sandy and Deb parted.

It was John Bestwick. He didn't know Jeremy and Leanne, so Sandy introduced them.

"Jeremy is my lawyer," Sandy said to John. "When I use the scanner in your office, I'm sending papers to him."

"I'd do anything I could to help Sandy,"

John said. "She's one of the best teachers in the school."

"That doesn't surprise me," Jeremy said.

After another minute of small talk, John moved on. Leanne leaned in to Sandy.

"I like him," Leanne said.

"If anyone wants to date my mother, they'll need my permission to do it," Jeremy cut in jokingly.

"He's a good man," Sandy said. "But I haven't had a date in years."

"Come on," Leanne said, touching Sandy's arm. "You've got a date with a couple of kids."

"I thought we were going to wait until Jeremy talked to his mom in Charleston."

"We are waiting as far as telling them who you are," Jeremy replied. "I'll introduce you as a teacher who I know."

"Are you sure?" Sandy asked. "Won't they feel lied to when they find out the truth later?"

"If you don't want to —" Jeremy began.

"No," Sandy said. "There's nothing I want more in the world than to see them."

"Zach won't care about finding out in stages," Leanne answered. "Chloe will think it's great once I suggest it's like something from a book."

"She likes the imaginary world?"

603

Leanne rolled her eyes. "Big time."

"When I was her age, I had an elaborate fantasy life," Sandy said. "I even invited my best friend Jessica to join me there."

Leanne looked at Jeremy. "It's a relief to know where Chloe gets it."

"You still have an active imaginary life," Jeremy said. "Your imagination was in high gear at lunch in Atlanta the other day."

"No." Sandy shook her head. "That thought came from who I saw sitting in front of me."

"What are you talking about?" Leanne asked Jeremy.

"I'll let Sandy tell you later if she wants to."

They walked over to the children's church area that was in a one-story building. The hallway was filled with parents and children. They went to a large open room. Sandy saw Chloe sitting on the carpeted floor talking to three other girls. Zach, his arm still in a sling, was chasing another little boy.

"Zach!" Leanne called out. "Slow down!"

The little boy scampered over to them. To Sandy his approach was like a cup of water in a desert place. She drank him in.

"Zach, this is Ms. Lincoln," Jeremy said. "She's a schoolteacher."

The little boy's face had the combination

of exuberance and innocence that only a child can display. Sandy leaned over.

"Hi, Zach," she said.

Zach moved a step closer to his mother and touched her leg.

"Hey," he replied.

Chloe approached with athletic grace that wasn't typical for a girl her age. When Jeremy introduced them, Sandy extended her hand, and Chloe shook it decisively.

"I understand you like to read," Sandy said.

"Yes, ma'am."

"What are some of your favorite books?"

As they walked away from the room, Chloe mentioned two titles, both familiar to Sandy, who then commented on each one.

"Are you a librarian?" Chloe asked.

"No," Sandy said and smiled. "I teach English at the high school in Rutland, but I've always loved to read."

Sandy and Chloe continued to talk about books as they walked.

"Have you read that series?" Sandy asked the girl.

"No."

"I think you'd like them. I'll bring the first one next Sunday for you to try."

Chloe rewarded Sandy with a smile that melted her heart. The girl looked so much like Sandy at the same age. The group reached the parking lot.

"Oh," Jeremy said to Sandy. "I almost forgot. We're meeting with Maria tomorrow afternoon at four. She needs to get together with me forty-five minutes early so I can prepare her."

"Where?"

"The conference room at the courthouse we used the other day. Can you let Maria know to be there?"

"Yes. Do you want me to come?"

"No, you'd better not. Dusty is going to use the translator who helped me the other day. She did a good job, and if we end up taking a deposition, the translator will need to be licensed and certified."

"What about Maria's father?"

"That's up to him, but if he tries to keep Maria from talking to Dusty, it means we have to drag her to Atlanta for the hearing in front of Judge Tompkins on Wednesday. Sooner or later, she's going to have to speak for herself and make it stick. The simplest way to take care of that will be for Dusty to see she's clearly competent and capable of making up her own mind about the pregnancy."

"I'm hungry," Zach said.

"Please let me know that Maria will be

there," Jeremy said as he unlocked the van and the children hopped inside.

"Okay."

Jeremy opened the driver's-side door, then turned around, leaned over, and kissed Sandy on the cheek.

"Thanks," he said. "I enjoyed seeing you with the kids."

From the middle seat of the van, Sandy heard Chloe ask her mother a question.

"Why did Daddy kiss the teacher?"

The door closed before Sandy could hear Leanne's response. As Jeremy backed out of the parking space, Chloe was inspecting Sandy closely from the window beside her seat. Sandy waved, and the girl slowly lifted her hand in response.

During the return trip to Rutland, Sandy called Maria and told her about the meeting on Monday.

"Will you be able to get there?" Sandy asked.

"Yes. One of the girls has to go to the dentist, so Rosalita is getting off work early."

Upon arriving at home, Sandy received a phone call from Jessica.

"Get on your computer again," her friend said brusquely.

"I just took a bite of my sandwich," Sandy

said, her mouth half full.

"You can chew while I tell you what to do."

Sandy went into the craft room and turned on her computer.

"What is this about?" she asked after she swallowed.

Jessica rattled off the address of a website.

"Slow down," Sandy said.

Jessica repeated the information. In a few seconds, a picture of a young woman with dark hair began to appear on Sandy's screen.

"Is the picture up?" Jessica asked.

"Yes."

"That's Lydia Abernathy Duncan," Jessica said. "Do you think she looks like Dusty?"

"No."

"The next photo is of Lydia and Dusty with their father. Press the arrow at the bottom corner of the screen."

Sandy brought up the image. The elder Abernathy had white hair; however, there was no question Lydia was his natural daughter.

"She looks like her daddy," Sandy said. "What is this site?"

"Lydia is an amateur photographer who posts photos on the web. I took you directly to a picture she took of herself. Do you see the box that says 'My Family'?"

"Yes."

"Click it."

Sandy moved her curser to the spot. A narrative blog post opened. She started reading it.

"Are you there?" Jessica asked.

"Yes. Skip all the stuff about the trip to San Francisco and go to the paragraph at the bottom that talks about Dusty's birthday party."

Sandy scrolled down the page to a sentence that read, *We got together at a gorgeous spot on the Chesapeake Bay to celebrate Dusty's birthday on April 5. Click here for pics of the festivities. Warning! No amount of Photoshop editing could remove some of the blurry eyes caused by a killer punch bowl.*

"April 5," Sandy said numbly.

"You were right," Jessica said. "The personal info about Dusty on the law firm website is incorrect."

Sandy was speechless.

"What am I going to do?" she managed after a few seconds passed.

"Did you keep the phone number and address I gave you for Lydia?"

"Yes."

"Either call her or have a much more

specific talk with Jeremy."

"I can't do that."

"Then I will," Jessica responded.

"You'll do what?"

"Contact Lydia. She won't know who I am, and I won't mention your name. I'll ask her if her brother was adopted. If she hangs up on me, then we're at a dead end. If she says yes and listens, then I'll tell her I know the woman who is probably his mother."

"That sounds crazy."

"But it's the truth."

Sandy hesitated. "No matter what she says, you won't mention my name."

"Right."

"Are you going to tell her your name? If you do, Dusty will connect you with me."

"I'll try not to unless it's absolutely necessary."

"It's courageous of you to offer." Sandy sighed. "But I don't want to upset the Abernathy family if they want to maintain the status quo. I had the same fear about Jeremy."

"And how did that turn out?"

"Wonderful so far, but his mother doesn't know about me yet."

"From what you've told me about her, she'll handle it with class. I know you will.

If you don't try to find out the truth about Dusty, you'll always —"

"Okay, do it," Sandy interrupted with surprising firmness. "Make the call to Lydia."

"Are you sure?"

"Yes. You're right. Everyone deserves the chance to know who they are."

"I didn't say it that way, but I agree with you. I'll phone her as soon as we hang up and before I lose my nerve."

"Then you'll call me back."

"Yes, Sandy," Jessica replied patiently. "I'm doing this for you."

"I know, I know. Thanks."

Jessica hung up. Sandy nervously wrung her hands. She returned to the kitchen. Nelson was taking a nap on his bed in the corner. No longer hungry, Sandy threw the rest of her sandwich into the garbage and began pacing back and forth across the room.

Thirty-Six

Five minutes passed. Ten minutes went by. Sandy looked at the clock on the microwave as the elapsed time approached fifteen minutes. Jessica would have called back if she hadn't made contact with Lydia. Sandy became more agitated. Different scenarios for the conversation between the two women raced through her head. After twenty minutes, Sandy opened the kitchen door to get some fresh air. By this point, she doubted the wisdom of pawning the job of making the call to Lydia onto Jessica. It was something Sandy should have done herself. Clutching her cell phone in her hand, Sandy hit the speed-dial button for Jessica's phone. No one answered, and when the call went into Jessica's voice mail, Sandy hung up without leaving a message. After more than thirty minutes, her phone beeped, and Sandy jumped. It was Jessica.

"I talked to her," Jessica said. "And get

this. She and her husband are in Atlanta this weekend visiting Dusty. They were sitting in the living room at Dusty's townhome when I phoned. As soon as I told her why I was calling, she left the room so we could talk privately."

"Privately?"

"Yes. She's known Dusty was adopted for almost ten years. Her father told her when she was in college. He'd had a heart attack and wanted Lydia to know the truth in case he didn't survive. It turns out his wife was the one who wanted Dusty to think he was their natural son."

"Why?"

"She got pregnant with Lydia when Dusty was about eight months old. It was a total shock because they'd been told they couldn't have children. The mother was a very insecure person who was afraid Dusty would feel second-class and decided not to tell him the truth. She died when the children were teenagers, and her husband kept quiet about it for years afterward."

"How did Lydia react to your news?"

"Surprised, but then she started thinking about Dusty. She believes he has a right to know he's adopted but is concerned that he'll be upset with their father."

"Is she going to tell him you called?"

"Better than a fifty-fifty chance. I could sense relief in her voice that she finally has a reason to say something to him. She's not been comfortable carrying around a secret this big for so long. She thanked me for calling. I believe she meant it."

"What did you say to her about me?"

"Nothing except that you're not seeking to barge into Dusty's life and create problems; that you're healthy and have your own income."

"Unless all the trouble his client has stirred up causes me to have a nervous breakdown and lose my job. What else?"

"She asked about siblings, and I told her Dusty had a twin brother who had met you. I didn't say how recently."

"Did she ask why I sent them to separate families?"

"It didn't come up. Oh, she knows my first name and that I live in Georgia. My area code came up on her phone, and I would have had to lie to deny it."

"I wouldn't want you to do that, but Dusty is a smart guy. Once she tells him about the call, he's going to remember my questions from lunch."

"Maybe. Men aren't as quick to connect the dots as women. Lydia is going to let me know if Dusty is interested in finding out more about you and his brother."

"Did she ask how you found her?"

"Yes. I mentioned the Internet and the genealogy site, which seemed to satisfy her. At some point she's going to realize I had to know something to do the searches in the first place. If she wants that kind of information, I'm going to pass her along to you."

"Okay. You've done more than enough." Sandy paused. "But this creates a whole different set of problems."

"About keeping the men apart?"

"Yes, I don't want to act like a superstitious teenager, but . . ." Sandy didn't finish the sentence.

Sunday afternoons were usually a time for Sandy to relax. But not today. After the call with Jessica ended, she sat at the kitchen table and debated whether to call Jeremy. However, she knew what his response would be. Once convinced of Dusty's identity, Jeremy would want to bring everything out into the open and get to know his brother. That thought gave Sandy cold chills. Concern for Chloe and Zach made her fear increase.

Sandy started walking through the house. By 4:00 p.m., she'd paced so much she felt more tired than she did after a long walk with Nelson. She went into the living room and stretched out on the sofa. Closing her eyes, she prayed for divine guidance, but she heard nothing, and no written message appeared on the ceiling. All she saw was a long, thin crack that needed to be patched the next time she painted the room.

Sandy fixed a salad for supper and forced herself to eat a few bites. Her cell phone was on the kitchen counter. It beeped, and Sandy shot out of her seat, almost tripping over the leg of a chair. It was Jessica.

"Lydia called back. She told him."

"How did he take it?"

"Skeptical until they called his father in California, who confirmed everything, including the fact that Dusty was born in Atlanta. Lydia said that blew Dusty's mind, since he had no interest in the city before his law firm sent him there."

"Was he mad at his father?"

"Not according to her. The secrecy bit made sense to him based on their mother's personality. She was a very private person who kept her feelings to herself. I think she was hard to live with."

Sandy felt a twinge of guilt that she'd sent Dusty to a less-than-ideal family.

"Does he want to meet me?"

"He's still in shock. This time Lydia had a lot of questions about Jeremy. I told her as little as possible."

"Did you talk to Dusty?"

"No."

Sandy leaned against the kitchen counter. "It surprises me that he let his sister do all the talking. He seems superconfident."

"Maybe he felt more like a little boy today."

"Poor guy," Sandy said. "I feel sorry for him."

"Once a mother, always a mother," Jessica replied. "Thirty-three years doesn't erase the slate. He's still the baby you didn't get to hold."

"Jessica!"

"I'm sorry. All I meant is that your feelings are real. You wouldn't be the person you are if you didn't have a maternal response to what Dusty is going through."

"What else did Lydia say?"

"Not much. She gave my first name and phone number to Dusty in case he wants to contact me."

"Do you think he'll be able to find out where you live?" Sandy asked quickly. "That will lead him directly to me."

"You knew there was a chance that would

happen when we talked earlier today, didn't you?"

"Yes," Sandy sighed. "I just wonder if he'll do any digging before he comes to Rutland tomorrow. He and Jeremy are scheduled to meet with the pregnant student."

"Are you going to let Jeremy know what's happened?"

"I'll have to at some point," Sandy said, "or maybe I won't."

"What are you thinking?"

"I'm not sure."

After the call ended, Sandy took out a sheet of paper and started writing down the things that were important to her. At the top of the list was taking care of Jeremy and his family. She wasn't sure what that meant except that she needed to do what she could to prevent anything bad from happening to him or them. Her feelings for Dusty, while real, were much weaker. Sandy didn't have the same intense desire to get to know Dusty that she felt for her younger son. If she had to make a choice, she would give up any possibility of future contact with Dusty to protect Jeremy.

A heaviness of heart she couldn't shake greeted her when she awoke the following morning. Her normal cheeriness toward

Nelson was absent, and she stared blankly across the kitchen while she sat at the table drinking her morning coffee.

At school, Sandy felt distracted all day. If she'd been a student teacher being observed by one of her education professors, she wouldn't have received a recommendation for a teacher's license. She gave her students busywork so she wouldn't have to focus on delivering a lecture. All she could think about was Dusty coming to Rutland and the meeting with Maria and Jeremy. As sixth period was winding down, Sandy looked at her phone, which was sitting in the top of her purse. It showed an unread text message. It was from Jeremy: *Here at courthouse. Where is Maria?*

Sandy quickly entered a reply that she'd notified Maria of the meeting and didn't know where she was.

Can you try to reach her? Dusty will be here at 4.

As soon as her class was over, Sandy called Maria's cell phone. No one answered. Sandy left a message and then called Jeremy.

"Is she there yet?" Sandy asked.

"No, and Dusty will be getting here shortly. I need to prepare Maria first."

Sandy hesitated. "I'd like to help, but the cheerleading squad meets for an hour and a half immediately after school."

"What is Maria's address? Maybe I should try to track her down."

"She lives in a trailer park. I'm not sure how the trailers are numbered, and she stays different places."

"I don't want to waste this chance," Jeremy said abruptly.

"I don't either," Sandy replied quickly. "I'll try to find a substitute to cover for me and see if I can track down Maria. Call me if she shows up. I made it clear to her where to go and when she needed to be there."

Sandy walked as fast as she could to see Kelli Bollinger. The Spanish teacher didn't know anything about cheerleaders, but she could be an adult presence in the gym during practice. Her room was empty, and the lights were out. Hoping John Bestwick would be there, Sandy continued to the gym. The basketball coach was rolling a rack of balls toward a storage area.

"Am I glad to see you," Sandy said with relief.

"I feel the same way," John replied.

"I hate asking you at the last minute, but can you cover cheer-leading practice for me?" Sandy said.

"Yeah, I've watched the cheerleaders a lot from my spot on the bench. Just tell me what to do."

Sandy smiled. "Huddle with Meredith and Candace as soon as they get here. They'll run the practice."

"Done."

"Thanks," Sandy said. "I really appreciate it."

John waved his hand toward the door. "Do what you need to do and don't worry about this place."

As soon as she was in the hallway, Sandy phoned Jeremy again.

"Dusty just got here, but there's no sign of Maria."

"I'm leaving the school. What do you want me to do?"

"Try to find her. If we don't get started in the next thirty minutes, we'll have to scrap everything."

"I'll go to the trailer park and see if I can locate her."

Sandy left the school and walked rapidly across the parking lot to her car. Her phone beeped. It was Maria.

"Where are you?" Sandy asked. "Jeremy is waiting for you at the courthouse."

"I'm at Rosalita's trailer. It took longer than she thought at the dentist's office."

"Can she bring you to the courthouse right now?"

"No, there's no one who can watch the little girls. The neighbor who was here while we went to the dentist had to go to her house."

"Can't her oldest daughter babysit?"

"She doesn't feel well. She got a shot in her mouth and had three teeth filled."

"Okay. Stay there, I'm on my way to get you. You're very late."

"I don't want to go," Maria said.

"That's not an option!" Sandy raised her voice. "I'm coming to get you!"

Maria didn't respond.

"And don't hang up on me!" Sandy warned.

Sandy looked at the phone. The call had been disconnected. She hit the Redial button and the call went to Maria's voice mail. Sandy wanted to throw the phone out the car window. She then called Jeremy and told him what had happened.

"What are you going to do?" she asked.

"Just a minute," he said. "Let me ask Dusty."

Sandy nervously shifted in her seat while she waited for the two men to talk.

"We'll go to her," Jeremy said. "I think she'll come around when we're there in person."

"I'm not sure that will work."

"It's worth a try. Can you swing by the court house? If the meeting with Maria doesn't happen, Dusty can go back to Atlanta, and you and I can spend time getting ready for the hearing next week. If Maria doesn't want to come to court voluntarily, she can be forced to appear."

Sandy drove as fast as she dared across the school parking lot and into the street. As she approached the courthouse building she saw Jeremy, Dusty, and a woman she assumed was the translator standing at the top of the steps. The two lawyers were both wearing tan slacks and blue sport coats. They could have been part of the same college fraternity. The sight of Jeremy and Dusty dressed alike and standing so close together sent chills down Sandy's spine. Jeremy motioned to her and came down the steps to her vehicle.

"Can I ride with you?" he asked. "Dusty is going to take his car. You can help us find out if Maria is going to cooperate, and we're going to leave the translator on standby. If we end up taking Maria's deposition, can we use Ben's conference room?"

"Probably, do you want me to call him?"

"No, let's talk to Maria first."

"Okay."

Jeremy settled back into the passenger seat.

"Things are never easy," he said. "Why do you think Maria balked?"

"She didn't say, but I'm sure she's afraid. This is all so unknown and intimidating to her. I blew up when she told me she wasn't coming. That probably won't help when we get there."

"I have a good rapport with her," Jeremy said, turning around to look out the rear window of the car. "Dusty is behind us. Let's go."

The trailer park was on the east side of town. Sandy stopped for a red light next to the veterinarian's office where she took Nelson.

"The more I get to know Dusty, the better I like him," Jeremy said. "I've met a lot of lawyers like Dusty. He's ambitious and doesn't know what's really important in life. But I think he'll listen to me if I tell him about my faith."

Sandy gripped the steering wheel tightly with her hands. The light turned green.

"I wouldn't expect you to be able to separate the lawyer from the man at this point," Jeremy continued. "But you may get a chance to see him in a different light in the future."

"I already do," Sandy replied grimly.

"Good." Jeremy nodded. "That's hard for someone in your position to do. What brought about the change?"

Sandy turned her head toward Jeremy for a moment.

"Do you really want to know?" she asked.

"Sure."

"It started with a phone call I received yesterday afternoon from a good friend who knows you're my son."

Sandy told Jeremy about Jessica's conversation with Lydia. When she glanced at his face, he appeared slightly pale.

"And this is legit?" he asked.

"Why in the world would his sister lie about it?"

"Yeah," Jeremy admitted. "When are you going to tell him?"

"I don't know. He's only known that he's an adoptee for twenty-four hours. You've had a lifetime to adjust to that fact. Just promise that you won't say anything to him until we agree it's time to do so. I think it's my right as his birth mother to break the news to him."

"Maybe, but only if you don't wait too long."

"I'm not negotiating with you," Sandy replied firmly. "Trust me. All I'm thinking about is you and your family."

Jeremy had a puzzled look on his face.

"What does that have to do with telling Dusty who he is?"

Sandy didn't answer.

Thirty-Seven

They reached the intersection for Haggler Road.

"It's not far now," Sandy said.

"Are you going to answer my question?" Jeremy asked. "Is there something you're not telling me?"

Sandy sighed. "You and Dusty may be twins, but as people you're from different planets."

"That can happen even when siblings grow up together. It doesn't change the fact that we're brothers."

"And you have to think about your family first. Before me, Dusty, anybody."

"You're not making any sense."

Sandy turned into the trailer park. "Right now you need to focus on Maria. We can talk later."

"That's going to be a challenge after the bombshell you just dropped on me."

Sandy glanced in the rearview mirror.

Dusty was behind them. It hadn't rained recently, and the cars were kicking up dust. Sandy slowed down and stopped.

"This is Maria's trailer."

"Let's check there first," Jeremy said.

There were two battered pickup trucks parked in front of the trailer. Sandy squeezed between them. Jeremy got out and walked up to the door and knocked. No one came. He banged the flimsy door harder with the side of his fist. It remained shut. He reached down and grabbed the knob.

"No," Sandy said under her breath as Jeremy tried to open the door.

It was locked, and he descended the steps. He went over to Dusty, who lowered the window of his car. Sandy couldn't hear what the two men said to each other. Jeremy returned.

"Where is Rosalita's trailer?" he asked.

"Down this row and to the left," Sandy said as she pointed.

"We agreed to try one more place. If Maria isn't there, Dusty is going back to Atlanta."

Sandy drove slowly between the trailers.

"It was odd talking to him just now," Jeremy said. "It's not right that I know and he doesn't."

"Jeremy, please —"

"Relax. I'm going to obey my mother. For now."

They reached Rosalita's trailer. Her car was parked out front. There was no sign of activity outside.

"I think Maria was in the other trailer and didn't want to answer the door," Jeremy said.

"Maybe, but she spends a lot of time with her cousin."

"I'll check."

"I should come," Sandy said. "Rosalita knows me."

Sandy glanced over at Dusty, who opened his door when he saw them both get out of Sandy's car. He joined them. There was barely room for the three of them on the rickety wooden landing in front of the door. Sandy knocked and waited. There was no response. She knocked louder.

"Rosalita!" she called out. "It's Ms. Lincoln from the school!"

A window near the door was covered with a flimsy curtain. Sandy thought she saw movement as the curtain was quickly moved back, then closed.

"Someone is there," she said. "Rosalita has several children."

"Try again," Jeremy said.

Sandy banged on the door.

"Rosalita! Maria!"

Jeremy put his ear to the metal door.

"There's someone inside," he said. "I can hear a voice speaking in Spanish."

"But if they don't want to open the door, there's nothing we can do to make them —" Jeremy reached for the door handle.

"No!" Sandy said. "Stop!"

Ignoring her, Jeremy turned the handle and pulled the door open a few inches. Before Sandy could see inside the trailer, the door was shoved violently into them, knocking Sandy off the landing onto the ground. Dazed, she looked up as a stocky young Hispanic man with closely cut hair appeared in the doorframe. He had a pistol in his hand. Jeremy stepped back. Dusty inched toward the edge of the landing.

"What are you doing here?" the man demanded in Spanish, pushing the revolver into Dusty's chest.

Dusty raised his hands and gave him a blank look.

"Looking for Maria Alverez," Sandy replied in Spanish, her voice trembling. "If she's not here, we'll leave."

The man glanced over his shoulder and swore. He pointed the gun at Jeremy, then Sandy.

"Get inside. All of you. Now!"

"He wants us to go inside the trailer," Sandy said.

"What do you want?" Dusty asked.

"Shut up!" the man shouted in English. "No talking!"

Sandy gingerly got up from the ground. She'd landed on her tailbone.

"Are you hurt?" Dusty asked from the porch.

Before Sandy could answer, the man with the gun shoved it into Dusty's stomach so hard the lawyer doubled over. He grabbed Dusty by the arm and dragged him into the trailer.

"Lie down!" he commanded in Spanish.

Dusty, still stooped over, hesitated, and the man sharply kicked the back of Dusty's legs, causing his knees to buckle.

"Stay on the floor!" Sandy said to Dusty in English, then repeated the phrase in Spanish.

The man looked at Sandy and nodded. Holding on to the thin wooden railing, Sandy climbed the steps. Jeremy took her arm to steady her. As soon as they were inside the trailer, the man jerked Jeremy to his knees and pointed at the floor. Jeremy lay down on his stomach beside Dusty. They were in a small living area with the kitchen to the right. A tattered rug partially covered the floor. There was no sign of anyone else inside the trailer. Sandy started to lie down too, but the man held his arm in front of her and shook his head.

"Don't move!" he said to Jeremy and Dusty.

Sandy translated. The man was wearing a dirty gray T-shirt, ragged jeans, and cowboy boots. His pants were held up by a belt with a large shiny buckle. He'd not shaved for days. Sandy heard a muffled sound down a hallway to her left but saw no one.

"What do you want with Maria?" he asked.

"To talk to her," Sandy said, unsuccessfully trying to keep her voice from shaking. "But we can leave and come back another time."

"And call the police?" the man sneered. "I am not a fool. Tell the men to give me their cell phones."

"He wants your cell phones," Sandy said.

Jeremy slipped his phone from the front pocket of his shirt and slid it across the floor, faceup. The wallpaper picture was Jeremy with his arms around Chloe and Zach.

"Mine is in the car," Dusty said.

Sandy translated. The man kicked Dusty in the side of the face. Dusty cried out in pain. The man then leaned over and quickly ran his hands along Dusty's body while the lawyer moaned. He took out Dusty's wallet and car keys and placed them on a small table near the door.

"Where is your cell phone?" the man asked Sandy.

"In my purse in the car."

The man eyed her for a moment, then raised his foot in the air and smashed Jeremy's phone with the heel of his boot. The plastic cracked at the impact, and the picture disappeared. Sandy glanced into the kitchen and saw the refrigerator.

"Move apart," the man said to Jeremy and Dusty. "About three feet."

Sandy translated, and the two men moved away from each other. The man with the gun stopped Jeremy by putting his foot on top of Jeremy's head. He pushed down for a moment but didn't kick him. Sandy racked her brain for something to say.

"You can tie us up and take my car," she said. "I have over two hundred dollars in my purse."

The man grabbed her face and pointed the gun at a spot between her eyes.

"And how far do you think I would get?" he asked.

The tight grip the man had on her cheeks

kept Sandy from answering. She looked in his eyes. They were cold and dark. He released his grip and roughly shoved her head to the side.

"Go into that room," he said, pointing down a short hallway. "And bring me the roll of gray tape that's on the table beside the bed."

Sandy moved slowly down the hall. Her tailbone was aching. When she neared the door, she glanced back at the man, who motioned for her to go forward. The door to the room was open. When she looked inside, she saw two of Rosalita's girls, their wrists wrapped in duct tape and their mouths taped shut, lying on their backs on a small bed. Their eyes were red and filled with fear. Sitting on the floor beside the bed was Rosalita. Her hands and feet were wrapped in tape and her mouth covered. Across the room from Rosalita, Maria was similarly bound. She looked at Sandy and sadly shook her head.

"Is that Emilio?" Sandy asked in a whisper.

Both Maria and Rosalita nodded. There was a large roll of duct tape on a nightstand beside the bed where the two girls were lying. Sandy picked it up.

"Hurry up!" Emilio shouted.

"Is your gun still on top of the refrigerator?" Sandy asked Rosalita as she leaned over to get the tape.

Rosalita nodded.

"Is it loaded?"

Rosalita nodded, then shook her head.

"Are there bullets in the gun?" Sandy repeated.

Her eyes wide, Rosalita grunted. Sandy reached for the tape to pull it back from her mouth.

"Get out here now!" Emilio shouted.

Sandy left the room and hobbled down the hallway with the tape in her hand.

"Come on, come on," Emilio said impatiently.

When Sandy reached Emilio, he grabbed the tape and pushed her against the wall. A sharp pain went through her lower back.

"Stay there," he ordered. "Keep your hands by your sides and don't move."

Emilio grabbed Dusty's wrists and taped them together behind his back. He then bound Dusty's feet together, rolled him over, and slapped a piece of tape across his mouth. For a moment Emilio had his back to Jeremy. Sandy saw Jeremy reach out toward a stool in front of the small table. He got his hand around the leg of the stool, all the time keeping his eyes on Emilio.

"Don't!" she called out.

Emilio swung around, saw Jeremy's extended hand, and stomped it with his boot. Jeremy cried out in pain and grabbed his wrist. Emilio threw the stool across the room and then kicked Jeremy in the stomach. He put the gun to Jeremy's head and threw the tape onto the floor.

"Get over here," he said to Sandy. "Put the tape around his hands and feet."

Sandy picked up the tape and knelt on the floor.

"Feet first," Emilio ordered.

Sandy wrapped the tape around Jeremy's ankles several times while Emilio watched.

"Now his hands," Emilio said. "Behind his back."

When Sandy picked up Jeremy's right wrist, he cried out. It was tilted oddly to the left. Tears rushed into Sandy's eyes.

"I'm sorry," she said.

"Shut up," Emilio said.

Sandy gently held Jeremy's wrist in her hand and brought his other hand closer. She wrapped the tape once around his wrists, trying not to put too much pressure on the bones. As soon as she brought the tape around once, Emilio pushed her away. He made two more quick rounds with the tape, each one causing Jeremy to cry out in pain.

Emilio stood up, leaving Jeremy lying on his stomach with his face pressed against the floor. Emilio didn't put any tape over Jeremy's mouth.

"Get Maria and Rosalita and bring them here," Emilio said.

"Can I take the tape off their feet?"

"Yes."

Sandy returned to the bedroom. She knelt in front of Maria and was about to ask another question about the gun when she saw Emilio out of the corner of her eye watching from the doorway. Sandy's hands shook as she ripped the tape away from Maria's ankles. Maria stood up. Her hands were bound behind her. Sandy moved to Rosalita and freed her feet.

"Do you know who I am?" Emilio asked while Sandy was still kneeling in front of Rosalita.

"You're Emilio."

They returned to the front room.

"Lie down on your stomachs," he commanded Maria and Rosalita.

The two women lay with their faces to the floor.

"Tape their feet," Emilio said to Sandy. "Make sure it's tight."

Emilio watched as Sandy bound the women.

"We have a big problem here," Emilio said as Sandy finished with Rosalita. "I came back to town to get my money and found out that people were asking bad questions about me and Maria. Is that your fault?"

Sandy remembered her conversation with Mimi Randolph.

"Yes," she said, then pointed at Jeremy and Dusty. "They had nothing to do with it."

"You brought them here, didn't you?"

"But they don't know what you did to Maria."

Emilio hit Sandy in the face with the back of his hand. She staggered sideways. Emilio then glared down at Maria, who turned her face away from him toward the wall.

The blow stung, but Sandy felt strangely calm. Emilio stared at her for a moment, then gestured toward Jeremy.

"I can hit you, but it will hurt you more if I do something to this one, right?" he asked.

Sandy didn't respond.

"What about this one?" Emilio stepped over and nudged Dusty with his toe but kept his eyes on Sandy's face.

Dusty's face was turned away from them. There was a nasty red welt forming on the side of his face where he'd been kicked.

"I care about both of them," Sandy said.

"But they can't help with your big problem. I can."

Startled, Emilio looked at her. "What can you do for me?"

"I don't want Rosalita or Maria to hear. Can we go into the kitchen and talk?"

Emilio eyed her suspiciously.

"You can still see them from there," Sandy said.

Emilio waved his gun across the bodies on the floor.

"Nobody move. I'll be watching."

Sandy moved slowly into the kitchen. The refrigerator was on the left. It was decorated with school artwork by Rosalita's daughters. Sandy moved past the refrigerator and stopped. It wasn't a large unit, but Emilio was directly in front of her, and she couldn't sneak a look on top.

"I can help you get what you want and then get away without getting caught by the police," Sandy said. "Are you here for the money Rosalita's husband owes you?"

"Yes," Emilio answered in a low voice. "Rosalita has hidden it. I'm going to the bedroom where her children are. When they scream, she'll tell me where it is. And I'm not going to leave Maria here. She's coming with me. I told her I would take care of her, but Rosalita filled her head with lies."

"Let me talk to Rosalita about the money. And Maria can go with you, but she and Rosalita can't know what you're going to do or where you're going to go. Here is my idea —"

Sandy stopped and glanced past Emilio into the area where Jeremy and Dusty lay on the floor.

"Don't move!" she called out in English.

Emilio spun around. When he did, Sandy ran her hand across the top of the refrigerator. She felt the cool metal of a gun and grabbed it. She pulled back the hammer and held the weapon out in front of her with both hands.

"It's okay," Emilio said as he turned back toward Sandy. "They're still tied up —"

He saw the gun in Sandy's hands, and his jaw dropped open. Sandy closed her eyes and pulled the trigger. She didn't know if she would hear a dull click of the hammer hitting an empty magazine or the roar of exploding gunpowder from a bullet. The sound of the gun discharging in the enclosed area was deafening. When Sandy opened her eyes, Emilio had stepped back and was leaning against the kitchen counter. Sandy rushed past him toward the door. If she could make it outside, she could run for help.

"Stop!" Emilio commanded.

Sandy tripped over Dusty's legs and fell to the floor. The gun slid out of her hand and down the hallway toward the bedroom.

"Go," Jeremy said through clenched teeth. "Get out."

Sandy scrambled to her feet and faced Emilio, who was standing at the edge of the kitchen with his gun pointed directly at her. The calm Sandy felt earlier returned. Instead of running, she waited for Emilio to pull the trigger. Then she watched in horror as Emilio's hand moved away from her and downward toward Dusty's upper body.

"No!" she cried out in English. "He's my son!"

Sandy threw herself across Dusty as the gun went off.

Everything went black.

Thirty-Eight

Sandy felt suspended in space, surrounded by a wonderful fragrance, a heady aroma that permeated the atmosphere. The scent was vaguely familiar. Somewhere, at some unknown time, she'd experienced a hint of the delightful odor before. Then, into the darkness a shape appeared. The shape moved gracefully out of the shadows. A face and form came into focus. The darkness turned to light.

It was the old woman from the gas station.

Sandy knew her immediately, but there was something different about her. The woman's entire being was wreathed in a glorious radiance. Her blue eyes remained bright; her snow-white hair was still pulled back in a bun. But the wrinkles of Sandy's teenage memory were gone. And Sandy knew she had been wrong. The woman wasn't old; she was ageless. She didn't live on earth; she came from heaven. Words emanated from the angel and traveled straight to Sandy's heart.

"You chose well."

And in an instant a limitless flow of divine affirmation washed over Sandy. Enveloped in pure love, she felt herself being lifted up and carried away. She'd chosen well. Not once, not twice, but at every critical turning point when self-sacrifice required her to lay down her life for her sons. She opened her arms wide.

She'd followed the path of her highest destiny.

Click. Silence. *Click.*

The sound seemed to come from a long way off. Sandy opened her eyes a fraction of an inch, then closed them without seeing anything. She longed for the light, the fragrance of glory, but the blackness returned.

Click. Silence. *Click.*

This time the sound was more distinct. Sandy waited for it to repeat but heard nothing. She moaned slightly and opened her eyes. The scene was fuzzy. She closed her eyes again. Someone touched her hand.

"Sandy," a faraway voice said.

She opened her eyes. A male face swam

into view. It was Ben.

"What?" she managed.

"Don't try to talk. You're in the hospital."

Sandy returned to the darkness. She wasn't sure how long she stayed there. She heard other sounds. Voices came and went. She opened her eyes again. The lights in the room were dimmed. It was night. She slowly moved her head to the side. Ben was leaned back in a recliner beside her bed. His eyes were closed.

And Sandy remembered everything.

"Ben," she managed in a hoarse voice.

Her brother turned his head. He jumped out of the chair and came to her side.

"The surgeon said you'd be coming around soon."

"Dusty?" she asked. "Is he —"

Ben took a deep breath. Fear came into Sandy's face.

"It was touch-and-go. They lost him on the operating table, but he came back. He's in intensive care now. They wanted to transport him to Atlanta, but it was too risky."

"Dusty died in the operating room?" Sandy asked weakly.

"Yes."

"But he's alive."

"Yes."

"I'm just glad Dr. Molitor was on call. He returned a few months ago from a tour of duty in Afghanistan, where he treated more gunshot wounds in a year than some surgeons see in a lifetime."

Sandy closed her eyes for a moment of thankfulness.

"And Jeremy. Where is —"

"They were able to set his wrist without surgery. He's on the orthopedic floor and should go home tomorrow."

"He's okay?"

"Yes."

Her boys had survived. Two tears forced their way past Sandy's eyelids and ran down the sides of her face. She felt a soft cloth against her cheek. Ben was wiping away her tears with his handkerchief. Sandy could see that her brother's eyes were red too.

"I was scared —" Sandy started.

"Of course you were."

"But then I felt strangely calm. I knew what I had to do." She paused. "Then I saw her."

"Who?"

Sandy closed her eyes and didn't answer. She longed to return to the place of fragrant light, but all she could smell was a hint of antiseptic. She took a deep breath. Pain shot through her chest. The thought of paralysis flashed through her mind. Sandy wiggled her fingers and toes. They seemed to work fine.

"What happened to me?" she asked.

"You were shot in the abdomen. The bullet sliced through you into Dusty and stopped within a fraction of an inch of Dusty's heart. If you hadn't shielded him, he'd be dead."

Sandy could see tubes coming out from beneath the covers near her hips. The clicking noise she'd heard was coming from the device attached to a bag of IV solution.

"You're stitched and bandaged up," Ben continued. "The surgeon told me the bullet destroyed one of your ovaries."

"An ovary?"

"I know," Ben said and managed a slight smile. "If you had to lose an organ, I guess that's one to pick at your age. There was quite a bit of internal bleeding, but no extensive damage to your colon or small intestine. The doctor cleaned you out, and you're getting a heavy dose of antibiotics."

"What about Maria and Rosalita and the children?"

"They're fine. The man you shot also had surgery."

"I thought I missed him."

Ben shook his head. "According to the

police, you hit him in the thigh. The bullet severed an artery, and he passed out on the floor right after he shot you. The sound of the gunshots brought police and emergency medical crews to the trailer park within a few minutes." Ben paused. "There's something to be said for living in a town with no traffic jams and a hospital that's two miles away."

Sandy's gratitude went much higher and deeper.

"Mama and Linda are on their way from Florida and should be here in the morning," Ben continued. "I'm going home in a few minutes, and Betsy is going to spend the rest of the night with you."

"She doesn't need to do that."

"Do you think I could stop her?"

"No. Does Jessica know?"

Ben patted Sandy on the arm.

"Yes, along with several million other people. The triple shooting at a trailer park in Rutland was the lead story on the eleven o'clock news on every TV station in Atlanta. Media trucks are still in the hospital parking lot. I guess they want to file follow-up reports about my heroic big sister in the morning."

"I'm no hero."

"That's right. You're something better."

Ben took Sandy's hand in his and looked into her eyes. "You're a mother."

By noon the next day, Sandy's hospital room was a swirl of activity. Local florists brought in so many flowers that Sandy asked the charge nurse to start sending them to the rooms of patients who didn't have any. Sandy's favorite card was one designed and signed by every member of the cheerleading squad. The most extravagant floral arrangement was from John Bestwick. Sandy had it positioned so she could look at it whenever she liked. One of the first things she wanted to do when her appetite returned was let the basketball coach take her out for a steak dinner. The arrival of Sandy's mother and her aunt Linda elevated the hospital's already high level of care.

Sandy was propped up in bed eating a few bites of soup broth when the door opened, and Jeremy, a white cast on his right wrist and lower arm, came into the room. Directly behind him was Leanne. As soon as Leanne saw Sandy, she burst into tears.

"I wasn't going to do that," she said, rubbing her eyes with the palms of her hands.

Jeremy came to the bed, leaned over, and kissed Sandy on the forehead.

"I love you," she whispered. "I'm sorry about your wrist."

"The broken wrist probably saved my life."

Sandy's mother and Linda were standing by a chair in the corner of the room.

"This is Jeremy and his wife, Leanne," Sandy said to the two women. "The last time you saw Jeremy, he weighed four pounds, ten ounces. He's gotten a lot bigger and stronger since then."

Sandy watched as her mother and Linda met Jeremy and Leanne. Her heart overflowed.

The morning of her third day in the hospital, Sandy awoke to shafts of sunlight streaming into her room. She was drinking a cup of weak coffee when Jeremy came in to see her.

"Do you want to go for a ride in the wheelchair?" he asked.

"To the baby nursery?" she asked with a smile.

They'd made several trips to inspect the latest crop of newborns.

"No, but your older baby can have visitors."

"Let's go," Sandy replied immediately.

Although Sandy was able to get out of bed

and go to the bathroom, she wasn't walking more than a few feet on her own. She put on her robe and brushed her hair.

"I look terrible," she said as she came out of the bathroom.

Jeremy held the wheelchair steady for her to sit down.

"That's not what I think. I can't believe I have a mother as young and attractive as you are."

"That's sweet. Even if it's not true."

"Don't argue with me. I'm a lawyer."

As Jeremy wheeled Sandy down the hallway, virtually every member of the hospital staff paused to greet her. She was getting used to the attention but longed to return to anonymity.

"Dusty's father and sister ate supper with Leanne and me last night," Jeremy said. "They enjoyed their time with you."

"It was fun answering their questions," Sandy replied. "Lydia is a sharp young woman."

"She and Leanne really clicked. I think they're going to become friends even though we're not related. To me, it's confirmation that you made the right decision to separate Dusty and me. How else would we connect with these people?"

"You really think so?"

Jeremy patted her on the shoulder. "Don't second-guess yourself now. It won't change anything."

Even now, Sandy didn't understand everything, but she could still be grateful. They reached the elevator, and Jeremy pushed the button.

"I'm nervous," Sandy said. "I feel like this is the first time Dusty and I are going to talk. How alert is he?"

"You'll see."

The third floor housed the cardiac and cancer patients. Rutland had few serious trauma cases, but when they occurred, the severely injured people were placed on the third floor where the staff-to-patient ratio was higher. Jeremy pushed the wheelchair to a locked double door and pressed a button. A woman's voice asked who they were.

"Jeremy Lane with Sandra Lincoln," he said. "We're here to see Dusty Abernathy."

A buzzer sounded, and the door opened on its own.

"No one calls me Sandra except my mother when she's telling me what to do in the kitchen at Christmastime."

"Okay, I promise not to call you Sandra if you can fit my family into your schedule this Christmas in Charleston."

"Did you clear that with your mother?"

"It was her idea."

"But I haven't written her a letter yet."

"You can tell her in person."

They passed several rooms. Sandy clasped her hands together in her lap.

"Here we are," Jeremy said when they reached a room on the left. The door was closed. "This is a bit tricky for a one-handed man."

Jeremy pulled the heavy wooden door open with his left hand and then held it with his right foot while he pushed the wheelchair ahead. Sandy leaned forward as they entered the room.

Dusty was sitting up in bed with his eyes closed. The first thing Sandy noticed was the deep bruise on the side of his head where Emilio had kicked him. There were multiple tubes coiled around him. Dusty turned his head toward them and opened his eyes.

"Come in," he said in a surprisingly strong voice.

Jeremy rolled Sandy to the side of the bed. She didn't trust herself to speak. All she could do was stare at Dusty and marvel that he'd died and come back to life.

"Hey," he said.

"Hi," Sandy responded.

Never had such a simple greeting held

more meaning. Sandy reached out and touched Dusty's hand. He had long, strong fingers. He looked over at her and smiled.

"I liked you the first time I saw you in the snack shop in Atlanta," Dusty said. "I thought you looked like a nice lady."

"And I thought you were a cocky lawyer," Sandy replied in an attempt to keep from bursting into tears.

"We were both right," Dusty said.

Sandy gently stroked his hand.

"I'm glad you're alive," she said softly.

"Me too."

Dusty turned his palm up and closed his fingers gently over Sandy's hand.

"I've thought about you a lot since I came out from under the anesthesia," he said, looking directly into Sandy's eyes. "I want to thank you for giving me life thirty-three years ago and saving my life four days ago."

A tear rolled down Sandy's cheek.

"I know what's happened is going to change me," Dusty continued. "I'm not sure how, but I want you to be part of who I am from here on."

Sandy squeezed Dusty's hand. Jeremy touched Sandy on the shoulder.

"Make that three of us," Jeremy said. "We're a family."

By the time Sandy got out of the hospital, the women's organization in Atlanta had dismissed the petition against her and dropped the juvenile court action against Maria. Jeremy told Sandy their new lawyer admitted that the threat of negative publicity generated by pursuing a claim against Sandy Lincoln far outweighed any precedential benefit of a court order muzzling a public school teacher.

Ben and Betsy took Sandy home from the hospital. Nelson ran in circles of excitement when he saw her slowly get out of the car. Sandy's mother, who was staying an extra week to help out, opened the kitchen door. Ben helped Sandy up the steps.

"What have you done to my kitchen?" Sandy asked as soon as she entered and saw that some of her things weren't in their usual places. "I won't be able to find anything."

"I'll go over everything with you. You'll see the improvement. It's easy to get in a rut and miss an opportunity for efficiency."

Seven months later, Sandy returned to the hospital. This time she went to the labor and delivery suite. Maria had been able to complete the school year before her pregnancy kept her at home. A late-term ultrasound confirmed that she was going to have a little girl. With Emilio out of the picture, her father's attitude changed, and he supported Maria's decision to have her baby and bring her home. Sandy had already started to coordinate child care so the new mother could return to high school the following year and graduate. Jeremy, Dusty, and Ben had pledged financial support.

Maria's father nervously camped out in the waiting area while Rosalita and Sandy stayed with Maria. Shortly after suppertime, Maria began to push. Forty minutes later she delivered a six pound, five ounce baby girl. Sandy and Rosalita were on opposite sides of the new mother when the delivery nurse placed the tiny infant in Maria's arms.

"You did great," Sandy said as she looked down at the mother and child. "And she's beautiful."

Maria softly kissed her little girl on the cheek.

"Tell her," Rosalita said to Maria.

Maria took her eyes off her infant for a moment and looked up at Sandy.

"My mother is dead. Will you be my little girl's adopted grandmother?"

"Yes." Sandy nodded. "That would be an honor."

Maria gazed again at her baby.

"And I've already picked out a name for her."

"Wonderful. What is it?"

"I'm going to call her Sandy."

A NOTE FROM THE AUTHOR

Thank you so much for taking the time to read *The Choice.* It's my desire to write novels that encourage, inspire, and entertain. Before you place this book on a shelf or pass it along to a friend, I want to share a few personal thoughts with you.

The sacrifice a woman makes to bring a baby into the world (along with the previous nine months!) is incalculable. One of my main goals in writing *The Choice* was to honor mothers. I've never had greater respect for my wife, Kathy, than during the birth of our first child. If you're a mother, please allow a few drops of praise and appreciation to rain down on you.

The titles of books and movies often contain a touch of irony. There is intended irony in my selection of *The Choice.* Within the abortion movement, the word *choice* is a rallying cry for the right of women to terminate a pregnancy as an acceptable form of birth control. In this novel I want to show that the same word can apply to a woman's decision *not* to abort her baby. Sandy is unselfishly "pro-choice." She chooses not to go to the women's clinic in Atlanta and prematurely end her pregnancy; she chooses to place the baby boys for adoption because, in the context of the story, it is the best decision for them; she chooses to place her own life in jeopardy to save her sons when she meets them as adults. Sandy's actions at key points illustrate practical ways to redeem the word *choice*.

My ultimate hope is that readers of this story, regardless of age or gender, will be encouraged to make unselfish, sacrificial choices. Laying down our lives for others, in big and small ways, is at the heart of Christian living. Jesus said, "Greater love has no one than this: to lay down one's life for one's friends" (John 15:13 NIV). Wouldn't more of that be a good thing?

ROBERT WHITLOW

ACKNOWLEDGMENTS

My wife, Kathy, profoundly influenced the writing of this book. She is the mother of our four children and an adoptee who found her birth mother. Without her insight I could not have told this story. Special thanks to Allen Arnold, Natalie Hanemann, and Deborah Wiseman for their invaluable advice in crafting the novel and making it better.

READING GROUP GUIDE

1. The story opens with the young Sandy and her mother waiting in a doctor's office for news that will change their lives. Put yourself in their shoes in 1974 small-town Georgia. How would you feel if you were the mother? If you were the pregnant, unwed girl?

2. Sandy's journey through the first half of the book is filled with challenges and choices. Have you or someone you know ever dealt with a situation like this? What was the outcome?

3. The meeting between Sandy's and Brad's families doesn't go very smoothly. How could that situation have been handled differently? If you were involved, what would you advise?

4. Brad tells Sandy that he loves her and wants to marry her. Do you believe him? Do you think that sometimes women may ignore red flags? What would you tell

Sandy in that moment — when Brad tells her "I can't live without you"?

5. On her way to Atlanta, Sandy meets a strange woman in the gas station. How would you react to a stranger predicting your future? Would you take it to heart as Sandy does, or would you brush it off as lunacy?

6. Linda selflessly invites Sandy into her home in Atlanta and supports her through her pregnancy. How does this experience affect Sandy's future?

7. Sandy goes home to spend Christmas with her family and attends the Christmas Eve service at their church. She realizes a correlation between her own pregnancy and Mary's. In what ways are their situations similar? How does this one night change Sandy's outlook on her pregnancy and her life?

8. After Sandy gives birth, her mother is persistent to see and hold the twins. She even begs Sandy to take at least one of them home. Would that have been a good choice? If your mother tried to force something on you that you didn't agree with, how would you handle it?

9. As a teacher and the cheerleading coach, Sandy plays an important role in the lives of her students. She develops a friendship

with Maria and helps her through a difficult time. Do you think there should be laws in place defining the relationships teachers are allowed to have with their students? Discuss the implications.

10. Do you think it was a coincidence that the lawyer Sandy visits turns out to be one of her sons? She is overjoyed and unsure what to do with her newfound knowledge. What do you think about her spying on the family and following them to Chloe's soccer game? Can you imagine doing something like this?

11. Sandy asks Dustin Abernathy if he was adopted, and he says no. Later we find out that he was adopted but his parents never told him. Do you think children need to know if they were adopted?

12. Even though Sandy wasn't fond of Dusty, she sacrifices her own life for him. Would you do that for your child? Would you be able to sacrifice your child for someone else?

13. In what ways does Sandy's story relate to the biblical story of Jacob and Esau?

14. Discuss the choices you see throughout this story that change its course. For example, Sandy chooses to believe the strange woman's prediction about her sons and acts accordingly. Later, Sandy

continues to help Maria even though Sandy could lose her job. Which choice do you consider the most pivotal?

ABOUT THE AUTHOR

Robert Whitlow is the best-selling author of legal dramas set in the South and winner of the prestigious Christy Award for Contemporary Fiction. A Furman University graduate, Whitlow received his J.D. with honors from the University of Georgia School of Law where he served on the staff of the Georgia Law Review. A practicing attorney, Whitlow and his wife, Kathy, have four adult children. They make their home in North Carolina.